Rockets of the Reich

**Novels by
Kim Kinrade**

Ice Break
Beneath the Plains of Abraham
The Millennium Man
Rockets of the Reich

NEW MILLENNIUM WRITERS SERIES

Rockets of the Reich

A World War II Action Novel

by

Kim Kinrade

BAINBRIDGEBOOKS

Philadelphia

Published June 2000
by
BainBridgeBooks
a division of
Trans-Atlantic Publications Inc.
311 Bainbridge Street
Philadelphia PA 19147

Website address: www.transatlanticpub.com

PRINTED IN THE UNITED STATES OF AMERICA

© 2000 by Kim Kinrade
All Rights Reserved

No part of this publication, except short excerpts for
review purposes, may be reproduced in any form
(including photocopying or storage in any medium by
electronic means) without the written consent of the Publisher.

This is a work of fiction.
Any resemblance to any person living or dead is purely coincidental.

ISBN: 1-891696-14-9

Library of Congress Cataloging-in-Publication Data:

Kinrade, Kim
Rockets of the Reich : a World War II action novel / by Kim Kinrade
   p. cm. – (New millennium writers series)
   ISBN 1-891696-14-9
   1.World War, 1939-1945—Fiction.
   2. World War, 1939-1945—Nova Scotia—Fiction
   I. Title. II Series
PS3561.I572 R63 2000
813'.54—dc21   99-462337

Cover and Book Design by Graphic Decisions Inc.

for
Heather

ACKNOWLEDGEMENTS

For much of this research, my deep appreciation goes out to Ed Michaud, President of Undersea Research and Recovery in Framington, Massachusetts. He provided me with documents pertaining to OPNAV and information on U-boats — especially the Type XIB-U-cruiser; a boat that, until recently, was thought to have existed only in diagrams at the Kriegsmarine "K" Design Office. His archive is quite extensive, including the information on the "Towed Launch Array" — mentioned in this novel — which actually existed. Ed's company and Sub Sea Research, LLC, are presently making plans to raise a huge U-cruiser that was sunk off Cape Cod on August 25, 1944.

I would also like to credit the resources of the Canadian Coast Guard, Canadian Navy, Halifax Regional Libraries, King's College Library, Maritime Museum of the Atlantic; and Chuck, Tom, Brooke, Robert and Mary Ellen at Shearwater Aviation Museum in Dartmouth, Nova Scotia. As well, thanks to the United States Coast Guard and Navy.

Guomundur Helgason and Tonya Allen get a gracious nod for http://www.uboat.net, a great site for information on the Kriegsmarine; and thanks to Kelly Miller for providing much of the German translation.

In addition, I would like to mention the following authors and persons whose works were instrumental in this story: Richard Hough, Michael Gannon, Captain John M. Waters, Otto Kretschmer, Konrad Dannenberg, Brigadier-General Denis Whitaker, DSO & Bar, CM, ED, CD; Mike Mullen, and Jak Mallmann Showell.

My gratitude also goes out to my family: Heather, Samantha, Tony, Shane and Brett, my greatest source of inspiration; to Ron Smolin, W. Lane Startin, and the fine people at BainBridgeBooks and Trans-Atlantic Publications; Danny Morton and Doug Fawthrop at White Point Beach Resort; Steph and Dave at Broad River Cottages; John Swain and Peter Gibbs at Survival Systems Training in Dartmouth, Nova Scotia; Lewis MacKenzie, for his encouragement; and my good friend Neville Gilfoy for keeping me focused.

This book was written at White Point Beach and Broad River, on the South Shore of Nova Scotia.

KK
January 2000

"They marched without fear and without hope"

*- The soldiers of
Napoleon's Grand Armée
on their way to Waterloo*

PROLOGUE

March 23, 1944
Potsdam, Germany

Upon reaching the crest of the knoll, the occupants of the two Daimler-Benz convertibles were awestruck by the wreckage of the large bomber. Dotting the scene were shabbily dressed workmen who ripped at the dull-green, aluminum skin and the innards, stripping the behemoth as a pack of army ants would ravage a dead seagull. The bomber's entrails of conduit, torn aluminum and other equipment were strung out behind it for hundreds of yards

The four-engine Boeing B-17G "Flying Fortress" was one of 669 "heavies" which bombed Berlin the previous day, the third huge raid by the United States Army Air Force in as many weeks. It had been crippled by several successive bursts of flak, and the commander had made sure every one of its seven crewmen got out before thinking of his own safety. By that time he was too low to jump. He crash-landed the bomber in a farmer's field outside this western suburb of Berlin and didn't survive.

The entourage and motorcycle escort gingerly edged over the top of the knoll and began down the other side. Most of the three dozen-odd workers stopped to follow the progress of the motorcade, which sported bright Nazi banners that fluttered in the cool, early spring air. It was not often that they were treated to such high-ranking guests. Usually on a crash site, a Luftwaffe captain would be considered a visitor of note. Mostly, onlookers consisted of interested farmers and the odd fighter pilot who had come to inspect his handiwork.

Four BMW motorcycles came to a stop first as helmeted soldiers in black-leather trench coats dismounted from the saddles and sidecars. *Schmeisser* submachine guns were pointed in the direction of the workers, who immediately froze with fear.

When the limousines finally halted, four of the black-jacketed guards ran to open the doors while two stood vigil, machine guns at ready, scanning the area for danger. Out of the vehicles stepped four officers with peaked caps. One was a large man in a powder-blue greatcoat that accented his rotund, pear-shaped figure. He was speaking as he stepped off the running board, much like a personal tour guide would, accenting his words with wild waves of his gold-encrusted baton. The object of his attention was a much smaller and slimmer man sporting a camel-colored topcoat of a civilian cut. This visitor seemed to be ignoring the dissertation.

The other two occupants of the vehicles, military officers of slight build, sported similar black, leather coats and were adorned with the same swastika-emblazoned armbands. They too acted as if the big man were invisible.

Giving no hint of his intentions, the small man in the light-brown coat suddenly moved forward in long strides. Caught unawares, the others scurried to catch up like large chicks chasing a hen. His head nodded as he took determined steps in the soft turf. Then, suddenly, he stopped and his eyes bore into the downed bomber.

"As you can see . . ." continued the large man, stopping in mid-sentence for a few seconds to catch his breath, "the Luftwaffe's deadly flak batteries have taken their toll on the Americans. My fighter squadrons have paved a corridor from here to the North Sea with the metal of their wrecked bombers. This is but a token of their victories." His big, cherubic face then bobbed up and down several times as if trying to convince himself that what he had just said was, in fact, true.

For the moment, nobody said anything. Then the slim officer with the gold, wire-rimmed glasses asked, "Would these be the very same squadrons that the American fighter escort chewed up when the bombers flattened Charlottenburg?"

The big man was standing slightly behind the other three so they never saw his eyes blink nervously.

"What I mean to say is – "

"I remember what you once told me in the spring of 1940," the small man interjected, coldly. "You said if bombs ever dropped on Berlin, then we could call you Meyer."

"But, I –"

"Enough!" his accuser barked, his attention still fully on the fuselage of the wrecked bomber. After an uncomfortable pause, he suddenly strode the rest of the way down the hill.

Adolf Hitler surged across the soggy field and did not stop until he came to the large tail plane of the aircraft. He slowly raised his eyes up the huge fin, finally resting them upon a large "A" in a white box, which sat atop the serial number of the bomber. "These gangsters come all the way from America to destroy my new city," he mumbled. "And they do it as casually as if they were going to a nightclub."

Reichsführer Heinrich Himmler doffed his glasses and quickly polished them with his handkerchief. He shoved them back on his slender nose while his eyes, mole-like dots on his face, grew under the magnification. "Our vengeance weapons are close to being ready, *Mein Führer*," he offered. "Then, I assure you, we will devastate London for what has happened here."

The Nazi leader threw up his arms and turned on the commander of his personal guard. "You assure me?" he spat, holding out his arms as if about to embrace him. "And where have I heard that before?" He shot a menacing glance at Hermann Göring who was dabbing his forehead with his handkerchief. "From *Herr* Meyer, here?"

It had been a long time since the Luftwaffe commander had been in the coveted inner circle of Hitler's confidants. This new daylight onslaught by American bombers, so deep into the Reich, pushed him even farther toward the periphery.

His thin, ashen face contorted with fury, Hitler suddenly spun around and slammed down his gloved hand on the stabilizer of the B-17. The dull thud of his attack echoed throughout the wreck and caused his subordinates to flinch. The workers watched in fascination as the leader of greater Europe hit the aircraft again. Even one of the battle-hardened SS guards was taken aback by the emotional exhibition.

As he spread his gloved fingers out on the cold, aluminum surface, his hands trembled, a symptom of Parkinson's disease. In addition to the beginning stages of this affliction, stomach cramps plagued him more these days and he was well into many of the 92 drugs that would be prescribed to him by his doctors during his last year of life. These included pervitin cut with amphetamines and cocaine-laced eye drops.

"Yes, I want London in ruins," he breathed, slowly turning his face to Himmler. His eyes seemed supported by ashen bags. His trusted adjutant glanced over to the others and was about to signal for assistance to help Hitler back to the car when, suddenly, the Nazi leader slammed his hand down for a third time.

"But I want Roosevelt and his cross-bred American hordes to feel my wrath for what they've done to Berlin!" he ranted. "I want to bring down such a plague on the cities of America that the citizens will string up that cripple in the White House and leave England to wither on its own bankrupt vine!"

After the echoes died down, Hitler lowered his head and pressed against the horizontal stabilizer of the bomber with his palms. His arms were outstretched as if trying to push the whole aircraft forward. His mannerism was odd enough to make even Himmler's pulse quicken. The spectacled man searched to find the right words to placate his leader.

However, before Himmler could speak, Hitler was on the move again. As if he were window-shopping, he peered through the smashed Perspex dome of the nose and examined the damaged bombsite. A red, tartan thermos bottle lay amongst the wiring and a belt of .50 caliber ammunition for the nose turret hung out the opening. Moving his eyes horizontally, he came face-to-face with the colored photograph of a scantily clad, dark-haired woman. Large letters below the picture spelled out *Steady Letty,* and Hitler huffed as he tried to pronounce the words. Then he bent over to read the artist's name: Milton Caniff.

"Barbarians," he breathed, pulling his gloves off to test the texture of the paint. A trained artist, he was always curious about the materials used on any painter's palette.

After a few seconds, Hitler took a deep breath and slid his hand out of the hole. Then he calmly turned to his three subordinates, his small, Chaplinesque moustache twitching comically as he took in all their faces. "I want them to pay," he breathed, his liquid-blue eyes suddenly turning skyward.

Himmler stepped carefully forward and then sidled up to the raging Hitler. Out of earshot of the others, he whispered, "They will pay, *Mein Führer.*"

"What?" asked Hitler, his attention back on the workings of the bomber.

"They will pay for their attacks on Germany," continued Himmler, puzzled by Hitler's sudden absent-mindedness.

"When?" Hitler asked, running his hand over a bent blade of the propeller. He suddenly looked up and saw the two .50 caliber Browning machine guns in the undamaged top turret, still keeping a vigil against airborne intruders even though the gunner had long-since bailed out.

"Late summer," Himmler answered. "The Japanese will be ready by then."

Hitler spun around and faced him. To Himmler's relief, the Nazi leader's eyes were now back to their intensive gaze. "And von Braun's program?"

"I have a good man at the whip," returned Himmler, confidently.

"Make sure he uses it now and then on that arrogant blue blood," Hitler spat. "Von Braun is like a temperamental thoroughbred and needs to feel a cold steel bit in his mouth."

"With pleasure, *Mein Führer*. And rest assured, the Americans will be in for the surprise of their lives!"

Hitler nodded and rubbed his cold hands together. Somewhere, on the other side of the aircraft, he had dropped his gloves. "Good, good," he said, approvingly, as if the past five minutes had never existed.

Then he added, "I think it's time for a warm meal," and walked away, directly past Göring and the SS colonel, to the waiting limousine. The smile on his face surprised both of them.

CHAPTER ONE

Off Great Point, Nantucket
Three miles outside US territorial waters
August 15, 1941

The scene in Gus' mind played over and over again and, of course, the outcome never changed.

* * *

Four elk were crossing the frozen mountain lake, frantically trying to get up some speed but being held to a slow, clumsy pace by the deep snowdrifts that coated the ice. The 14-point bull, his massive antlers shoving at the young spike in front of him, snorted violently like a locomotive, the vaporous breath forming great clouds with each loud exhale. In front of the large calf, two cows struggled through the thick, white barrier, which might well have been made of tar rather than snow.

Jim Keegan and George Blondin, his best friends, displayed a wide-eyed excitement as they slammed the cold bolts of their rifles shut with echoing metallic clicks. His huge jacket hood almost covering his entire face, Jim turned to him and chirped, "This is going to be a turkey shoot, Gus!" Without another word, he brought up his Remington and fired. A thunder erupted in the stillness, echoing down the range of mountain peaks in a series of smaller explosions.

In his exuberance, Jim's bullet missed its intended mark — which had been the rib cage of the great male — and struck the much-smaller spike elk in the haunches. The back legs of the young animal, who was a few months shy of a year old, suddenly went out from under him and his back end slumped down, placing him in a tragically comedic seated position.

The instant the animal dropped, the trajectory of the mushrooming bullet became instantly clear to the boys as a red cone-shaped spray painted on the snow beyond the animal. The stunned elk sat there for a few seconds before his body began to quiver in convulsions. Then came a series of unearthly cries from the animal.

The others in the small family just stood there. They were stunned, unable to comprehend what had befallen their youngest member. One cow nervously nuzzled him, sniffing at his blood-soaked hair. Then, a few seconds later, her nostrils went up and flared in the frigid air. It was at that moment that her eyes locked on the three boys. Completely ignoring the bleating and thrashing of the wounded elk, she wheeled and plunged ahead into the snow. The others, sensing her fear immediately, redoubled their own efforts to escape.

For almost 10 seconds Jim, George and he watched the turmoil of the animals, so awe-struck by the handiwork of Jim's bullet that they seemed unaware of the 20-below air on their bare hands. In their excitement to ready their weapons, they had forgotten their discarded mittens. They also never heard the scolding of a flock of ravens and a duet of whiskey jacks, hardy winter birds whose peaceful existence had been shattered by the resonance of the loud shot.

It was George who finally broke the mood, the lad spurred on by a rocketing rush of adrenaline. Seeing him in his school clothes, one would not have taken him for an outdoors man, but the thick, padded coat and fur-lined cap transformed his skinny frame into that of a beefy mountain man. In a move that made Gus shiver, George suddenly threw his bony head back and let out a loud, piercing cry. It sounded unearthly, a primeval response to the bawling of the calf, and it sent chills up the backs of his two companions. When his whoop ended, he calmly looked at Gus and said, "Let's get 'em all."

* * *

In an effort to regain his night vision, Lieutenant Commander Augustus Anthony Lanton squeezed his eyes shut for a few seconds before bringing his binoculars back up for another look. The ocean breeze was now in his face and the smoky residue from scorched oil attacked the insides of his nose. Stifling a sneeze, he searched the moon-soaked swells to the north of the burning tanker, straining to find what he feared would be the conning tower of a German submarine.

"Mr. Kennan?" he barked, lowering the binoculars to his chest.

"Nothin' yet, sir," piped the adolescent voice of Able Seaman Matthew Kennan, one of three lookouts Gus had posted up on the forecastle. "But it's gotta be a sub. Tankers just don't blow up like that on account of a leak or tossed cigarette."

"Ain't that the truth," Gus replied under his breath, rubbing the loose skin on his large face. Although he was still a few years away from middle age, his face was beginning to sag with jowls. A small fold of skin hung below his jaw line. This seemed to exaggerate his already anxious-looking countenance.

"What do you see coming from the tanker, Mr. Kehoe?" he asked, suddenly peering over his right shoulder at another sailor, while carefully keeping his eyes from the bright flames emanating from that direction.

"Lifeboats coming down, sir," answered Harvey Kehoe, the bosun's mate, one of his veteran sailors. From his perch, Kehoe had a better view of the inferno, which was now a thousand yards off the starboard beam.

"I count . . . one . . . two . . ." Kehoe was silent for a few seconds, then added with a tired lilt in his voice, "Just two, sir. They tried to get another one off but it's not moving down. The davits must be rusty."

Gus reached into his pocket and pulled out the remains of a cigar. Then he began to chomp on it. Even without smoking the tobacco, he felt its calming effect. His wife, Ginger, used to tease him about his habit, calling the old cigar butts his "soothers."

"Men are beginning to jump off the gunnels now," Kehoe continued. "There's maybe a half-a-dozen guys swimming in the water and —"

He paused for a second and then Gus heard a strangled cry from the sailor. "Christ in heaven, sir, they're on fire!"

"Thank you, Mr. Kehoe," Gus replied, trying to keep his tone matter-of-fact. "Keep your eyes sharp. With three more sitting ducks to shoot, that sub won't leave on our account."

"Aye-aye, sir," the bosun's mate replied.

Having to stare down a fully armed U-boat had never been in Gus' wildest thoughts when he began the patrol last evening — especially on the shakedown cruise of the first in a brand new line of United States Coast Guard cutters. He was just supposed to "let it air out," and go over the modern systems with his crew.

Most of the *Montauk*'s crewmen had been with him for two years on his previous vessel, the USCGS *Cape Cod,* a small patrol cutter operating out of Portland, Maine. When Gus was promoted to the large Hamilton-class cutter, the new ship was still being finished in the dockyard. So during the four months they had been beached, Gus had drilled his core crewmen on the new weapons systems, especially the anti-submarine technology. Then he brought on the new recruits and blended them in with the trained crew. Now both vets and "kids" stood side-by-side on the gunnels, able to load live depth charges on the racks and K-guns, a far cry from the rock-filled practice barrels they had used a week before.

"Mr. Myers," he bellowed into the communications pipe at chest level. "Prepare to lower a whaler with three crewmen and Doc Hayes!" Even as he mouthed the words, Gus knew it would be too late to save the poor souls who were thrashing around in the burning oil, but it was better for his crews' morale that he went by the book and sent along Hayes.

Lieutenant Martin Myers came up to the forecastle two steps at a time, his shoes making a slap sound, unlike the muffled thump of a sailor's sneakers. The 29-year-old Myers had a small-featured face like a Chihuahua, and his brown eyes were always darting in their sockets like two miniature cameras searching for clues. Tonight, he was adding conning officer to his job of duty officer.

"Whaler ready, Commander." Myers was a southerner who hung onto every vowel with a laziness that seemed odd during a period of crisis. He pronounced Lanton's rank as "Comman-dah."

Like Gus Lanton, Marty Myers was a landlubber, hailing from Conway, Arkansas, where he was well versed in running small boats on the lakes. A Montana man, Gus was familiar with lakes as well, but his kind was usually a mile above sea level and surrounded by mountains.

Removing the stogie for a few seconds, Gus inhaled the cool ocean air, which was so much different than the crisp mountain air of the Rockies. It never bit at his face like the frigid mountain breezes, but found its way through his government-issue summer jacket and chilled him to the same effect. He silently mused that if they were a mere 50 miles to the east, he would have his jacket off, basking in a balmy breeze brought on by the Gulf Stream.

But here, off Nantucket, his body trembled, nearly in rhythm with the *Montauk*, whose slightly vibrating deck felt like a living organism. He hoped his shaking was due to the cold wind and not the fear building in his stomach.

Until this moment, his most dangerous adversaries had been smugglers' ships, mostly two-bit bootleggers whom he could easily outgun with one .50 caliber machine gun. A German sub, on the other hand, was the perfect killing machine. Like the ocean's most formidable predator, the shark, it operated in a three-dimensional world, using the surface of the dark water to conceal its presence until it could strike. Then it used the same medium to make good its escape. It was in the middle of this dangerous world that Gus and the 165 sailors on the *Montauk* hovered like men swimming in water when they knew that a predator lurked somewhere beneath the surface.

However, unlike the ocean carnivore, a U-boat did not have to reveal its presence to kill its victim. When a shark struck one tuna, the school instantly became aware of its comrade's killer and escaped while the shark gorged itself within a cloud of blood, seemingly oblivious of the others. A submarine just kept killing until either all the ships were sunk — or had escaped — or until the torpedoes were used up. Worse still for its intended prey, a sub could surface and destroy unarmed freighters with volleys from its 15cm deck gun.

"Very well, Mr. Myers," Gus said. "Prepare to lower the whaler, but make sure you arm your party with Thompsons. The Jerries might decide they don't want the merchantmen manning another ship and they may come around to finish the job." A batch of submachine guns did not add up to the firepower of a surfaced U-boat but, like having the doctor aboard, it was a positive factor in preserving crew morale.

"Would they do that, sir?"

"Well, Marty," sighed Gus, "let's just eliminate the chance of whether they do or don't. Besides, we won't be far away so just fire a flare the second you spot something."

"Aye-aye, sir."

* * *

George Blondin fired before he drew another breath, the 30.06 round taking the bull elk in the neck. The great animal shuddered, and then bellowed loudly when the pain registered a millisecond later, but it held its balance. Seconds later, it seemed to recover from the shock, frantically pounding with its hoofs to gain traction on the slippery surface.

* * *

"U-boats rarely attack when they're submerged, so this guy's gotta still be on the surface," Gus said, absent-mindedly, thinking Myers was still within earshot. "But without that new radar system we were promised, we have only our eyes."

Right then, he silently cursed his superiors for not including his Hamilton-class cutter in the batch of those ships chosen for the new Radio Direction and Ranging apparatus, or radar. The fleet had made it clear that the Navy had first dibs on them but gave Gus the impression that there were enough for the Coast Guard cutters as well.

However, the staff at headquarters had counted wrong, so the Navy hogged all the radar despite Gus' protests that his ship needed the system to combat submarines. Gus took the matter right to the top.

"Don't be daft, Gus," laughed Rear Admiral Stokes, his superior and Coast Guard representative to the US Navy appropriations board. "Submarines go *under* the water, or don't you know what the prefix 'sub' means?" After this belittling at the hands of his own boss, the argument turned out to be extremely one-sided and Gus sheepishly left the meeting without his precious radar.

However, even without the means for surface detection the *Montauk* was still a formidable opponent for any sub. It was outfitted with the Type 29 ASDIC, a newer version of the British/French-designed underwater search device. In the United States, the Navy decided it would be called *sonar* — for Sound Navigation and Ranging.

The system on Gus Lanton's ship, despite being on the leading edge of technology, was only effective only up to 1300 yards. And those specifications had limits. The ship had to be traveling up to 15 knots speed in good sea conditions where malfunctions could be kept to a minimum. In Gus' favor, he had a well trained crew and his sonar man knew the new instrument as well as he knew the lines on the palm of his hand.

In addition, the cutter was outfitted with the new high-frequency direction-finding apparatus, or HF/DF. The "Huff-Duff," as the sailors called it, enabled an escort vessel to track down a submarine by detecting its high frequency transmissions when the U-boat surfaced to send either radio or navigational signals. One ship with HF/DF could alert the convoy about the presence of a U-boat and its distance away, but if two surface ships got a contact, an accurate fix could be made and the coordinates radioed to aircraft or ships closest to the spot. These attack craft could then close in on the submarine.

"Let's get those men out of the water," Gus suddenly remarked. "Come right to zero-zero-five."

"Come right to zero-zero-five, sir," echoed Myers, directing the orders to the helmsman.

"Steady on zero-zero-five."

"Steady on zero-zero-five, aye."

The *Montauk* eased gently to starboard before settling back into a straight course, making a slight curve in the wake off the stern. The forward gun crew, bedecked in asbestos fire hoods and helmets, leaned with the course correction. To Gus, they looked like medieval pikemen readying a catapult.

"Commander!" barked Kennan from the forecastle. "Contact off the starboard bow. I confirm it's a submarine!"

"Contact has been made off the starboard bow!" reiterated Gus. "Ready all guns!"

"Gun crews, action stations!" replied the gunnery watch officer, Petty Officer Harris Fontaine. He straightened his hood and stepped in behind the forward gun crew, preparing himself to supervise the firing procedure.

"Both engines back two-thirds, steady as she goes!"

With the call to action, Gus suddenly felt warmer and noticed his shakes were gone. His eyes suddenly sharpened and he felt as though he could see clearly in a dark cave. It was a feeling that many commanders experienced going into their first battle: a rush of adrenaline compounded with the exuberance of putting every ounce of training and past experience to the test.

"Both engines, back two-thirds, steady as she goes, aye!" the conning officer chimed, the helm responding to command.

From his perch on the forecastle, Gus still could not make out the low-slung shape that lurked ahead of his vessel, but it was not due to his natural eyesight. The burning tanker caused a blind spot in that direction and the glare had eroded his night vision again. "Mark target!" he shouted.

"Target still in sight, sir!" returned Kehoe, whose eyeballs were still glued to the enemy boat.

"Fine, Mr. Kehoe," Gus returned, his feet carrying him slowly aft. "Mr. Kennan, get a position on those life boats and set a beacon. We'll have to come back for them." The crewman began readying a floatable carbide lamp to toss overboard.

"Mr. Myers, signal that sub. First, identify our ship and inform them that they are approaching the waters of a neutral country. Then order them to break off their attack immediately, as we mean to go in and pick up survivors."

"Aye-aye, sir!"

Fontaine scanned the surface where the gunnery watch had first spotted the contact and asked, "Sir, shouldn't we fire off a couple of flares to see where the sub is?"

"Negative," Gus replied. "That could be taken as a provocation. Our friend out there is probably gun-happy enough right now and I don't want to do anything that might be misconstrued as a hostile action."

"Besides," he added. "the flare would light us up also, and we sure as hell don't want him to see all our cards in case we have to fight him."

As the cutter wheeled around for the new course change, the front half of the dying tanker came into sight. It was now at a 45-degree angle, with the bow pointed toward the star-studded sky. The air in her forward compartments was compressed to such a high degree that the glass portholes were exploding and could be heard as a series of pops above the roaring flames.

In the calm water around this last vestige of what once was a home to 33 sailors, the great fire was spreading slowly, igniting in great patches as the thick black cargo bubbled to the surface. The two lifeboats were, thankfully, now well upwind. But there was no hope for the crewmen who thrashed in the water directly in its path. In a short time the creeping fire silenced their screams.

* * *

The spike pawed at the slick surface under the snow in an effort to keep upright. It had stopped bawling, as if trying to conserve its energy for another try at standing. In the area around him and the dying bull, the confused cows stamped at the snow, trying to beat a path that would enable the wounded elk to escape.

George howled like a wolf as he slid another 30.06 cartridge into the chamber, slapping the bolt down with his half-frozen hand. Raising his rifle, the teenager looked over at Gus, who had yet to lift his gun. "Come on, Gus, you gotta have a shot at this!"

* * *

You gotta have a shot at this!

The words buzzed through his brain as he watched the fiery bow of the ship and the flaming waters around it — an inferno whose radiant heat was coming across as a welcome summer breeze on the unseasonably cool night. In a cacophony that only could have been orchestrated by Satan himself, the loud hissing of steam offset the low rumble of the oil-fed flames and boiling water.

Just when he had steeled himself to the macabre din, a sudden crack of thunder rocked the night and a flash added a brilliant exclamation to the orange and yellow pyre. As Gus eyed the origin of the blast, a ship approximately 500 yards beyond the sinking tanker, a second denotation obliterated it in a blinding eruption that lit up the horizon like it was midday. A split-second later, the aftershock hit the *Montauk* and shoved the cutter over into a steep list to starboard. Then a sound like thunderclaps attacked his ears.

Gus Lanton was a stocky man, bearing a muscular 220 pounds on a six-foot frame, but the hot blast of air tossed him against the bulkhead as if he were a pillow. Excruciating pain shot through his shoulder almost making him black out. For several seconds, as spots danced before his eyes, he thought he would throw up. Every piece of equipment that was not lashed down came crashing down onto the decks as a loud series of hollow-sounding smashes and clattering arose from the vents leading to the lower decks.

The US Navy had known about his physical condition when Gus had applied to Annapolis almost 20 years ago. His grades were impeccable but he was refused entry because of what they termed as "unacceptable physical limitations" — which meant that his right shoulder drooped because of a gunshot accident in his early teens. The esteemed US Naval Academy found it difficult to accept that a lop-sided cadet could fit the image of the modern sailor. However, the Coast Guard had no objections to allowing the barrel-chested young farm boy in their ranks. So began his dream of becoming the commander of a ship.

The *Montauk* righted itself with a rocking motion, and the terrified sailors grabbed for anything sturdy within reach. In the process, some lost their footing and slid into bulkheads, while the others clung to guardrails to prevent themselves from being pitched over the side.

Finally, the cutter settled into gentle pitching, each motion gentler as the effects of the blast receded. When he had recovered his balance, Gus surveyed the spot where the freighter had been. For five long seconds his sight was limited to a collage of bright blotches, unable to see anything.

He closed them tightly. A few seconds later, he opened them to witness a sky full of flaming wreckage that was gently drifting down onto a waterborne inferno that seemed to consume the ocean itself. He now knew for sure that a second of the four ships had been hit but, unlike the tanker, this one was completely destroyed by its volatile cargo.

"Damage control!" Gus yelled, still blinking his eyelids in an effort to focus in the false twilight. The call was echoed through to midships.

The lanky Marty Myers appeared before him as a spotty ghost. "Damage control reports no harm to the ship other than broken dishes and one hell of a mess in the kitchen, sir."

"Casualties?"

"Everyone accounted for. Two headed for sick bay with fractures and seven with lacerations." Miraculously, none of the crew had gone overboard.

"Thank God," Gus breathed. Just then it struck him that the whole port side of his ship and the horrified faces around him were bathed in a flickering yellow light. The strange illumination gave them odd masks that seemed to expound their fears. Like him, these were Coast Guard sailors, trained for search and rescue and for rooting out contraband. Although he had trained them to detect and fight submarines, none of them had believed their routine drills would be put to the test. Nor had they been prepared for the abhorrence of war — like seeing living men on fire. After all, America was not at war.

As he wrestled with the options he watched the anxious faces again. Many months ago, his fellow officers had thought it was radical move for Gus to put his crew through anti-submarine drills, exercises that sometime precluded other training schedules in the Coast Guard directive. For some reason, he felt it important for them to know how to fight submarines, as if someone had tipped him off that war with Germany was a foregone conclusion. So, while other ships were practicing their gunnery, Gus' men were studying ASDIC operation and acoustic sounding. But despite all their static training, none of the crew had been prepared for what they were witnessing at this point.

"Sir," Myers continued, "we were flashed a message in English just before the explosion but Walker never had a chance to deliver it." The OOD reached over to hand him the piece of paper but Gus waved for him to read it. His eyes would never be able to focus well enough to read right now.

In his southern drawl, Myers read the hastily scrawled note. "It says, 'We are operating in international waters, stop. This is none of your concern, stop. You may pick up survivors when our business here has been concluded, stop.'"

* * *

The great elk lay still, his head and huge antlers hidden by the newly fallen snow. All that showed was his mountainous back — like a dark-brown island on the lake. Just behind him, the spike seemed resigned to his death and sat with his head lowered like a contented dog awaiting a biscuit from his master. Short puffs of frozen air, like translucent balls, popped from its nostrils in quick, regular intervals as if the dying animal were a small, animated steam engine.

The disoriented cows circled them once more, now smelling death in the large bull and the certainty of it in the younger one. With this registering in their brains, the instinct for their own survival slowly began erasing the memory of their family members. A few moments later, they suddenly plunged into the deep drifts toward the safety of the far woods.

"Dammit, Gus, if you ain't gonna shoot, we're gonna take 'em, ourselves!" cried Jim, raising his rifle and aiming at the rump of the fleeing cow on the right."

It was now snowing so hard that Gus could hear the snowflakes touching his earlobes. His rifle and gloves were now coated in the fluffy stuff and appeared to him as part of the scenery. He turned around to his friends and said in a low, calm voice, "No more shooting."

George looked away from his aim and asked, "Huh?"

"I said," Gus repeated, in a louder tone, "no more shooting."

"Says who?"

"Says me," Gus growled. "Hell, we've got more meat here than we can cart out in two days. Killing them makes no sense. It's just plain murder."

"Yeah, well you ain't my boss!" spat Jim, returning to his aim.

"Me neither!" echoed George. Both boys now had their sights on the bobbing haunches of the bounding cow elk, which had not gone far in the deep snow. At less than a hundred yards, even through the curtain of falling snow, they could hardly miss. What they never could have foreseen, however, was a determined Gus wading out through the deep snow toward the animals, flailing his arms and shouting as he walked.

At the sight of Gus, the frightened elk redoubled their efforts in the opposite direction, putting Gus between them and the shooters. As the boys readjusted their rifles, Gus came into their sights. "Holy smoke!" cried George. "What in Hell are you —"

The report of Jim's gun cut him off and the surprised boys saw Gus' body lurch forward. In a grizzly remake of the scene with the spike elk, a conical spray of red stained the otherwise pristine snow.

* * *

"Commander Lanton?" Gus looked into the bright, jaundiced-like faces of Myers and Able Seaman Walker. "Sir, how should we answer them?" Myers asked.

Gus' attention flipped back to the sinking tanker. In a few scant minutes, the *Montauk* had moved to the right of the scene, where the flaming debris from the destroyed ammunition ship was now being slowly smothered by the gentle swells. If he did not put down the whaler soon he might overshoot the lifeboats and risk losing any waterborne survivors from the ammunition ship. The floating carbide lamp would only show them where to pick up burned bodies.

"All stop!" he said, his voice suddenly exuding confidence. He knew his crew was ready. All they needed was a commander.

"All stop!" The pitch of the cutter's twin engines rose as the propellers were reversed. The ship's progress slowed somewhat, but Gus did not wait for a full stop.

"Lower both whalers!"

"Lower number one and number two whalers!"

The two small rescue craft were winched down the steel rails of the davits. There were three crewman in each, one petty officer, one seaman and one medical officer, all busily sorting out the blankets and first aid supplies as they descended. When the small hulls touched the water, the crewmen unfastened the davit ropes and then began rowing toward the waning flames.

When the whalers had gone approximately 30 yards away, Gus suddenly shouted, "All ahead two-thirds!"

"Sir?" asked Myers, in a puzzled tone.

"I said, all ahead two-thirds . . . now, Mr. Myers!"

"Aye-aye, sir!" Myers answered, and *Montauk* was soon underway, much to the surprise of the six crewmen in the whalers.

"Mr. Kehoe!"

"Sir?" replied the gangly youth, dropping his binoculars.

"What's our contact doing now?"

"He's proceeding west at about 12 knots, sir. I figure he's maneuvering for a shot at the remaining two freighters."

"Christ, that's fast," Gus growled, knowing that Kehoe's prediction was right. International waters or not, the U-boat's skipper wanted to kill these remaining ships and then get his boat as far away as possible. No doubt the distress calls from the ships had been received and would bring out Royal Canadian Air Force bombers from Nova Scotia before first light. They may not save the ships, but the stubborn Canadian aircrews, in their rugged PBY flying boats, would either kill the sub or harangue it into the deep, keeping it there until Royal Canadian Navy corvettes could reach the area.

"All guns prepare to fire on my command."

"All guns prepare to fire on command!"

Seconds later, Myers turned back to Gus and said, "Gunnery watch officer reports all guns ready to fire on your command, sir."

"All right, Mr. Myers," Gus said, peering out over the dark swells. "It's time we took control of this little dance. You tell that Kraut sonofabitch that we have two rescue craft in the area and he is to break off his attack immediately.

"And add this: The rescue craft are American and any further action on his part will be construed as act of aggression upon a United States vessel and *will* be met with extreme force."

"Aye-aye, sir," grinned Myers. He stretched the last word out to "sa-ah."

Gus took a deep breath and fought off another bout of the shakes, but this time he knew from where it came. The cold had worked into the old wound in his shoulder. His right side was as stiff as an old oak door.

As he looked to the bow, Gus saw the readied gunnery sailors in the Great War-era British "Tommy" helmets and bulky flak jackets. It was then he realized that he had neglected to put on his own battle dress. He immediately gathered up his kit from a large box affixed to the bulkhead, donning his Mae West and then plunking the slate-blue steel helmet on his head. The dull pain sharpened as he raised his arm but he ignored it.

The old floatation vests never gave him comfort. For they were long past their prime and, in terms of specific gravity, he calculated they were probably on par with an anchor.

But Gus was confident they would never need the life-saving equipment. The armament of the new Hamilton-class cutters was not only formidable for a Coast Guard ship, but could rival many smaller naval vessels. There were the smaller Ready Guns: two .50 caliber machine guns manned at all times; one rapid-fire three-inch gun forward; and two 20mm anti-aircraft guns, one on each side. In the event of a battle, three more three-inch and two five-inch guns could be quickly manned — which required only the addition of one more crewman and the removal of the waterproof covers.

"Torpedo! Bearing one-nine-four!"

"Hard to starboard!" barked Gus, lunging for the railing to get a better look. He clamped his fingers around the tubular steel willing him to resist the fear that wrestled with his stomach.

"Hard to starboard!" echoed Myers. The ship lurched and, as if protesting the sudden move, a sharp pain lanced through Gus' shoulder again. He ignored it as he had the discomfort in his stomach.

Just then his eyes caught the white wake of the projectile moving through the black swells. Thankfully, fire was behind them so they could track the white wake.

"Come on, turn," Gus uttered, trying to goad the new ship into a tighter circle. He was aware of the hissing of the water and its cold spray on his face as the cutter's bow bit into the swells.

Ten heart-stopping seconds later, the bubbling wake of the projectile could be seen crossing the bow of the *Montauk* and heading out to sea.

"Holy Hanna!" cried Myers, his eyes locked on the foaming trail.

"Contact fuses," deadpanned Gus, his large chest beginning to pound like a boxer's speed bag. "Probably fired from its rear tubes and meant to scare us off."

"You reckon?" countered Myers.

"Sure," responded Gus, his nervousness making his voice a higher pitch. "If he wanted to kill us he would have used a magnetic exploder. They're driven by electric motors and meant to pass under the ship and go off below the keel, breaking the ship's back. They're slower, but you can't see them coming."

And then you're dead, Gus wanted to say. *And then you join those unfortunate merchant crewmen in the drink, waiting for the cold water to sap out your life or to fry slowly in burning oil.*

"Can I help you to sick bay, sir?" Myers asked, his smallish eyes perusing Gus.

"Uh, no, I'm just winded, Mr. Myers," Gus responded lazily. "You go up to the bridge. I'll be along shortly."

Gus watched the last of the white stream disappear and felt the emotional rush fade with it. Pushing back from the rail, he began to take deep breaths. In less than half a minute, the shaking had stopped and the nausea was gone.

"Thank you, Lord," he sighed, glancing upward. Then he trotted up the steps to join Myers on the bridge.

"All ahead full," he said, calmly, his feet now braced and back erect as if he were one of Nelson's captains whose ship was moving in to engage the French and Spanish fleets at Trafalgar.

"All ahead full, aye!"

"All right, Mr. Fontaine," Gus said, confidently, "fire a five-incher across her bow."

"Fire a five-incher across her bow, aye!"

A loud report came from the front of the ship, combined with a bright yellow flash. Seconds later, a white geyser broke the silvery swells 200 yards away. Without the fiery glare and smoke from the flames of the stricken tanker, the dark conical shape could be seen clearly. However, the last two freighters were just as visible, silhouetted against the lights of the coast.

Gus silently cursed the government for allowing the seaside resorts and highway commissions to use power as usual. The effect was like drawing a big gunsight on every coastal freighter trying to get up the coast from New York, New Jersey or as far away as Texas.

In a veiled attempt to aid Great Britain, President Roosevelt had ordered a Neutrality Zone for 300 miles out from the American continent, but Hitler's U-boats routinely ignored the ruling as contrary to international law. Many America First advocates lobbying in Washington felt that Germany could not be expected to adhere to a unilateral declaration of ocean sovereignty such as the Neutrality Zone.

Even though the United States adhered to the Neutrality Act, Gus and his fellow Coast Guard officers knew that war between the United States and Germany was as inevitable as the coming winter. They also agreed that not only was the United States *not* ready but some influential American politicians seemed to be swinging back the other way in an effort to placate the German lobbyists in Washington. This meant that some congressional committees were too jammed up with arguments between isolationists and those who felt war with Germany was just around the corner to come up with a sound plan for war when it started.

Just then a flash appeared from the running submarine and there was whistling sound over the bow.

"Come left to zero-one-four!" spat Gus.

"Come left to zero-one-four, aye!"

Turning at 15 knots, the *Montauk* shoved over like a race car overshooting a corner.

"Range of contact?"

"Range of contact . . . 150 yards . . ."

"Commander, she's diving!" bawled an excited Kehoe, his loud voice barely heard over the thrumming engines and machinery vibrations of the charging cutter.

Gus glanced at his watch and marked the time. He never wavered with his next order. "Fire guns!"

The flashes attacked his eyes from the full compliment of guns that were brought to bear. All roared to life except for the starboard machine gun and rear three-inch cannon. In the distance he could make out dozens of geysers straddling the low form and bright yellow and blue sparks flashed where hits were being made on the steel conning tower. Then the form slid under and was gone.

"Both engines ahead flank, steady as you go! Stand by depth charges!"

The gunners scrambled from their perches and raced to their alternative posts, the depth charge racks in the stern and the K-guns along the sides. The K-guns used a charge to fire the barrel-shaped depth charges in an upward angle out and away from the ship.

"Make ready a four-four spread. Set depth charges for 150 feet." At that depth a hydrostatic pistol-fuse would detonate the charge in each canister.

As he watched his crew go through their paces, Gus suddenly realized that this was the first live action they had ever been through. His orders were very clear: if fired upon by a belligerent, use any and all force available to defend your ship and crew.

Gus cocked his head in the direction of the radioman. "Send the following transmission to COMINCH, Commander-in-Chief of the Navy," he said. "USCGS *Montauk* fired upon by German U-boat at six-nine-degrees-45-minutes-west stop 42-degrees-15-minutes-north stop *Montauk* presently engaging stop."

Then he added. "Send in plain language."

"Aye-aye!"

Gus checked his watch again, his eyes glued to the second-hand. "Ready depth charges!"

"Depth charges ready, aye!"

"Three . . . two . . . one! Away depth charges!"

"Away depth charges, aye!"

A series of small explosions shot the T-shaped launchers from the K-guns, hurling two depth charges out into the air on each side of the ship. The large cans came down and hit the waves 50 feet out. At the stern, four 600-pound barrels were rolled off into the churning wake of the cutter.

Moments later, falling at a rate of 16 feet per second, the bombs went off in rapid succession, churning the black water into huge, white geysers and causing tremors through the *Montauk*.

"Commence echo ranging. Search 150 through 220."

Petty Officer Harry Collins, the ASDIC operator, sat in an open compartment aft of the bridge and listened intently to his headphones. For his commander's sake, he had the sonic sounds piped through the bridge speakers. The ASDIC instrument was housed in a dome on the underside of the hull. It sent out sound signals that, when they struck an undersea object like a U-boat, returned a pulse echo that gave the objects bearing and range. It could not, however, measure depth, so Gus had to rely on the second hand of his watch, and it had been 42 seconds since the submarine disappeared.

PING-ping . . . PING-ping. The sound of the pulses almost caused his teeth to chatter.

The 35-year-old Collins was another of the "old crew" whose skill with radios had made him a natural choice to operate the temperamental ASDIC. "Contact bearing one-six-five, four-nine-two yards."

"Helm, bring her about to one-six-five and hold steady."

"One-six-five and steady!" The second turn of the cutter was even a tighter circle than the first, causing pots and pans to rattle free in the galley as crewmen lost their footing and grabbed onto overhead pipes for balance. It would be the second time they would have to clean up the galley in less than a half hour.

As the ship finished her turn, Gus spied the carbide float lamp that had been set to show where the first spread had been dropped. He had trained his crew well enough in these maneuvers not to be surprised by their diligence. The illuminating speck was 10 degrees to starboard, which showed that the course of the submarine was still toward the freighters and would most likely attempt to use them as a screen to lose the *Montauk*.

"Commander," interrupted Myers, running onto the bridge. "I thought you should know that, in another 1,000 yards, give or take a few, we'll be in US territory."

"Thank you, Mr. Myers, you've just made my day." Fortunately for the freighters, they had run toward the American shore and were now just inside American waters. But, in the heat of battle, it was doubtful if the U-boat commander had realized this. Or maybe he would conveniently ignore the fact.

"Left cut, one-eight-oh."

"Left cut, one-eight-oh, aye!"

"What's happening down there, PO?"

"Signal's strong and getting stronger. She might be hurt."

Collins gripped the earphones to his head for a dozen more seconds. Suddenly his body jerked up ramrod straight. Looking up at Gus, he announced, "Instantaneous echoes!"

"Another eight-pattern charge!" Gus blurted out.

"Another eight-pattern charge, aye!"

The sound of exploding K-guns echoed along the metal bulkheads as more of the depth charges flew out laterally, their launchers falling into the waves behind them. Seconds later, eight more rapid explosions shook the sea as the canisters of highly-explosive Amatol detonated.

Gus looked toward the shore and saw the small, stern-view outline of the freighters making for the sound. In this direction, devoid of the glare and smoke from the burning oil, the sky was much lighter. In about 20 minutes, a squadron of American bombers from Weymouth would be overhead to shepherd them into Canadian waters.

* * *

As he fell, Gus saw brief snapshots of the rumps of the cow elk, their white and tawny brown color mellowed by the spray of fine snow smashed into a mist by their hoofs. He couldn't see his friends; however he knew they must be angry because one of them had hit him hard behind the right shoulder.

To their credit, the quick-thinking 14-year-old boys had tightly wrapped their scarves around Gus' wounded shoulder and placed him on the toboggan they had brought along to carry back any animal they shot. As they pulled him along, his last memory was of two ravens landing on the snow-covered shoulder of the large elk. The birds were pecking at the oozing blood.

Luckily for Gus, the freezing air had helped to staunch the flow of blood from his shattered shoulder. When they reached the horses, four miles back down the mountain, Gus' sled rope was then tied to the saddle horn and he was pulled along to the rangers' station. The park official gave him first aid. Then he put him in the back of his pickup truck and drove down the mountain to the hospital in Columbia Falls.

The doctor had to make three layers of stitches and graft the clavicle with a piece of Gus' rib, a radical treatment for a small Montana hospital. It took almost a year to properly heal but the shoulder would always be slightly lower than the left one.

* * *

"U-boat surfacing off the starboard stern!"

"Hard to port. Gun crews, action stations!"

The *Montauk* made another tight turn, again throwing anything not fastened down to the starboard side. When the cutter was almost at the second carbide light, he saw the water boil not 300 yards away. In the dark slate sky, the conning tower of the submarine became clearly visible. Then the whole boat broke the surface.

"Prepare to fire forward guns!"

"Prepare to fire forward guns, aye!"

Gus squinted to get a better look at the dark figures appearing on the conning tower. He was just about to give the order to fire when a shout broke his train of thought. "Commander. Someone's waving a sheet of some kind! I think she's surrendering!"

A loud cheer went up from the crewmen and several of them began jumping up and down in merriment. Marty Myers entered the bridge and lightly slapped Gus on the back. "You did it, sir! You got us a U-boat!"

But Gus just scoped the boat in silence. It was as if he were looking beyond the surrender flag for some trick. A few seconds later he simply said, "Prepare all stop."

* * *

"My name is *Kapitänleutnant* Lothar Stahl and I desire to lodge an official protest with the German embassy in Washington."

Stahl's English was very good, with only a light hint of an accent with his *s*'s. Unlike Americans, who pronounced "is" as "*iz*," Stahl verbalized them as "isss," like the hissing of a snake.

Stahl was far from the imposing masculine figure Gus had imagined he would be when the German commander appeared in his ready room. Instead of a six-foot-two, blonde, blue-eyed superman — as portrayed in the German newsreels — Lothar Stahl was under six feet by a couple of inches, his face was gaunt and he had dark hair and a matching beard. His eyes were a light chestnut color that flashed gold when the light hit them.

The German officer was also soaking wet, having refused the invitation from the *Montauk* crewman to go below and get dry clothing. He was in definite need of a bath, his body odor exacerbated by the stink of wet wool. At the moment, however, his personal hygiene did not seem to concern Stahl.

But his mannerism seemed to fit the bill, as if he were acting out some Teutonic play in order to impress the American of his importance. The U-boat man was expressing his outrage at having his command destroyed by the vessel of a country that, he thought, should have remained neutral in this situation.

At 30, the lithe Lothar Stahl had been a lover of U-boats for nearly a quarter century. As a youngster, he used to sneak into the naval yards in his hometown of Kiel and watch the submarine crews returning from battle. The image of the shabby, bearded men in fishermen's sweaters lined up on the decks of a sleek *Unterseeboote* was firmly lodged in his mind. He envied them for the cheering crowds who threw flowers at the "knights of the seas" and the bands which provided the joyous and proud atmosphere for their grand returns.

He remembered how the crewmen grinned through their beards and pointed at the hastily painted numbers on the conning tower, denoting the number of ships they had sunk during that voyage. In those days — in the late summer of 1918 when the German land forces were in retreat — they were the last symbol of German invincibility. And in the end, when the armistice was declared, they remained undefeated.

Stahl entered the U-boat service when it was a ghost force, a secret part of the German armed forces which was not supposed to exist by order of the Treaty of Versailles. It was headed by his uncle, Karl Dönitz, a torpedo boat captain and former seaplane pilot, who had also been a U-boat ace in the Great War. After the war, Dönitz was chosen by Wilhelm Canaris — head of the intelligence service of the High Command of the Armed Forces — to assemble quietly a new *Unterseebootewaffe*.

In 1934, after the Nazis came to power, parts were smuggled in from the Netherlands, Spain and Finland to build 10 boats. Lothar Stahl, a bright 23-year-old midshipman, was asked to join this elite group and spent most of the next two years involved in espionage and the transport of contraband. When his Uncle Karl was made *Führer der U-Boote*, Stahl was given the rank of lieutenant on Günther Prien's *U-47*.

On his first mission, the *U-47* sailed into Scapa Flow, the heart of the mighty Royal Navy, and sank the battleship *Royal Oak*. Shortly afterward, Prien and his crew were given a parade in their honor in Berlin where an awestruck Lothar Stahl shook hands with Adolf Hitler. However, that was two years and nearly 40 victories ago. Now he stood as the captive of an amateur.

"At this time, commander," replied Gus, in a very officious tone, "your embassy has been advised of your situation and, when we dock, there will be representatives of same to meet you. We should be at the pier around 0915, in roughly five hours."

Gus noticed that Stahl had a habit of rolling a gold ring around his index finger. A quick glance at the emblem on the ring confirmed it was a hooked cross, the Nazi symbol.

"And my boat?" he asked, the nervousness not showing in his question. It was as though he were asking for the train schedule from a conductor.

U-329 was the latest version of the Type VII, the *C*-class. Gus knew the specs by heart. It displaced 761 tons, had four torpedo tubes in the bow and one in the stern, a surface speed of up to 17 knots and a range of more than 9,000 miles if traveling at 12 knots. This craft, and a 100 like it, were responsible for sinking over three million tons of British shipping in only two years of warfare.

"My chief engineer has confirmed that the leaks in your boat's inner hull have been sealed and it should withstand the trip to port. Two tugboats are presently on course to tow it in."

"I would, of course, like to accompany it," added Stahl, as if it were a foregone conclusion.

"That is not possible, sir," replied Gus. "Even though you are not considered an enemy, you shall remain under scrutiny until the politicians decide what to do with you. My superior has informed me that this procedure will be handled exactly as it is written in the Neutrality Act. That being the fact," Gus went on, "I cannot let you back into a position where you could possibly escape or do harm to your vessel."

"But, I must see to the pumps," Stahl countered. *What he really means,* Gus thought, *is that he wants to finish the job he began before the boarding party crashed his demolition exercise.*

When the Americans had first gone aboard, the U-boat crew were burning documents. The sight of submachine guns made them stop. However, a weighted case hit the water and disappeared before the Americans reached the open hatch in the bow area. Gus figured it was the Enigma coding machine and cursed his own careful, but time-consuming, procedure in preparation for boarding the craft. If he had sent them in two minutes earlier, the cipher machine would have been in his hands — and with it, the secret of the German Navy code.

Forty-seven of its officers and crew had been offloaded to the *Montauk* and were now in the aft compartments under guard. The merchant sailors were being kept in the front to avoid a chance meeting. If that happened, no amount of persuasion, other than armed intervention, would keep the surviving victims of the two torpedoed freighters from mauling the submariners.

"Negative, commander, you —"

"You have breached several high seas laws!" Stahl rebutted, angrily. "Right now, your government is probably figuring out what it will cost the American people to compensate Germany for this act of piracy."

Gus never took the bait. "Be that as it may, commander," he countered dryly, "you are still my prisoner and I have control of your boat until my boss says otherwise."

Then turning to the husky non-com behind Stahl he said, "Petty Officer Harris, take the commander down below and see to it that he receives food and dry clothing."

But Stahl wasn't finished. "Commander Lanton," he said, his teeth clamped as he spoke, "do you realize what you've done?"

"Yes, I do, Commander Stahl," Gus replied, his eyes unblinking, "and if there were any aberrations in my conduct I will have to answer to my own commander for it."

He then flipped open his package of Lucky Strikes and pulled out six. Handing them to Stahl, who accepted them, he added, "Now, the only thing I have to worry about is how I'm going to keep 47 British and Norwegian sailors from getting to your crew. It seems that they want to have a rematch on a level playing field."

Stahl's brownish-green eyes flipped up from the cigarettes in his hand and met the hard stare from the American. Instantly, he knew that what this man lacked in combat experience would be amply made up for in intelligence and tenacity. He also knew he would never underestimate the Americans again.

Just then, two muffled explosions caused them both to turn their heads toward the dark shape moored off the starboard side of the cutter. As they ran to the railing, they saw water boiling around the U-boat. Less than 10 seconds later, the bow came up like a giant black cigar and the submarine slid by the stern from sight below the gray swells.

"Shit!" snapped Gus, his dark-brown eyes burning into Stahl's face. "Your engineer was still down there!"

"He was a brave man, commander," Stahl added wistfully. "He gave his life to scuttle your prize."

CHAPTER TWO

August 19, 1942
9:33 AM
In the English Channel off Dieppe, France

For some reason the E-boat never challenged them again. The German torpedo craft may have had problems maneuvering in the shallow waters, or it may have been that there were other, fatter targets to go after. Either way, two of Captain Wyn Parsons' men were writhing in pain on the floor of the landing craft from the earlier attack, blood squirting out on the rusty steel deck in a red slick. A couple of soldiers in the tightly-packed group lost their footing on the greasy floor and had to be held up by their comrades.

Two medics squeezed in among the bunched soldiers and were already cutting away the wool tunics to get at the wounds. But it was not very precise workmanship. The landing craft was pitching in the mid-morning swells, the combined see-saw and rolling action inducing more than a few of the Canadians to lose their breakfasts — thus adding to the unsure footing.

"Peters is gone," yelled Corporal Guiness over the drumming of the engines, a red cross on his white armband.

"Who's the other one?" shouted Parsons over the rumble of the engines, pushing the woolen-clad soldiers aside as he leaned over to speak with the medic.

"Medchuck," returned Lance Corporal Addison, the other medic. "A 20mm round smashed his hip. It musta gone through Peters and ricocheted."

Wyn Parsons swayed with the motion of the boat, the warm breeze hardly compensating for the stifling hot jacket. *These bloody uniforms are too hot for the summer and too cold for the winter,* he thought.

Wyn's dull blue eyes peered out from under his net-covered battle helmet like two hardened stones. "Get Peters to the back and patch Medchuck up quickly so we can get him there too. It's almost time."

Wyn was feeling queasy as well, but he never heaved. His stomach felt the same way he did when he had worked on his great uncle Jimmy's fishing boat in the waters off Shelburne, Nova Scotia. It ached from his groin to his heart and reminded him that, from his earliest recollections, he never liked being out on the water.

That was why he had joined the Army — and the day after he made that move was when he realized he had gone from the frying pan into the fire. First, there was the troop ship across the Atlantic, then the amphibious landing drills off Dover and now this waterborne attack on Dieppe, on the other side of the English Channel.

His upbringing in a southern Nova Scotia fishing community started off ordinary. He was baptized in the United Church as a boy of eight, as his parents decided that the new church would be good for their young Wynton.

Within two years, however, the happy family was torn apart. His mother died of tuberculosis, her prolonged death throes causing his father great pain. Spiritually shattered, George Parsons sunk into a deep depression, finally killing himself with a shotgun blast in the mouth.

For an instant, as he glanced at Peters' blood and viscera sprayed on the ramp of the landing craft, Wyn pictured his father's headless corpse. It was for this reason the scene didn't horrify him as much as it did his seasick soldiers. It merely steeled him to the job at hand; just as his father's death had made him tough for the abuse he suffered later on in the orphanage. In his eyes, his father had taken the easy way out, leaving young Wyn with a burden that no motherless, 10-year-old child should ever have to bear.

When he stood upright in the rocking boat, Wyn was a husky six-foot-one. The three long years of training in England had filled him out and now, at 22, he was a muscular 210 pounds. His freckled, angular face and his strawberry blond hair gave him the look of a boy in a man's body. But when looking into his slate-blue eyes, people saw a hardness that offset his youthful looks.

"Check your rifles and ammunition!" he barked. A series of clicks followed his pronouncement as the platoon members checked their ordnance, both in the wedge-shaped clips of their Lee Enfield rifles and the long lateral magazines for those wielding Sten guns.

Placing his foot on a protruding bolt in the gunnel, Wyn lifted himself up to see the objective bobbing in front of the rocking craft. The sun was now high enough to bathe the starboard side of the boat, and he winced at its cutting brightness. A cross-channel breeze gave him a brief respite from the growing heat but it also brought up the unpleasant smells from the bottom of the landing craft — ones that accompanied fear, motion sickness and death.

Wyn was but one of almost 150,000 Canadian soldiers who had been based in England since the fall of 1939. Originally, they had formed the backbone of the force that was ready to repel the expected German invasion in 1940 but now, two-and-a-half years later, they were the most over-exercised and under-utilized troops on either side in the war. In addition, their inactivity was a breeding ground for discontent within their ranks and among the local population of the surrounding areas where they were barracked.

The Dieppe invasion, code-named *Jubilee*, came at an opportune time, not only for the bored soldiers but for the Canadian people as well. Prime Minister Mackenzie King and his wartime government were itching to get into battle like their Commonwealth partners, New Zealand and Australia, which were facing Rommel in North Africa. For a country like Canada, whose troops had spearheaded every major Allied breakout in the Great War, being left in a stagnant defensive position was more than a little demeaning.

The attack was supposed to be carried out on an 11-mile front, with the town of Dieppe as its center, but the planners could not have picked a more formidable target. Two high promontories flanked the beach at the town and to each side were unscalable chalk cliffs. Added to these natural defenses, the Germans moved in heavy batteries, poured cement pillboxes and implanted deadly anti-aircraft guns.

During the many briefings, Wyn was informed that the troops opposing them were inexperienced German recruits and old Wehrmacht soldiers unfit for regular combat duty. There was also talk of Polish conscripts who would surely turn their guns on the Germans at the first sign of an Allied invasion.

Admiral Lord Louis Mountbatten, a cousin of the King and a former destroyer commander, was in charge of Combined Operations. He managed to meld it into a cohesive force, but his inability to convince the heads of other departments, such as the RAF, to cooperate with the initiative led to a diminished version of the original concept.

The plan called for landing six infantry battalions, one tank regiment, two commando outfits and a multitude of support units. The commandos would knock out the big coastal guns to protect the invasion fleet and then two of the Canadian units were supposed to take out the guns on the headland promontories. That would lead the way for the main Canadian force which would land in a frontal assault.

Mountbatten visualized the attack on Dieppe to be a shining light in a sea of despair that had plagued Great Britain in the past year. Nazi Germany was at its zenith, having conquered virtually all the land between the English Channel and the Black Sea, from Normandy to the outskirts of Moscow and up through Norway to the Arctic Circle. There were over 400 million people under the swastika, and it looked as though Rommel's Afrika Corps was going to push the British all the way across North Africa into Egypt.

In the Pacific, things had not gone much better. The Japanese had taken all the British possessions in Southeast Asia and with its indomitable air power had easily sunk the *Repulse* and *Prince of Wales*, two of Great Britain's greatest battleships. So, after three years, war-weary Britons needed a victory.

In the late night hours of August 18th, the moon shone down on an invasion fleet of 237 Royal Navy ships. In a few hours, with a calm sea ahead of them, nearly 5,000 Canadian infantry and tank crew, 1,100 British commandos, a handful of Free French, 50 American Rangers and some German expatriate interpreters would be landing in France.

However, disaster struck shortly after the ships set sail. Just after 0300 hours, 23 landing craft of No. 3 Commando ran into an armed German convoy. Wyn saw the faint glow from the flares and heard the furious gun fight, finding it odd that the invasion had begun so early. He never knew that No. 3 Commando, in their wooden landing craft, had been severely mauled by German naval guns and would be in no shape to take the coastal guns when, and if, they landed.

The beach was now about 2,000 yards away. To his dismay, Wyn saw that the clouds of black smoke blanketing most of the area were not from German positions, but from destroyed landing craft and broken Canadian tanks. They lay on the beach like crippled whales, with light-brown forms interspersed all around them, far from their objective: the white facade of the casino which lorded over the beachhead. *Why didn't they get up and get to the safety of the wall?* he wondered.

A sound like a small locomotive went over Wyn's head and he quickly ducked his head. He turned around and heard a muffled explosion as a huge spray of seawater came down on one of the Royal Navy crewmen who operated the unwieldy boat.

The young landing craft skipper readjusted his cap and signaled for Wyn to come to the back. The Canadian captain squeezed his way through his men, taking in the fear in their eyes. He not only knew each of them by first name, he knew their parents' names and, with some, had even memorized the faces of their wives, sweethearts and kids. These were young men with whom he had been living for three whole years, and he suddenly found it difficult to look at them as just a bunch of soldiers in net-covered tin hats.

Wyn pulled himself at the stern up to get close to the pilot and ducked again as another artillery round pasted the ocean. The navy man, his white gloves so soaked that they were almost transparent, leaned down and yelled into his ear over the thrum of the engines.

"Captain," the boat pilot said, "I have orders to stand by."

"What does that mean?" queried Wyn, his body bumping the gunnel railing as the craft hit a large swell. The heat increased by the minute, and the sweat began to run in small streams down his body.

"It means that they're calling the show off, that's what it means," answered the British sailor, his temper worsening by the second. "Take a look for yourself. Your pals aren't even off the beach."

Wyn pulled himself up for another look, his boots slipping on the gunnels. The craft had gone more than 50 yards since he last had a peek and he now could see the reason for the lines of Canadian soldiers lying on the shore.

They were all dead.

A few groups were huddled up against a sea wall, but he saw no more because of the smoke. A geyser erupted on the ocean directly in front of him and his face was hit with a blast of cold water. From the intensity of the shooting, Wyn surmised that the German artillery piece had singled them out for practice. Along with many things that had been promised this day, he had been assured that there would be no big guns when they arrived. The commandos and the RAF were supposed to have taken them out.

Two more rounds roared overhead and then a closer explosion in the water threw him back onto his men who, luckily, held their footing and prevented him from hitting the steel floor. Another near miss rocked the small boat, slamming the men together.

Ten seconds later, small arms fire began hitting their boat, sounding like a group of elves striking the thin, steel-coated wooden hull with tack hammers. Wyn lowered his hand to the men, signaling them to crouch as low as they could to avoid any ricocheting bullets. In the next instant a small shell hammered the loading ramp out front, shaking the craft as if it had just collided with a floating log.

As he looked back at the acne-scarred face of the landing craft driver, his eyes locked on the patch on the man's arm which read: Royal Navy Voluntary Reserve. With his perpetual grin, the young man looked like Donald Duck.

"How long have you been in the Royal Navy?" Wyn asked, his mind temporarily distracted from the landing site.

"A year . . . on and off," was the reply.

"On and off?" asked Wyn incredulously. "What's your real job?"

"I'm a tailor," replied the driver, expecting a smart remark from him.

However, Wyn ignored his comment and unrolled his small, waterproof map. At least the man had got them to the right beach. But they seemed to be the only ones going in.

"Captain!" yelled the other Royal Navy man, a husky lad of no more than 19. He was clutching his headphones, as if to drive them further into his head.

Wyn pulled himself up again, his helmet netting catching on a cable. He suddenly wondered if his unwieldy steel headpiece could stop a bullet.

"Captain, I have orders to turn back!" the young man yelled.

"What?" Wyn protested. He had heard the man, but the thought of it never registered through his brain. The Hamiltons had been practicing for this show for a year. Before that they were either guarding English beaches against a possible German invasion from France or training for another go at Norway. It was three years of training and boredom waiting to get at these very same Germans who were just a few hundred yards away. This was it.

"For crissake, captain," he pleaded, "take a good look at the situation. Your men are getting bloody well murdered."

Wyn peaked at the beach again and his heart dropped. He could now pick out scores of men's bodies bobbing against the shore and each other. Through the smoke he could see others taking refuge behind the wrecks or nuzzling up against the seawall, their main obstacle in taking Dieppe.

They were members of his battalion, the Royal Hamilton Light Infantry and, if not for the balls-up navigating of the Stooges — as he now referred to his Royal Navy entourage — they all should have all landed together. *Major Fairweather must already be there,* he thought.

During the regimental meetings concerning the Dieppe operation, Fairweather had used a model of the town and the German defenses. During one of these meetings, the commander of the 2nd Canadian Division, Major General Hamilton Roberts, was present and he assured them that the RAF would bomb the German guns into oblivion. Also, one British battleship and three destroyers would pound the beaches before the landing took place.

Well, Wyn had heard no airplanes, except for the odd buzz early in the morning. And there were certainly no British ships in the area otherwise the fast E-boats would not have had a chance to take a crack at them.

That little detour had cost them an hour. And when you add to that the lost time spent while the Stooges tried to figure out where they were, that would have put them three hours behind schedule. Now it was fully daylight and the Germans were wide awake.

Wyn glanced at the sea around them and noted that the two other boats, just 200 yards behind them, were executing long turns to port. These landing craft had followed Wyn's boat figuring his navigator knew the way. It was a classic case of the blind leading the blind. Now, with clear orders to return, they were cutting out.

In all this confusion, there was one thing Wyn knew for certain: *If they turned back, who will take the troops off the beach? Are we just going to turn tail and leave our comrades to perish or be taken prisoner?*

Out of the corner of his eye, he saw the navigator's white-gloved hand go up and the man rotate his index finger. The pilot nodded and Wyn heard the engines being cut in preparation for turning the craft about.

In a sudden fit of pent-up rage, the boyish-faced Wyn pulled his Webley pistol and pointed it at the driver's head. "Get those engines going," he screamed above the cacophony, his strained voice taking even himself by surprise. "We're getting those men off the beach before we go anywhere!"

The frightened British pilot immediately gunned the engines and began making for the French beach again. As bullets careened off the bulkhead, his fear began to transform to anger.

"Don't you know we're all going to fucking die, you idiot!" the sailor yelled.

Wyn just raised the gun higher until it was eye level. "Prepare to lower ramp!" he cried. Beside the driver, the frightened communications sailor numbly nodded and reached for the lever.

As the winch motor groaned in preparation, Wyn regarded the anxious faces of his men. What he was doing was contravening a God-given reprieve on his men's lives in order to send them into a maelstrom which could turn out to be an ill-fated attempt to save their comrades.

Lowering his pistol, he waved his two lieutenants over and they squeezed through the tense khaki bodies and over to his side.

"Fredricks," he yelled to the young officer, making his plan up as fast as he could think, "when we hit the beach . . . just before the ramp lowers, you launch a dozen smoke grenades. Then get your men out and under cover, and begin to lay down fire at the German positions above the seawall. I want everyone back here in five minutes."

"Check," Fredricks replied.

"With 90 seconds left, send up a flare and then throw out some more smoke grenades. Get your men back to a defensive position around the landing craft."

"Check," he repeated.

"Hawthorne, you get your men moving as soon as the ramp hits. Get to as many of our guys as you can. You have only five minutes, so check your watch. When you see Fredricks' flare, you will make your way back for embarkation. The ramp goes up whether you're here or not. Is that clear?"

Nodding heads signaled their understanding. Suddenly Wyn felt scared. He could call it off right now, making up any excuse he wanted and no one would think anything bad of him. They could be back drinking hot coffee aboard ship in less than an hour.

"Ramp!" yelled the disgruntled sailor. The engines were immediately cut and 22 soldiers of the Royal Hamilton Light Infantry made ready to jump to rescue their brothers-in-arms. When the thought of their small numbers hit Wyn, his groan blended with the grating sound made by the sudden slowing of the craft as it slid into the shallows.

Wyn leaned over to Sergeant O'Brien and said, "Billy, you stay and supervise the loading. Get them in quickly."

He added: "And keep a gun on our chum here. If he tries to leave before five minutes, shoot his friend."

"It would be a pleasure," replied O'Brien, shoving a bullet into the breech of the Lee Enfield and slamming the bolt shut. The navigator recoiled in horror as the rifle came up. The Disney character was instantly gone.

"You know," added O'Brien, with a chuckle, "back in Ireland in 1916, my father used to shoot at your kind for sport."

"All right!" yelled Wyn as he pushed through the forest of khaki. "Let's get our friends!"

The rattling of chains signaled the lowering of the ramp, which dropped like a falling slab of cement onto the rocky beach. Wyn was the first one out into the smokescreen and, for an instant, was enveloped by a choking gray mist. Crouching as he hit the beach, his feet sunk up to the ankles in the large round gravel. But he never pondered the traction of the shore for too long. Bullets began smacking around him, sending up sprays of stinging round stones the size of large playing marbles, hastening his sloppy steps. A metallic ringing in his right ear signaled that one had careened off his helmet.

Suddenly, the whole war seemed to be situated in the small area around him. His comrades had suddenly vanished and Wyn's world became a series of snapshots of the landscape as he ran: a calm, dead face; blood running from three torn bodies into a tidal pool; the opaque-gray of exposed intestines; a head with a red maw for a face.

The soundtrack was just as disjointed. There were no explosions and yelling as there had been in training. Instead, his ears rung with snaps, cracks, whines, pops, and human cries. His eyes smarted from the whiffs of oily smoke.

From that time on, Wyn never thought about what he was doing. The years of training took over. His legs moved unconsciously as he became an animal akin to a crab or badger, using his left hand to help him scramble sideways toward the murky image of a tank. A few feet of crabwalking later, the air began to clear and the pictures began to grow together.

Suddenly, the scope of the devastation began to register in his mind for the first time. Bodies were strewn from the shore to the seawall; he saw dozens of muzzle flashes above the wall. Almost none of the German defenses had been neutralized.

His leather heels rolled and lost their traction on the billiard-ball sized rocks — like running over coarse ball bearings. An instant later, he was safely behind a damaged tank whose burning fuel, thankfully, added to the smokescreen. Sucking in an unintended lungful, he began coughing uncontrollably, almost dropping his rifle. Then his eyes focused through the mist on three petrified soldiers staring out from under the tank. He recognized them instantly.

"MacNeil!" he hacked at the nearest one, wincing at the soot in his lungs. "Where's the major?"

Before Private MacNeil could answer, a mortar round went off 10 yards away peppering them with rocks. One smacked Wyn above the right eyebrow and a stream of warm blood spilled down into his eye and ran down his cheek in a wide, red stripe.

"Captain, you're —"

"Bugger it!" cried Wyn. "Where's the major?"

"He's up at the wall!" the private answered, lowering his eyes. He half expected a verbal onslaught for his cowardice but Wyn's bloody face softened and he asked, "Are you hit?"

There was no answer.

"Okay, then," Wyn continued, "run to the landing craft. It's going to take you home."

He then peered around the front of the tank and was confronted by the dead face of a tank crewman whose body was sprawled out of a hatch. Looking past the corpse, he saw a group of Canadians huddled together at the high breakwater. From the cinnamon-colored bodies lying around in thick heaps, he could see that many had tried in vain to get over its 10-foot height.

Interspersed with the dead were a few satchels and several lengths of six-by-six-inch logs. Wyn's heart dropped when he saw them. They were the sappers' tools for blowing a hole in the seawall. He was now certain that the engineers outfit had never even made it halfway to their destination.

He swiped at the blood clogging up his right eye and peered at his watch. Two and a half minutes had gone by. "One, two, three!" he shouted for encouragement. After "three," he let out a roar, digging his feet into the gravel and pushing with all his might. His powerful legs pumped and his line-of-sight narrowed to the cluster of khaki figures bouncing in his field of vision.

In an odd flashback, the maneuver reminded him of hockey practice when he was a kid; the pushing off during stops and starts. His coach had made the team go over the tedious drills, which entailed starting from a standing position and skating to a full stride, and then quickly stopping. He made the team do this for half an hour at the start of each practice before he allowed them to touch a puck.

Hockey had been his way out of the small Nova Scotia town. A scout from the Hamilton Steelers had seen him play in Moncton and sent him a train ticket. In his exuberance, Wyn purchased another one for his girlfriend, Laura, boldly thinking that she would elope with him. But he had been wrong about that. He had put her in an awkward position. Tearing a 17-year-old girl away from her parents for a life of uncertainty was too much to ask, even for someone who cared for him as much as she did. She stayed at home, and he never saw her again.

Hockey had been his way into the army. In April of 1939, the 19-year-old Wyn had been ejected in the first game of the playoffs for fighting. Then, when the other player in the confrontation wanted a rematch in the second game, Wyn thrashed him again, but was thrown out for the rest of the series for his efforts. His team subsequently lost and the owner took it out on the rebellious Wyn, unceremoniously dumping him from the Steelers. With no job and no money, Wyn walked into the nearby armory and enlisted. That was on August 19, 1939, exactly three years before.

As the ground moved past him, his mind raced back and forth from hockey, to Laura — who was now married to a fisherman from Port Mouton — to his mother and father's wedding picture, his father's shattered body, and then to a baseball game between Shelburne and Springhill, one in which he scored the winning run by sliding into home plate head first.

The battle sounds returning to his mind, he suddenly leapt and his body traveled in much the same horizontal trajectory that had won that game only five years ago. He seemed to be airborne for minutes, hearing every slapping bullet, smelling a variety of things from smoke and spent cordite to blasted flesh.

Faces grew in his eyes. They were not just forms anymore; they grew into Major Fairweather, Sergeant Gentry and Captain George James of D Company. Then he landed on his chest and felt the wind blast out of his lungs.

"Parsons!" cried Major Fairweather, as three sets of hands reached out and dragged him to the safety of the wall. His run seemed to have attracted some attention as a machine gun began stuttering. Rocks spat up and danced around their position.

"Where have you been?" the major shouted, looking him over for any wounds.

"We had a party with the German Navy," Wyn replied, his lungs still aching from deeply inhaling the smoke.

"Major," he said, firmly, glancing nervously down at this watch, "we have just a little over a minute to get back to the landing craft."

"What?" the major asked. "Our orders are to wait for the tanks." It was obvious he did not know about the recall. Looking over to his right, Wyn saw the reason. The radio was smashed.

"They're not coming, sir," Wyn replied, his breathing slowing down. "The mission's been called off."

"Called off?"

"Yes," he replied, shooting a glance at the men farther up. "Now please, sir, we have to get these men back before the landing craft leaves. I only gave them five minutes."

"What about the others?"

"My boys are gathering as many as they can, sir. After that . . ." His tired voice trailed off.

Fairweather stared for moment at the sandy-haired Parsons, gathering the situation more from his gray blue eyes than his words. The major was a tough career soldier, a veteran of the Great War who had seen many battles.

In less than 10 seconds, Fairweather had messengers scurrying to others who were farther up the breakwater and, one by one, the men peeled themselves away from their safety pocket and began picking their way back through the smoke. A few wounded men were helped along but those that were badly hit were leaned against the seawall and given cigarettes.

"I guess we better get going, too," sighed the major, staring at the dozens of corpses. As for the wounded, he said, "We'll have to leave most of these guys for Jerry to look after. At least they'll get hospital care. God knows what might happen if we try to move them."

Whether it was from the smoke or the tragedy of the situation, the major's eyes were brimming with tears. "So many good lads butchered," he sighed.

A spark appeared through the lazy smokescreen, which was now thinning at a rapid rate, and blossomed into a pink flare.

"Major," interrupted an impatient Wyn, "we have to go."

"Right then!" Fairweather chirped, his chin suddenly set. "Let's go!"

At 52, the major was old for his rank but was in excellent shape and maneuvered quite deftly around the wreckage as bullets zipped by. Wyn and the other three scampered behind, all peering through the smoke for any other survivors.

It was more to good fortune and the drifting tide, than to the pilot's credit, that the landing craft was now parked behind the burning tank. For the moment, it appeared as though the German gunners had lost it in the smoke. This fortunate circumstance enabled the retreating Canadians to get on the boat unscathed.

However, a breeze began slowly to move the smoke in another direction and the landscape began to show through. The blasted hulks of three more landing craft appeared through the mist revealing dozens of bodies that bobbed in the oily water. Some had been cut down by machine gun fire before they could get out of the water and away from their doomed vessels. Still others drowned under the weight of their equipment and were now bumping against each other on the shoreline, joining the silver masses of dead fish that lined the shore.

Luck still remained on the side of the landing craft. The drifting smoke continued to hide it from view of the German gunners as the men streamed on without incident. Once aboard, they jammed against each other until it was evident that the ramp would not be able to close properly.

"All right," yelled Sergeant O'Brien, his rifle somewhat more relaxed and not aimed at the pilot anymore, "some of you get up here and slide in beside our Navy chums."

A sudden change in wind direction began to erode the shroud and, with the smoke now clearing, German mortars began to target the boat. Shells began blowing small craters on the beach and the running major went down just before he made it to the ramp.

The other men in the fleeing group had not seen him get hit and were now pressed up against the solid brownish-green humanity in the landing raft. But

Wyn, pulling up the rear, dropped down beside him and quickly checked him over. The major's right leg was mangled, with his thighbone protruding like a bloody spear.

"Get out Parsons!" Fairweather cried. "I'll take my chances with Jerry."

Through the mist, Wyn could see that the ramp was beginning to go up. He ignored the major's pleas and yanked the officer's arms around his neck, nudging his helmet under Fairweather's chest. With a shove of his athletic legs, he had the man up on his back and was moving toward the landing craft.

"What are you doing, Parsons?" scolded the major, his face wracked with pain.

"Stops and starts, sir," coughed Wyn, pumping his legs under the weight, "Stops and starts."

"The captain's coming!" someone yelled and dozens of soldiers craned to see around the smoldering tank.

"Stop the ramp!" yelled O'Brien, raising his gun again. The terrified Royal Navy sailor, his hand shaking, stopped the winch. "We're all going to die!" he screamed.

"Fine," replied O'Brien, "but if you touch that lever before the captain gets in, you'll go first."

With the ramp up to waist height, Wyn rolled the major into the waiting arms of the packed troops and then pulled himself over. The same hands pulled him in.

"Okay, go, go, go!" yelled O'Brien, putting his gun down. At that instant, the landing craft wrenched back and the ramp came up and slammed tight. Five seconds later, it was clear of the beach, maneuvering between the damaged hulls of two tank carriers. The sea was speckled with bodies, and the squeamish driver flinched with each one that slid under his boat.

Now out in the open, bullets smacked against the hull with greater frequency, the larger 20mm rounds making screeching sounds when they scraped along the steel-sheathed surface. Feeling like a duck in a shooting gallery, the Navy man drove the boat with his head barely over the bulkhead, just enough to see where he was going. But his crouched position would not help him.

A mortar shell hit behind the steering area and exploded, throwing his torn body against the steering controls. When O'Brien looked up, the man was dead, his accusing eyes staring at the sergeant. The two soldiers behind him had disappeared, just a red paste against the bulkhead where they had been leaning.

The navigator was shielded from the blast by his partner's body and now he quickly took up the controls, pushing the dead sailor away as if he were an old mattress rather than a former friend. He then gunned the engines and the craft was soon moving into the channel.

For these weary survivors of the Hamilton Light Infantry, it seemed as if God were playing a game of craps with the Devil, and each tick of the clock was a winning throw against the Prince of Darkness. Every second was another 20 feet to safety.

From the headlands on the flanks of the town, German artillery crews were now picking up the retreating boat. They brought their captured French 75mm guns to bear and soon huge geysers of water began erupting around the fleeing craft. The rapid firing cannons were initially designed for use as flak guns against enemy bombers. These were the guns that were responsible for decimating the Canadian tanks on the beach area. Instead of lobbing a shell, as a mortar did, the shells went in a straight trajectory so that the gunners could aim their guns as a rifleman might. Their firing rate was a quick four shells a minute.

While the gunfire pawed at the boat, some of the soldiers in better shape were helping the badly wounded, who were scrunched up against the ramp. Others prayed and a few cried. For what they had been through, and were now experiencing, there was no wrong way to act.

A minute later, the range was too great for the small arms and mortar fire. But the 75's still worried the craft. The Royal Navy man drove through the swells like a motorized cork, weaving around the waves in an attempt to throw off their aim.

"How many did we get?" Wyn asked, as he sidled up to the exhausted Hawthorne.

"Well, we came with 22," the lieutenant replied, "Tremblay and MacDonald never made it back and, with the two we just lost, plus the ones we got off the beach, we're now at 40."

"So, with Peters gone on the way in," Wyn calculated, "we're going back with only 19 of our platoon."

"We also lost the driver," the young lieutenant reminded him, his eyes flitting with fear. Wyn suddenly thought that the young Hawthorne should be back in Ontario, minding his father's horse ranch.

"Yeah," sighed Wyn, his conscience tugging at him.

He stood up and pushed through the crowded soldiery, smiling and offering encouragement to the many faces he saw in the bobbing boat. The pained face of the major came into his view and, at first, Wyn thought he had died.

"Is he —?"

"No, he's alive." Despite the constant rocking, Corporal Guiness had successfully secured Fairweather's leg and was carefully applying the splints. The major almost passed out from the morphine and his head lolled with the motion.

"It looks like the femoral artery's been nicked, but I've stanched the flow," shouted Guiness. "He's lost a lot of blood, but he'll make it."

Wyn examined the face of the man responsible for his officer training. The fatherly Fairweather had seen something in the recruit and picked him off a gun emplacement on the Dover cliffs for his own unit. Who would have known way back then that they both would be bouncing around in a blood-and-puke spattered boat.

"It's too early to tell if he'll keep the leg," added the corporal. "The bone's quite busted up, but we've got some good doctors at —"

Guiness never finished his sentence. A 75mm shell ripped through the hull and exploded among the packed soldiers.

* * *

5:40PM

"No armed Englishman remains on the continent."

— from the diary of Field Marshal Gerd von Rundstedt, Commander-in-Chief of the German Army West, who assumed the attack was an all-British force.

CHAPTER THREE

December 13, 1942
1201 Greenwich Mean Time
USCGS Montauk
Convoy ONSJ-142
About 390 nautical miles southwest of Iceland

"Try to get another sun shot. We must've gone too far."

Commander Gus Lanton chomped on his cigar and sucked some hot, smoky air into his chilled bronchial tubes.

The week's docking in Hvalfjordur, Iceland — "Valley Forge" to the Americans — should have given him time to rest and soothe his month-long cold. However, every minute away from home Gus devoted to his job. That was why he squandered the respite on personally supervising his ship's repairs and meeting with the other escort officers.

Most of time these interviews, which included the crews of B-24 Liberators and PBY Catalina Flying Boats, were 'lubricated' by various types of European liqueurs and too much second-hand cigar smoke in the offing. Hence his poor lungs never had a chance to recover.

"Hate to tell you this, skipper," replied Lieutenant Martin Myers, in his southern drawl, "but our man Dougie is right on the money. We're bang on top of ICOMP."

ICOMP stood for Iceland Convoy Meeting Place, and it was where the small convoy was supposed to join up in formation with Convoy ONS-142. A week ago, the larger, westbound group of ships had formed off Oversay, a small rock formation jutting out from the British Isles, and had been observing radio silence ever since. Calculations were one thing, but everyone knew that the weather in the North Atlantic sometimes decided events that had originally been put into place by either military planners or, at worst, the U-boat command — who seemed to know their every move these days.

There had also been a late blast of the Foehn Winds, a meteorological phenomena that usually came in the late fall in the North Atlantic. Because of the

Gulf Stream, which flowed around Iceland, a semi-permanent storm center called the Icelandic Low formed in the vicinity of the large island and, for the next few months, spawned one howling storm after another; complete with low temperatures and high winds, sometimes up to 100 knots. This was a terrible hardship on the crews as these factors combined for a minus-10 degree Fahrenheit wind chill. To make things worse, the gale force winds and high waves could slow and scatter a convoy of even the most powerful ships.

Gus had been advised by Iceland that the convoy was last seen on the 11th, two days before, by a patrolling RAF Sunderland aircraft. The aircraft navigator guessed that it was a day and a half behind schedule. This being the case, prudence required that Gus' group hold on to the course of the big convoy until dawn, in case it passed by the group during the night. It was now high noon.

It was not only the timing of the big group of ships that worried Gus. The other snag was that his own navigator had not been able to perform a star or sun shot since leaving Iceland three days ago. This meant that they were now operating on dead reckoning, and without a break in the clouds there was no possibility for an accurate reading of their position. They could very well be the ones who were hundreds of miles off their destination — not the delayed ONS-142.

"Jeeze, would you look at that!" chimed Myers, pointing upward. At that instant, Gus squinted as a beam of light attacked his eyes and his dark eyebrows grew into one crooked line. Two huge cloud banks began parting and the pale blue sky was rapidly expanding.

"Get Johnson up here, quick!" Gus barked, raising his binoculars to scan the broad expanse of ships in the convoy. The swells were now an endless expanse of gunmetal gray mountains whose foam-capped tops were instantly blown into spray by the high winds as the waves reached their peak. The showers of seawater made the decks slick and seeped into every fold of the crews' jackets, caressing them with icy tentacles. On a day like this, a warm mug of coffee was tantamount to a hot bath on "Civvy Street."

Myers yelled down a pipe to the navigator, who instantly popped up the passageway like a large gopher. Myers quickly retrieved the chronometer and sextant from the bridge and had it ready for Johnson as he stepped on the bridge wing.

Lieutenant (jg) Douglas Johnson, a native of Oklahoma, slipped on the icy surface but Myers steadied him and they both leaned against the bulkhead to brace themselves against the motion of the ship.

Satisfied that Myers could provide an anchor for him, Johnson lifted the delicate instrument, using his body as a shield against the spray. Then, moving the sextant to the southern horizon, the round-faced, 20-year-old "Okie" squeezed his eyes against the glare of the sun.

"Stand by, mark!"

Quartermaster Petty Officer Billy Stevens jotted the time and date nervously on the clipboard, moving his knees to hold himself steadily against the rocking of the ship as the navigator read out the sun's altitude from the sextant arm. "Nine degrees, 42 points, seven minutes."

Then, as if the weather god had decided that Johnson should only have one go at the coordinates, the clouds squeezed shut again and the gray shadow regained its former mastery. There would be no second reading for a confirmation.

Suddenly, the navigator felt the urge to check the figures he had called out. Forgetting Myers was holding him, he quickly spun around and grabbed the paper from the PO. Myers fell back, his hands unclasping from the navigator's waist as Johnson turned into a fierce gust of wind which threw him into the canvas-padded bulkhead. He remained upright but, as luck would have it, the valuable slip of paper shot out of his fingers, up into the slipstream and disappeared.

"Oh, shit!" he cried, his eyes wide open in terror.

At first, Gus could not believe what he just witnessed. Then, oblivious to the icy deck, he bolted over and grabbed Johnson by his skinny shoulders. "Did you remember the coordinates, Dougie?"

By this time, Johnson was so upset his mind was not registering Gus' words. His heart was drenched with the realization his fumbling could well have cost the small convoy its rendezvous with ONS-142. No navigator, regardless of his skill, could swear to his location on dead reckoning.

To compound Gus' worries, two of the short-run destroyer escorts were running low on fuel, and the valuable tankers needed to replenish them were sailing with the main convoy. They would have to break radio silence soon and find the convoy, or the big ships would have to turn back. And if a German wolf pack found them with only three small escorts, all the zig-zagging in the world would not save them.

"Well, we had our shot," sighed Gus, struggling to keep his emotions in check. To say any more would be to further demoralize the already distraught Oklahoman. Instead, he looked up at the clouds and mouthed a short, silent prayer. When his eyes returned to his anxious officers a grin spread out over his face.

"Mr. Johnson, I think it's time for lunch and an afternoon siesta," Gus said, nonchalantly. "And I'll do the same. Mr. Myers, you have the watch."

"Aye-aye, captain," returned a puzzled Myers. If he had been the commander he might have choked the life out of Johnson.

* * *

December 14
0921 GMT

"Captain, there's a PBY inbound from Iceland!" reported the helmsman, Able Seaman Freddy Parker. The pimply-faced Bronx native had only been out of high school two years but was already a dependable sailor and a veteran of seven trips to "Valley Forge" and back.

Unlike the southerners, Johnson and Myers, there was more of a sense of urgency in his movements, especially in his speech. Myers used to tease him by saying, "Well, if y'all gotta be a Yankee, make sure it ain't a New Yawkah. They's always pissed at somethin'!"

Known for his quick wit, the sandy-haired Parker would have liked to reply but he knew that sailors rarely teased their officers back without suffering extra duties of some sort. Besides, as he had grown accustomed to southern humor, the subtle quips became funnier the more he thought of them. Back home, witticisms were used like fists, a way to get one up on the other guy or to hurt him. Living on a ship had taught him that on a long, cold watch, humor could be another way to deal with the loneliness and fear.

"Thank you, Mr. Parker," replied a stiff Gus Lanton, tossing onto the night table the book he had been reading before he drifted off to sleep. He slowly raised himself from the inclined bunk and gently massaged his right shoulder. The ship was riding easier now and the familiar sound of wind whistling around the forecastle hatch was gone.

Gus never slept lying flat down on his bed. Halfway down his bunk he had installed a wide, padded board, which was raised to a 45-degree angle. On this, he propped his mattress and bedding. It made the process of sleeping that much easier on his stomach. Although his superiors never would have known, Gus was susceptible to seasickness and felt queasy anytime his ship was in motion. The board gave him a better chance at having a prolonged sleep and made getting upright a less traumatic experience than trying it from a horizontal position.

"When's your watch?"

"Ten minutes, sir."

"Well, grab a cup of java and we'll see you on the bridge."

"Aye-aye, sir." The young New Yorker had just gone through the hatchway when he stopped and turned around again. "Oh, yeah, I almost forgot, sir. Lieutenant Johnson said to inform you that he got a star shot early this morning and knows where we are."

"Well," chuckled Lanton, feeling instantly refreshed, "I guess a good night's sleep does more than just give you rest."

As he had done on thousands of occasions since his youthful accident, he stretched carefully, lifting his right shoulder in a slow, circular motion to get the juices going. While performing his calisthenics, his eyes caught Ginger's picture, a professional one taken for the marquee at the dance studio. "I'm a lucky man," he grinned, kissing his finger tips and placing it on her face on the poster.

As he got up, the book he had been reading slid off the stand and he caught it before it hit the deck. Studying it for a few moments, he said, "You're some smart sonofabitch." Then he slid it in among the books on the shelf above his bunk. The title on the spine of the book read:

Herd Tactics: a Naval Treatise by Captain Karl Dönitz
German Imperial Navy
English Translation
US Naval Academy

* * *

"So, that makes the main convoy 23 miles due east?"

"Yes sir," replied Myers. "It was just as you figured. The gale must have slowed them down a half day."

Gus took his first look over the easy gray swells. The Foehn Winds were playing a trick on him, he thought, trying to ease him into a false comfort zone. It would be well into the new year before he could see them calming down for good. For now, he would be content to get the destroyers fueled before the enemy caught wind of their position.

His jacket kept out the wet cold but it bit his nose and neck. For an instant, he cursed his friend, Jim Amor, who commanded a small cutter in the warm waters off San Diego.

"Very well, any signals from the other escorts?" he asked, the azure seas off California disappearing from his mind.

"Just the status quo, sir: keep sailing and let them catch up."

Riding a roller coaster some 600 miles out on the ocean, it now seemed awfully strange to him when he thought of the reasons he moved from the Rockies. He explained to his friends and mates that it snowed too much, and he felt claustrophobic in an area surrounded by tall mountains.

But nothing in the Rockies had ever prepared him for the kind of cold one experienced in a North Atlantic winter. Except for the crewmen down below, no one on the *Montauk* ever complained about being too warm, even in the summertime. It stayed with a person like a dye or a stain that could not be purged by walking into a warm room. Only a prolonged stay in the engine room could begin to take the chill away.

Gus drained the last of his coffee and wondered, for the 10,000th time, why he drank the acidic brew. It had to be wreaking havoc on his bowels after all these years. Ginger never made it for him when he was on shore leave. Instead, she made him a Chinese tea which was supposed to calm the nerves and make him sleep better.

He suddenly felt homesick for his place in Bar Harbor, Maine, and longed for the feel of his wife's body as they danced to *I'll Never Smile Again*, her favorite record. The tune by the Dorsey orchestra and its singer, Frank Sinatra, was always the last one she put on the phonograph before they went to bed. It was a sailor's dilemma: wishing for home when you were at sea, and wishing to be back at sea after a few weeks at home.

They lived in a small house on five acres overlooking the ocean, just south of town. Ginger, a dance instructor, also worked at the hospital for a few days a week. With no children, it helped make his absences go by that much quicker.

When she did come home, she sat out on the deck and gazed over the expanse of water from their deck, much in the same way as sailors' wives had done for eons. Then she fell asleep listening to the radio, sometimes envisioning how Gus and she would dance to the song that was playing.

"Captain?" It was Myers. "Jimmy's got an ASDIC contact bearing three-two-six."

"Sound general quarters!" he bellowed. The clanging of the alarm bell went echoing through the ship.

"Now hear this!" cried Myers, the OOD. "All hands to submarine general quarters!" Less than five seconds later, the cutter lurched forward with the increased speed throwing everyone slightly starboard. A huge spray of ocean swathed the foredeck drenching the newly arrived gun crews.

At the first sound of the bell, the dozen or so staff officers having lunch in the wardroom threw down their sandwiches and bolted through the series of watertight hatchways that led to the bridge. They would be the support crew for the men on duty who had already made the contact. Just before they made it upstairs, they heard the first depth charge explode. Then the ship wheeled hard to port, throwing two of the officers against the padded bulkhead.

"Glad you could join us, gentlemen," mocked Myers, as the shaken group materialized on deck. Flipping a switch on the intercom he said, "Sweep bearings three-two-oh to three-five-oh. Alert the convoy about the situation."

The search continued for an hour with the *Montauk* keeping merchantmen far off to port and, hopefully, out of harm's way. The charges had obviously driven the sub down and, with any luck, away — unless it was part of a pack. Luckily, there had been no other reports.

"Sir, it was a *good contact* at 3,500 yards," sighed Myers, taking a sip of hot coffee. Then he added, "It had to be lining up two of the outside merch's for a shot when we wrecked the party."

Gus' serious brown eyes stared at the chart again, following the lines where the ship had made its search. After a pause of three minutes in which he scribbled light notes along the azimuth, he said, "I know in my gut we hit her. She's either limping home or sailing to the bottom. I'd bet on the latter, but we can only put in the report that we drove her down." Then he added, "Good work, gentlemen."

"Sir," replied Myers, "we could make another sweep. I'm sure we could re-establish contact."

"We could," returned Gus, "but that would put us dangerously low on fuel. Besides, it would leave our southern flank with one less escort for a half hour, and that German may have a friend or two on the other side. We got all our lambs safely to this point. I don't want to start trading U-boat kills for freighters. If she surfaces, maybe one of our aircraft might finish the job."

Gus strolled out to the bridge wing and instantly felt the stinging of the cold on his nose and forehead. His hands warmly gloved, he took out his binoculars and scoped the surrounding ships. The other escorts, the cutters *Ingram, Babbit* and *Leary,* were still dashing around the convoy to set up a screen. It would take a U-boat skipper with iron balls to take up that challenge — and there were, thankfully, few of those anymore.

"Mr. Myers, resume base course and inform the others of my intentions. We have to find that big group before we end up towing our destroyers."

"Aye-aye, sir."

* * *

"Dive! We have to go deeper!"

"We can't, *Kapitänleutnant*. The external pressure connection for the quick diving tank is broken and the port outboard tank has been punctured. To go any deeper would be suicide!"

The dim lights made the water vapor appear like a liquid atmosphere in the small, fetid confines of the submarine. Through it flickered the gaunt, bearded face of *Leutnant* Lothar Hessler, his head bobbing as a pair of overexerted lungs pumped the fetid air in and out. His breathing apparatus hung limply around his neck but he was too busy supervising to think of using it. Water leaked from joints in the overhead piping and steadily dribbled on his shoulder but he ignored it as if it were a common, everyday occurrence.

Then the power went out for a few seconds. When it returned, it was only in an intermittent state. A pulsating short in one of the generators made the tense situation that much more horrific by causing the lights to strobe. To the boat commander, Joachim Beltzer, Hessler and the bosun looked like frantic puppets in the flickering lights.

"If that ship makes another pass we'll never withstand the punishment," complained a stressed Beltzer.

"I know," Lothar replied, his voice backed by the groaning of a couple of wounded crewmen. "But *if* they attack again, their depth charges will be set for a target much deeper. They won't be expecting a hunted U-boat at barely 80 meters and their ASDIC doesn't calculate depth."

A sly smile came over Beltzer's flickering face. Like Hessler, he too had a thick, wet beard which gave him the look of a rain-soaked animal. "Once again, Lothar, your reasoning astounds me."

But the attack never came.

"Sir, the escorts are moving farther away!" announced a relieved crewman through the pipe from the radio room. "They must be nine or 10 kilometers from us."

"Thank God," sighed Beltzer. "Up to periscope depth."

The commander spent 10 minutes scoping the surrounding seas and sky for intruders. "Prepare to surface."

With his eyes still stuck to the viewer the U-boat broke the surface. "Officer of the watch! Start diesels! Hatches! Gun crews!"

Lothar gave the order to the helm and then shifted over to the cluster of funnel-shaped speaking tubes. Putting his mouth up to the one that was labeled, *Sprechen Dieselmotram,* he informed the engine room of the speed and course of the boat. Normally, the orders for the operation of the twin nine-cylinder, 2,170-horsepower diesel engines were relayed electronically from the control room to the engine-order telegraph, but because of the damage the machinists were operating the electrics manually. Then, he bolted aft to check on the wounded. Three men had been injured but the only serious casualty had a broken arm.

As Lothar made his way through the narrow confines, men disappeared into every crack and hollow to let him pass. The crewmen were like frightened night creatures, their eyes flashing fear with every step he took. At his feet, water sloshed back and forth, pushing fruits, vegetables, and other flotsam.

When he reached the engine room, he sighed with relief. The big stacks were thrumming normally and the leaking water had been curtailed. The older *Maschinistmaat* looked up and gave him a brief grin as he scampered through. Hans Schumman was a veteran of "The Happy Time" and a miracle worker with a wrench. Sparks flew from the dynamotors as Schumman and another machinist soldered a large cable. If the older man could not fix it, Lothar knew it was not serviceable. Burnt electrics and diesel fuel, mixed with the faint odor of chlorine gas, attacked his nostrils which, by his standards, was far better than the puke and urine smells in other parts of the boat.

"How much longer until we have them operational?"

"Not much longer, *Leutnant,*" replied Schumman.

Just then the pump gave out a loud banging noise and quit working. Lothar stood in stunned fascination as the most vital organ of the U-boat stopped. Without it, they could not operate the diving systems.

"Damned compressors," spat Schumman. "When we get back to base I'm going straight to the Junkers office and tell them what a piece of shit this machine is!"

At almost the exact instant, the sweet smell of ocean air wafted in from the open hatch covers and Lothar and Schumman momentarily forgot about the compressor.

CHAPTER FOUR

June 18, 1943
Port Pleasant,
South Shore of Nova Scotia

"Elroy's bringin' her in some fast, he is," quipped Jimmy Enslow, shoving his old black pipe back into his mouth. The old fisherman shifted his weight on the Maple Leaf butter box, digging his rubber boots into the worn planks on the pier for stability.

At 79, Jimmy was the last of his generation of Grand Banks schoonermen. The younger men, ones who fished for haddock, lobster and tuna off the islands of the south Nova Scotia town, treated him as a sort of sage of the sea. His white beard still had some curl to it and, like most of his former mates, he still preferred the facial foliage without the moustache. "It gets sloppy when I eats soup," he always said.

The old fisherman was far from infirm, even for his age. He still could lift lobster traps with men half his age — if they would let him — and his eyes could pick out a sail or plume of smoke as well as most men.

"The sad truth is," he liked to confide in visitors and others who heard the story time and again, "I got hit in the leg by a revenuer's bullet. Right here ..." Then he'd pull down the top of his boot to reveal a worm-like white scar below his knee cap.

"Cut my tendon clean in two," he would add. What he would call a "revenuer" was actually an American Coast Guard official who had called out to Jimmy's boat to heave to one foggy night while Jimmy was hauling rum down to "the Boston states," as the locals called New England. He really had nothing to lose by running rum. His wife had died of pneumonia the previous spring while he was off the Labrador coast. His only son, Dave, was long dead in an overseas war.

The incident with the American officials was 13 years ago. And the remarkable thing was, Jimmy had kept right on going when a sou'wester blew up a fog bank. His crewmate, Phil O'Hern, tied a tourniquet around Jimmy's leg, and they made their rendezvous with the contraband ship and sold their lot of alcohol.

The closest relative Jimmy had was his wife's nephew, Wyn Parsons. And Wyn was, as Jimmy would say, "as gimped as me." No one really knew the circumstances behind Wyn's return to Port Pleasant, but there were rumors — plenty of rumors.

Some say that Wyn won a medal at place called Dieppe, in France. They said he saved a bunch of soldiers from the Germans. Others whispered that Wyn was kicked out of the Army — not because of his wounds, but because he got a bunch of his own men killed for nothing.

Jimmy didn't bother trying to find out which story, if any, was correct. He was just happy to see him when Wyn got off the train after three years in England.

Wyn, of course, would never talk about the fighting and Jimmy knew why. Enslow had been over in South Africa in 1899, fighting the Boers with the First Canadian Rifles. That had been a bad business as well. Boers, Germans, he thought, it didn't matter who they fought, it was all pretty stupid. His best friend, Billy Michaels, had died at a place called Ladysmith. Eighteen years later, his only son, Dave, died at Amiens, in France. Both had got it within three months before their respective wars ended. That was why Jimmy had tried to talk Wyn out of going.

"Fighting with the British will only get you dead, Wyn," he had said the night before Wyn got on the train. "The Limeys pick stupid wars to fight. And if that ain't bad enough, they kill off all the best men, leavin' the stupid ones to run the country afterward."

It was to no avail. Wyn left in October 1939 and then stepped back on the same platform three and one half years later, his arm in a sling and limping from a small wound in his leg. His dark blue eyes were even darker and the fresh young face, once so full of freckles, seemed hollow — just like the look of the boys who came home from the Great War in the spring of 1919; the group with whom his son should have returned.

Nope. He never asked Wyn what happened. He just clamped his hands on Wyn's shoulders and told him he had fresh haddock for dinner. That was almost six months ago, and Jimmy never made mention of the war again. Wyn had gone off and confirmed what Jimmy knew along but there was no use gloating. Two other area boys had died at that Dieppe place. Good boys, they were, and damned good fishermen. Yes, he thought, the British pick stupid wars, and they either kill off their best, or send them home as gimps. That was the way Jimmy saw it, and no one was ever going to tell him anything different.

As Jimmy watched the small packer come in, he wondered if Elroy Gladman remembered about the afternoon breezes. Too much mainsail and you could keep right on going into the jetty.

Just then there was a chorus of shouts followed by a cracking noise as the packer struck the old, creosoted logs at the end of the pier.

"Told ya," mumbled Jimmy, and stuck his pipe back into his teeth.

* * *

"Haddock's up a penny a pound today."

"How's that?" Wyn asked.

"Government's buying everything we can catch. Hell, once Weeb gets 'er unloaded we're out for more."

Shifting to his good side, Wyn grabbed the teapot off the black potbellied stove and gave Angus Cotter another pour. The young, bearded Cotter was the only fisherman Wyn had ever seen that drank tea from a tin cup. Even the crustiest seagoing men had enameled ones. Most carried a porcelain mug.

"Thanks Wyn," he added, gulping down the tea then quickly wiping his brown whiskers with his flannel shirtsleeve. "Just mark down the oil to me and I'll be back Monday to square up." With that, Cotter tromped off across the oiled-plank flooring, his rubber boots squeaking as he walked.

Through the large, dusty glass window, Wyn watched him saunter down toward the pier. Then he picked up a pencil and carefully wrote Cotter's name in the ledger, taking as much time as would a first-grader.

Satisfied with the entry, he put down the pencil and reached for a broom. Sady would arrive in a half hour and he knew she hated dirt and dust on the floor.

Working the broom with his right hand it occurred to him that cleaning was one of the few occupations he could do without much practice. As he had always been a lefty, learning to steady his right hand enough to perform such precise duties as writing took a bit of time to master. Now, even as slow as he was, his penmanship was as good as it had been before he lost part of his left arm.

Roddy Palmer in Liverpool, 20 miles up the Canadian National Railway line, lost a right arm after it was crushed in a loading accident on the dock. The doctor took off the upper arm halfway to the shoulder and, a few months later, Roddy was fitted for a prosthesis. Now, one year afterward, he worked the clamp-like appendage as well as a man could use his fingers. At least that was the word in Liverpool. Wyn had never met the man, but so many people had informed him of Palmer's situation that he felt he could probably carry on a good conversation with him if they did finally meet. Wyn glanced at the stump midway down his left forearm and chuckled at the thought of he and Roddy buying their gloves together.

The flannel sleeve was pinned back so that the extra cloth would not flop around and catch on anything in the shop. The doctor in London had told him that he could fit him with an artificial arm, but Wyn had declined. With the tension of the court martial proceedings, he didn't want the added stress of learning how to use a hook.

The rest of the summer and fall of 1942 was a blur of faces: doctors, nurses, Canadian and British officers, military policemen, solicitors and Canadian government officials. But he remembered clearly the faces of the capital officers on military tribunal and knew they had been forced to make a difficult verdict. They would have been justified in sentencing him to prison at hard labor for his actions on August 19th.

While witnesses gave their testimony in the dank mess hall that served as a courtroom, he sat stoically, his tunic drawn up so that only with careful scrutiny could anyone see that he had lost part of a limb. Some who were there that day gave glowing comments about his leadership abilities under fire, while others, like the Royal Navy sailor navigating the landing craft, accused him of gross insubordination and murder.

The judges had weighed three items while deciding his punishment. The first was his dedication and heroism during the actual beach activity; the second was the injury he had sustained; and the third, and most important, was how it would play in the Canadian press. The debacle at Dieppe, no matter how it had been handled by Lord Louis Mountbatten's public relations people, had not been well received in Canada and there was a fear that sending a Canadian officer to jail would hinder recruiting.

Major General Hamilton Roberts, the divisional commander, visited with Wyn in the hospital on several occasions, each time informing him how sorry he was about what happened on that hot morning in France. He was a respected military man who had supported a good attack plan only to see it erode before his very eyes as the different players pulled away from it. Stripped of the very essentials which would have garnered success — air and naval support — he was still pressured to go ahead with the piecemeal effort.

Despite Roberts' condolences on these visits, Wyn felt never felt sorry for himself, nor his predicament. He had made a choice, and was now paying for it. Roberts, he surmised, was carrying the guilt of the whole Canadian officer corps, and Wyn began each visitation trying to comfort him. Both knew what was in store. Someone had to answer for Dieppe. So when the dust settled, the "soldiers' general" would be blamed for the botched attack and would probably never get a field command again.

That was the way the game was played. Lord Louis Mountbatten, Chief of Combined Operations and the overseer of the Dieppe planning, had lost his destroyer a year earlier in the Mediterranean — but he was a Royal and nothing more was made of it. Not only that, they made a movie about that very incident with Noel Coward in the lead. It was designed to boost morale.

So after the Dieppe attack they had to protect him again, at the expense of Hamilton, a fine officer — but a colonial officer. The Canadian was the scapegoat and Lord Louis' film made him a legend.

Not that Mountbatten was distancing himself in any way. He had once sat in on one of the interviews held before the court martial proceedings, interrupting only once to ask Wyn about the condition on the beach that day. Wyn had been respectful in his dissertation and, at the end, the Chief of Combined Ops simply said, "Don't blame the Royal Navy for your own misdeeds, Captain." Then he got up to leave as if Wyn never existed.

Unperturbed by the commander's quip, and just as unimpressed by the gold braid, Wyn simply replied, "You knew it would fail, didn't you, Admiral?"

But Mountbatten pretended he didn't hear. He just turned and walked out. That was when Wyn finally snapped. Before the guards grabbed him, he stood up, as if to follow him, and shouted, "The blood is on your hands, Lord Louis, not on General Roberts!"

If the British Admiralty had the final say, Wyn would have gone to prison for the duration of the war, and then some. However, his charges were somehow stayed. Days later, when the doctors deemed he was fit to leave, he was quietly shuffled out of the hospital and placed on the next available boat back to Canada. There had been no stopping at his barracks. His duffel bags were waiting on the ship.

The discharge papers were civil, never mentioning his court martial. His lawyer, a Major Krebbs, never called on him again. In fact, the only proof showing that he had ever been in the army was a regimental photograph — taken in Hamilton, Ontario — in his kit bag and an official paper stating that he was unfit for further action. There was no documentation that he had ever gone to England at all.

As he stood at the railings of the departing merchant ship as it slid out of Portsmouth, Wyn suddenly realized why the last three years had been officially blocked out. In a newspaper article he read in the hospital, the military had succeeded in playing off Dieppe to the public as "a raid" and its participants dubbed heroes. To have a dishonored officer from the action would surely attract Canadian reporters and stir up controversy. So, no jail, no dishonor, no battle record. As for his lower arm, the official report was that it was "amputated after a training accident in Hamilton."

The far-off train whistle shook Wyn from his daydream. Glancing at the old wall clock he saw that the timepiece was three minutes fast. It had to be; the CN was rarely late.

Wyn plunked the dustpan on the floor in front of the pile he had accumulated. With the toe of his right foot he dragged the small shovel over and positioned it between his ankles, then swept the pile into it. Disposing of the sweepings, he scanned the shelves of the small store, with its tins of bully beef and chicken haddies on one side and fishing supplies on the other.

Things were a lot easier now than they had been six months ago. With the Sicily landings and the success against the U-boats, not only was the mood of the people more upbeat, but some foodstuffs were easier to come by.

In the summertime it was not that bad. Everyone had a garden and so vegetables were plentiful and eggs were easy to get because most places had a chicken house. And now meat was available in small quantities and could be bartered for fish. However, it was other things, the small luxuries that added a sparkle to life that were missed: nylons, sugar, coffee, and good tea. These things were also beginning to show up in small quantities.

Restrictions on gasoline were obviously still in effect but that did not interfere with Wyn because he never had a car. For most places he wanted to go, he could take the train, and other destinations, such as Kejimkujik, his favorite place for camping, he could borrow a horse from Jack's Stable. Jack Thompson would trade him labor for usage of a horse. Even a one-armed man was a bonus when all able-bodied ones were in uniform or away working in war industries.

Wyn took out a clear bottle and poured some vinegar on a clean rag. Dabbing the wet piece of cotton in the water pail, he began to clean the large front windows, careful not to apply too much pressure to the painted red letters which spelled *LeBlanc's General Store* backwards on the inner pane. Sady

LeBlanc was proud of the artwork and she would say, over and over again, that it had been worth the whole two dollars. "Good sign painters, like men," she reminded him, "are hard to come by these days."

Wyn's employer could be slightly overbearing for many people, but Sady's moods did not rankle him. One day, the 55-year-old Sady was cranky, the next silent. And then there were the times when she would come in beaming with happiness. But those times were not that often. Usually, she would just walk about the store and complain about everything: prices, shortages, and men.

As Wyn finished up the last pane of the segmented window, he brushed the dead flies onto the dustpan and, walking behind the long counter, threw them into the can of sweepings. His eyes caught Laura as she entered the store.

"Sure hot, isn't it, Wyn?"

The sound of the voice almost made him dump the ashcan as he suddenly found himself struggling to maintain his balance. Self-consciously, he turned to hide his left arm from her direction. In the same motion, he took a swipe at his sandy red hair and looked at the woman in a print dress who was wearing a straw hat.

"I'm sorry I startled you, Wyn," Laura Finer said, her face holding a smile even though it was obvious to Wyn she was feeling quite awkward. He knew exactly what her next words might have been, had she been brave enough to say them: "I thought Sady would be in at this time of the day."

There were many courses of action he could have taken at this time. He could have come right to the point and asked her why she had gotten married so quickly after he had left — especially to a buffoon like Barry Finer. And he could have tested her true feelings for him, a gentle probe that might give him a small opening to begin easing her away from her husband.

However, his training as an officer saved him from causing her emotional trauma. In times of extreme duress outside a combat situation, he had been taught to stuff it and let the gentleman take the lead.

"She'll be in a little bit later. She had to care of some personal business," he replied, locking onto her smooth, tanned features. It was obvious that she had been working outside throughout the hot days. She looked healthy and vibrant and, for an instant, he thought an errant facial expression on his part might slip out and break the tacit truce. "And you're right, it is hot."

Laura had not changed that much in five years. She had lost the little girl look, which made her more desirable to him. Her long, cinnamon hair was tied back under the wide-brimmed hat revealing her large dark eyes and tanned brown porcelain face. Her pale cream dress fit loosely at the waist and he could tell by the light material that her figure had not been altered by the birth of her two children.

"Well, I just came in to pick up my allotment of sugar," she explained nervously.

"Sure," he answered, unable to curtail the smile on his face or the warmth he felt. "Coming up."

This was the most contact he had with Laura in six years, since that awkward goodbye in September 1938. In the past year, he never saw much of her, just a glimpse as she passed by in the passenger's side of her husband's truck. However, usually one of the boys was hanging out the window, laughingly trying to cool off his face and blocking the view of her.

"Ah, Wyn?" she asked, her face widening with a perplexed smile.

"Yeah?" he answered, his voice sounding lazy.

"My sugar?" Laura held out her porcelain sugar jar.

"Oh!" he laughed, shaking his head and accepting the container. "I was just thinking about the price ... to see if it had come down this week." It was a lie but it covered. Another officer reaction.

He reached down and scooped into the sugar barrel, placing a portion into Laura's jar. Then he repeated the process.

"Could I see your ration card, Laura?" This time his tone was slightly officious.

"Right here," she replied, reaching over to replace the lid. As she did, she peeked into the jar.

"Wyn, there's a lot of sugar in there," she said, her voice becoming serious.

"Well, Laura," he answered calmly. He loved rolling her name over his tongue again and a nostalgic rush went up his back. "The truth is, I don't use sugar so I would like to give you my ration so you can make extra cookies for those handsome boys of yours."

"Oh my, Wyn," she replied, her face flushed with embarrassment at his generosity, "I don't know what to say."

After six years, he had an opening, a chance to redeem himself, or apologize, or do whatever it took to regain some of the old magic. For a brief instant, he was 17 again, flushed with the same pins and needles he had felt when she agreed to go out to the barn dance with him. However, the feeling vanished when he looked up and saw him standing in the doorway.

"Shove that sugar up your ass, Parsons!" shouted Barry Finer. Then to Laura, "And you get the hell out of this store!" grabbing her by the arm with his meaty hand and yanking her back.

"Barry, he was just being nice!" she bleated, her terrified eyes avoiding his.

Wyn wanted to reach out for her hand but knew that it would have been unwelcome. She would just get into more trouble with her husband, he surmised, but he still cursed himself for his inaction.

Instead, he straightened up and slowly slipped his hand under the old wooden counter. There, his fingers fondled a piece of doweling. A calm feeling washed through his body, a tide of knowledge that his next action would be carried out all the way. That was another thing the Army had drilled into him: When fighting in close combat, *always finish off your enemy.* And at this moment, Finer was his enemy.

"Like, hell, you stupid cow!" Finer continued his rampage, twisting her arm so that she spun around to face him. "That gimp's been ogling you since they threw him out of the Army!"

Finer was a bear of a man, six-foot-three, 250 pounds, and a fisherman who owned two boats. Originally from a fishing village down past Shelburne, he had spent a year in the merchant marine and was excluded from military service because he was the only son of a fisherman. He had married Laura in 1940 and, a year later, her father had died, leaving his boat to his daughter. With fish prices steadily rising, Finer's two boats brought in a handsome income.

Barry Finer's head sported a thatch of dark-brown hair coming down to within inches of his heavy eyebrows. The eyes were bright blue, which made him seem that much more intimidating to the locals, especially after he had been drinking. It was obvious to Wyn that Finer had been in the Sable River Inn for quite a few.

"Isn't that right, gimp?" he snarled, snapping Laura's head back. The smell of rum was heavy on his breath but he seemed extremely capable.

"Please, Barry," she pleaded, softly, "you're hurting me."

"Look," Finer snapped, maintaining his grip on her, "I told you I didn't want you coming in here while —"

"That wasn't her fault," Wyn cut in, his voice firm, but not loud. "I wasn't supposed to be here today."

"You should just keep your mouth shut, you weasel, and stay away from my wife. You're just lucky you're only half a man or I'd knock the piss outa you right here and now!"

Wyn acted like Finer had never spoken. "Sady usually works this shift," he went on, with a slow, deliberate meter in his sentence. "She had a doctor's appointment so I filled in. How could your wife have known that?"

"That's what I'd like to know," Finer grunted, letting go his wife's arm. "You just stay away from her, that's all."

Wyn just stared; the freckles on his face and neck making him appear like a schoolboy but his worldly eyes firmly set and without fear.

Rubbing her sore limb, Laura tried to avoid eye contact but could not help herself from one last look at Wyn. What she saw made her shiver, the look scaring her almost as much as Finer's temper.

"Will that be everything?" Wyn said to her, his eyes unmoving.

"Yes, thank you," Laura replied, looking down to balance the sugar jar in her left arm.

Without warning, Finer reached over and knocked the porcelain container out of her hands and it went over onto the floor. It didn't break but it spilled most of the sugar out on the dark, oiled floor, the grains shining like millions of minute diamonds in the solid band of daylight.

Laura shrieked and went down on her knees to retrieve the jar. As she did, Finer quipped, "Just grab the jar and let's go. The stuff on the floor belongs to the gimp here and we don't take no presents from cowards."

"He's no coward!" Laura replied, her voice showing an uncharacteristic defiance.

"That's not what I heard in Liverpool," he snapped. "And you just better watch your tone with me, woman!"

Wyn remained unmoved by the exchange. He still had the same expression on his face as before. Finer added, "See for yourself, Laura, the gimp's too scared to even help you out. Maybe that's how he got himself shot, just standing there like a scared duck, while the Krauts took shots at him. I heard they shot him while he was runnin' away. Hell, maybe his own guys did it."

The band of light suddenly went dark and Finer and Laura looked around to see the huge image of Sady LeBlanc at the door. Despite the heat, she was not fanning herself. A newspaper was clutched in one hand, as if a club, and in her other hand was her large carry bag, which she had poised to swing if the need arose.

She wore an oversized pink summer hat that matched the color of her tentlike dress, and it gave her the appearance of a very big child. Her eyes had a mournful tilt, as if their whole field of vision was enshrouded with sadness.

"Laura," she finally said, as if a teacher speaking to a pupil, "run along with your sugar."

Flushed with embarrassment, Laura lowered her eyes and shuffled past the big woman. Sady shifted aside to let her by.

At first, Finer was taken aback by Sady's entrance, but he eventually broke free of her spell. "Y'know," he said, pointing at Wyn, "That gimp you hired should mind his own business."

"Well Mr. Finer," she sighed, "that gimp, as you call him, is a good worker and the only one with any brains I can get to help me out. So, I'll thank you not to call him that again."

Wyn picked up the broom and dustpan, seemingly ignoring the remark made by Sady. He rounded the counter, walked up to Finer and stopped, staring him full in the face. "I'm going to clean up the sugar now. Would you step back, please?"

Something in Wyn's eyes made Finer involuntarily retreat a few steps, something that he could only describe using a comparison to the blackish eyes of a deepwater fish. Except Wyn's eyes were grayish-blue.

A few seconds later, the floor was back to its dark, oily appearance. Wyn deposited the waste sugar in the ashcan and, ignoring them, went behind the counter and into the stock room.

As Finer was about to leave, Sady piped up, "You know, Mr. Finer, that boy has seen himself a mountain of misery, and all of it was none of his doing. Now, it seems to me that a grown-up man like you, in good physical shape at that and with sound financial means, could find better things to do than to degrade another man less fortunate than himself."

"Look Sady," blurted Finer like a school boy in trouble, "that Parsons has been after my wife since he got back and, if he wasn't all shot up, I would have knocked out his lights a long time ago."

Sady just shook her large head. "Well," she huffed, "if you think that, then you're a bigger ass that even I see you for."

"Look, you can't talk to —"

"Mr. Finer," Sady replied, throwing her hands on her generous hips, "you may be a big man, and one with money at that, but if you think that your wife of yours has a wandering eye I wouldn't go blamin' Wyn for it. I would look straight in the mirror."

"I don't have to take this from you," Finer snorted, wheeling to go out.

"No you don't, Mr. Finer," she replied, "but if you were to use that big head of yours for thinking instead of as a doorstop, you would know that your wife comes in here every Wednesday afternoon, like clockwork. And if you were to think even deeper, you would know that this is the first Wednesday afternoon I haven't been in the store since before the war began.

"Not only that," she added, "Wyn Parsons' usual job on Wednesday afternoon is helping his uncle, Jimmy, repair nets on the wharf. He only filled in for me so I could go to the doctor. Now, put that in your pipe and smoke it."

As her large form edged around the counter, Finer swatted the air in disgust and stomped out. She took a good, hard look at Parsons as he came in from the store room.

* * *

"Come on Wyn, that woman has a husband."

Sady raised the small, green bottle of Coca-Cola and drained the contents in two swigs.

"You know better than that, Sady," replied Wyn. "That's the first I've laid eyes on her in months. Laura was another lifetime for me. So is this place. Once Jimmy gets his pension through, I'll light out."

"Oh, Wyn," she sighed, fanning the air, "you don't have to go just because some bully like Finer spouts off at you." Once the words had passed her lips she realized her slip. "Sorry, I didn't mean to insinuate that you backed down from him."

"No offense taken, Sady," grinned Wyn, his boyish face reminding Sady of the freckled lad who once pitched a no-hitter against Liverpool in 1937.

"I got a letter from Halifax which says my war benefits are going to start next month. So with that and the money I made in town the last year, I can buy that property on Ashton Island. Wilbur Corkum, the lighthouse keeper, is selling a chunk of it."

"Ashton Island? Come on, Wyn, Wilbur and Lottie Corkum are great people but it's too cold in winter out there and you'd get lonely bein' stuck in a house on the other side of the island." Sady reached over to the cooler and slid another Coca-Cola down the rack. Then she pulled the dripping green bottle up through the gate of the pop cooler. The cold water in the tank swirled around her fingers and eased her discomfort somewhat.

"Want a pop?" she asked.

"Nah, the owner might walk in and catch us pinching colas."

"I guess owning the place takes all the fun out of it," laughed Sady, snapping off the cap. The small bottle was almost lost in her chubby hand as she lifted it for a drink. Before it reached her lips she said, "I was kinda thinking of gettin' a new owner."

"Really?" returned Wyn.

"The doctor says I gotta change my ways or else I'll soon be a sack of arthritis," she went on, puffing as she readjusted her bulky form. "As it is now, I can barely open the jars or crank down the awning without a handful of aspirin. So, after 30 years, I think it's time to retire the LeBlanc name."

"Someone already offer to buy you out?"

Sady began drinking and Wyn watched in amazement as she finished the whole bottle in a series of large swallows.

"I was kinda hopin' you'd take it," she said, nonchalantly.

"Me?" asked an astounded Wyn.

"Well, for a real good price," she beamed, priming herself for a good sell job. "I would finance the building for you and you'd pay off the stock when you liked."

Wyn let out a slow stream of air. Outside, a trickle of cars began to go by signaling the men returning from the dockyards in Shelburne. The large Liverpool/Shelburne bus lumbered after them puffing smoke from its exhaust. To add to that clatter the large clanging bell from the train locomotive echoed off the promontory. It was like that at five o'clock every day.

"I don't know, Sady," he replied, as the noises went on around them. "As I said, I just stayed on as long as I did to see that Jimmy got settled. He's the only one I got left now. Mrs. Buchanan will take him in as a border. Old Alf Chetwynd stays there, and he and Jimmy can talk their fishing and play dominos. I'll bring him out to the island now and then when I get a place built."

Sady drained another cola and plunked the greenish bottle down. "When you going?" she asked, resigned to the fact she could not make him change his mind.

"Two weeks."

CHAPTER FIVE

Saint-Nazaire, France
June 19, 1943

There was no escaping the fact that many things had changed in the last three months. Dressed in their gray leather coats to fend off the late spring chill and sporting their navy blue, boat-shaped Schiffschen atop their heads, the returning crew stood just as proudly on the deck as they had on previous missions when their U-boat slid passed the quay. They smiled through shaggy beards at loved ones lining the pier. Waving from the antenna, just behind the officers in the *Turm* — the conning tower — were the familiar, triangular tonnage pennants: trophies of combat which showed that no fewer than six Allied ships had gone down under the explosive blasts of *U-497*'s torpedoes.

However, on this occasion, there were no bands to greet them with the triumphant *Kretschmer March* — named for the famed U-boat ace, Otto Kretschmer — as had been the custom in the past. Actually, the atmosphere had a funereal air, the families and friends waving as if they were greeting a boatload of ghosts. Also missing were the throngs of officials in dress uniforms with lanyards, or "monkey hangers," as the irreverent U-boat crews had been calling them.

Replacing the traditional trappings were the interested stares of dockworkers and representatives of the many manufacturing companies which supplied equipment for the submarines. They silently calculated how much punishment had been inflicted on *U-497* and how long it would take to repair her. Many things caught their attention, especially the area just above the starboard navigational light on the conning tower. There was a large blackened scar embellishing the rusted hole where a cannon shell had gone through the *Turm*. The light was gone and so was the horseshoe-shaped life preserver that was fastened above it.

As the submarine moved toward her slip in the massive concrete bunker, more holes were visible to the onlookers, and other signs of battle became evident: twisted railings of the *Wintergarten*, a smashed breech on the 105mm cannon, a crumbled bowsprit and, oddly, no periscope.

Twenty minutes later, the U-boat was safely with the confines of the fortified concrete pens and the thin, bearded figure of *Kapitänleutnant* Joachim Beltzer sauntered up the gangplank. His pearly teeth exposed in a great smile, he doffed his dirty, white-crowned cap and pulled his small, dark-haired wife, Rhoda, out of the milling crowd, ignoring several naval officers who had come down to into the dank, dimly lit pens to greet him. After hugging and rocking back and forth, Beltzer pulled his head up and kissed her several times. What he wanted to say to her was, "I thought I'd never see you again," but his discipline prevented him from letting on to both her and the relatives that there was anything other than business as usual.

"Kapitänleutnant?"

Beltzer looked up from his tiny wife as his fierce blue eyes locked onto one of the men in the dark blue uniforms. Unlike the man's adjutant, who wore several medals, this thin, dark-haired officer simply exuded a quiet strength that needed no extra military baubles.

Suddenly recognizing him, Beltzer stiffened. *"Guten Tag, Herr Konteradmiral!"* he said, raising his hand to his head in a crisp military salute instead of the straight-armed party one. Taking another glance at the battle-damaged U-boat, he envied the commander for having the chance to fight the enemy instead of administering pins on a map as he did.

"And to you, Joachim," Godt replied, clapping the commander on his thin shoulders with both hands. "I am pleased to see you looking so well." Then looking down at the U-boat commander's wife, he added, "Rhoda and I have had quite a chat while waiting for you to dock."

The loud, thrumming engines of a squadron of Messerschmidt *109* fighters passing overhead diverted their attention for a few seconds. Godt glanced down at his watch and, as the droning of the Daimler-Benz engines softened, he said, "I know three months is a long time, Rhoda, but could I bother you for just 20 more minutes of Joachim's time?"

"Only 20 minutes!" snapped Rhoda in a mock scolding. Despite the blackout on American radio and movies, she wore the latest hairstyle from the American cinema, a side-parted Greta Garbo coiffeur that her hairdresser had seen in a *Life* magazine she had purchased on the black market.

"Thank you, Rhoda," Godt replied, his fatherly eyes filled with understanding. "And wonderful to have seen you again."

With his easy going nature and preoccupation with the people underneath the uniforms, Eberhard Godt could have been mistaken for a church leader or college professor of the arts. He had joined the Imperial German Navy at the end of the Great War, becoming a U-boat commander in 1935. This was an exciting time for the Navy because Hitler had just repudiated the Treaty of Versailles, opening the floodgates for German re-armament.

When the war began in 1939, Godt was the first staff officer to Karl Dönitz. Under the direction of these two men, the small submarine operations department quickly rose in significance to be one of the most important of the Naval War Staff. To the U-boat crews, it was called simply, "U-boat Command."

There had been many changes in the past few years, from "the Happy Time" when their U-boats had ruled the Atlantic waves up to now, when each returning boat was like a blessing from Heaven. Godt had noticed the teary-eyed members of the crowd waiting for men who would never return. They came down to the docks daily, braving the threats of Allied air strikes, hoping that the reports were untrue and that their loved ones' boats would come sliding triumphantly into port.

For Godt and his boss, there were other, more pressing considerations which sapped their time allotment to the U-boats. Their focus changed drastically the previous January when *Grossadmiral* Erich Raeder resigned as Supreme Commander-in-Chief of the German Navy — after 14 years of service. Hitler had harangued Raeder over the failure of his surface force — led by two heavy cruisers — to destroy a Royal Navy Arctic convoy. The Führer went on to threaten him with scrapping all the big ships of the fleet. Raeder, a proud veteran of the old Imperial Navy and the great Battle of Jutland in 1916, quit the post.

A professional to the end, the old battleship man, knowing that the German fleet was much too small to duke it out with the capital ships of the Royal Navy, suggested to Hitler that Karl Dönitz, the competent U-boat man, be his replacement. U-boats, Raeder reasoned, could be built cheaply and quickly in only a few months, while cruisers and battleships took years and were a drain on steel supplies.

For Dönitz, it was a double stroke of fortune: not only did he finally have his finger on the pulse of German naval production, he also had direct access to Adolf Hitler. Important agendas, such as the building of new U-boats and quality control over torpedoes, would never again be buried amid stacks of paper on a bureaucrat's desk.

In terms of operations, Dönitz no longer needed to seek approval from the Naval Staff because he now had complete authority over them. This cadre of professionals had often overruled U-boat command directives by diverting precious boats for patrols in unprofitable and overly dangerous waters. Dönitz would now concentrate his boats and make the tonnage battle the main thrust of the operation, bringing it to bear where the most cargo ships could be sunk with the least losses to the U-boats.

However, the new appointment had its drawbacks. Until his new assignment, Dönitz had been a hands-on commander, setting up his *Befehlshaber der Unterzeebooten*, or BdU, in Kernével, 25 miles northwest of the French port of Lorient. Inside the country château, U-boat operations were designed and conducted from two situation rooms. Entire walls were papered with ocean charts divided into grids and studded with hundreds of colored pins and flags, each denoting a boat at sea.

Dönitz's change in station was not the only factor in his distancing from the U-boat crews. In March of 1942, a British raiding party had attacked the pens at St.-Nazaire, making an impression on him as to how vulnerable the *BdU* could be. So, reluctantly, his HQ was moved to Avenue Maréchal Maunoury in Paris, far away from enemy espionage — but also from the U-boats.

In the spring of 1943, in a move to centralize the navy's structure after his promotion, U-boat Command was moved even farther east — into the Hotel am Steinplatz in Charlottenburg. The staff was later moved into Koralle, a bombproof bunker some 30 kilometers from the Reichschancellery, near Bernau.

For the U-boat crews, the loss of their familiar father-figure whom they called *Onkle Karl* or *der Löwe*, "the Lion" — a man whose very image inspired a loyalty unknown in the other branches of the armed forces — was felt by the crews as they returned home from their sorties with their tonnage flags flying.

For the easy going Godt, the change was equally monumental. As head of *BdU*-Ops, his job took on a rapid metamorphosis when Dönitz incorporated the U-boat Command into the Naval Staff as its No. 2 Section. That was five months ago, but it felt like a lifetime to Godt. For the energy required for the reorganization of the *BdU* — and the surprising Allied successes of the past month — had aged the gentlemanly navy man well past his 42 years.

Returning submarine commanders were now referring to the great convoy battles of May 1943 as the "Great U-boat Death." The recent operation against

Convoy SC-129 had cost two U-boats for every merchantman sunk, an amazing turnabout from the dozens of Allied freighters sunk per loss during "The Happy Time" in the first year of the war, and the "Second Happy Time," when the unprepared Americans had entered the battle for the convoy lanes.

Beltzer left his wife happily chatting with another officer's spouse and trotted past the guard house on his way over to where Godt and his adjutants were waiting. After two months at sea, Beltzer's appearance was far from official looking. His disheveled figure in this restricted area might have been enough to prompt the elite *Kriegsmarine* guards to shoot first and ask questions later. They were very young, and their fierce dedication to their mundane work was obviously a result of their Hitler Youth training. Two of the guards immediately shouted out a challenge to stop but Godt immediately waved them off. Reluctantly, they let Beltzer pass.

At first, the U-boat commander was content to walk past them. Suddenly, he stopped and wheeled around to face the young sailors. "You will salute when an officer passes!" he bellowed. In an instant boots slapped together and two long arms shot out in the Nazi gesture.

Beltzer flipped up his hand as if it were an annoyance and eyed the anxious youths up and down. Then he growled, just low enough for the guards to hear, "Hey kiddies, the real war is that way." When he was satisfied his point had been understood, he turned and sauntered over to Godt's side.

"I need a favor from you, Joachim," stated Godt, in a more officious tone than he had been using at the docks. Without waiting for an answer he added. "I need the services of one of your officers, a Lieutenant Lothar Hessler."

"Hessler?" answered Beltzer, rubbing his shaggy beard. "Well, I would hate to lose him, but it's about time he was promoted. The man is as well versed about submarines and tactics as I, maybe more so. He should have had a command a year ago. Why he was assigned —"

"*Kapitänleutnant*," interrupted Godt, "there are some things that are better left unsaid."

"*Jawohl, Herr Konteradmiral*!" was the reply, as Beltzer shifted into an official posture. He silently chided himself for his casualness. Being cramped up in a submarine for weeks on end tended to dull an officer's sense of priorities for the world ashore.

"Come, walk with me, Joachim," Godt said, putting his arm around the U-boat commander in a fatherly fashion and steering him away from the other officers. With this unexpected closeness, Beltzer was suddenly glad that he and his crew had a chance to clean themselves before they had arrived. Added to that was his insistence that everyone travel with an extra uniform for homecoming — if not a well-worn one.

"I have to tell you something that must be held in the strictest confidence," Godt went on. "Do you understand?"

"Yes, of course," answered the bewildered skipper.

"Good." Godt uttered so low it was difficult for Beltzer to hear. The loud diesel engines were still rattling around in his brain. "Now, officially, as far as the fleet is concerned, Hessler does not exist."

"What?" Beltzer blurted out, catching himself as he saw the stern face of Godt.

"Joachim," the older man tried again, "Hessler is not the man's name. He is a former U-boat commander who was accused of a capital offense two years back. Dönitz had no say in the outcome of the matter — not even the chance to appeal his conviction."

"Why, what was the reason?" pushed Beltzer, his shrewd eyes peering out from the hair under his cap like a child's.

"Before war was officially declared with America, his boat was depth charged and captured by an American Coast Guard cutter. He did manage to scuttle it, but Göbbels was furious. At the very moment the incident hit the newspapers, it seems some of our operatives inside America were meeting with the America First group — which included the famous pilot, Charles Lindbergh — at a hotel in New York."

"And *that* was a capital offense?"

"The political situation at the time was tense, Joachim. Lindbergh opposed the United States becoming involved in a war with Germany and was a prominent spokesman against Roosevelt's policies.

"Therefore, having one of our U-boats being captured by the Americans at such a delicate time was seen in Berlin as a great humiliation to the Propaganda Ministry and a setback for American groups pushing to oust Roosevelt. Well, Göbbels was so incensed, he ordered the commander executed."

As a year of U-boat duty with Hessler reeled through his head like a fast projector, the bewildered Beltzer nodded slowly. "No wonder he was so secretive."

"He had to be," sighed Godt. "If Göbbels knew that he was still alive, he might have sent Hessler's family to a concentration camp. As it is, they were harassed by the Gestapo for nearly a year afterward."

"Would you and the Grand Admiral have been indicted?"

"There would have been some serious tongue lashing, I suppose. But even Hitler wouldn't tamper with the success of the U-boat campaign by sacking Dönitz over one of Göbbels' tantrums."

"Poor Lothar," replied Beltzer, his voice grating with anger. "If there ever was a capable commander, then it is he. He saved our boat from a spiral dive when depth charges caused a breach in our outer hull and damaged our stabilization systems. While men were screaming in terror all around him, Lothar handled the hydroplane wheels, un-sticking the bow stabilizers. When the boat finally leveled off, he went aft to assist with the malfunctioning air compressor.

"Hans Schumann, my machinist, said he had never seen anyone so mechanically skilled as Hessler. The Lieutenant tore the compressor apart as if he had designed it himself and got it back together and working in less than two hours. If we would have had to limp back home on the surface, there is no doubt in my mind we would have been spotted by one of those damnable English patrol aircraft."

Godt nodded thoughtfully. "Worthy of a Knight's Cross, then?" he said, pointing to Beltzer's medal.

"What is a bauble compared with saving the lives of a U-boat crew, sir?"

"I know," replied Godt, lifting his cap and running over his slicked-back, dark hair.

"So," shrugged Beltzer, "does Hessler get a command or does Göbbels get another head?"

"I doubt if the Propaganda Minister would get any mileage at this time from pursuing a U-boat commander who once sank ships in American waters, even if he did lose his boat."

"By the way, did you know he was an ace?" added Godt.

"No, I didn't. I just figured that Hessler —"

"His real name is Lothar Stahl."

"Stahl!" Beltzer gasped, excitedly shaking his head. "Why he's a legend! Knight's Cross with Swords. He was one of the first to sink over 100,000 tons."

"Twenty-one ships for 114,201 tons, to be exact," Godt added. "All in 14 months. He was also a lieutenant with *U-47* during the Scapa Flow victory at the beginning of the war. The reason they got the *Royal Oak* was in no small part to Stahl's navigating through the narrow passages."

"I know the story well," sighed Beltzer. "How many skippers, including me, would give up everything they own to sink a British battleship in her own home harbor? I should have recognized him from his picture in the newspapers."

"Well, that is the past," Godt said, tiring of reminiscing. It just made the defeats of the past month more painful. So many U-boat crews blasted to a watery grave — so many friends gone.

This was a troubling time for Godt and for Germany. In a mere six-month period, the Russians had captured the German 6th Army at Stalingrad, the British and Americans had thrown the Afrika Corps out of North Africa, and occupied Europe was bombed by the Americans during the day and by the British at night — and now the horrific losses of U-boats in the North Atlantic. He surely did not envy Dönitz's meetings with Hitler.

"It goes without saying, Joachim, that it is my continued wish that Stahl does not exist — for the present, anyway."

"I understand completely, *Herr Konteradmiral*."

* * *

He almost knew Paris as well as he knew his home in Berlin. Both cities were similar in many ways, having been built during the imperial phases of their respective histories. The thinking of their planners was to build capitals to show off the glory of their cultures and intimidate people that may want to conspire against them.

However, unlike the German capital with its austere martial trappings, there was a casual vitality to Paris. Except for the odd Nazi banner, there were few hints that the world was at war. Uniformed Paris policemen, in the distinctive *kepis* and white gloves, directed the traffic at major intersections and strolled in front of the shops with the rest of the citizens. There was the occasional German uniform, but most of these were soldiers playing tourist, some with pretty French girls on their arms. The perfume of blossoming roses wafted on the air. Even the gray ceiling of clouds could not diminish the luster of the world's most famous city, a metropolis that was now a Nazi playground.

"When was the last time you saw Paris, Lothar?" Eberhard Godt asked, his tired body stretched out on the leather seat beside Lothar Stahl.

"Summer, '41," replied Lothar. His light green eyes panned the tree and rows of rose bushes as they flashed by the windows of the low-slung Duesenberg limousine. In the distance, the familiar postcard image of the Eiffel Tower rode along the skyline.

The officers sat in the back of the luxurious car while a driver and guard sat up front. On the road ahead as well as behind the cars, a total of six motorcycles made up the escort, each of these with a sidecar carrying a guard with a mounted machine gun. Unlike the intimidating shiny black leather raincoats of the SS, the *Kriegsmarine* guards wore the soft gray coats that adorned naval and U-boat crews. Missing too were the Nazi armbands, but swastikas were prominent on the red navy banners which adorned the hood of the limousine.

Lothar, like most U-boatmen returning from a long voyage, was extremely gaunt and pale. His face was thinly shaped, centered with a long nose that appeared longer because of his hollow cheeks and protruding brow. The Adam's apple was prominent as well, as if Lothar had swallowed a pingpong ball.

"Well, we'll have to get you to go out tonight," quipped Godt, noting that Lothar should include lots of food with his recreational activities. "Parisian women are quite hospitable."

There was an awkward silence, as there had been throughout the short trip from the coast to the capital. Stahl had slept through much of the hour-long trip on the Folk-Wulfe Condor, a pitiful rest after the long, sleepless days he had spent helping to keep the U-boat from foundering.

Ten minutes later the limousine pulled up in front of a huge apartment complex on the Avenue du Maréchal Maunoury. Large *Kriegsmarine* banners fluttered in the spring breeze above a pair of navy footmen, similar to the ones that had guarded the U-boat base. To the submariner, it defied logic to have the headquarters of the U-boat commander-in-chief so far inland.

* * *

"You look well, Lothar."

"Thank you, sir."

"Come, stand here and let me look at you. It's been a long time, my boy. Your family will be ecstatic to see you."

The mention of his incarcerated family caught him off guard. He suddenly wished to be back with Beltzer. It was as if this man — his idol — were goading him. *Had Dönitz changed this much in two years?*

Grossadmiral Karl Dönitz had a higher than normal voice, one that some dedicated cinema fan might say matched his protruding ears and his rather small stature — like one of the Keystone Cops. Hitler's top sailor was definitely not a physically imposing man. He was of average height and thin enough for his uniform to hang on him as if he were a store-window mannequin.

However, his hawk-like features and Prussian deportment seemed to transcend the admiral's non-military body structure. These qualities made him seem larger, more intimidating, a fitting demeanor for a man whose empire stretched from the Arctic Circle to the Bay of Biscay off Spain, some 3,500 miles of coastline.

Dönitz joined the German Navy in 1910 when he was 18 years old. Although he was raised in a middle-class family with no tradition of military service, he quickly adopted the focused and rigorous discipline of the Prussian officer corps. The marriage of his background and the military regimen proved a winning combination as he retained the human qualities of his upbringing, allowing him to express concern for the welfare of his subordinates. Although treating every man with respect was not a trait of the Prussian Junkers, this unique ability earned him steady advancement within the German Navy — whose hierarchy was somewhat removed from the Spartan attitudes of their Army counterparts.

When the Great War began, Dönitz was in the naval air service as an observer and soon became commander of a seaplane squadron. He got his first submarine command in 1918. Unfortunately, while on patrol off Sicily on October 4, 1918, his boat was beset by mechanical problems. To make matters worse, he surfaced his malfunctioning submarine among a throng of enemy warships. He and his crew were captured.

In July 1919, after spending half a year in a British interment camp, Dönitz returned to the German navy station in Kiel. The vaunted naval service that he had known so well for the past 10 years was a pitiful skeleton of its former glory, plagued with mutiny and mass desertions by Communist sympathizers.

Dönitz's next surprise came when he was asked to stay on when more experienced men were being passed over or mustered out of the service. As the Versailles Treaty did not permit U-boats, Dönitz became a torpedo boat captain.

Meanwhile, a peacetime German Navy had gotten around the naval embargo by forming the Dutch Submarine Development Bureau, a contrived organization where Germans in civilian clothes, former U-boat crewmen and boat workers, built subs in Holland for sale to other countries. For reasons of safety and quality control, they made sure that they practiced on them first.

In 1934, with the Nazis running Germany, enough submarine parts were smuggled to Spain, Finland and the Netherlands to build 10 boats. Then on June 18, 1935, a day which Hitler said was the happiest of his life, Germany repudiated the Versailles Treaty and began a conscription campaign for an army of 35 divisions. Not wanting to push Britain too far, Hitler made an agreement with his former nemesis that Germany would build a fleet with no more than 35 percent of the ships then operated by Britain. By agreeing to this naval pact, Great Britain had added a second happy day to Hitler's life. The signing of this treaty caused a crack in the Stresa Front, the British and French alliance against German aggression. The seeds of mistrust between the old allies were now in the ground.

In that same year, Dönitz turned 44 with over 25 years of service. During the rush to build the new navy, he was moved into the position of Submarine Flotilla Commander. Then, in 1939, he was made full captain and was able to concentrate entirely on the U-boat flotilla.

With a renewed vigor, he drilled his crews in advanced firing techniques and new tactics which saw the submarines grouping together into a wolf pack to counter enemy convoys. He wrote a book on this new strategy which he called *Die Rudeltaktik*, literally "herd tactics."

To counter the new British/French ASDIC, Dönitz drilled his crews on the skill of coming up to the surface at night and firing at 600 yards away, thus nullifying the effects of the new enemy weapon — which could not get a reading for them while surfaced.

Under his command, the *U-Bootwaffe* became the most feared arm of any military force in the world and, in the first two years of the war, was responsible for almost strangling Great Britain to death. This he had done by formulating a strategy he called the "tonnage war" — in which attrition of Britain's lifeline could be attained by sinking 700,000 tons per month. Although this rate had not been achieved, flotillas of U-boats succeeded in decimating Atlantic convoys and American coastal shipping to the point where fighting his boats became the primary objective of the war in Europe for the United States and Britain. This had the added bonus of diverting men, ships and materiél to the battle and alleviating the pressure on German forces in other theaters of the war.

However, three years after the first Allied ship went down from the explosion of German torpedoes, his whole stratagem was reeling under the blows of a concerted Allied strike against his submarines. And as if his troubles were not enough, his son, Peter, was missing with the crew of *U-954*.

* * *

Lothar observed the situation room, noticing the pins and flags on the huge wall chart, markers which were being moved around by the *Kriegsmarine* staff as he stood there. Subconsciously, he shifted the gold ring in his right hand, spinning it around his middle finger. As his life stood now, it was his most cherished possession, a gift from his mentor, Günther Prien; a man who risked his reputation to defend him two years ago and a submarine ace who was now dead, his luck finally running out against his surface enemies.

Clean-shaven, Lothar Stahl lost the veneer of a deadly combatant. He looked to Dönitz like a malnourished college student, a much younger man than his 31 years. However, one long stare into his bottle-green eyes and the admiral saw something that few men outside the *U-Bootwaffe* would ever see: a man who was not only a ruthless hunter, but one who has also been as ruthlessly hunted. There was no other occupation in warfare where a man went out and goaded death day after day with as much enthusiasm as did the U-boat men. It showed on their faces with much more emphasis than all the battle ribbons and medals they could ever display.

Except for his rank, and the lack of an ace commander's Knight's Cross, Lothar had all the accessories of a veteran boat skipper: navy blue dress jacket, white shirt, tie, *Leutnant zur See*'s gold rings on his sleeves, flotilla insignia, national eagle pin with swastika and — most important to a U-boatman – *Das U-Bootskriegsabzeichen*, the gold Submarine War Badge.

His white-crowned cap, which now rested on his left knee, was the only thing he allowed himself from his old rank of *Kapitänleutnant*, and this was the first time he had taken it out of his footlocker since he was court-martialed. To many in the *Kriegsmarine*, it might have seemed like an act of mutiny for a mere sub-lieutenant to wear a commander's headgear. But Dönitz was not about to reprimand Stahl for this bit of impropriety. There were some things, he knew, that a man earned — and Lothar had earned the right to wear that cap.

"I'm sorry, Lothar," sighed the U-boat chief, clenching his fists while addressing his nephew. "So much has happened since we last saw each other that I forgot, momentarily, about the circumstances of your leaving."

The lieutenant just nodded, a polite way of accepting the admiral's apology.

"Of course, Lothar, you couldn't have known that your mother and brother are now free and living in your family house in Charlottenburg."

"What?" he gasped, his ring spinning as quickly as a top. "They're alive?"

"Yes," Dönitz replied, grinning like an amiable baker. "They were held by the Gestapo for a while. But when war with America came, they were left alone. Suddenly, it seemed unpatriotic for the Propaganda Minister to continue to harass a family because one of its members fought an 'enemy' ship."

"So, my family knows I'm alive?" Lothar gasped, his eyebrows raised like those of a child on his birthday.

"Oh yes," smiled the admiral. "Unfortunately, you were not told because I was always working on a way to get you reborn, as such, and the opportunity did not come up ... until now."

Lothar took a deep breath and stopped turning his ring. The room seemed to take on color and he could even smell the coffee in front of him. Coffee. It was the real beverage, not the artificial grain that everyone had been drinking since the war began. And his ears heard the chirping of a bird outside the window, even with all the clamor of telephones ringing and feet shuffling across the floors.

After a moment of thought, his expression changed back to his normal, unsmiling look. "I just heard about Peter, *Onkle*," he said, almost as an announcement, but with a deep feeling in his voice. "I'm truly sorry."

"I know," uttered Dönitz, his mood suddenly deflating. He truly appreciated the gesture but there was never a good time to offer condolences. "You and he were quite the pair when you were growing up, weren't you?"

"Before the war, he was one of my best friends," returned Lothar, his mind locking on the image of Dönitz's son.

"Yes, well, I guess there's still hope he has been picked up and is a prisoner of war."

The picture faded and so did the clarity of his other senses.

"We can always hope," Dönitz added, steeling his tone.

He then motioned for Lothar to sit down. The U-boat man pulled a chair away from the ornate walnut desk and waited for the commander to retrieve his before sitting down. In the next rooms, telephones rang and uniformed men and women walked in and out of the various rooms down the hallway. One lieutenant walked in, clicked his heels, and went straight to one of the charts. After marking on one of the western Atlantic grids labeled "AJ," he turned to the admiral, clicked his heels again, wheeled smartly, and walked out.

"Life goes on," Dönitz shrugged. Lothar thought it laudable that the admiral would not leave the pulse of activity for a private meeting.

"How is Joachim?" asked the admiral.

"He is well and sends his regards," replied Lothar, his spirits perking up with the query of his skipper and good friend. The younger man's dirty turquoise eyes found those of Dönitz and he managed a brief smile.

"He's one of my best," added the admiral. He reached over and picked up his ornamental baton, the symbol of his station as Commander-in-Chief of the Navy. The half-meter short cane was adorned with gold anchors, eagles and Maltese crosses in symmetrical rows.

"Do you know what this 'stick' is?" Dönitz asked, his keen eyes taking in every twitch in the young navy officer, as if looking for some small fault in the man. With his large cap off, Dönitz's ears, hanging lower than his eyes, looked as though they were peeling off his head.

"Yes, of course," answered Lothar. "It is the baton of the *Grossadmiral*. Please accept my profound and, I regret, late congratulations."

"Yes, yes, thank you," sighed the admiral, waving it as though it were a flyswatter. "But it's also a pain in the behind because now I seem to be too busy flitting around Europe to spend time with my U-boat crews as I used to."

"I'm sure they understand that, sir," offered Lothar, being polite. Dönitz's presence on the docks in the old days was a great morale builder and it was no secret that he was sorely missed.

"The Allied convoys are, at present, proceeding unmolested to England and back," Dönitz continued, ignoring Lothar's statement. "But that will change in a couple of weeks. We have new technologies at hand and we will soon be sinking 750,000 tons a month."

"May I venture to ask —"

"Well, for starters, we have two new torpedoes. One type can find a ship by following the sound of its engines and the other that can be guided to the target by the submarine captain. This is a great leap forward for us, don't you agree?"

"Truly," Lothar replied, his mind going over many incidences when faulty torpedoes had either not detonated against enemy hulls or had gone off by merely passing through a ship's wake. It had always astounded him that these incredibly important pieces of ordnance had changed little since the end of the Great War. Dönitz had finally been able to get the Navy to assign a top priority to the torpedoes although it had taken a couple of years. In effect, this bureaucratic incompetence on the part of the naval command — whose collective minds were on battleships — had meant that many dozens of Allied ships had gotten through with their cargoes.

"And to combat Allied aircraft, all U-boats will be outfitted with 20mm anti-aircraft batteries."

"But sir," interjected Lothar, impressed with the torpedoes but visibly uneasy with the latter announcement, "even a heavily-armed U-boat would be taking a chance to fight it out with aircraft. The best solution, in my estimation, is a submarine that can stay under water longer and does not need to surface at night to recharge its batteries. As it is now, the Allied aircraft can find us in the dark."

"I know," uttered Dönitz, "at first I refused to believe it but after losing 41 U-boats in May —"

"Forty-one!" Lothar blurted, surprising himself at his loss of composure. No wonder the pens in Saint-Nazaire were empty.

"Yes," the admiral sighed, tapping his baton on the desk. "That is the figure we have now that nine more have not reported in."

Lothar shook his head in disbelief. Sixteen hundred trained crewman gone. "It's as if they can read our radiograms."

"No," replied the admiral. "That I know is impossible. I could have believed it with the old *Enigma*, but since we added a fourth rotor to the code machine it is mathematically impossible for the English to figure out what we are sending."

"Maybe it's our radio waves," countered Lothar, an excitement to his voice at his new thought. The ring in his hand was spinning as he spoke, causing a puzzled look from Dönitz. "Maybe they can locate our boats by following them."

"Not according to the High Command," replied the admiral. "The English and Americans, they say, have radio waves which can detect ships and aircraft, but they assure me that no other such technology exists in the enemy camp."

The admiral rolled the baton on the dark oak table, the large gold ends making a rattling sound as it moved. "However, this 'stick' allows me to do what I want with my fleet and, with the permission of the Führer, build as many boats as I want. With the new weapons we will regain the upper hand by the end of summer. The Americans were once soft, Lothar, but they learned quickly from their experiences and now are a formidable enemy. That is why the *U-Boot-waffe* has to press on."

"But our boats, *Onkle*," badgered Lothar, his heart still aching at the loss of U-boat crews. "We still —"

"Lothar, I know what you want to say on that issue and, believe me, I have a surprise for you. But first, I want to finish what I was saying about your situation. You see, another of the powers of this baton is that I can right past wrongs."

He let that sink in for a few seconds, then said, "And we all know what that means."

Lothar shrugged at the suggestion. Rank and societal position did not mean much to him anymore. But it had occurred to him during this visit that, if he returned from the dead, he may not fit in with his old friends in Berlin. Too much time and experiences had passed.

"We all know the Propaganda Ministry thought that you were executed and your family sentenced to a re-education camp," the admiral continued, in a low voice.

"However, a few of us in the *BdU* know differently. It was a mere slight of hand, with some favors granted to a couple of officials who ran Dachau prison camp."

Lothar remembered the rest: a midnight ride to the train station beside the Zoological Gardens, a private car back to France, some false identification papers and pay book, and a quick meeting with Beltzer, the U-boat skipper.

"Does my family know that I was not a traitor?" Lothar ventured.

"Yes. Eberhard took care of that for me. He also has a friend in the Berlin Gestapo who, at the time, agreed to back off them. Your family house was eventually returned to them and they were left alone. With you 'dead,' the officials had bigger fish to fry rather than bother your family. Besides, with the success of the *U-Bootwaffe*, I began to have some political clout. And how would it have looked to Hitler to have the sister of his U-boat commander in jail for crimes against the Reich?"

"When will I be allowed to see them?" Lothar asked, a twinge of excitement in his voice.

"At the appropriate time, Lothar, we will have a family reunion," smiled the admiral. "It will be soon, I promise."

A long ladder on wheels was pushed across the wall by another of the plotters, who then climbed up and moved some pins out from the map of France into the Bay of Biscay. The admiral looked up for a few seconds to comprehend the change and then returned his gaze to Lothar. He was staring at the desk, a hundred questions whirling around in his head.

Dönitz suddenly raised his hand and a young officer came over to the table with a uniform jacket on a hanger. "I think this will fit you," the admiral smiled. "Try it on."

When Lothar stood up and examined the tunic, he saw the stripes of a *Fregattenkapitän* on the sleeve. Also, an Iron Cross hung where his used to be, right above the Submarine Warfare Badge.

"As of this moment, the slight against your record has been wiped clean and you have been promoted from Junior Lieutenant to Junior Captain. Four grades. Quite a leap, I would say."

Then he chuckled, "I would love to see the look on Göbbel's face if you showed up a party function — a *Kriegsmarine* version of Lazarus. That would put that goggled donkey in his place."

Lothar could scarcely believe it. He just kept staring at the four stripes of gold on the sleeve as if the empty uniform was to be worn by another man.

"Well, put it on!" laughed the admiral.

Lothar took off his old tunic and the adjutant took it from him. Then Dönitz helped his newly-promoted nephew into his new coat. "It's off the shelf," quipped the lieutenant, who was around Lothar's age. "But we'll get a tailor to fix it for you."

Dönitz then stood up and walked around his desk, stopping in front of the dazed Lothar. Another officer walked up with a polished wooden book and opened it, so that the contents were facing the admiral. Dönitz then took out a medal with a bright red-white-and-black ribbon.

"I am returning your Knight's Cross with Swords and, for your valor last month, you are awarded the Oak Leaves as well. The way you were sinking ships, you would have earned it within two patrols anyway." He placed the ribbon around the stunned Lothar's neck and then saluted him.

"*Fregattenkapitän* Stahl," the Admiral continued in his formal tone, "you are hereby transferred to U-boat Headquarters in Berlin. You are to report there immediately for your assignment."

"A new boat?" he asked, his eyes lighting up.

"In a matter of speaking," Dönitz replied, "but first we are going to put you through an engineering school of sorts."

"Why?" he asked, shrugging his shoulders. "Is there some new boat design of which I should be made familiar?"

"That is in the works but not right now. There's another, more pressing assignment for a man of your engineering skills in a place called Pennemünde, an island in the Baltic."

Dönitz shrugged. "But there are no U-boats there."

"If there are no boats," Lothar ventured, "can I ask the Grand Admiral what type of engineering I will be involved in?".

His uncle leaned over and whispered. "Rockets."

A disoriented look came over the U-boat commander. "What?" he asked in an astonished tone. "A man of the sea is to learn about flying?"

"I couldn't have put it better, myself, Lothar."

There was an awkward silence in which Dönitz turned to peruse the new convoy positions on the large wall chart. Then he spun back to his nephew and noted that Lothar was staring at his striped sleeve.

"But first," added the admiral, a smile forming on his hawkish face, "I am granting you a one week furlough to see your mother and father."

CHAPTER SIX

March 1, 1944
Bar Harbor, Maine

"Once there was a little girl who lived next to me . . ."

Ginger Lanton's voice followed the notes and words on the sheet music with melodic precision. However, her right-handed piano accompaniment was jerky and she forgot to flatten the B on the word "to." Instead of stopping and going back, she just paused and shrugged her padded shoulders. Then she leaned forward again and began playing, her eyes jumping from the ivory and ebony keys back to the music.

"And she loved a sailor boy. He was only three . . ."

She grinned at navigating the next passage without a mistake but the last note was off-key and she made a mental note to get the old mahogany Willis upright tuned.

"Now he's on a battleship in his sailor's suit . . ."

This time she remembered the natural sign and a finger deftly landed on a white key.

"Just a great big sailor man but he's just as cute."

Ginger Lanton envisioned Gus' big, serious face as she mouthed the last word. A Vic Damone or Frank Sinatra he was definitely not, and she grinned when the image of him dancing came to mind. But no man danced as well as her Gus. That was because she taught him everything he knew: quick step, rhumba, foxtrot, tango and waltz.

"Bell bottoms trousers, coat of navy blue!" she sang, giving up on trying to follow with the piano.

"She loves her sailor, and he loves her too!"

Ginger flipped the sheet music shut with her left hand, and the cartoon images of four singing sailors popped out at her. Turning the booklet over she saw an advertisement for new songwriters. It claimed that they could earn $1,000 in advance royalties.

"For Pete's sake," she sighed, "I should enter that. I could write a better song than this."

Ginger was tall, even without her heels – 5'11" — which was why in her younger days men tended to avoid her at dances. She usually wore her long, sand-colored hair pulled back and tied with a bow, in the manner of her favorite singer, Martha Tilton. She even copied Tilton's style of singing, catching her every time she performed on *Maxwell House Coffee Time*.

Gus thought Ginger's resemblance to Tilton was uncanny and made sure he had all her recordings. On many occasions, just before they went to bed, he would put on *You and I* and they would dance.

"Gus?" she called out across large living room to the open bedroom door. "It's almost eight and you told the Stokes' we would be at the club by a quarter after."

A groan greeted her query. "Come on sailor boy," she chuckled.

Ginger got up and straightened her jumper, watching it fall just above the knees. The length and the low neckline were a bit daring for an inter-service function, especially since it was not good form to show up the wives of more senior officers. But then she was always the talk of the Coast Guard dances because she went to have fun and did not care about scoring points for her husband's career.

Gus sauntered out of the bedroom resplendent in his dress blues.

"You look wonderful, darling," she cooed. "And on the very first try."

"I had a good teacher," he grinned, taking a breath of the cool sea air that wafted through the screens on the front porch. Beyond that was a lawn that gently sloped downward to the water. The Atlantic Ocean, a misty gray in the late winter evening, touched on almost half a mile of his land, most of it sandy beach.

The real estate had cost them dearly, but an inheritance to Ginger and the sale of Gus' Montana farm got them the land and house without a mortgage. The Coast Guard income could easily keep up the house and the '38 DeSoto, while Ginger's dance academy in Bar Harbor brought in the funds for all the extras.

"Gus," she started, her tone becoming more serious, "why do you think we're being invited to a *Navy* function?"

"Who knows?" he replied, walking up the mirror in the hallway. He rested his cap on his head and then carefully maneuvered it to regulation fit. "Maybe they want to see how well the Coast Guard dances."

It was no secret among the people of Bar Harbor that Ginger and Gus could dance. They had been partners since a spring night in 1936 when an awkward ensign went into the Broadway Dance Studio in Bar Harbor to learn a few steps for the Admiral's Ball. He had no problem with her height, and she thought his clumsiness was endearing as well as a challenge to her skills as a teacher. He took three lessons and, to her dismay, went back out to sea. But on his next leave he signed up for nightly instruction with dinner afterward. From then on, they were an item.

"Should I dance with all the four-stripers and stars this time or pretend I'm lame?" she laughed.

"Jitterbug 'em to death, baby" he replied, as if a judge passing a sentence.

"Aye-aye, Commander," she saluted.

As Gus fussed with his tie again, Ginger pulled a record out of the cardboard sleeve and walked over to her RCA console. Gus had bought it for her on their fourth wedding anniversary, two weeks before the sinking of "that German submarine," as she later called that particular episode in their lives. The action had brought Gus within a hair of being demoted and subsequently relegated to buoy tending or running a lightship. The inquiry had lasted over two months with Gus being put on indefinite leave.

There had been three departments involved in the inquiry: the US Coast Guard, the US Navy and the State Department. Watching from the wings were two members of Congress and a senator, all from Maine. The politicians were on hand to make sure Gus was getting due process as a citizen of their state. Maybe Washington was tip-toeing around the issue of German submarines, but they were a real item off the waters of the northeastern state. Since the inquiry was not a court martial, civilians were allowed to attend and, in their eyes, Gus was a hero.

On October 17, the day when the inquiry was about to hear testimony from officials of the German embassy, news of a U-boat attack on the US destroyer, *Kearny*, headlined the local news services. Eleven American sailors lost their lives. This lead to a week-long recess while the military adjudicators and politicians attended briefings in Washington regarding amendments to the Neutrality Act. They had only been back a few days when another American destroyer, the *Reuben James*, was sunk by a German submarine while escorting a convoy from Halifax. This time, 115 servicemen died. The instant that the members of the inquiry heard of the sinking they adjourned the proceedings indefinitely. Gus went back to work the next day.

Ginger let the stylus float down and gently closed the polished walnut doors to eliminate the mechanical noises of the record player and the hiss of the needle on the heavy, black disk.

"The doctor's report came," Ginger said, her voice muffled from speaking into his shoulder.

"What did he say this time?" Gus asked.

"Inconclusive," she sighed. "Either you don't have the stuff or I can't catch it."

"Now what?" Gus replied, his mood somewhat dampened.

Ginger cocked her head. "Oh, I did call an adoption agency while you were gone."

"You did?" The sudden announcement took him by surprise.

"Yup. It seems with all these single men running around in uniform there are even more young women faced with unexpected families."

"So we do our patriotic duty and adopt one of these unintended kids, is that it?"

"Yup."

"Shuddup and dance with me."

"Yup," she giggled, burying her face back into his shoulder.

The last strains of music faded out. Without a word, Gus held out his hand for her and they both skipped down the stairs to the waiting DeSoto.

* * *

"Gus, it's no secret that your name is up for a fourth ring. Hell, if it hadn't been for that damned sub incident in '41, you'd have made captain when the war started. Those America First sonofabitches got to some Navy bureaucrats on that one. But hell, the *Reuben James* was sunk and, a month later, Pearl Harbor was bombed and everybody forgot about you. In a strange sort of way, you could say that a U-boat got you into that mess and one got you out. Well, with a little help from the Japs."

Vice Admiral Clayton Stokes flipped the ashes from his cigar, missing the ashtray by a good six inches. In his late 40s, Stokes was a bald man with heavy wrinkles on his forehead that would rival the facial skin of a bloodhound. His nose and cheeks were heavily veined from bourbon, with jowls that quivered when he spoke. Yet his crystal-green eyes alerted all within eye-shot that the liquor had not dimmed his mind.

"It's a damned good thing for the convoy program they left you alone," he continued, stopping to suck on the fading cigar butt. "With two German U-boats to your credit, and two probables, that makes you about the best sub hunter on this side of the Atlantic — which is another reason why you've been passed over a few times."

Gus just shrugged and took another sip of his rum. Since his days escorting convoys to Iceland, he had adopted the traditional drink of the Royal Navy, finding it smoother than the bite of corn liquor. His wandering eyes found Ginger winking at him in mid-stride as she two-stepped with Captain Dan Malick, a friend of his who was once a lieutenant on a small patrol cutter Gus commanded in the '30s. In addition to the Coast Guard faithful, the floor was crowded this evening with naval officers from two destroyers that were in port. One of their commanders was seated at the next table and he and Gus were in line for the next available dartboard.

"Now, our troops are getting ready to invade France and they'll end this thing sometime around Thanksgiving. But there's no sense taking a good dog off the hunt just yet, is there?"

"No, Clay, not yet," Gus finally responded. "I mean, I'd just get bored with all this great food and seeing my wife every night."

Stokes chuckled and slapped Gus on the back. "You know, Gus, one of these days, you'll look back on the war as the best time of your life, you mark my words."

Gus just nodded, somberly, a smile cracking his face for the first time. He liked Clay Stokes. The man was a good commander and had taught him more about operating a fighting ship than all the other courses and instructors combined. He fought for Gus at the inquiry, risking his own career in doing so. No man could ask for a better friend than that.

"All right Clay," Gus said, plunking his glass down on the oak table, signaling the end of the friendship preamble. "Why did you drag me out here tonight when you knew I had an armament inspection lined up for the *Montauk?* You could dance with Ginger anytime."

"Gus," he sighed, "I need a favor."

"Shoot," replied Gus.

Stokes tapped the ashtray with his fingernail.

"The Navy wants me to loan you and your ship to the Canadians," he said bluntly.

"What?" Gus answered, leaning over to the admiral as if the acoustics were better on the other side of the table. "You invite me on a social outing to talk business? I thought you wanted me to help you move, or lend you money, or something."

"Gus," he whispered, "what I'm telling you is confidential and, if I went through proper protocol and called you into my office, I'd have to write it down for Washington to see, and then someone down there would hit the fucking roof. And my ass would be toasted."

"Clay," Gus sighed. "You're not making any sense."

"All right, I'll try to explain it better," he continued, glad that he had stopped himself with one bourbon. "U-boats are still a big problem in Canadian waters."

"Really?" Gus replied. "I thought the Canucks were doing quite well."

"They are to a point, Gus. Between their ships and aircraft they can sink subs as well or better than any in the Allied forces."

"So what's the problem then?"

"U-boats are still wreaking havoc in the Gulf of St. Lawrence and up the St. Lawrence River. The Canadians need some assistance, a ship with an up-to-date sonar to counter the new German subs."

"Why the secrecy?"

"Political. The Canadian government doesn't want panic to spread just when they've convinced their people that the waters are safe again. If it got out that we were helping them —"

"Helping them, Clay? Those corvettes can find a U-boat as well as anything we got."

"In deep water, sure," the admiral countered. "But in the shallows, especially where there's a lot of noise from the river, it's hard to track them. Somehow, they've got a sub that can stay under water while both running and recharging. Intelligence confirms this."

"But their air crews are deadly on subs."

"Not against this new one. Like I said, it doesn't have to surface."

"I see," sighed Gus, stopping to stare at his wife as she flowed across the dance floor. He was supposed to be on coastal patrol — out for three days, maximum, in for three. "So the rumors are true. Jeeze, with those snorkels they can run submerged for days. And when they do surface, the rubber coating on their conning towers cuts down on the radar signature."

"Yes, Gus, but the good news is our newest SG radar can pick up a paint bucket on the water so we will have something new for them."

"I think you're over-optimistic on that one, Clay," Gus breathed. "That's only if the surface is like glass. If you start getting heavy swells it would be hard to pick up a conning tower let alone a can of paint."

"Gus," Stokes growled, "I can't order you to do this, and I wouldn't even if I had the authority. You've done your duty in the worst water the world has to offer and it's time to let someone else carry the load. Hell, there are more guys now chasing fewer subs so we're not in trouble of having a shortage. But this request come straight from the top."

"Washington?"

"Yep," Stokes growled. "It seems Roosevelt read about that Newfoundland ferry being sunk and all those civilians killed. So, the president offered to help and this is what I got saddled with. But it's not a bad assignment. Four months at the most. I can even sweeten the pot. You take your ship to Sydney, in Cape Breton, and we'll give you and your crew four days furlough every three weeks. I can arrange for you to fly home on a PBY or Ginger can join you there, whatever you want."

Gus watched Ginger and the officer doing the tango. That was one of the dances that his bum shoulder was hesitant to let him try. They looked so good dancing together that he suddenly felt a pang of jealousy.

"Will you give my crew a furlough starting tomorrow?"

"Sure. I can write it down as time off for a partial refit for the *Montauk*."

"You know, Clay," Gus sighed as he watched his wife flowing with the music, "if the Jerries have this boat in any numbers, it's a whole new ball game."

"That's what I want you to find out."

CHAPTER SEVEN

May 19, 1944
Pennemünde Island
Baltic Sea off the North German coast

Lothar Stahl was jostled by a bevy of scientists in white laboratory coats who scampered past as if he were merely a post in the concrete bunker. Another scientist, much larger than the rest, stood in the middle of the room and issued reams of orders, his commands echoed by three or four more of the technicians as they went down their respective checklists. In the ensuing cacophony, the U-boat skipper wondered if any of these men knew what they were doing.

A few minutes later the shelter was oddly quiet, most of the technicians having gone to perform their respective duties. Two of the remaining ones stood in front of the control panel, working several potentiometers and reporting their adjustments to the big man who instantly processed the information and spat back refinements to their information as a tennis player would return a volley. This robust man, although only 31 years of age, was one of the world's leading authorities on propulsion systems, and his career would outlast that of his masters' by decades. He was Wernher von Braun.

Von Braun's interest in rocketry went back almost as far as the program itself. When he was 18, the bright student became involved with a collection of Berlin theorists calling themselves the Society for Space Travel. During the 1930s, even when this type of research was regarded as a waste of precious resources, the society produced Germany's first liquid-fueled rocket engine. Coinciding with von Braun earning his engineering degree, he participated in the launching of the group's first significant rocket, the *Mirak-1*.

Beginning in 1936, he was the resident researcher at Pennemünde. His A-4 became slowly refined and finally, in 1942, it lifted off successfully for the first time and flew in a great arc over the Baltic Sea.

"Today the spaceship is born!" General Dornberger, the Army overseer had announced to the press. But Wernher was heard to utter, "Oh yes, we shall go to the moon but, of course, I dare not tell Hitler yet!" His productive partnership with the Army and Dornberger would end in January 1943, shortly after a visit by Heinrich Himmler.

To the left of where Lothar was standing was the stiff, authoritarian figure of Klaus Deckler, the commander of the project and a colonel in the *Schutzstaffel*, or SS. However, with his black uniform and polished black boots covered by the long lab coat, he blended in with the other scientists who, unlike von Braun, seemed to be all of the same stature: thin and about five-foot-ten inches.

But even white lab coats cannot hide everything. Because of the long and narrow shaping of Deckler's graying, short-cropped head, the dark eyes seemed too close together. and many men cringed when they looked into them. His thin, almost effeminate, eyebrows further enhanced this illusion.

* * *

Lothar never saw the rocket take off. He felt the ground vibrate and clutched his ears at the tremendous roar of the engines but the clouds of vapor obstructed his view. Ten seconds later all he saw was the scorched metal framework that had been the launching tower.

"Well," sighed von Braun, his tinted goggles still strapped to his head. "So far so good. If it clears 15,000 meters, then the range projections will hold."

One of the scientists clutched at his headphones. "Air observation puts it now at 9,000 meters at a speed of 740 kilometers per hour."

"Good," replied von Braun. "It just shattered the airspeed numbers of the A-4. At this rate, it will achieve the sound barrier in a few seconds."

Moments later, the phone rang. The technician who answered it piped up, "Sonic boom detected at 01:13:23."

"Good work!" beamed von Braun, over a chorus of subdued cheering. Scientists were never ones for ecstatic shows of joy. Von Braun yanked off his goggles and bent down over the console to monitor the tracking.

"Now, let's see how the new gyros work," he announced.

"Ceiling goal attained. Now leveling off for designated target."

Lothar peered over the shoulder of one of the scientists and stared at the small, green cathode ray screen that von Braun was observing. A small, flickering dot moved across it in a westerly direction, denoting the flight path of the rocket. If all went well in the next few minutes, the A-7 would have surpassed the farthest distance made by the A-4, or, as the Allies would soon come to know it, the V-2 — or "Vengeance Weapon-2"

"What?" cried the technician with the headphones. Shortly afterward, his face seemed to melt and his eyes drooped like a basset hound's. The blip on the screen faded to a blur.

The technician shifted in his chair to face the others. With a sad tone he uttered, "The rocket exploded at 01:29:56."

"Damn!" cried von Braun, hammering his right fist on the palm of his other hand. "Another month wasted." If the rocket genius had bothered to look over at Deckler, he would have seen that the pensive expression on the SS man's face was unmoving, like a frozen mask.

Unlike von Braun, who had grown up in a privileged family and held the title of a count, Deckler had fought his way up in the Nazi Party, beginning with Ernst Röhm's SA, or Brownshirts, in the early 1930s. Röhm was Hitler's contact with ex-Great War servicemen and drew many of them into a private Nazi army which provided scare tactics to persuade politicians and business people to support Hitler.

Deckler had survived the purges of June 1934, when Röhm and many of his SA thugs were executed by Hitler's new security arm, the SS. The loyal Nazi enforcer had become an embarrassment to Hitler, an obstacle to the party gaining support among Germany's elite, with names like Junkers, Siemens and Krupp. Röhm and his hierarchy were therefore eliminated. The men who survived, like Deckler, were welcomed into the SS organization and rewarded with a military rank.

Not that the lithe, 49-year-old Colonel Deckler was just another bureaucrat with a military title. He had served with distinction in the Great War, reaching the rank of lieutenant when hostilities ended. Deckler was also keenly aware that those above him were now wreaking havoc on commanders who, they felt, had not performed up to Hitler's timetable. These were the ones who now had the ear of the SS chief, Heinrich Himmler.

As the last trace of the blip on the green monitor disappeared he was already composing the story he would tell Himmler. Personally, he liked the scientists. Although they were true academics who constantly complained about the lack of resources — and ones who almost never gave the party salute — their honesty was refreshing. And it was very rare these days to find anyone who was not covering his behind.

However, Himmler never thought so. In their meeting of two months ago he ranted, "Klaus, I want you to bring these traitorous scientists to heel. And the way I see you performing this task is to arrest that obnoxious von Braun and make sure he's never seen again."

When caught between his personal feelings and his duty, Deckler knew there was no option. Following the order to the letter, he personally arrested von Braun.

Deckler then had him taken to Berlin but, as it turned out, von Braun had friends in powerful places who interceded with Hitler himself. The scientist was dressed down for his arrogance, and the many failures of his experiments, but Hitler was convinced by them that it was only because of this young Prussian that England was now being terrorized by the V-1's — and even the Führer wouldn't tamper with that success.

Deckler had survived as well. Himmler wanted him demoted and sent to the Russian front, but Albert Speer, Hitler's new War Production czar, wanted the rocket team to stay intact. Deckler kept his rank and job — for the moment at least.

Lothar watched von Braun carefully. The world authority on rocket-propelled vehicles began to jot down some figures on his notepad, drawing long strokes to represent the sides of a rocket.

"The structural configuration of the rocket alters slightly after it proceeds through the sound barrier," he uttered, more to the notebook than to anyone in particular. "But just enough for the walls to buckle ever so slightly as to press onto the engine. The resulting friction from the vibration builds up a static charge which ignites the fuel cell."

"How can you be sure?" queried Deckler. "This is 12th time this has happened."

"Nineteenth," corrected the scientist with a shrug. "All the other options have been covered. It must be this. If we strengthen the walls around the fuel cell with a molybdenum or chromium alloy, it should alleviate that problem."

"True," piped up one of the other scientists, an older man named Müller who barely came up to von Braun's chest. "But before we send the next one up we should look for a method to send the static charge out into the atmosphere."

"But Herr Müller," countered von Braun impatiently, "if we strengthen the hull there won't be a charge."

"How do we know for sure that is the source of the static charge or, for that matter, the explosion?" Deckler cut in.

"Because," replied von Braun, his voice sounding more irritated as the discussion wore on, "we have tested the propulsion system with great care. In my estimation it should run for more than three hours without malfunction. In fact . . ."

To Lothar, these discussions were commonplace after a launch, successful or not. However, despite their length, the banter never was boring. The submariner's grasp of the rocket program had grown exponentially at Pennemünde and he could now keep up with their conversations.

* * *

An hour later, Lothar was standing on the pier looking out over the calm Baltic Sea. During the past year, he had eased his thirst for operational duty through his travels to the building yards in Bremen where he monitored the construction of four newly-designed U-boats. But he longed to be standing on the conning tower with a pair of Zeiss binoculars in his hand, his U-boat racing through the churning ocean in anticipation of battle. That was what he was born to do and every day he spent away from his boats made him miss it that much more.

"You will be out there soon, Lothar." The U-boat man turned to see the big, smiling face of von Braun approaching him. The scientist looked clumsy without his white smock, and his civilian clothes were not those one would associate with a baron of Prussia.

"Too bad I won't be going with you," he sighed. "Although, at the present time, I feel it is a drain on precious resources and time, part of me wishes I was overseeing the program."

"But you will be, Baron," countered Lothar. "Every piece of equipment has your stamp on it."

"Oh, because I have made more than 50,000 alterations to the rockets?"

"Wasn't Thomas Edison asked why he kept trying to perfect electric lighting after failing that many times?"

"I see your point, of course, Lothar," chuckled von Braun. "Like Edison, I could answer that I have now ruled out options as to why it will *not* work – 50,000 of them."

The longer days seemed to lighten Lothar's spirits, a change from those dark few days last winter when the SS seemed to be ransacking his office at every turn. It was if they were in concert with Göbbels and the Gestapo about his past, but he knew neither the Propaganda Ministry nor the Gestapo had anything to do with Pennemünde. This was Himmler's operation and the SS chief tolerated no outside interference.

Sometimes the guards would speak to him, curious young men not far removed from the Hitler Youth who yearned for his tales of U-boat action. However, they would quickly become mute when an officer happened by as they had been instructed not to be on friendly terms with the scientists. Some of Deckler's officers even deemed the rocket academics as necessary evils. But to these soldiers, Lothar was a warrior and they routinely bent the rules so that he could take the ferry across to the mainland to get out for awhile.

"I'm afraid Deckler is not going to get the rocket he wants," sighed von Braun, watching the light-hearted kibitzing of the crew of an anti-aircraft battery. The 88mm weapon and the huge searchlight beside it were manned by junior high school students, lads of 14 and 15.

"Size has its limitations."

"Size? How?"

"Well, as it is, the A-4s are manufactured at Mettelwork."

"Yes," replied Lothar, "the concentration camp. So, are the laborers doing shoddy work?"

"I detest the system of slave labor, but it is what I am given to work with. This includes the transportation system, which also puts constraints on my program. You see, a larger shell could withstand the pressures but we are limited in the size of the vehicle by the conditions of the European roads. The rockets can only be a certain size because they have to fit through tunnels and underpasses on their way here."

Lothar was astounded at von Braun's words. Problems such as this were never encountered in his end of the project because U-boats were built at the water's edge and then each one is launched into its environment from a close proximity. Only torpedoes require transportation from inland Germany to the naval bases. Everything else of size is manufactured and repaired locally.

"It's the same with fuel," continued von Braun. "Can you imagine what the world would think if they knew that the A-2s now hitting England were powered by the labor of farmers?"

"I don't understand, Baron."

"Ethyl alcohol, the fuel for the rockets, was not my first choice but it was what was available in large enough quantities. We have no oil wells nearby and, with the Allies bombing everything that moves in Germany these past few months, every drop of petroleum product goes to the Luftwaffe, Wehrmacht and your U-boats."

Lothar still did not understand.

"When you first began to drink with your friends, Lothar," von Braun chuckled, "what was it that you brought to parties?"

"Wine and beer."

"How about when you wanted something stronger?"

"Moonshine, of course."

"Correct. Ethyl alcohol. So now you are one of the privileged few who know that my rockets operate on potato squeezings." The big man paused to laugh at Lothar's amazed look.

"Oh, it works," von Braun shrugged, his mirth receding, "but the A-7 engine is too refined to run on moonshine. It requires a better propellant, but I do not have the resources to produce such fuel in the time allotted. Therefore, with those two constraints, I'm afraid your project will have to be altered somewhat."

The big scientist crouched down and reached for a twig nearby. Drawing figures in the dust he explained his diagram. "Here," he added, sketching a rough picture, "is North America and this is Newfoundland, where we had initially planned to base the rockets, and New York is farther down here. We chose Newfoundland first because it fit the projected range of the A-7s. Secondly, there are large areas which are not populated, so it would take the Allies weeks, maybe months, to figure out the firing location. Before that time, given the destruction of the payloads on US territory, peace negotiations would supposedly be in progress.

"Now, we know that the distance the rocket has to travel is 1,000 kilometers and that it has to carry a ton of Trialen. However, with the structural and fuel problems we are having with the A-7, there is no way it will be ready in the time that Deckler has assigned us. We need another four months, minimum."

"Four months?" sighed Lothar, his knees cracking as he squatted down beside the scientist.

"Or more if the Allies continue bombing the supply routes and our test rockets and materials keep getting delayed. Remember, the A-7 has to be shipped without fins and final assembly here takes time."

"So does that means the mission will have to be scrubbed?"

"The present scenario, yes," replied von Braun, tapping the stick on the diagram. "However, a modified version, one which I had already submitted to Deckler three months ago, could still work."

"You sent him another plan while working on the A-7?" asked Lothar incredulously.

"I know what you are thinking, Lothar. It probably was a naïve move after all the trouble we were in at the time but I am a realist and the laws of physics aren't subordinate to the plans of the Third Reich. As you might have guessed, Deckler called me a defeatist and threatened to begin the whole business of treason again."

"My God!" blurted Lothar, his exclamation drawing interest from one of the patrolling guards. The young man tipped his head to get a better look at the diagram and, after ascertaining that it was just scientist drivel, shrugged and walked on.

"Lothar," continued von Braun, his voice a low monotone, "sometimes your lapses in decorum are quite unnerving."

"Sorry, Baron," the U-boat man said sheepishly. "Please continue."

"As I was saying, there is no way we can meet the proposed deadline but I am going to put forward my plan to Deckler, with a few modifications. What I am proposing is to shorten the distance to the farthest range of the A-4s, vehicles that we know are reliable."

"But by having the effective range, that would put us somewhere in Nova Scotia or out in the ocean."

"That is quite correct on both parts, Lothar," replied Braun, the point of his stick digging into a spot equidistant.

"Now, from what the High Command reports, there is a Norwegian-manned weather station right here in Canadian territory, in Nova Scotia." Von Braun then drew a straight line down toward him and stopped halfway down the diagram.

Suddenly Lothar's eyes lit up. "Baron, it could be done," he said, picking up another twig. "I know the area on the southern shore of Nova Scotia quite well and I am familiar with many of the fishing villages. There are hundreds of small, virtually uninhabited islands off the coast. It will, of course, be right under the noses of the Allies, but it could work."

"It will achieve what the High Command wishes to accomplish with the A-7," continued von Braun, impressed with Lothar's grasp of the situation. "I will show you the expanded version of the plan this evening."

As they both got up and let the blood run back into their legs, von Braun added, "But that is only *half* the plan."

"There's more?" Lothar asked.

The scientist drew several small ovals to the right of this spot. "Right here, Lothar, approximately 500 kilometers out from New York, is where an operation called *Sea Scorpion* will take place. Here is how it works . . ."

* * *

Lothar never let on he knew what the scientist was talking about. However, seven months before, it was he who had first brought the idea to Grand Admiral Dönitz in order to get a high-level opinion of his brainchild. His uncle Karl was quite receptive to the idea but then drew it out on a piece of paper in front of an astonished nephew, almost verbatim.

"U-boat men think alike, Lothar," Dönitz had confided. "Therefore, firing rockets from a submarine is the next logical next step in their weapons development; in the same way that building better batteries is for their increased time of running submerged. In other words, we already thought of that and have designs already drafted to fire a rocket from a submerged platform."

"You do?" Lothar had asked of the Grand Admiral, feeling like a child who had been made to share his favorite toy with his brother.

"Yes, the name of the project is *Sea Scorpion* — and I can't emphasize enough the top secret status given this plan. This is not 1941 when the antics and loose lips of irreverent captains in the U-boat service would be grudgingly overlooked. Nowadays, men are being hauled in for not giving the proper salute. There's no telling what would happen to someone whom the Gestapo suspected had knowledge about an idea that was supposed to be an official secret."

His uncle then took out a piece of paper and, as he wrote, said, "Since you now know that a little knowledge is dangerous, take this to Admiral Godt and he will get you in to see the project firsthand. He is supervising the building of the undersea launching systems as we speak — the system called *Sea Scorpion*. The successful launch of missiles from the ocean, combined with a land operation, will deal a stiff blow to American confidence. What do you say?"

Lothar sighed as he was passed the document. "What I really want is a transfer back to active duty. That way I won't be tripping over the SS at every turn."

"Yes, I know, Lothar. I feel bad about the way Himmler has put his foot down on those creative geniuses at Pennemünde, dedicated men whose ideas are essential to winning the war. I should have let you in on the seaborne program earlier, but that would have meant you having to put up with meaningless interrogations from the bureaucrats, maybe even unearthing your old feud with Göbbels. And there's no telling what may have happened. But to get clearance, one has to go through the drill.

"However, this is a slightly different matter because it is based entirely on the *U-boatwaffe*. Whenever U-boats are involved in a combined operation, I have total authority over the allotment of security clearances. As of now, you have that designation. I need someone I can trust to see that our boats aren't squandered by someone outside the service. That is why I need you to stay on."

CHAPTER EIGHT

July 9, 1944
1129:30 German Summer Time
1236 nautical miles west of Portugal

"What is the status of Scorpion Two?"

"Seven hundred meters off the port stern, sir," replied the operator in the hydrophone room. He was 19 with a wispy beard barely covering his chin.

"Good, they're catching up." Lothar Stahl studied the face of his watch for a long moment. His beard had grown enough that it had stopped irritating him.

"All stop," he said as the second hand touched the top numeral.

"All stop, sir," replied Siegfried Weidling, the chief engineering officer, in a nasal voice. The twin electric dynamotors of the new Type IXD boat were shut off and each of the 500-horsepower power plants whined down in a steady decrescendo. A minute later there was a ghostly silence.

"Signal Scorpion Two Leader that we are stopping and that he and his transports are to continue running until 1129:50. At that time, they are to stop and await instructions.

"*Jawohl, Kapitän.*"

"Bring her up to 15 meters."

Ten seconds later, Weidling, a tall, slender man in his mid-20s, announced, "The boat is at fifteen meters, sir."

The two submarine groups, Scorpion One and Scorpion Two, consisted of two huge Type IXD U-boats, each shepherding two underwater transport boats. Lothar Stahl, the captain of Scorpion One, depressed a button on the side of the periscope and the metallic cylinder began to rise up from the deck in a snake-like hiss. Flipping his white-crowned cap around backward, he eased his forehead into the black, rubber eyepiece, flattening his long nose in the process. Then he began to scan the ocean surface using a familiar search pattern. He was immediately relieved to see that the sky was overcast with a high, even cloud cover. This was favorable because patrolling aircraft and ships would be highlighted by the background and spotted long before they had a chance to attack.

The *U-1409,* a 1,200-ton Type IXD *Atlantikboot,* was the world's first true modern submarine. From its commissioning in May, the 254-foot boat was nicknamed *Seekuh* because its ungainly profile when surfaced reminded some sailors of a manatee, or sea cow. Lothar disliked the term and had snapped at one of his subordinates who had the bad luck to use the word while he was within hearing distance.

Unlike its predecessors, the Type IXD contained a high-capacity battery system that allowed it to travel submerged for greater periods of time. This gave it a range of 15,000 nautical miles at a speed of 12 knots. However, battery storage came secondary to another, more profound, feature.

"Siegfried, prepare to raise the *schnorkel.*"

"*Schnorkel* ready, *Kapitän,*" he replied.

The *schnorkel* — a twin-piped device enabling undersea craft to take in fresh air and expel exhaust while underwater — derives from a German slang term meaning "nose." But it was neither a German invention nor an improvement made by marine engineers of Lothar's country.

Fifty years prior to being installed on the new U-boats, a primitive American submarine ran an internal combustion engine underwater by taking in air through a hose. In the 1930s, the Royal Dutch Navy ran experiments with floats which would automatically close the openings and shut off the diesel engines if the level of the water ran over top. The data from these trials was discovered by Nazi intelligence operatives when the German army overran Holland in 1940 and the technology began showing up on U-boats in late 1943.

"Up to eight meters."

After a few moments came the reply. "The boat is at eight meters, sir."

"Raise *schnorkel.*"

During the deadly spring of 1943, many U-boats were destroyed or damaged from being caught on the surface replenishing their batteries by conventional venting methods; that is, opening engine room covers and allowing natural airflow to vent the big diesels.

This worked well enough for the first three years of the war. That is, until the Allies came up with technology to counter the mostly surface-dwelling U-boats. In late 1942, anti-submarine bombers were fitted with a portable version of the ship-borne radar units. The aircraft could then sweep their designated areas at night and other times when human vision was impaired, such as in foggy conditions.

When on a nocturnal patrol, a surfaced U-boat could be attacked by the radar-guided aircraft aided by a brilliant spotlight called the Leigh Light. This powerful search lamp illuminated the surface of the ocean, catching the hapless submarine completely by surprise. Using the *Schnorkel* reduced the radar signature from a large conning tower to a mere rubber-coated stick, thus thwarting both Allied inventions.

Unlike the type of *schnorkel* fitted to the transport boats, which folded down across the deck, the apparatus on the long-range Type IXD was installed when the boat was being constructed and telescoped into the hull in much the same way as the periscope. When the valve reached the surface, a float dropped, exposing the submarine to the fresh air while the engine exhaust and hull gases could be sent out via the second pipe, which was placed lower and farther aft.

"Valve clear," Gerhard announced.

"Fans on."

"Fans on, sir."

"Start engines."

A small vibration began in the lead boat as the air compressors were engaged to start the large diesels. A loud rumble echoed through the dank chambers of the U-boat when the first of the 2,200 horsepower, nine-cylinder engines began to run. This intensity increased when the second one kicked in. In a few hours, the 60 tons of storage batteries, arranged under the interior deck plates, would be replenished.

Using the *schnorkel* was a delicate process, even in the calmest of water. Depth had to be strictly maintained because if the U-boat went too low, the head valve would shut off and the internal combustion engines would begin taking air from inside the hull. This would create a vacuum, which could have serious effects on the crews' eardrums. But another, more deadly, hazard of a closed valve was a buildup of carbon monoxide gas.

Every night, the two escorting U-boats surfaced for navigational updates and ran on their engines. In this way, the batteries could be charged while maintaining progress toward their destination. But Lothar feared the new American radar, which was said to able to pick up objects as small as the pipe valve of a *schnorkel,* and so nervously watched the NAXOS screen while the boats were surfaced.

The trip had begun on July 1st, at St-Nazaire, a full month ahead of schedule because the Allied landings at Normandy on June 6th threatened the sanctity of the U-boat pens. Himmler was still convinced that the invasion would be thrown back into the sea but *Grossadmiral* Dönitz wanted the mission advanced because of increased air attacks on all U-boat pens.

Six U-boats were lined up abreast at the dock; two *Atlantikbooten* and four stubby Type XIV *Milchenkuh* — "milk cows," or transport U-boats. As Lothar stood on the deck with his crew and five rocket technicians, 20 hand-picked men of the *Waffen SS* were escorted aboard two of the transport U-boats amid much fanfare from an orchestra. Once they were on the rubberized deck of the *Atlantikboot,* Colonel Klaus Deckler was presented by Himmler as "a Nazi hero." The *Reichsführer* went on for five minutes on how the fate of the mission rested upon the shoulders of Deckler and the SS men without once mentioning the 20 *Kriegsmarine* guards, the four scientists or the U-boat crews.

However, toward the end of his monologue, his voice began to be rivaled by the sound of music wafting up from the open hatches of the *U-1409.* Lothar smiled when he heard the familiar strains of *The Kretschmer March.* To their credit, the crews waited until Himmler had stopped talking before they began to sing along with the music. No one admitted to playing the phonograph, but Lothar knew that Siegfried Weidling had remained below to maintain the systems.

Lothar never sang but, being the captain, Himmler singled him out and glared at him through his round spectacles. This indignant display was matched by Deckler's cold stare and it was all Lothar could do to keep from smiling. *Onkle Karl* could not be there because he was supervising the battle that was being presently waged between his U-boats and the Allied escorts for control of the English Channel. But his crews sang as if Dönitz were standing in Himmler's spot.

When the boats were safely out to sea, Deckler, who had naturally chosen to ride along on the lead boat, had tried to chastise him for the interruption. "Find the person responsible," Deckler had said, "and bring him to me."

Lothar had simply replied, "Colonel Deckler, this is my U-boat and you are its passenger. So hear me on this: the law of the sea requires that until such time that your feet touch dry ground again, I am in command and you will conduct yourself in a respectful manner to both myself and my crew. Do you understand?"

Unused to the confines of the boat, and feeling a touch of seasickness, Deckler conceded the point and backed off — but he did not forget.

Today, they were nearly halfway to their destination, and Lothar was proud of the progress of the commanders of the other boats. Never had he been involved in such a difficult mission as keeping six boats together for nearly 3,000 miles.

It was an exhausting affair that required precision timing and constant communication. During the day, the boats kept in contact by sound pulses at 15-minute intervals. At night, Lothar's boat and the other *Atlantikboot* would run surfaced and signal the transports with focused light flashes picked up by their commanders watching through periscopes. Then, each using their *schnorkel*, the four *Milchenkuh* would recharge while shepherded on the surface by Lothar's boat and the *U-1410,* the second *Atlantikboot.* So far, they had been stealthy and had not attracted the interest of any enemy craft, even though an occasional ship had been spotted on the horizon. This would be the plan while they were in the mid-Atlantic. In another 700 miles, they would be within reach of air patrols and the escorting U-boats would not have the luxury of running surfaced, even for an hour.

Scorpion Two, the other flotilla of three boats, always maintained a distance of one kilometer behind Scorpion One. In the same manner as Scorpion One, the hydrophone operators kept in touch with each other with a series of minute sound pulses, to both avoid collisions and prevent the break-up of each pack. It was a tedious process that could easily be disrupted by a storm — or discovery by an enemy ship or aircraft. But, so far, they had been lucky.

Besides the unwieldy size of the underwater convoy, the other impediment to the effectiveness of this mission was that two of the transports each towed a pod behind them, an object half the length of their boats. These trailers were, in effect, half submarines — hollowed-out U-boat shells with a small system of ballasts to keep them at a steady depth. They followed along like mindless children tagging behind their respective mothers. The pods could be jettisoned if trouble arose, but finding them again would be extremely difficult. And they carried key components to the success of the Sea Scorpion mission.

The two other transports, one in each group, carried barrels of ethanol and, because of their sheer weight, were a handful for their skippers. Added to their maneuvering woes, an Aphrodite radar decoy trailed behind each one at a distance of 50 meters. The Aphrodite was a hydrogen-filled bladder from which aluminum strips streamed behind. These noisemakers were designed to emulate the underwater signatures of a U-boat conning tower, and trick an enemy ship into depth charging a phantom. However, in this operation, the Aphrodite served constantly to alert the hydrophone operators in the two escort boats as to the location of the boat farthest back.

The escort boats kept to the sides of their respective transports, shepherding them from a distance of half a kilometer away. In the *Hydrophone room.* of each *Atlantikboot*, the frequencies of the pods and the Aphrodite trailers were constantly charted. By using this system, each boat in the "herd" could be notified by sound pulse if it was out of position.

"Report?" Lothar asked.

"Our transports are *schnorkelling*. Scorpion Two reports the same."

"Very well, Gerhard. You can get out your prayer book and ask God to keep the weather nice for another seven days."

* * *

July 12, 1944
0102:34 GST

"*Kapitän*, I am picking up a radar signal, 11 kilometers at two-five-four!"

"Sound the alarm!"

Until that moment, the night had been one of the calmest Lothar had ever witnessed on the Atlantic. The submarine sat almost perfectly still in on the water like a toy ship on a mill pond. An amazing array of stars plastered the night sky overhead, a summer constellation that Lothar wished he could have seen at another time when he could lie back and enjoy it.

However, the sound of distant aircraft engines soon chased away this idyllic pause in his life. It was a faint drone and it was soon lost in the bustling of the crew as they cleared the conning tower and prepared to dive.

One by one, three of the transports disappeared beneath the surface in a flurry of foamy water. The fourth was settling slowly and its conning tower was still fully exposed. Like a diligent dog, the other escort vessel remained off the port bow, refusing to submerge without its "tardy lamb."

"Signal Beltzer and Baumann to dive immediately," bawled Lothar, irritated that the two U-boats had not disappeared yet. He raised his binoculars toward the ghostly image of the *U-1410* and then over to the transport. It was not like Joachim Beltzer to be so reckless; he already knew there was problem.

* * *

"Action stations!"

A Royal Air Force B-24 began a slow descent to verify the odd array of signals that had suddenly appeared on the water to the southeast. The four-engine Consolidated Liberator Mark V was the latest in a line of very-long-range aircraft operating out of Bermuda. To increase its range to 2,400 nautical miles, items were stripped from the standard bomber such as the fuel tank seals, armor-plating, belly gun turret and turbo-superchargers. At this operational weight, the Liberator could cruise at 150 knots, carrying 2,000 gallons of fuel on takeoff with eight 250-pound depth charges. The bomber was usually cold and drafty, even in the summertime, but the crew liked the freedom of the huge bomber over the confines of the smaller Hudsons.

The flight navigator, Sergeant Alfred Boles, squinted as he studied the smears on the glowing green screen. Flying a mission on an antisubmarine patrol required a strict routine of rotating visual and radar watches, especially the latter where the radar operator's position was rotated every 45 minutes. "Captain, there's something wrong with this thing," Boles complained. "I see up to six images now."

"Jimmy, go back and have a look," replied Captain Phil Hardy. As the co-pilot squeezed out of his seat, Hardy banked the aircraft and began to descend from his 5,000-foot altitude. A few minutes later, when the Liberator had reached 300 feet, he leveled off and banked in the direction of the contacts. The bomb bay doors slowly opened revealing the sticks of Torpex that would be unleashed on the enemy below. The second radar operator, Corporal Eddie Andrews, a Cornish baker's son, was already below in the nose turret, readying the 50-caliber Browning machine guns.

"Jimmy, what have you got?" Hardy asked.

"There were six contacts, captain," Lieutenant James MacDougall replied in a thick Scottish accent, "But now there are three."

"Ready the light," Hardy replied without reservation. "Set depth charges for shallow."

* * *

Lothar knew what Beltzer was doing and sent one last frantic signal to get him to back off. But there was no response from the radio of the *U-1410*. If Lothar could have had night vision, he would have seen the veteran U-boat skipper high in the conning tower, snapping out commands while his gunnery crews hurriedly ripped the covers off the deck gun and the two 20mm anti-aircraft guns. That completed, the battle-ready men began accepting shell boxes from the forward cargo hatch.

Lothar had used his influence with his uncle to get Beltzer on this mission. With such a difficult operation ahead of them, he needed the best available and, with permission of the *BdU,* Beltzer gladly came along. And like the dedicated

U-boat skipper that he was, Joachim prepared to meet the danger without a second thought.

"God go with you, you crazy bastard!" Lothar cried, his voice disappearing in the hum of the approaching aircraft. He could make out the silhouette of the boat in the distance and a lump hardened his throat. An instant later, he slid down the hatchway into the control room The last look-out wheeled the hatch shut and followed him, his palms squeaking on the ladder as he shot downward.

Almost immediately he was confronted by the stern face of Deckler. His brow was heavily-furrowed and his upper teeth were clamped on his lower lip. "What is going on?" Deckler demanded of him.

"An aircraft is making ready to attack us," Lothar replied curtly, pushing past him to get to the periscope. "Depth?" he shouted, his voice suddenly hoarse with emotion.

"Depth now 20 meters."

"Ahead flank." Then Lothar shot a look at the chart and locked his eyes there for what seemed like minutes, but it was actually two seconds. "Maintain bearing two-four-nine. Notify the other transports to join on this course. Flank speed." Then he locked his eyes to the periscope.

"Stahl!" barked Deckler, his thin face reddening in anger.

"You may call me *Kapitän* while on my vessel, Colonel," Lothar replied, as civilly as he could under the circumstances. He then glanced over to check a cluster of gauges as the sub picked up speed.

"I will have you up before the *Reichsführer* when we get back!"

"Fine," Lothar growled. "Now you will shut up and get out of the way before I have you restrained."

Locking his eyes back on the periscope he could see nothing but the stars and the darkness of the ocean through the periscope. "Where are you, you flying vermin?" he breathed, sending his ill wishes to the enemy via telepathy.

Deckler eased up beside him, silently berating himself for allowing his SS guards to go on one of the transports instead of accompanying him. *If they were here*, he sniffed, *Stahl would be in irons now*.

"It seems that the enemy's radar is more up-to-date than our NAXOS detector," Lothar quipped to no one in particular, his chin flattened on the oily steel of the periscope tube. With cap reversed, he resembled a comedian in a silent movie. "And they caught us with our pants down."

He suddenly pulled away and glanced over the six colored lines on the graph paper as if the knowledge had suddenly come to him that each represented a submarine with crew, passengers and materiél. "What is the status of the transports?" The periscope slid down like an obedient animal.

"Numbers One, Two and Four are proceeding at six knots, and adjusting to two-four-nine ..." The crewman's voice trailed off as he listened to the hydrophone set. "Number Three has just begun to dive . . . *Kapitänleutnant* Baumann signaled that the diving planes were reacting sluggishly but he's got them free now."

"It might be too late," Lothar sighed. He pushed by a confused Deckler and hit the periscope button again. The shiny tube reversed direction and stopped at the appropriate height. Like his fellow commanders, Baumann was an experienced captain. However, the malfunction in his diving planes had cost his boat at least 200 feet of depth.

Jamming his face to the eyepiece, Lothar snarled, "Colonel, at this moment, we have a transport full of fuel barrels that is approximately half the depth of the others due to an equipment malfunction. Also, my friend, Joachim Beltzer, is up there trying to draw off the enemy aircraft by fighting it. It's plain suicide."

"*Kapitän*. It's a message from *U-1410*," announced the hydrophone operator.

Lothar broke away from the periscope so quickly he bumped his long nose on the eyepiece. The smarting caused his vision to blur for an instant and he felt the familiar trickle of blood out his right nostril. "Yes?"

"*Kapitänleutnant* Beltzer says ... " began the radioman, hesitantly, "'Kiss Rhoda, Heinz and Wolfie for me.'"

"*Scheiss!*" spat Lothar, wiping the film of blood from his lip and smearing his cheek in the process. Seeing the animal-like fierceness in his eyes, Deckler backed off, almost tripping over the helmsman in the process. In effect, Lothar was like a wolf whose companion had turned to fight off a grizzly bear to save its cubs. He could either help his friend and risk getting sunk in the process — thereby leaving the transports defenseless and the mission without its submarine leader — or slink away and complete the mission. Prudence demanded the latter, but the thought of it stung him worse than the throbbing of his nose.

*　*　*

"Ready the light," Captain Hardy said. During the dive, the pitch of the engines had raised from a steady drone to the snarl of disturbed bees. Inside the fuselage of the hollowed-out Liberator, the sound was amplified and the increased vibration made every loose piece of gear rattle.

His altimeter was now dead on 150 feet.

The first gun to open up from the *Atlantikboot* was the 105mm forward gun. Beltzer was hoping that the pilot might be inexperienced and the big flash might throw off his aim, or, more fortuitously, cause him to back off until the other U-boats had reached a safe depth.

However, Hardy was not dissuaded by the big gun. The 27-year-old pilot was a veteran of the convoy battles of 1943, flying a Short Sunderland out of Reykjavik. His one-and-a-half kills and three probables made him one of the top antisubmarine patrol commanders in the RAF, and Bermuda was his plum assignment for living through three Icelandic winters.

Ten seconds later, Beltzer's crew spotted the dark shape looming out of the horizon and the fast-firing 20mm anti-aircraft batteries on the boat opened up. Then came the chattering of the U-boat's machine guns.

"All hands ready?" Hardy asked, his voice a hollow ring in each crewman's headset. His query was answered by a chorus of three excited voices. Bright 20mm and machine gun tracers arched under the bomber but as the aircraft got closer the Germans would be making hits.

"Light ... on!"

The instant the switch was thrown, a surge of electrical power from seven 12-volt, 40-amp-per-hour, Type D Vickers storage batteries shot into a 24-inch, narrow-beam searchlight. The resulting 50-million candle-power Leigh Light illuminated the calm seas in a sun-like incandescence, revealing the stark presence of *U-1410* as if it were sitting in the middle of a salt flat.

"Remember Jimmy," he yelled into the intercom as the Liberator skimmed low over the water, "add 50 feet to the drop site for every five seconds of submersion. The swirl of white water from the diving boat will be your marker."

* * *

"*Das verdammte Licht!*" bellowed Lothar, rubbing his pain-struck eyes as he ripped himself from the periscope.

* * *

Beltzer's men suffered the same malady, and one dazed, gun crew ceased firing momentarily. The huge, blinding illumination grew larger and more intimidating with each second and two of the U-boat gunners felt streams of urine run down their legs. It was like the sun had suddenly appeared in the night and had begun diving to earth. But then the firing continued.

***

"Eddie, fire forward guns!" snapped Hardy.

At the lower nose turret of the Liberator, Eddie Andrews felt the buck of the twin .50-caliber Browning as he instantly obeyed the command. Brass shells bounced off the deck and soon the inside of his Perspex bubble reeked with the biting odor of cordite.

As they got closer, the determined German gunners began making hits on the huge four-engine bomber. Suddenly, the Perspex windscreen in the cockpit exploded and Hardy was thrown back against his seat, his chest a mass of red in the glare of the cockpit lights.

"Jesus!" yelled Lieutenant Jimmy MacDougall, as Hardy's lifeless body slumped forward. It never bent at the waist like a normal person's torso would. The spine was shot away so it folded over halfway down the chest.

In the next instant, the panel began sparking and the warning light for Number Three engine came on. Glancing to his right, MacDougall's heart almost stopped when he saw flames begin to lick at the cowling of the 14-cylinder Pratt & Whitney Twin-Wasp power plant.

***

Twin streams of deadly .50-caliber bullets from the damaged Liberator raked the crowded tower and *Wintergarten* — the anti-aircraft platform — blowing bodies apart and tossing others overboard in a bloody spray. In less than three seconds only one 20mm battery was still firing, its gunners screaming at the infernal light as if they were challenging the Devil himself. Above the din, the bloody face of Beltzer was a demented mask. Although mortally wounded he implored them to continue. *"Angreifen! Ran! Versenken!* — Prepare to dive!" he bawled shaking his fist at the blinding ball.

Then, suddenly the light went out and the night became a series of polka-dot flashes for the stunned survivors.

***

As he fought to keep the Liberator airborne, the silvery-black image of the submarine grew steadily in his windscreen. The Leigh Light suddenly went out in a shower of sparks and the ocean became a black maw.

"Jimmy!" MacDougall knew Andrews' voice but he never expected the strangled scream that came through the intercom. A second later, the wounded gunner slipped out of the smashed turret and his body was sucked into the four-bladed propeller of Number One engine.

"Eddie! Eddie! For Christ sakes answer me!" the Scot cried. But the only sounds he heard were the screeching of two tortured engines and the hurricane blasts of air whistling through the damaged bomber. As far as he knew, every man in the crew was dead.

Tears streaming down his terrified face, MacDougall reached for the lever and pulled for all his might. It did not matter to him that there were proper procedures for dropping the sticks. In his catatonic state, he never saw the swirls of the recently submerged submarines and could not calculate the time necessary for properly dropping the depth charges as he had memorized on so many missions. Training never entered his fractured mind. His unleashing of the bombs was reduced to a fear-driven reflex.

The first two sticks went down immediately but, somehow, the remaining four took two seconds longer to unhook. One and two hit just ahead of the white whirlpool left by the slowly descending *Milchkuh* with the damaged bow planes. They were set for shallow detonation and caught the transport at 80 feet. The expanding Torpex-gas bubble hit the forward deck with the shock of a perfectly-aimed torpedo, splitting it wide-open. A second later, 45 barrels of ethanol exploded in a chain-reaction.

Beltzer was still alive when the four remaining sticks straddled his boat. His last sensation was that of being lifted in the air by a huge spray of water. Then he was thrown through air, a shattered corpse.

* * *

"What is going on?" yelled Deckler, as the boat pitched and rocked. They were now almost a half kilometer from the blast of the transport but the shock wave of the exploding rocket fuel was like the near-miss of a depth charge. All lights went out and a red mist returned. The smashing of electric bulbs and gasping of crewmen greeted Deckler's ears.

"Damage report?" Lothar shouted. At first, he was answered by the shrill metallic sounds that were reverberating along the length of the boat. Then he heard a human voice.

"There is water in the forward torpedo room but, other than that, the boat functions are fine. Some of the crew have a few bumps and bruises, but everyone is all right."

Lothar raised the periscope and, at first, saw nothing. Then a small explosion caught his attention.

* * *

The water-borne explosions made little impression on the B-24 as it was well beyond the strike point to be affected by the concussions. After the Liberator had made its run, it rumbled on as if the two blackened engines, one on each side of the fuselage, had never been started in the first place. The fire extinguishing systems had doused the flames and the slapping sound of the flames was gone — but the smell of heat-tortured steel and oil attacked his nostrils.

His heartbeat slowing down, MacDougall felt the warm air rushing through the hole in the right side of the cockpit in an eerie howl. Then it struck him: he was alive. Despite the punishment doled out by the U-boat guns, the remaining outer engines seemed to be running well. The control panel sparkled with electrical shorts and the wheel was heavy, but MacDougall was confident he could make it back to Bermuda

First, he feathered the propellers of the dead engines to lessen the airborne drag. He felt another ripple of relief warm him as the vibrations lessened. Next, he shut down the electrics to the damaged power plants and cut off the fuel mixture.

Then, with anticipation, he tried the intercom. But it was dead. The fourth crewman, Sergeant Boles, the primary radar operator, was either dead or too wounded to come forward. He gave a brief glance to the pilot's seat. Hardy's body had slumped under the wrecked control panel and was almost invisible in the dim glow of the remaining cockpit light. He knew then that he might well be the only survivor.

To MacDougall's good fortune, he had many hours as a navigator before he went in for a pilot. And although there were no instruments in which to help him back to base, he knew he could get a plausible reading from the stars to guide him back to Bermuda. It may not be the base but he knew he could pick up a few familiar islands and find his way home that way. At least the instruments showed he had enough fuel.

"Yes, Jimmy, me lad," he sighed with a renewed confidence, "we can find our way home."

But that feeling only lasted another few seconds. A crack in the shell-damaged port wing root caused the aluminum spar to twist and the huge wing went up in a 90-degree angle. The great Liberator immediately flipped onto its back and bounced on the calm surface of the ocean, the tearing of its unprotected wing tanks sparking the remaining fuel. The bomber exploded before it could bounce again.

* * *

"What happened?" begged a panic-stricken Deckler. His hands were shaking and his thin face was bathed in sweat.

The light-systems had returned to normal conditions exposing the frightened white faces of the crew. In that moment, a strange thought buzzed through Lothar's mind, a flash brought on by shock. For the men resembled a mime troupe, their silent actions exaggerated as they regarded each other. For they too were trying to comprehend the events without having witnessed the carnage that their commander had seen. And he would have to inform them that, in less than a minute, one-third of the Sea Scorpion's first phase of operations was gone

"The rocket fuel just blew up," quipped Lothar, drawing a sleeved arm across his sweaty forehead. Everyone within sight froze.

"All of it?" Deckler asked, shakily.

"No, just Baumann's boat." Lothar wanted to add that he had trained Baumann at the U-boat School in Pilau, East Prussia, and that he had attended the Pomeranian lad's wedding in 1939. But he knew Deckler wouldn't care — no more than he cared about Beltzer. And Lothar's mind quickly zipped past the thought of his old friend and commander. That would just compound the pain.

"What of the pod?" Deckler demanded. "was it damaged?"

Lothar glared at the SS officer for a few seconds and then look past him to the sound room. "Begin contacting the others," he sighed.

Within five minutes the one remaining U-boat of Scorpion Two, the transport carrying the Waffen SS guards, signaled that they were in good condition. "Fine," Deckler announced, almost happily. "Scorpion Two's pod was not damaged. All we've lost is fuel and we can get more of that."

"All we've lost?"

This time Deckler chose to ignore Lothar by walking out of the control room.

CHAPTER NINE

August 5, 1944
Shelburne County, Nova Scotia

"Good to have you home again."

Billy Whinot could barely be heard over the coughing of the small one-cylinder Make and Break engine that struggled to propel the Tancook whaler, the large former lifeboat which doubled as a ferry and supply ship when Billy was not out fishing. The old-timer's right arm hugged the bleached tiller, gripping the smooth handle under his armpit as if it were a swagger stick. An errant wavelet splashed over the gunnel, hitting him in the face and causing his prune-like face to scrunch up tighter than it already was.

Jesse Corkum sat with her back to him, fixated with the growing shape of Ashton Island. The ocean breeze floated her long chestnut curls which were fused into a ponytail with a red-patterned, paisley scarf. She squinted her brown eyes to avoid the saltwater spray and the glare from the bright haze.

She turned around to the old man, a family friend since she could first remember, and replied, "I missed you, Uncle Billy. I missed you, Mom, Dad, the water, and Ashton Island. Even the smell of your boat!"

Jesse's eyes grew large as she spoke, two gold-flecked, cinnamon irises coming to life as her long dark lashes parted. Her face was round, like a young girl's, but her slender chin and thin nose gave her the mature beauty of a woman a few years older than her 21 years.

"Oh that," Billy chuckled, "I should have hosed down *Mabel* better. I was haulin' sole yesterday and never got to it. Me and the boys went right to playin' poker after we came in and the rum was runnin' free."

"That's okay, Uncle Billy," she replied, taking a deep sniff. "It's the smell of home."

"You mean it smells better than that school you been teachin' at?" Billy laughed, flashing a toothless smile, the result of a fishing accident when he was a teenager.

Jesse laughed at his inference then turned forward again to view the approaching island. It was dark green, the color of the trees that covered most of the land off the shoreline, with the exception of the lighthouse grounds. The 20 acres around the light encompassed the exposed rocks on the ocean side, the wild side of Ashton, which seemed so far removed from the tranquil waters of the inshore bay. This had been home to Jesse since before she could remember. For her father was the keeper of the Ashton Light.

Through the misty horizon to her left was a smattering of small islands connected by shallow passageways and shoals which were deadly to oceangoing ships. The Ashton Light warned coastal freighters of the impending danger, showing them the deeper water off the point.

On the right, just around the head and tucked into Shelburne Harbor, was McNutt Island, the home of two large coastal guns and a battalion of American soldiers. The Cape Roseway Lighthouse showed the safe passage into the port of Shelburne, a bustling town that had grown larger since the war began.

The kidney-shaped Ashton Island was four miles long and barely a hundred yards wide at its narrowest. The southwest portion was rough rocky coastline, hewn by the winds and post-hurricane waves which visited on a yearly basis, usually in the late summer. On this outcropping was where the lighthouse sat.

On the other end, to the northwest, was a bulge of coastal lowlands made fertile by tons of kelp and fish life stranded when it was once a small bay. Years of wave action had ploughed a rift of round rocks up high enough to seal the tiny body of water off from the sea. The evaporation of the sea bottom exposed a rich humus, the salt leeched out by hundreds of years of rain. Jesse knew the 300-odd acre area as simply as "the Knob."

A forested area separated the Knob from the Department of Transport enclave — which featured the lighthouse, a sturdy four-room house and a large shed for storing supplies and lifesaving equipment. Some of the trees were throwbacks from another era — one was over 1,000 years old.

When the motorized skiff was 100 yards from the beach, Billy cut the engine and slid in alongside an old, faded-red dory that was tied up to a cork buoy. From here on in to shore the bottom came up quickly into a long sandbar, too shallow for his craft, or any others with a keel. To Jesse, this was just part of returning home.

"Sure you can get her in?" quipped Billy. Before she could say anything he added, "Sorry, I kinda forgot who I was speakin' to."

Jesse just shrugged as she put a leg over and steadied the paint-blistered punt with both hands clamped on its narrow gunnels.

Jesse reached for the oars and slid them into the locks. "Thanks for the ride, Uncle Billy. I'll tell Mom to be expecting you for dinner."

"Really?" replied Billy, scratching his head. "Why? Is there a christening or engagement party happening out there?"

"Nope," she quipped. "Just me coming home." With that she shoved the punt away from his boat and began to row.

Today, her thoughts were not final exams or finding a teaching position. She had one of those. This time she was worried by a more longterm decision she had to make: should she accept Allan Blakey's marriage proposal and live in a fine house in Halifax with a well-off husband who practiced law?

Now lightened by her absence, the punt was easily pulled the rest of the way to shore and up onto the gravel with a flick of her wrist on the rope. As she had done a thousand times, Jesse hopped two more stones and then landed on the moist sand of the shore.

Once the punt was securely tied, Jesse began the 20-minute walk to her parents' enclave. For many, the mile-long stretch through the woods was an inconvenience, a gauntlet of mosquitoes and other pests through an exhaustive walk. Jesse viewed it as a long welcome mat, a runway that would lead to her favorite place in the whole world.

As she trudged up the incline where the high-water mark met the forest, she glanced over her left shoulder at the Knob. She stopped and drew a hand over her eyes to shield them from the brightness. Viewing the broad area she saw, to her surprise, that it had been planted. Her mother usually had a garden to help with the food requirements but never could she and her father, together, have planted so much and then have expected to tend and harvest it all.

Jesse stared in amazement at the sheer quantity of plants. There were acres of potatoes leading up to a thick forest of corn, both of which stopped just before the crest of the gentle hill. Her father's small garden had stopped there because the nor'easters would rip the tops off the plants during a storm.

A movement caught her eye and she was surprised to see the head of a man moving quickly among the immature corn stalks. Squinting her eyes to cut the glare, she saw a shiny, powder-blue tractor exit the corn patch and then turn toward her. The man driving the machine bounced around as if he were trying to stay on an unfriendly horse. When man and tractor reached the flat, the gyrations ceased and the machine moved smoothly. As it got closer, Jesse heard the roar of the engine over the whistling wind.

The brand-new tractor stopped 10 feet from her. A sandy-haired man leaned over and turned a key, which immediately killed the engine.

He was shirtless, sporting a bronzed, muscular body. He neither smiled nor waved at her, but just stared for a few more minutes. Then he threw a leg over and dismounted. As he did so, she saw that he was missing part of his left arm.

When his feet hit the ground, the man ducked under the machine and pushed at a loose rubber hose. Satisfied, he stood up and walked toward Jesse. As he got closer, she made an effort not to look at the arm. She was suddenly uncomfortable, but not because she thought he might do her harm, but because he was here — on her domain. This distress was further deepened with her guilt about the man's disability.

"Hello," he said, a timid smile causing his brow to crinkle.

"Hi," she answered, finally getting the courage to look him in the eyes. They were blue with brownish flecks, and the right brow had a scar above it which appeared as a pinkish smear. He swiped at a lock of reddish hair and let a faint smile break his pursed lips.

"I'm Wyn Parsons," he said. "Can I give you a lift?" His tenor voice was relaxed, a smooth timbre that was almost boyish.

"Well, no I'm . . ." Jesse was suddenly stuck for words.

"You're Jesse Corkum, Wilbur and Lottie's daughter," he announced. "I saw your picture in their house. They talk about you all the time."

Jesse kept her eyes on his face, dreading to look at the man's amputated limb. "What are you doing here?" she asked, suddenly feeling angry at his presence on the island. In the next instant, she felt violated and wanted to be away from him more than anything else, a feeling even stronger than wanting to see her parents.

"I was invited," he answered, his eyes drifting off toward the town. "Seeing as your father and I are partners he —"

"Partners?" retorted Jesse, her voice almost cracking from the stress. "Why would a light keeper need a partner? He's got my mother."

"Because," Wyn explained, taking no offense by her outburst, "I bought this piece of land from your father, and part of the deal was that we split the crops and whatever wood I cut."

"But father would never sell a piece of Ashton!" she bleated, her voice filled with emotion. "Why it's been in our family for almost 100 years!"

"I'm sorry if it upsets you, Miss Corkum," he answered, his voice still calm, "but we, that is, your parents and I, thought it was a pretty good deal all around."

"Well I don't!" Jesse spat, turning her back on him and picking up her two bags. Looking over her right shoulder, she added, "I don't know how you harassed my father into parting with the land, Mr. Parsons, but I assure you that I will not rest until you and your machine are off our island! Good day to you!"

Wyn just watched her trudge up the rocks without saying another word. He had not been interested in looking at women since he had seen Laura Finer again. However, even though he had been instantly tried and found guilty of land fraud by this woman, he could not take his eyes off her until she disappeared into the trees.

"Well, Mr. Ford," Wyn chuckled as he slapped the large, shiny-blue fender of the tractor, "it seems we didn't make a very good impression."

* * *

"You said that to Wyn Parsons?"

"Yes, I did, Mother," replied Jesse Corkum in a self-righteous tone as she lifted her teacup to her mouth again. When she had swallowed another sip of the hot liquid she added, "And it doesn't matter to me if he is missing part of an arm. I think people like him should be locked up for preying on old people."

"Yep, we sure are old," Lottie Corkum quipped, nonchalantly placing another stitch on her quilt. "Your father and I are getting measured for our pine box any day now."

At 50, Lottie was a graying copy of her daughter. Her eyes were the same dark mocha sprinkled with auburn flecks and were just as attentive. Only a cluster of laugh lines around each eye and slightly rougher skin betrayed the fact that she was a quarter-century older than Jesse.

"Wyn's a nice fellow just —"

"Just trying to steal this island from us," Jesse snapped, her fingers busily kneading the lace napkin under her teacup.

Wilbur Corkum raised both of his large hands up in a surrendering motion. He was a tall, scarecrow-like man and his gesture filled the room. "Will you two please now let me speak?"

At 51, the lithe Corkum had spent all but five of those years on Ashton. His father had been the keeper before him and had lived here, except for a couple of years schooling and three years in the Great War. It had always been his lifelong ambition to step into his father's occupation.

"Seems to me, Missy," he started, his voice much dryer in contrast to the rich, lyrical tones of his daughter, "that there is a whole lot of presuming going on in this room."

To emphasize his point, he waved a hand around in the bright yellow kitchen. Lottie never looked up from her stitching. She rarely did during family conversations, except when something startled her enough to put the quilt down and either defend or expound her views.

"With you gone these past few years, it's been mighty tough to run this operation, 'specially with the goddamn war on. The Department of Transport rarely sends us any supplies and so we have to grow much of our own vegetables and use the rest to trade for fish and meat, when we can get it."

This was one of the occasions that prompted Lottie to look up. "Wilbur," she scolded, "please curb your language." The lighthouse keeper ignored her.

Jesse had lowered her eyes. She suddenly felt ashamed at going away to become a teacher when she could have helped her parents.

"Now, Wyn Parsons is a fine man who just happened to lose his arm defending his country," Wilbur went on. "Even with that, he can still work as hard as any man I ever saw."

"I never said he couldn't," Jesse pouted.

"Well all I ask is that you listen to our deal before you make a judgment," he continued, his hands lowered now. Using the long index finger of his right hand he tapped on the old oak table.

"I sold him The Knob for $900 cash and a share in the crops he harvests. As well, he will thin out the dead fall for firewood and fill my wood box when needed."

"But I could have come up with the money if you needed it that bad," Jesse replied, still stunned that any part of Ashton could be spoken of in terms of mere money.

The light keeper stood up and lifted a steaming kettle from the old black stove. He was wearing the same red tartan flannel shirt that Jesse had bought him at the Hudson's Bay Company store in Halifax five years before. She had used some of her cranberry money from the previous fall. His suspenders were the only pair she had ever seen him wear and his dungarees were twice as old as the shirt.

He refreshed his tea and glanced out the window at the sky, more from habit than of interest. As Jesse watched him she thought how much he had aged since she had first gone away to the Halifax Academy. Two years there and then another two at the Teacher's College in Truro. Added to that was a teaching position in Bridgewater which brought her closer to home but far enough away that she could only get back once or twice more than she had when she was farther away.

"Here's where I get to the point, Missy," he sighed, his dark blue eyes looking older than his years. "Your mother and I are getting too old to work this whole place on our own."

"Now there you go again with that old stuff," teased Lottie, trying to lighten up the conversation.

"Well," he replied, pointing his finger in his wife's direction, "the doctor's been warning you to stop running around this place as if you were two 25 year-olds with good hearts instead of a 50 year-old one who always forgets to take her pills."

"Pills," she snorted, holding up the edges to admire her handiwork "They just make me nauseous. Anyway, I haven't had a dizzy spell in over two years and it sure had nothing to do with the pills."

Wilbur just threw up his hands. "When you were young, Jesse, we had your grandmother and Uncle Billy to help run things. We also had money from the Department of Transport for things like repairing the jetty and hiring men for other projects such as rebuilding the barn. That left me and your mother to see to the light and outbuildings."

"Why didn't you ask my opinion?" Jesse asked, hurt that all these decisions were made without her input. She had known about her mother's lapses in health but always assumed that there was a worker who came over to help out. It just struck her that the war would have drawn off most of the available men who were young enough to do work the heavy labor on the island.

"Because times change, Missy," he continued. "You're a teacher now and we would never have asked you to give that up to come out here. It's gettin' so that we hardly see anyone anymore. How would a young woman like you handle it?"

"You're forgetting the Norwegians on Raddall Island," Lottie piped up, "A few of them were over last week."

"Norwegians?" Jesse asked.

"They're manning a weather station over there and have a radio set up to report weather to the military."

Seeing Jesse's bewilderment Wilbur said, "They're nationalist Norwegians, men who were on ships or escaped their country when Hitler took it over. They have a couple of bases around here. One up Lunenburg way as well."

"It's nice to see such pleasant fellows in uniform," Lottie added, turning her quilt over to inspect her skill.

"Anyway," Wilbur continued, "what I was tryin' to say is that there'll be no one in the family to take over here when I finally pack it in. And if you get to talkin' with people the way I have, you'll not find many who'd want to come out here do this kind of work. The war's brought lot of high-payin' jobs and light keepin' is not the life young people want anymore.

"So, Wyn heard I was lookin'. He came at the right time and offered me a deal that was too good to refuse. Here's what we decided as far as your mother and I are concerned: I stay on as light keeper and he does most of the work. When he gets the crops in, he'll busy himself with maintenance jobs and building his house. When I finally retire, he wants me and Lottie to stay in this house and he'll run the light. In other words, we get to stay as long as we want."

"Will he own the whole island?" Jesse asked, cautiously.

"That's up to you, Missy. When I re-wrote the deed, I gave you the other third. You can sell it to him, rent it out, or just sit on it. That's your choice. When we go, you'll have our third."

Just then there was a knock on the door and they turned to see the uniformed figure on the other side of the glass. He was average height and light-brown hair leaked out from under his cap.

"That's Jan," Wilbur remarked. "He's one of the Norwegians."

* * *

Lieutenant Jan Johansen's eyes flashed gold as a ray of the late afternoon sun reflected off a pane of glass on one of the outbuildings. He was thin; almost too slight for his uniform jacket, and his nose would have been too long for his face had he not had the dark, close-cropped beard.

Lottie laid her quilt on her lap and reached over to pour him another cup of tea. Johansen nodded in appreciation and took another sip.

"In answer to your question, Mr. Corkum," he continued in almost flawless English, "With the invasion of continental Europe by the Allies, I think the U-boat threat is all but finished. The Americans are now attacking their bases on the French Atlantic coast."

Wilbur nodded thoughtfully, letting a plume of blue smoke escape from an opening in his lips. He tapped the bowl of the pipe on the old gray automobile piston that substituted for an ashtray and reached into his pouch for some fresh tobacco. As he did, he studied the foreigner, from his dark blue uniform to the crest of his cap. Johansen was not a large man but he carried an air of command that impressed the lighthouse keeper. That was one of the reasons why Corkum could agree with him that the threat of German submarines was pretty well over and that Hitler would be defeated before the snows fell.

The Norwegian looked over at Jesse again and smiled. Corkum's daughter returned the gesture but tinged with a shyness that came with the unabashed show of interest, the kind that Johansen was displaying.

"So when the war is over," Lottie interjected, her velvet eyes transfixed on her stitches, "will you boys stay in the Norwegian Navy or will you become civilians again?"

Johansen's smile formed creases on the cheeks above his beard-line, and his eyes squinted with mirth. "When the war is over, Mrs. Corkum," he laughed, "I will stuff this uniform into a trunk and become a plumber."

The others chuckled at his good-natured humor and his eyes shifted again to Jesse. She was about to say something to him, a few words hinting that his advances were welcome when a knock caused then all to turn their heads to the glassed door.

"Come in," Lottie piped, shuffling her quilt aside in order to greet the caller. As she made for the door she saw a familiar outline. "It's Wyn," she happily announced.

When Wyn entered, it took a few moments for his eyes to get used to the dimness of the kitchen. He was dressed in his usual work clothes: soiled dungarees, army shirt and infantry boots. His face had been unshaven for nearly a week, the stubble a reddish gold giving his eyes a deeper blue tone.

"Well, Wyn," chimed Corkum, "come in and have some lemonade."

"Thank you, Wilbur," Wyn answered, eyeing the stranger in the uniform without acknowledging his presence. It should not have given him any cause for concern, as most male men of that age were in uniform, but Wyn found it hard to shake the uneasiness he felt at the moment.

"I appreciate the hospitality, but I just came to let you know that I can get to sealing the glass on the light anytime you want. That's all."

"Please sit with us, Wyn," Lottie said, placing her hand on his shoulder. "We hardly see you anymore."

In the next instant he caught the Norwegian's eyes. They were pale green marbles in process of sizing him up and hinted neither animosity nor friendship. Lottie said, "Oh, Wyn Parsons, meet Lieutenant Jan Johansen of the Royal Norwegian Navy. He and a dozen other of his countrymen are manning that weather station on Raddall Island."

"I am pleased to meet you," said Johansen, standing up with his hand out. The two gold rings on his sleeve confirmed his rank. His gesture was cordial and correct. The beard, Wyn thought, was regulation for most naval officers.

Wyn nodded as he took the European's hand. The grip was firm but not trying to prove any manly intent. The two men's eyes were locked in mutual interest, each subconsciously recognizing something in the other, a trait each one felt but could not knowingly grasp at the moment.

On the surface, however, both had to shrug it off as being too suspicious. When he finally broke off the handshake, the Norwegian sat down and began to twist a ring around the middle finger of his right hand. It was out of sight of those seated but Wyn caught the movement.

Jesse gave Wyn a curt smile, a movement of her face which avoided showing her teeth. She was not intentionally trying to show her distaste for the man but he could have taken it that way — which he did and quickly forgot the slight.

"Good afternoon," he said, nodding in her direction.

"Pull up a chair, Wyn," said Corkum, pointing to an old painted one pressed up against the coal chute. "It's too hot to go working on the glass right now. The sun's turned the place into a greenhouse."

"Thanks, Wilbur," Wyn replied, awkwardly shifting his feet. His body was turned slightly to the left so that his lack of a limb on that side would not be so noticeable. All it did, however, was to focus everyone's attention that way.

"I should really get to doin' it because I have to get the shingles on my place before it rains."

"Well," Jesse interjected, "the lieutenant should be able to give us a forecast on the rain, shouldn't you, Lieutenant Johansen?"

"I guess that's my job," Johansen chuckled, his ring still rotating quickly. "I must say with pride, Mr. Parsons, that my men are quite good at what they do. From their forecast of this morning, I am happy to say you have nothing to fear. There will be three glorious days in which to work outside."

For the first time, Wyn let a smile warm his face. "Well, that makes me feel better, lieutenant," he said, his eyes wandering from the Norwegian to Jesse. She felt certain that her continued discomfort seemed to amuse him and she hated him for staying around.

"Speaking of my men," Johansen added, looking at his watch, "I think I should be getting back for the evening watch. A few of them were in Shelburne last night and their heads are rather large!"

"I know that feeling," chuckled Corkum, sliding his chair back.

"Not in a long time, thankfully" retorted Lottie. As she got up, Jesse remained the only one sitting. She was taking in the light-hearted banter as everyone said his or her goodbyes, but she was watching Wyn out of the corner of her eye. *What does he want?* she thought.

"Say hi to Sven for me," Corkum quipped.

Johansen paused for a moment and then answered, "Yes, I will." He looked over at Wyn and gave him a curt smile.

"Well, good day everyone," chirped Johansen to all, his eyes staying on Jesse for a few seconds. His gaze then shifted back to Wyn. As he positioned his hat, he said, "I hope I see you again, as well, Mr. Parsons."

"*Ha det*," Wyn said.

"*Vi sees*," returned Johansen hesitantly.

CHAPTER TEN

August 9, 1944
Ashton Island

The twilight had always been Jesse's favorite time of the day. The pinkish glow on the western horizon reflected on the small pond below the lighthouse, her sacred place when she was a girl. Her father had even stocked it with trout one summer but none of the fish was ever eaten because Jesse would cry when her father caught one. He would always throw it back. In time, the ospreys got most of them, but she never minded their presence. She'd rather have the big birds of prey eat the pet fish than her family.

On the protruding promontory, the trees came down from the forests hesitantly, becoming grayer in color and scragglier as the granite rocks took hold. Wild grasses and weeds grew in hollows where dust had collected over the centuries and finally petered out in clusters of large white rounded boulders.

A timeworn path led up to the lighthouse, a stark white obelisk that shone with the purplish sunset taking on its pastel color. Twenty feet below, the cold Atlantic waves lapped against the barrier of smooth stonework that formed the base for the beacon. The top portion of the tower was a checkerboard of red and white. It had four stories of slanted wall supporting the lamp, with another story and a half to the landward side, a landing that her father had built as an outdoor patio for warm summer days.

There were several outbuildings as well as the main house: a cowshed, a roofed-over pig pen, long disused, and a henhouse covered with an old fishnet to ward off birds of prey. The biggest structure was the oil shed which held the tanks of fuel to feed the light and parts for the lamp burners. And up toward the woods, standing on its own like a guard's box, was the outhouse.

This was also the time of the day when Wilbur went up the lamp to light up and set the rotor in motion. While he was busy readying the Ashton beacon, Jesse stood in the evening breeze on the promontory and smiled as she saw the other lights begin to sparkle. Cape Mersey, to the left, was usually the first to arrive, a bright flash visible each time it turned in their direction. Then Sable Head, to the far left across a small bay from Cape Mersey, came on with a rosy-red glow. Raddall Island, off the head to the far right, was always the last of the outer beacons to light before her father lit the great beam above her. The Ashton Light guided ships past the shoals leading into Port Pleasant

In all the years she had been here, Jesse had never met a soul from any of the other lights. There was no association or annual get-together, as much as her father had spoken of organizing such a thing. However, the unknown lighthouse people were her friends, welcome signs of civilization and companionship during those rare times when loneliness overwhelmed her.

This was her world, a festival of textures and lights brought to life by the shimmering sea. And when the storms came, the taut guy wires screamed in the wind and the waves crashed about the base of the tower. It also gave her a proud reminder of her family's accomplishment on this sliver of land stuck out in the Atlantic: to ensure the safe passage of hundreds of souls through the treacherous shores and inland waterways of southwestern Nova Scotia.

At a precocious 16, Jesse entered the Nova Scotia Teacher's College and her instructors soon found that she had a better command of her subjects than many of her older peers did. The isolation had done wonders for her reading skills. During the winter months she would devour works of prose and poetry on a daily basis.

If there was any downside to her upbringing, it was that the isolation made her depend upon the island and her parents for her emotional support. During the long stays away from Ashton, she found she had to steel herself against sliding into bouts of homesickness.

And her parents missed her as well. When the war began, their hired workman, Joe MacDougall, a 30-year-old from town, had joined the Army. And most of the other men were busy in occupations which supported the war effort. That left Wilbur with no one except for those times when Billy Whinot could get out to lend a hand. So when Lottie had one of her spells, it left the whole operation to Wilbur.

Lottie had nearly died of rheumatic fever when she was four and her heart had been weakened as a result of the trauma. Her second brush with death was when she gave birth to Jesse. The doctor in Halifax had saved her life and was more than a bit relived when he found out that complications during the difficult birth had prevented Lottie from being able to have any more than one child. The stresses surrounding a second pregnancy, he concluded, would kill her. As it was, God had given her 21 years to enjoy her daughter.

Lottie had been staring out the window watching Wilbur paint the shed when she died.

Her newest quilt was on her lap and she had paused for a moment to reflect upon her wonderful life with Wilbur. She knew he was going to be a lighthouse keeper when she first met him and, despite her parents' concerns, accepted his courtship. She could never imagine what her life would have been like without him and Ashton Island. And there had never been a time when a second guess had crossed her mind.

Jesse heard the timepiece mechanics of the lantern echoing within the hollow walls and looked up to see the beam of Ashton light bathe the twilight. Wilbur was on time, to the minute, as he always was. That was his job, his duty. It was a position of trust that linked him with the rest of the world. It was also a duty that helped him to cope with the death of his wife. If Wilbur had been a philosopher, Jesse thought, her mind ignoring the sound of meshing gears echoing off the house and outbuildings, the thought might have crossed his mind that the ocean had exacted a revenge on him; a sort of retribution for all the ships and human cargo that Ashton had saved by stretching its light into some of the blackest, gale-torn nights known to man. But Wilbur did not think in those terms. All he knew was that there was a big hole in his life, one that working the light, along with his memories of Lottie and his daughter's love, could never fully patch.

Usually, when a night's work had begun, Wilbur would climb down from the light to have his evening tea and listen to the CBC radio broadcast. Lorne Greene's "Voice of Doom" would greet the small kitchen with the latest news of the war, but there were also the other programs such as *Wayne and Shuster* which brought a smile to his face and would make Lottie laugh. The American stations had *Burns and Allen* and *Abbott and Costello*, and the latest big band songs. He and Lottie would never speak during the programs but would catch each other's eye when the punch line of a joke caught their attention. Even as a child, Jesse could remember their hearty laughs filling up the house after one of Jack Benny's witticisms.

Tonight, for the first time in her memory, Wilbur didn't come down from the light. Jesse waited almost an hour for him, until the moon began to take on its bright glow and lift off the horizon. The tea in the pot would be evaporated by now and the kitchen alive with the fuzzy sounds of different radio channels trying to gain the upper hand on their set. Without someone to tune them in it was just a cacophony of electronic signals.

Jesse slowly sat down on the smooth surface of the rock and adjusted her coat to give herself the most cushioning on the hard surface. Then she lifted her face to the moon and wailed, calling for her mother to come home.

* * *

August 12th

By the time the last of the funeral guests had left the island, Wyn Parsons had filled in the grave and covered the plot on the sandy hill with the dozens of flowers brought out by the mourners. Yesterday, he had spent the day in his machine shed carving an ornate cross out of wood which would stand as a grave marker until the permanent stone arrived. Wyn had fused the two pieces of oak slab so that it was difficult to tell if it was made out of more than one piece of wood. Then he had carved out Lottie's name and pertinent dates, using his knees to steady the cross while the sharp knife in his right hand chiseled. Finally, he used a rich stain to bring out the beauty of the wood grain before sealing it with varnish.

Wyn's shed was attached to his living quarters, a small room with a cot and stove. His plans for the winter called for building a larger structure with enough room to have two bedrooms, one for his great-uncle, Jimmy Enslow, to stay in on one of his visits from the home. His building chores would now be a bit easier. Jimmy had passed away a week after Wyn began living on Ashton.

The wood for the project was neatly stacked outside and the nails, hardware and glass for the windows were housed in the shed. Once the last of the hay and vegetables were in, he would begin building, only taking time off for hunting and helping Wilbur with the lighthouse repairs.

As Wyn put away his shovel and pick in the corner he heard a crunch of gravel outside. Someone was around the back of his living quarters. One peek through the window over his cot and he caught a quick glance of a navy uniform. Wyn waited inside for a moment, catching the odd footfall from through the wall. The visitor was not merely trying to find him; he was stopping at intervals as if to examine items.

The man in the navy uniform stopped just short of the door and turned around to view one of the last of the boats to leave the island. There were children aboard and they happily launched a blue kite in the afternoon breeze. It trailed behind like a bright yellow flame.

"I kinda miss flying kites." Wyn announced.

The startled visitor spun around to see the large, boyish image of Wyn leaning against the doorframe. He was wearing a sweat-stained undershirt so his sizeable muscles and mutilated arm were visible.

"Oh, Mr. Parsons," the smaller man said, a relieved smile splitting his face. "You startled me."

"Lieutenant Johansen," replied Wyn, the left side of his face turned up in a half-smile. "To what do I owe the privilege of this visit?"

"Why, to offer my assistance with the embarkation," the Norwegian naval officer replied, sweeping an arm out to the small flotilla of boats making their way through the gentle swells to the mainland. "But," he added with a sigh, "it looks like I arrived too late."

Wyn's sky-blue eyes studied him for an instant, and then he said, "Yeah, well it seems they got away without using anyone's help."

* * *

"It would seem so," Johansen nodded, scrunching his lower lip up as if in thought. For some reason, Wyn made him feel uncomfortable, however he could not put his finger on just what and this made his discomfort intensify.

"Join me in a shot of rum?" asked Wyn, reaching his right arm inside the shack. He retrieved an unmarked bottle and waved it as if it were made of gold. The invitation instantly brought the officer out of his awkwardness. "I would be delighted," he said, shrugging his shoulders. "I was returning from Svalbard Islands, a large Norwegian island group up north in the Arctic, with my frigate, *Lofoten*, when my radio man informed me of the British raid on Narvik," Johansen said, plunking his glass of rum on the table after taking a swig.

"I had been stationed there since September '39, patrolling the waters for suspected German naval activity. There was none at the time and the post was very boring — and cold! When the Nazis invaded Norway in the spring I was ordered home. We were 100 kilometers from Trondheim when a Stuka dive-bomber surprised us and mortally wounded our ship. A British destroyer picked us up and we spent the next two years in England before we got this assignment from the Norwegian government-in-exile. Besides our weather station crew, there are several hundred Norwegians up in Lunenburg and more in camps around Nova Scotia."

Wyn poured himself another drink and clinked glasses with the officer. "To a speedy return to your homeland," he said.

When they had drained that glass Wyn asked, "Where were you stationed in England?"

The ring on Johansen's finger suddenly began to turn, propelled by the side action of his thumb. "Portsmouth, mostly," he replied. "At first we were spotters for the RAF during the great air battles in the summer of 1940."

"Hell of a time," sighed Wyn. Johansen knew that the man could only be in his mid-20s, but Wyn's mannerism made him seem 10 years older. "I was on beach duty facing the whole German army. They were 15 miles across the English Channel, all loaded up in barges to invade."

"Is that how you lost your arm?" ventured Johansen, feeling he knew the man well enough now to ask such a delicate question.

"No, that was at a piece of French real estate called Dieppe."

"Oh," nodded Johansen thoughtfully. "I heard about that."

"Well, what they say about it probably took longer than the fighting itself." Wyn drained another half glass of rum and then added, "But now it's just another place on a map."

"Aren't they all?" asked Johansen. The Norwegian then glanced at his watch and remarked, "I have to get back to the station, Mr. Parsons. Thank you for your hospitality."

"No need," he replied. "But call me Wyn."

"Okay, Wyn."

As the officer was getting up to leave, Wyn quipped, "By the way, I used to see the odd group of Norwegians in a pub called *The Jolly Witch* in Portsmouth. We might had been in there together a few nights and never known it."

"It might well be," replied Johansen.

"I mean, it's kind of ironic that two people who are out on islands off the southern shore of Nova Scotia might have rubbed shoulders in a crowded bar in England."

"Very ironic," returned Johansen. The officer placed the cap on his head and adjusted the visor. "Well, Wyn, thank you again."

Wyn watched the man as he sauntered up the path toward the last boat in the placid anchorage. There was a crewman waiting for him and assisted the lieutenant aboard. Then he began walking toward the lighthouse.

* * *

"*Herr Kapitän,*" the SS corporal gasped, throwing his arm up straight in a salute, "there is an urgent message from the Colonel that everyone is to return to the island immediately!"

In a fit of rage Lothar grabbed his arm and threw it down. "You stupid baboon!" he seethed. "Don't ever give that ridiculous salute around here again! We are supposed to be Norwegians!"

"*Jawohl —*"

"Speak English!" Lothar spat as he sat down in the punt.

When the corporal had cast off the motor launch, he gunned the engine and headed toward the breakwater. Six miles past the line of huge rocks was Raddall Island.

Watching their departure was Wyn Parsons.

CHAPTER ELEVEN

7:07 PM
Raddall Island

Raddall Island formed the farthest point east of an isosceles triangle, with Ashton as its northeastern point and the equally distant Horn Island to the southwest. It was about the same size as Ashton but its trees were smaller and more ragged at the tops, having taken the brunt of many an ocean gale. The shoreline on the windward side was one long drift of beach stones, a small drifting range that raised up to nearly 15 feet.

On the leeward side of the beach, the land was rocky as well. But without the constant grinding action of the other side, the rocks were more irregular. Right in the middle of this shore was a sandy crescent where the crews of the buoy tenders could land a whaler to service the electric light guarding the shoal. Not many years before, the Department of Transport had heeded a call for the shoal to be marked because of the increased traffic in the area.

The corporal cut the engine of the punt and it slid easily onto the sandbar. Without waiting for his help, Lothar jumped into the ankle-deep water and trudged up the sandy beach to the path in the dark woods. Footfalls close behind signaled to him that the soldier had been ordered to shadow his every move.

When he had traveled 100 yards into the woods, he came to a man-made clearing in the dense brush that could not be seen from either the mainland or the other islands. Five large, green camouflaged tents were arranged in a straight line along the seaward edge of the forest and two steel frames rested in the center of the open spot. In the daytime, it was always twilight because of the heavy patterned netting covering the compound, giving the illusion from the air of a continuous seacoast forest. Just beyond the huts were more trees, with a path that led to the weather station and the light. At nightfall the area could be seen as groups of murky images.

Patterned shadows ran down his back as he made his way to the largest of the huts which was the original Norwegian weather station. It was sheltered by the trees but the front of the small building faced seaward and the natural light filtered in. Two guards, also in Norwegian uniforms, snapped their boots to attention as he walked to the door. They neither looked jovial nor morose as they made eye contact with him. As with many guards, their training did not allow for displays of human attachment.

The door to the steel hut opened easily and the hatless Colonel Deckler looked up to see Lothar give him a haphazard salute. He did not return it. And, at first, he did not speak. Instead, he raised himself formally from his chair and walked around the chart table, his bald head flashing under the dim electric light bulb, the only one allowed in the hut. His eyes were darker in the room and, with his brow furrowed in obvious distress, he looked like a doberman pinscher ready to strike.

"A bomb went off in a room where the Führer was conducting a meeting." Deckler's tone was officious as if the event were already part of an historical dissertation. Unlike the others of the expedition, he wore his black SS uniform and high boots, his way of making sure there was no mistake about which branch of the service ran this operation.

Lothar was stunned at the news but, unfortunately for him, had the discipline not to show it. This made Deckler even more suspicious and he began rapping his nails on the chart table as if deep in thought.

"That is terrible ... I mean, well, I do not know how to respond to that news, if it is true," Lothar responded blankly.

Deckler straightened up and picked up a written communiqué from the table. "That was not the answer I was looking for, Stahl."

Lothar's eyes wandered over to another guard, Sergeant Nagel, who was standing at the back of the small room. The man's machine pistol was pointing at him but Lothar felt neither afraid nor indignant. The SS always had reasons for considering someone suspect, and he had been in this very position with Deckler before that day last winter when the SS Colonel arrested von Braun, Müller and him.

"Are you waiting for me to say that I am appalled?" Lothar added, tiring of Deckler's game.

"Are you?" Deckler baited him, reaching into his jacket pocket for his silver cigarette case.

Lothar calmly said, "Yes, I am appalled ... as appalled as any officer could be whose commander-in-chief has been harmed."

"You haven't asked me yet," Deckler quipped.

"Asked you what?"

"If he is still alive."

The beginnings of a smile turned up Lothar's lips and his blue eyes opened wider. "If he had died," Lothar said, "or was mortally wounded, we wouldn't be having this conversation, would we?"

Now it was Deckler's turn to lighten up. "No, I guess not. I just would have shot you."

"No," rebutted Lothar, his voice showing some irritation, "I don't think you would have, Colonel."

"And how can you be so sure?" Deckler huffed, tossing the piece of paper back on the table.

"Because then you would have been all alone in enemy waters, wearing an SS uniform with a hostile government in power in Germany which would surely have put a price on your head by now."

Deckler's face fell at the sound of the ramifications of Hitler's demise. "What makes you think you are so important that you would know how a new government in Germany would act?"

"Because, colonel," Lothar went on, "a successor to Hitler would most likely be chosen from the Wehrmacht or Navy, branches of the armed forces with long traditions of serving the Fatherland. The Luftwaffe is Göring's creation and he would be one of the first ones arrested. They could not be sure about his subordinates, so they would all be suspect.

"If the Wehrmacht were to decide, they would most surely choose Field Marshal Rommel. The people love him and he is surely no friend of the SS."

Deckler cringed at Lothar's presupposition.

"Now, if the Navy chooses, then *Grossadmiral* Dönitz would take over. And I am his nephew. That would actually be more to your benefit than your detriment, colonel. Sure, you would have to trust me to overlook your Nazi nuances and hope that I put forward your exemplary knowledge of rocketry to the new government. But it would be better than to be brought back in chains."

Deckler glanced over his shoulder at the guard and waved his right hand. Immediately, the machine gun came down and Nagel relaxed.

"You know, Stahl," he chuckled, "you have more lives than a cat."

"I need only one more, colonel," Lothar replied, his eyes set. "And that is to see that my mission for the Fatherland is complete."

"Then tell me this, Stahl." Deckler continued, picking a Lucky Strike out of his case. "If Hitler would have died, what would you be doing right now?"

"The same thing I was going to do before you ordered me into your hut, colonel … my duty."

* * *

In the northernmost hut, now re-supplied by additional U-boats, large drums of ethanol were stacked so tightly that there was no way another one could be squeezed inside. Lothar checked the thermometer and was satisfied that the temperature was well within bounds for safe storage. Then he began to trot down towards the beach on the eastern shore.

The contingent relegated to off-loading supplies from the U-boat consisted of 20 men, four *Kriegsmarine* and 16 SS soldiers. At his command they had rolled out the new, collapsible supply boat and carried it down to the rocky beach with him in step behind them.

Going with him in the boat were the four sailors and two of the SS soldiers. No boat was to leave the island without supervision from Deckler's men. They pushed it into the incoming wave and, once cleared of the grinding white rocks, they all hopped in and started the small engine. Almost immediately the boat ceased to be inhibited by the tide and reluctantly moved forward against the incoming waves.

His face wet with cool spray, Lothar glanced down at his watch and then out to sea. If everything went on schedule, the process would be completed tonight — another flawless operation in the blackness of the new moon. They would have to thank lady luck as well, for the enemy had advanced radar. And the thundering of distant patrol aircraft could be heard from time to time.

As the waves lapped against the long freight carrier, Lothar's eyes scanned the black rolling water but his mind was back on Ashton Island. At first, he smiled when Jesse's face came into his mind. It had been a long time since he had afforded himself the luxury of having a girlfriend and, even though she was an enemy civilian, he could always go over and talk with her once and a while. And now that she was going to stay on the island to help her father, that idea was more than just a possibility. It would be complicated, but then nothing in his life had been simple since his altercation with the Americans three years before.

The little engine thrummed, propelling the boat more quickly once it had cleared the eddies of the shoal. Leaning out over the bow Lothar studied the dark sea, gauging the difficulty of the operation he was about to perform.

Then he saw it — a pinprick of light. Again, it flashed with such a minute range that it could never be seen from Raddall Island, let alone the mainland or the shore. Lothar raised his flashlight and returned the recognition signal. The thin light flashed twice more and then all was dark.

Suddenly, a rush of water much like a running brook sounded directly where the light had been. It grew louder with each second until, finally, Lothar saw the vague outline of a submarine conning tower. "Engine off, bumpers out," Lothar whispered. "Prepare to receive moorings."

From the shadows of the ominous anti-aircraft guns aft of her conning tower Lothar knew in an instant that the boat was a new Type XI-B U-cruiser and not a Type IV *Milchkuh*, which came four days ago. The great U-boat, the newest in the fleet, rose upward as if a great beast was surfacing in search of food, its twin armored turrets up forward giving it the impression of an undersea battleship.

Two vertical stacks ran parallel to the two periscopes. The first of these was the newest version of the NAXOS, a radar detecting device which could pick up the signals long before they reached their effective range. The second was thicker and curled over onto itself like a dark, candy cane. At the end of the curve was a float which automatically closed the vent when the water buoyed it upward. This was the newest version of the *schnorkel*.

With great skill, the four U-boatmen, all personal choices of his, maneuvered the skiff through the swollen waves until they were close enough to receive lines. These tied down, they eased the craft over to the great U-boat.

"Bumpers over," reminded Lothar. He chided himself for the stupid order as soon as it left his mouth. These men knew as much or more about mooring than any sailors alive.

On board the boat, the crewmen were scurrying to set up a large crane, their footfalls scarcely heard because of the synthetic-rubber coating on the deck. When he looked upward, a dozen or so ghostly figures were already standing at the four gun positions.

"*Kapitän* Stahl?" The voice sounded hollow, as if human sounds were forbidden on such a night.

"Here," Lothar replied, not recognizing the speaker. He only saw a group of men in the coveralls of the U-boat crews leaning down to assist in their boarding.

"I am Siegfried Beust, commander of the *U-2900*," continued the man. Lothar saw the outstretched hand and took it. He found himself unexpectedly propelled onto the rolling deck of the submarine and facing *Kapitänleutnant*

Beust, a bear of a man who, at first, seemed too big for the *U-Bootwaffe*. But then, the gigantic 3,630 ton Type XI-B *Der Schwarze Ritter* — The Black Knight — matched its commander.

"This is indeed a pleasure," beamed Beust, his pearly teeth parting his beard with a Cheshire smile. "I was in your class at Hamburg in '40, the one you gave on convoy tactics. All of us felt honored to be taught by a hero of Scapa Flow."

"Thank you, Beust," responded Lothar dryly. He knew the man had no hidden motive in flattering him, just to establish a link that might make their mutual work go much smoother. Trust was always established more quickly when both parties shared a similar period of their past, a reference point to begin their new relationship.

"No *Milchkuh* this time?"

"They are just for fuel and food. For a such a project like this I was ordered to assist with the *2900*."

"I sailed on one of these new boats on several training runs in the Baltic but I never knew they would be serviceable so quickly. I'm glad Dönitz restarted the U-cruiser program. This boat should have sailed in early 1940.

"Unfortunately, the Americans bombed Bremen and destroyed four incomplete boats, so two of the remaining U-cruisers, the *2900* and *1229*, were ordered to sea before their final shakedown. We carried extra mechanics to set up the instruments and calibrate the weapons systems while en route."

"Really?" Lothar replied, still overwhelmed at the sight of one of the secret boats he had a hand in designing. "I was a regular visitor at the 'K' Design Office when the blueprints for the *1229* were being finalized."

"You will meet with it in a few days," Beust announced. "It is to assist in *Sea Scorpion*."

"Two U-cruisers for *Sea Scorpion*?" Lothar seemed confused by the news. All the training had been performed on Type IXD boats and now they would have to waste valuable time readjusting to a new set of plans. "I was not told of —"

"What you were told has no bearing on the *new* mission, *Kapitän*."

Suddenly, Lothar saw that it was not the commander speaking, even though the voice was vaguely similar against the din of the waves and breeze.

"Who are *you*?" he challenged the murky figure.

"I am *Hauptmann* Heinz Fripp, SS," the man responded, officiously, "assigned to this project by *Reichsführer* Heinrich Himmler himself."

As he moved closer, Lothar saw that the man wore the same coveralls as an ordinary petty officer, except that he sported a dark officers' cap with the familiar badge of the SS that glinted when under the starlight.

"What I meant, Captain Fripp," Lothar sighed, "is that had we known that such a large vessel was coming, we would have put on a larger crew to assist with the loading."

There was no answer, just the tapping and dragging sounds on the deck of the boat. Finally, Fripp said, "Let's get on with it."

When Lothar walked forward he saw that a larger than normal cargo bay had been cut into the boat and its long hatch covers were wide open, exposing nearly 30 feet of the innards of the submarine to the open air. The two cranes had been assembled in minutes and were now lowering cable hooks into the hold.

It was Beust who spoke next, very quietly and directly into Lothar's ear. "Fripp was an add-on. Basically, an SS stooge along for the ride. This happened the day after we got word on the foiled assassination attempt on Hitler. That was over three weeks ago. Did you hear about that?"

"Yes, just today," Lothar whispered back. "We were under strict radio silence."

"Damnable business," said Beust. "Anyway, we got a radiogram from Berlin saying that we are to override Dönitz's instructions and that Fripp, here, is the new submarine commander. Himmler's orders, I guess. If we never knew it before, they wanted us to know that the SS is really in charge of Germany now. God knows what's going on back home. Probably a blood bath."

"Don't you know whispering is impolite," Fripp butted in.

"My apologies, sir," responded Beust in a low voice, "but I was bringing our friend up to date with the sub's specifications. He is a famous U-boat commander, you know, but unfamiliar with the new U-cruiser."

"I know all about Stahl," growled Fripp. "Joseph Göbbels once sentenced him to death for treason but his uncle saved him. If Dönitz had tried that with *Reichsführer* Himmler, he would have been hung alongside his nephew."

Lothar gently sidled up to Fripp, who at five-foot-ten was nearly the same height as Lothar, and spoke in a low voice. "Look Fripp, like it or not, Himmler needs the *U-Bootwaffe* for this mission so I suggest you stop this petty foolishness about treason or Himmler's pet project will never get off the ground."

"Do you realize who you are speaking to?" growled Fripp, raising his chin haughtily. Even in the darkness Lothar could make out his thin, greyhound facial features.

"Yes, I do," Lothar spat back, suddenly planting a vice-like grip on Fripp's skinny arm. The pain instantly registered on the captain's face but he was too surprised to cry out.

"I am speaking to a tin pot bureaucrat who is going straight to the bottom of this cold sea if he does not shut up and keep out of the way of men who are trying to do their duty."

"I'll have you shot for this!" bleated Fripp, struggling to free himself from Lothar's grip. Unfortunately for Fripp, none of the others could see or hear what was going on.

Lothar squeezed even tighter. "Fine. When I let you go, shoot me," he continued. "Then you can explain to your Colonel Deckler why you executed the only man who can finish this project." The officer tried to say something but was cut off.

"Now, get the hell out of the way!" Lothar sneered, shoving the man aside.

Fripp rubbed his sore arm and glared at the enraged Lothar. For the first time since he joined the Nazi Party, he could not think of an intimidating reply to counter the insubordinate remarks made by a mere Navy or Army officer. Even full colonels cowered before the black tunic of the SS. But this man's swift rebuke caused his bravado to freeze up.

"All right, Mr. Beust, are we ready?" Lothar said, ignoring Fripp.

"Just say the word, *Kapitän*," Beust beamed. He had seen the whole thing.

CHAPTER TWELVE

August 18th
Ashton Island

"Daddy, they say he's a coward."

"Missy," he sighed, "I want you to stop talking that way about Wyn. I don't believe that crap for an instant and you have to stop saying it too. He was wounded at Dieppe and was damned lucky to get out alive."

Jesse Corkum strained at the weight of the kerosene container as she labored with it halfway up the 47 stairs to the lantern. The climb was imbedded in her memory and she sometimes dreamed about the distasteful chore when she was at school, even waking up with sore shoulders as if she had actually performed the duties in her sleep.

Wilbur Corkum stopped on the 36th step and lowered his oilcan. The inside of the concrete structure was wet with condensation and smelled dank and moldy. When he looked down at Jesse he saw a determined 11-year-old who once lugged an evening's supply of oil up these very stairs without his knowing, just to prove she was going to run Ashton Lighthouse someday. Her features had never changed, just her body, which now took the form of a mature woman.

Even though his heart ached the day she first left for Teacher's College, deep down he never wanted to her to return to Ashton to live. Times had changed. He wanted his daughter to have all the luxuries that he and her mother never had: fine house, furniture, time to go to the movies, a big car. That way, she would have the best of both worlds — a comfortable city life with holidays on Ashton. Now with Lottie gone, he wished she'd stay with him forever, yet he knew this was no place for her and never could be.

"Daddy, will you please listen to me?" she bleated. "Allan called me last night and gave me the complete story on our Captain Parsons."

"Captain?" answered Wilbur, his heavy brow raising the wrinkles on his tanned forehead. "Wyn was a captain?"

"Yes, with the Royal Hamilton Light Infantry. It seems he disobeyed a direct order and got half his men killed. Then he was court martialed and sentenced to jail, but they relaxed the sentence and sent him home with a dishonorable discharge."

Wilbur looked up at the remainder of the steps he had to climb. Suddenly, he felt like abandoning the can and going down to the house, even if it meant not shining the light tonight. It was as if God were poised to hit him with that one final blow that would cause him to finally buckle.

"You know, Missy," he uttered, after a few second's silence, "my father once told me that you judge a man on what he does, not what other people say about him."

After he had his say, his strength seemed to return. He reached down and picked up the oil can, his shoulder muscles straining as he raised it. Still not looking down to speak to his daughter, he added, "It pains me to think that a daughter of mine would speak that way about someone like Wyn Parsons. Especially when it's based on hearsay. It seems that you will do anything to discredit him because you are too damned proud to admit you are jealous. For some asinine reason, you think he is after your birthright."

Wilbur's eyes dropped and burned into the anxious face of his daughter. "Your mother's only been gone a little over a week and the pain in my heart burns so bad that all the water in that ocean can't cool it down. So what I'm going to tell you is no treat for me. I want you to leave that oil can right there and go pack your bags. Billy's coming over later and, when he leaves, I want you to be on that boat back to the mainland. This is no life for you. Marry that Blakey fellow and come visit when you have time. That's what I want you to do, not stick around Ashton and whine and complain about things that you don't want to understand. There are more important things to attend to here and bellyachin' ain't one of them."

Wilbur slowly turned his back on her and continued his climb. As he turned up the spiral staircase, he saw her standing where he had left her, with the same expression on her face.

He stopped and sighed, "Come on, Missy, you better get packing."

* * *

"The very first lighthouse, I mean the one that lasted more than 10 or 20 years, was called Pharos. It was a 400-foot tower built in 300 BC on an island in the Mediterranean to guide ships into the port of Alexandria. It was done with slave labor and was one of the Seven Wonders of the World. Today, it would cost millions to make something that big.

"Instead of a light, it had an open wood fire that they say could be seen up to 40 miles and was supposed to have blazed for 1600 years."

Wilbur Corkum stood in front of the white sill, taking in the nuances of the approaching fog. The light room was decagonal in shape, with sides of heavy iron plate for the first two-and-a-half vertical feet. All the metal parts were a bright vermilion in color. On top of each steel side was a 30x36 plate-glass window set in steel brackets.

Wyn took the polish and dabbed a bit on the huge lens, rubbing the beveled glass gently. He winced as a sliver of light attacked his eye from the curved glass. A thin ray of the setting sun had caught a wavelet on the ocean swells, sending a flash of light to one of the glass rings and directly into his face.

"Quite an invention, the lenses," continued Wilbur, seeing Wyn's discomfort. "They are the heart of the light, made in Paris by Barrier, Renar and Tuienne. My dad got this one while I was away at war. Cost the government $38,000 in 1918."

Four great lenses set into a metal frame surrounded the central kerosene lamp. Each of the lenses was made up of five rings of beveled glass in a bull's-eye shape; each ring staggered one behind the other. The prismatic effect of the large rings refracted the lamp light, which shone in all directions, onto a horizontal plane and magnified it. Making sure these surfaces were cleaned regularly had more than a passing implication on the range. This lens was encased in a light carriage, which sat in a bath of mercury and rotated on this metallic cushion.

"The oldest light down this way is Cape Roseway, on McNutt Island. The keeper has lots to talk about now, with a battalion of American soldiers and two 16-inch guns for company!"

Wilbur sat down on the sill and watched Wyn buff the crystal faces of the glass. He studied the stump at the end of the younger man's arm, an appendage that wobbled with every movement, and the scar that made up most of his right eyebrow. Noticing that the talkative light keeper had stopped the conversation, Wyn ceased his strokes and looked up at him.

"Wyn," Wilbur sighed, "you were supposed to be a worker and a partner around here but, as it turns out, you've become a good friend. Now, either way, I never ever thought about prying in your business. Whatever was in your past was your concern as long as it never rubbed off onto us."

Wyn took a deep breath and lowered himself on his haunches, putting a knee down, the way he used to do it in the Army. Nothing on his face gave Wilbur any indication that the young man knew what he was talking about.

"That said, Wyn, I have to ask you this," Wilbur continued, his voice ringing with an official tone, "and then I'll never bring it up again."

Wyn just nodded, his expression remaining the same.

"What happened at Dieppe?"

He stared out at the deepening twilight for a few seconds and then said, "Y'know Wilbur, we might want to light up first, because it's a long story."

CHAPTER THIRTEEN

August 22
2131 hours Atlantic Time
43 nautical miles east off the Nova Scotia coast

Captain Gus Lanton strolled out to inspect the three-inch ready gun on the bow and relish the warm breeze of the early evening. His crew had performed admirably during the past two months and he had no doubts about their professionalism whatsoever. Three young crewmen snapped to attention as he approached.

"Gunnery watch reports that this gun is ready for inspection, sir!" the first one snapped, his eyes looking straight past Gus.

The early evening wind was a balmy breeze compared to the some of the cool blasts they had received in the Gulf of St. Lawrence in recent days. They were now within the Gulf Stream and the ocean was as warm here as the waters off South Carolina.

"Proceed, Mr. Taggart," he replied to the young man whose well tanned face and arms were a perfect metaphor for the past three months. Gus looked down at the second hand on his watch and waited for the start signal.

"Alarm!" yelled the watch, and the two sailors manning the gun broke from their positions and quickly tore the rubberized, canvas tarpaulin from the three-inch weapon. Once the gun was exposed, one of the sailors cranked on a wheel, which spun the barrel around smoothly. Then he snapped open the breech. The other one had opened the ammunition chest and was ready to feed the rapid-firing gun.

"Not bad," Gus remarked, not really paying attention to the timing but satisfied that they had completed the process correctly. "Stand down."

There were not many times on the North Atlantic when the air was so warm that crewmen walked around in short-sleeved shirts, even in the summertime. But today was different. The weather service had informed the ship this morning that a hurricane was brewing off Bermuda and would not play itself out until it had almost reached Maine. However, Gus was not worried about weather. He and his crew would be safely docked in Bar Harbor for a long period of rest before the storm system hit.

The Gulf of St. Lawrence had been a good tour for him and the 174 crewmen of the *Montauk*, just as Admiral Stokes had promised. Working closely with corvettes of the Royal Canadian Navy and the PBY's and Grumman Wildcats of the Royal Canadian Air Force, they had been on a dozen solid hunts and many wild goose chases. Piloting the cutter through the shallows and narrows of the St. Lawrence River had been a challenging experience for his crew. They had to maneuver in a flowing body of water, whose speed both accelerated and slowed the usually staid process, depending on whether they were going with or against the current.

They had been very successful. Two old Type VII's had been sunk and three more driven down, with the *Montauk* getting partial credits for all. But the U-boats had sunk seven freighters in the Canadian coastal and inland waters, adding a frustrating appendix to the tour. The U-boats may have been beaten as a massive anti-convoy force but one submarine in the right hands could still deal some stinging blows.

Now it was time for home, furlough and a desk. With the Allies pushing into Belgium, the Germans could not hold out past the fall, just as Stokes had predicted.

* * *

"*Kapitänleutnant* Beust, what is our position?"

"Sonar makes us one hour away from the rendezvous position."

"Good, that will give us just enough twilight to hide our silhouettes."

Lothar went to the chart table and made some quick calculations. The line drawn from Raddall Island met the other from Argentina in a neat stroke. He felt better in his uniform and cap again, relishing the new smells of the U-boat as they mingled with the old ones. Even the slight hint of mold and diesel never caused his face to sour. It was the smell of action; it was the smell of victory. And it got him away from Deckler for a few days.

Last night, they had received their first wireless transmission from the BdU in several weeks, a coded message ordering them to rendezvous with another submarine and pick up cargo from it. What bothered Lothar was that the entire message was not in German naval code. Certain parts of it were in a jumble which only Deckler understood. Immediately after reading it he ordered Lothar to command the *2900* and rendezvous with another U-boat at a certain map coordinate.

The thin figure of Captain Fripp leaned over the large sheet of paper and studied the bisecting lines. He was dressed in a fresh, black SS uniform and had taken the time to shave during the two-day trip. If not for the wrinkles around his eyes and his thinning blonde hair, Fripp might have been mistaken for a schoolboy. And standing next to the robust Beust, he appeared waif-like, almost fragile.

Looking up at Lothar he commented, "Since we are not yet there, are you not being a bit too optimistic?"

"My glass is always half-full, *Herr Hauptmann*," Lothar replied, placing the drawing instruments down.

Fripp never replied. He just peered at the chart as if he felt Lothar were trying to take them off on some other course.

For the most part, Lothar and the SS contingent had been getting along quite well for the past week. If not for the foreboding uniforms, Fripp and the soldiers could have passed for normal soldiers and sailors. They stayed aboard *U-2900,* coming in every second night to change with the other guards, while Fripp and Deckler held briefings.

Beust stayed on the U-boat at all times. It sat on the bottom during the day and rose to *schnorkel* depth at night to recharge the batteries and air out the submarine. Fripp would always take the punt out and stay on the submarine at night.

Lothar watched for a moment and then said, "I'm curious, *Herr Hauptmann*, why this sudden burst of paranoia? I mean, the Führer was not harmed and the perpetrators were brought to justice without one member of the *U-Bootwaffe* having been implicated. After you have witnessed all this work we have done right under the noses of the Canadians, why do you still doubt us?"

Fripp looked up from the table and stared blankly at the U-boat commander, his eyes resting on the Iron Cross. He suddenly remembered that this man had also won the Knight Cross of the Iron Cross with Oak Leaves and Swords, the second highest award given in the German forces. Only the addition of diamonds to the award would make him "the best of the best." But, as usual, his sense of duty caught up with him.

"Because we are the only ones who hold the sacred trust of the Fatherland in our hands," he replied. "We are the only ones who have sworn personal allegiance to the Führer and, until someone has done that, he will always be under suspicion."

"I see," returned Lothar, a gentlemanly tone in his voice. "But here's the point I would like to make, *Herr Hauptmann*. These men you see around you are the only ones in our entire armed forces who live in an environment where certain death is less than half a meter away. If something happens to a tank, the men can climb out. If an airplane is disabled, the crew has the chance to bail out and open their parachutes.

"But these men," he continued, sweeping his hand around the control room to give credence to the furry faces of the U-boatmen, "have to worry about getting out of a steel coffin at depths that would crush a man's lungs before he could get to the surface, even if he could manage to escape."

"That is very chilling, Stahl," Fripp replied in a bored voice, "but living in a tin can under the water is not an instant recipe for patriotism."

"Then —"

"*Kapitän!*" It was the second watch officer. "The sound room reports propellers!"

Lothar looked over to Beust and said, "I have the conn."

"*Jawohl, Herr Fregattenkapitän!*" he replied, snapping his bearish body to attention. A sly grin came over his face as he passed the command of his vessel to a man whom he considered the greatest living commander in the fleet.

"Bearing!" cried Lothar as he grabbed the handles of the periscope. Then he flipped his hat around so the bill was facing backward.

"Bearing three-two-two!" replied the startled navigator.

"Prepare to take her up to periscope depth!"

Beust turned to the helmsman, who was stationed on the forward starboard side bulkhead, and yelled, "Helmsman! Prepare to take her up!"

"Take her up to 20 meters!"

Beust echoed the call.

Fripp's eyes narrowed in concern at the action and he sidled up to Lothar just as the commander switched on the motor to raise the periscope. "Stahl, what are you doing?"

Lothar jammed his forehead against the rubber eyepiece and slung his arms over the handles, seemingly unaware of the captain's question. Finally, he said, "I want to look at this ship."

"That's foolish," Fripp announced. "He might spot us and the whole mission might be jeopardized"

"She might already have us on her ASDIC," replied Lothar, still involved with the periscope. The lens had just broken the surface and he was scanning the horizon for the source of the engine noise. "And if she's a warship, she'll soon zero in on us. I just want to have a peek at what we're up against beforehand."

"You can't just —"

"My job is to ensure the safety of this mission," replied Lothar, calmly, his head jammed against the mechanism as if he were viewing a Berlin peepshow. "Now, *Herr Hauptmann*, just move aside and let these men do what they're very good at."

Lothar patiently watched the glowing purple horizon until the form grew larger. Unfortunately for them, the sun was taking its time going down. Suddenly, he began to nod. "I can see her!" Lothar exclaimed. "It's a warship, a small destroyer . . . looks American."

"Battle stations!"

"*Auf Gefechtsstationen!*"

Suddenly, he realized that on this modified boat he only had rear tubes operational. And to save space, there were only two torpedoes, but both of the newer *Zaunkönig*, or acoustic-type, which homed in on the engine noises of a ship.

"Open rear doors!" he yelled.

Lothar adjusted the visor on the periscope against the setting sun. The dying rays framed the warship. "Ready torpedoes! Simultaneous shoot!"

Again, Beust yelled into one of the funnels. "*Torpedoraum*. Prepare to shoot both torpedoes at once!"

* * *

"Captain?" Taggart said, interrupting Gus' daydream.

"Huh?"

"Captain, you're wanted on the bridge."

"It's a strange signature, captain," Petty Officer Jimmy Ranford, the sonar man uttered, staring at the smeared blip on his green radar screen. "It could be a lone whale but it sure is big, if it is."

James Eldon Ranford and Marty Myers were the last of the old bridge crew, the ones who had been with the ship since she had taken her first voyage in 1941. Both could have taken more important assignments on other ships but wanted to stay on with Lanton. Myers could have had his own ship a year ago. Ranford had just joked that he was "too old to train another commander."

"Come right to one-four-two, Mr. Myers."

"Right to one-four two, sir!" Lieutenant Commander Marty Myers called out to the helmsman in his southern drawl. The diminutive stature of Myers made his command seem that much more urgent, like the barking of a small dog. The ship began to turn gently.

"Steady on one-four-two."

"Steady on one-four-two, aye!"

"Jimmy?" Gus prodded the sonar man, his chin resting on the sailor's shoulder. Ranford squeezed the headphones as if trying to work them into his skull. Each sweep of the jagged green line around the screen seemed to add another clue to his arsenal.

"It's a sub, captain," Jimmy finally said, his voice sounding somewhat confident. "He just changed course."

"Wouldn't a whale change course if he heard our propellers?" Gus asked.

"He might, captain," replied Ranford. "But away from us. This guy's coming right at us."

"Sound general quarters!" Gus bellowed.

"Captain!" Gus looked up to see the freckled face of Ranford. "Taggart's got a periscope dead ahead!"

"Both engines ahead flank, steady as you go! Stand by depth charges!"

* * *

"He's seen us. Crash dive!"

"*Alarm!*" echoed Beust, slamming the ball of his hand against the dive bell switch, which sent a shrill ringing through the boat.

"Vent main ballast!"

Fripp watched nervously as men jostled him, cranking wheels and pulling levers. Surges of water and air echoed through the control room as gas was exchanged for water to make the boat into a rock instead of a balloon. The helmsman pushed the planes into a steep angle and the boat suddenly tipped up, causing everyone standing to grab for the nearest stationary piece of hardware.

Straining to hold onto the shiny steel cylinder of the periscope. Lothar barked, "Hard to port!"

* * *

The scrambling sailors were like a blur of powder blue with orange flashes where their helmets caught the dying rays of the sun. Gus was now on the starboard forecastle. The adrenaline raced through him and, coupled with his sweat cooling in the warm breeze, he felt charged like a quarterback who has begun to call the numbers of a play out to his team.

"Make ready a four-four spread shallow. Set stern charges for 150 feet. K-guns for 300."

Gus cocked his head in the direction of the radio man. "Send the following transmission," he said. "USCGS *Montauk* engaging enemy submarine at six-nine-degrees-45-minutes-west stop 42-degrees-15-minutes-north stop."

Gus shook his watch free of his cuff and glued his eyes to the second-hand. "Ready depth charges!"

"Depth charges ready, aye!"

"Away hedgehogs!"

"Hedgehogs away, aye!"

A sudden series of explosions on the bow of the cutter signaled the release of 24 bulbous-headed rockets which spread out ahead of the ship, arched and then fell into the light swells.

"Hard to port!"

"Hard to port, aye!"

A series of waterborne explosions churned the water into white foam as the hedgehogs detonated at their preset depths.

"Three . . . two . . . one! Away depth charges!"

"Away depth charges, aye!"

Explosions from the T-shaped launchers hurled depth charges out into the air on each side of the ship. The large cans came down and hit the waves 50 feet out. At the stern, four 600 pound barrels were rolled off into boiling wake.

Moments later, the depth charges went off in rapid succession, shaking the *Montauk* and shooting up white geysers.

"Commence echo ranging. Search 140 through 280."

The heavy *PING-ping* . . . *PING-ping* rang through the bridge.

* * *

"*Wasserbomben!*"

Fripp clenched his eyes shut after the first bunch of hedgehogs went off. The sub rocked and shook with the 24 explosions. He held on to a railing with all his might, too scared to even yell.

Lothar had gambled correctly, steering away from the hedgehogs as the lethal depth charges exploded harmlessly a large distance from the diving U-boat. Other explosions were far enough away that they were only tremors. But when the four large drum charges from the stern of the cutter detonated, the U-boat shook like a dying whale and Fripp and the two SS soldiers cringed in terror.

"Two more!" Lothar yelled. "Hold on!"

The depth charges from the starboard side had been set for a far greater depth. They drifted down toward the U-boat at 16 feet per second in an intercepting pattern, mindless barrels outside the cutter's intended pattern meant to provide coverage if the target suddenly moved away from the kill zone.

The *U-2900* had done just that and was racing toward the bottom at a steep angle trying to outrun them. Each can was a Mark VII depth charge containing 250 pounds of a highly-explosive mixture: Torpex, Cyclonite, TNT, and aluminum flakes. At 450 feet, a preset hydrostatic fuse detonated the explosive compound, causing the formation of a spherically-shaped gas bubble with an initial temperature of approximately 3,000 degrees Centigrade, pushing a shock wave of nearly 50,000 atmospheres. The pressure surge rode to a peak level within milliseconds, moving through the water at the speed of sound, its energy dissipating in proportion with the distance traveled.

Because water cannot be compressed, the shock wave moved farther and faster underwater than it did in the atmosphere, pounding the boat with a shock amounting to what someone would feel in two small car accidents. One crewman slipped on the steel floor and was flung against a bulkhead. Two more were shoved into one of the soldiers and all three crashed to the rocking, steel floor. The lights went out and a soft red glow replaced them.

Fripp was wild with fear. Unearthly tones rose from his larynx and his eyes were closed so tight that every muscle in his face was sore. Then the deadly *swish, swish, swish* of the twin screws passing overhead cut through the crying.

* * *

Two huge plumes of white water flew up a hundred yards to the starboard side, spraying the forecastle with a fine mist.

"Helm, bring her about to one-seven-two and hold steady."

"One-seven-two and steady, aye!" The turn of the cutter was a tight circle, causing the usual noise of pots and pans to rattle free in the galley. The firemen and machinists mates in the engine room lost their footing and grabbed onto overhead pipes for balance. Because they were heading home, housekeeping and other non-war procedures on the cutter had been slack. Books, plates, personal items and food became airborne during the maneuver.

The western horizon was now a pinkish glow, the colored hues catching the cutter and the wave tops on the surrounding ocean and almost every member of the crew was searching the mottled dark blue and pink water for signs of damage to the underwater enemy.

"Mr. Ranford?"

"I'm getting a signal, bearing two-two-nine," replied the adolescent voice of the sonar man. "It looks as though he's trying to play possum."

"Possum, my ass," Gus bawled. "He's ready to launch. Helm, hard to port!"

* * *

"*Kapitän!*" Beust announced, running into the control room. "We have one crewman dead and five wounded. Presently, there are five leaks in the aft torpedo room. Two are still out of control.

"Compressor?" Lothar asked, as if completely ignoring the big man.

"No damage, sir."

"Ballast controls and steering?"

"They are fine too, sir, but the men —"

"Take us up!" Lothar answered, looking past him. His eyes were lifeless, like those of some deepwater fish. Beust just stared at him as he gave orders around him and the crewmen jumped to his command.

"Beust!" he said, after the submarine began to rise. "I want you to clear the control room of all unnecessary personnel."

Fripp was sunken on the floor with his arms still around a cluster of pipes. Beust reached down to help him up and, like a marionette, he rose in a series of jerky motions. His face was a gaunt blue under the emergency lights and he looked more like a Boy Scout in a black uniform than an SS officer. It was then he realized that he had wet himself and so stood very still against the bulkhead, his eyes panning the control room.

"*Herr Hauptmann,*" Beust said, "come with me to the —"

"I'm staying," Fripp announced indignantly. He looked over at his guards and, seeing their terrified faces, he waved them off. Like zombies they walked out of the small control room.

"Where is the ship now?"

"Two thousand one hundred meters, sir".

Lothar shifted, he had lived here over and grabbed the funnel which was labeled: *A.V. Torpedoraum.* "Stand by torpedoes." Taking a deep breath he looked up to see that everyone in the control room was looking at him. Beust turned his eyes away after a few seconds and pretended to check an instrument.

"Range now?" Lothar asked.

"One thousand eight hundred," was the response. "They are coming right at us, sir."

The faces in the room were sweaty, tired and afraid. In the dim lighting they looked more like the faces of miners who had just survived a cave in and were about to be told if they would ever be rescued. Unlike his charges, Lothar had witnessed this scene on four occasions. In his mind, there were only three earthly outcomes in a situation like this. The first was, you persevered and rode it out, no matter how terrible the urge was to surface and surrender. The second: you died in one of the most horrible ways imagined. And the third was: you killed the enemy.

In the old days, there was a very good chance that the hunting ship would lose. Or if the boat was damaged, surrender was possible. In these days, however, the enemy was too good at what they did and had the best equipment to find you. Hiding was simply not an option.

The nature of this very mission was all or nothing. If defeated, there would be no surrender. The secret would die with them and Deckler would have to go to the second option, which was solely a land-based attack.

"Range?" Lothar asked again, his eyes resting on a frightened 19-year-old with his hands on one of the control wheels. Every month they became younger and had less and less training. In the hands of a green commander, they might all be dead now. Many of those leaders might have tried to run or shut down and hide when the enemy attacked. It would be just a matter of time before they were sent to the bottom.

"One thousand, three hundred."

"Let me know when we are at 900."

Beust came back into the room, the eyes in his furry face betraying his fatigue. "The leaks have been sealed. Number Two generator is still out but Hans can have it fixed in a few hours."

"And the men?"

"The medic is seeing to them now," he sighed. "One broken leg and the other a gash to the head."

"Whom did we lose?"

"Feltner. A pipe fell on him."

"I'm sorry, commander," Lothar said, sincerely.

"One thousand meters!" cried the sonar man.

Lothar leaned beside the smaller, targeting periscope and pressed the telescoping button. A motor noise signaled the raising of it and he calmly adjusted the focusing. Range markers accompanied the view of the approaching warship.

Lothar turned to Beust and said, "Fire!"

"*Los!*"

* * *

The acoustic torpedoes were designed to home in on the cavitation noise of escort vessels, which usually traveled between 10 to 19 knots. The two *Zaunkönige*, "wrens," as the sailors called them, quickly picked up the frequency of the *Montauk*'s propellers and corrected course. The German naval acoustic torpedo moved more slowly than conventional waterborne projectiles; however its electric motor left no telltale wake, as did the compressed air variety. With the *Montauk* bearing down on the U-boat at 18 knots there was nothing to distract them.

* * *

"Captain, I'm picking up something . . . a drone of some sort coming toward us."

For an instant Gus' mind went blank but then a chill shot his back and he grabbed the microphone on the bulkhead.

"Hard to starboard!" Gus cried. Instantly, the ship lurched on his command, almost causing him to lose his balance.

"Now hear this, brace yourselves for torpedoes!"

The sudden shifting of the ship almost threw the torpedoes off the target but they veered with the *Montauk*. The earlier versions might have hit the turbulence caused by the turn and their sensitive detonators might have been set off. But these new models were not dissuaded. They exploded under the gearing box.

CHAPTER FOURTEEN

August 23rd
0115 Atlantic Time

The signals were received and verified through the latest *B-Dienst* code; Lothar ordered the dinghy out on the deck. The other submarine was a ghostly iceberg on the shimmering seas.

For this rendezvous, he appreciated this hint of moonlight. As they were more than a 150 miles offshore, the chances of aircraft were slim, and ships could be picked up by their own radar. Still, the formidable 37mm and 20mm guns of the *U-2900* were manned by able crews and lookouts dotted the bridge and deck areas. As well, the NAXOS antenna scanned the skies, its advanced radar detection abilities making Lothar feel the safest he had ever been in the railed *Wintergarten* — or anti-aircraft platform — of a surfaced U-boat.

As the two boats approached each other, both deck crews waved and broad smiles lit up their faces. They were not allowed to speak but their pantomimes were an acceptable substitute for the long times between furloughs when they could share their experiences with other U-boatmen.

"Are you ready, *Herr Hauptmann*?" Lothar asked, adjusting the ties on Fripp's lifejacket. Unlike their last nocturnal liaison, he could see the man in the moonlight.

"Let's get this over with," the SS man growled. After the battle, his haughty attitude had returned with the change of his wet trousers.

The rubber raft was lowered into the water and the two officers were helped down into the bobbing craft. Once comfortably seated they broke out the small oars and began paddling the 20 meters to the other U-boat.

* * *

"Willi, it's so good to see you!" Lothar said, his green eyes animated and watery.

"I can't remember ever meeting you in such calm and warm water," Willi Strauss replied. "Not like the freezing Foehn winds off Iceland, eh? This has to be a good omen!"

Kapitänleutnant Willi Strauss stood like a jaunty pirate against the iron rails of the *Wintergarten* of his Type VII boat. Behind him on this platform, the vigilant crews manning 20mm anti-aircraft guns gave further testament to this image. Lothar smiled as he recognized the familiar shark logo on the conning tower just behind him. The emblem was in cartoon form with the chubby image of Winston Churchill, in boxer shorts made from a Union Jack, crying because the smiling shark had the British leader's large posterior in his jaws.

He was the last of Lothar's friends from "The Happy Time," and experienced commander with almost 40 Allied ships to his credit. Also, the tall, autocratic Strauss had two U-boats sunk from under him. During his escape from the second one, he was captured temporarily by the crew of a British torpedo boat but managed to slip away from them during the night.

Fripp shot nervous glances between the two commanders and the alert gun crews on the Type VII boat. In normal times, he tolerated small talk but tonight the prattle between the two friends caused an anger to ferment deep inside.

Lothar finished up with a slight tease on Strauss' scraggly beard and then noticed Fripp's discomfort. Time, he knew, was very limited, as the distress calls from the ship he had just sunk would alert aircraft and ships to search the area. "Oh, Willi, this is *Hauptmann* Fripp. He is in command of the transport for the project."

Even though Fripp was disguised in U-boat coveralls and lifejacket, Strauss knew him to be SS the minute the man landed on deck, just as Lothar had weeks before on their first encounter. He just nodded in Fripp's direction.

Lothar turned to Fripp and said, "And this is Willi Strauss, the best U-boat commander in the fleet." He almost slipped up and said, "still alive," but had caught himself. Willi could read that in his words but, like all commanders under Dönitz, knew the reality of their profession. Although official channels would never admit it, both men knew that the *U-Bootwaffe* had suffered nearly 28,000 casualties — 60 to 70 percent of the entire force — in five years of war.

Willi pointed to a wooden trunk on the deck. Stenciled on the side of it were large Oriental characters. "Then this must be yours, *Herr Hauptmann*," he said, almost formally. "I was only happy to make the rendezvous with the Japanese sub. They are a very polite people and their commander gave us a crate of rice wine to go with the beef we took on in Argentina. I love these tours that take us to southern waters."

Fripp ignored him. He pulled a notebook from under his coveralls and flipped it open to pre-marked page. Squinting in the moonlight, he ran his fingers down until the exact characters came up on the sheet. "Yes," he answered, "this is definitely it."

"Then we better move," cautioned Willi, motioning to three of his crew. One man slipped down into the raft and the other two lowered the crate with a rope.

When Fripp was seated in the dinghy, Willi whispered to Lothar, "What is the SS doing here?"

"The assassination attempt on Hitler. The SS is in control of the armed forces now."

"*Scheiss!* I just heard about that last week in a communiqué from our transmitter in Portugal. I thought it was some just some crackpot."

"No, Willi, it was very organized," Lothar sighed. "So when you get back to Germany, watch yourself. According to Deckler, who is the commander of this project, rank and achievement in battle do not mean anything anymore."

"Then why wasn't some stooge put on my boat in Buenos Aires?" he whispered, not caring that Fripp was watching them.

"Because, to my knowledge, the Gestapo and other agencies don't know what we are doing."

Strauss gave a quick wave to his men and they all cleared the deck. "So just what are you doing, Lothar?" he asked slyly. "And what's in the crate?"

"I honestly don't know, Willi," he answered.

Lothar gave a quick glance at Fripp and the others. When he looked back at his old comrade he said, "Joachim Beltzer is dead."

Willi almost stumbled on the deck when he heard the news. "When? How?" he asked, his voice trembling..

"Unfortunately, Willi," Lothar sighed, "I can only tell you that he died saving my life and the lives of my crew."

"I could say so many things about him," Willi sighed, shrugging off the welling emotions. "It would take weeks."

Just then Fripp stomped down the deck and stopped at the two men, regarding them as if they were loitering. "We are ready," he announced.

"I'll be along shortly," Lothar replied, curtly.

Fripp eyed both men suspiciously. "Be quick about it," he snapped as he walked down gangplank.

Lothar gave Willi a knowing glance and then shrugged at Fripp's comment.

But not Willi Strauss. "Nazis," he chuckled, as Fripp began barking orders to the men on Lothar's boat. "They look so out of place in the real war."

A moment later, Lothar took his friend's hand and gave it a firm shake. "Take care of yourself," he said, then he stepped down the gangway.

"Prepare to dive!" Strauss shouted, as their respective crews threw back the line and began retracting the bridgeway.

"Goodbye old friend," Lothar replied to the lonely figure against the railing of the *Wintergarten* in a pose that had become one of a U-boat commander's most familiar trademarks.

An instant before he turned away, Lothar was certain he saw Strauss's eyes watering. If ever there was ever a picture of a wolf crying, it was now engraved in Lothar's mind.

CHAPTER FIFTEEN

August 23rd
0231 Atlantic Time

He could never remember his shoulder hurting this badly, not even after the hunting accident. The pain was as regular as the ticking of a clock, a sharp jab with each second that had passed. If he had been in colder waters, it might have numbed the throbbing, but also he might have succumbed to exposure hours ago. Instead, he hung on, the Mae West just holding his head above the gently rippling warm water.

The moon was a mocking sliver in the sky, its millions of reflections on the wavelets teasing his eyes. Many times he tried to sleep. But then his shoulder reminded him that any rest would be impossible.

He was not alone in the water. There was debris all around him and the odd body bobbing just out of reach. Most of the dead were face down and so he never knew who they were. But he did recognize Gordie Taggart, the gunnery watch for the evening, and Freddy Parker, the New Yorker who had his name in for Annapolis. Parker was one of the dead lying on his back, his eyes wide open and facing the Milky Way.

Gus also noticed that they were all deck crew, killed quickly by the explosions or the aftershock when their bodies were either slammed into the water or thrown up and dropped from a great height, the impact on the ocean surface snapping their necks or pounding the life from them, like Billy Stevens, the quartermaster, who flew past him in the explosion and had struck the bulkhead very hard.

None of the men who toiled below decks were visible. They never had a chance to get up the ladders before the *Montauk* flipped over and disappeared. In fact, many of the 174 crewmen might have survived if the bow of the great cutter had not suddenly shot up steeply and then folded back on itself; either entombing the struggling sailors below or throwing the deck crews like a great catapult. The disaster took only 13 seconds from the time the two torpedoes blew the stern off the *Montauk* until it slipped beneath the churning water.

Gus had been tossed overboard in the shock of the second explosion, which was barely a finger snap after the first. He had landed unconscious and underwater until his Mae West shot him to the surface, luckily with his mouth above the lapping water. He could not have seen either of the two whalers which had been blown free and had landed upright among the flotsam. A dozen of the crew had swum for the boats and then, once aboard, had oared the craft among the debris checking for live ones.

By this time, it was very dark as the thin moon had not risen high enough to brighten the area. The easy ones to find were the conscious sailors who had switched on their electric torches. The rest had to be turned over and checked for life. Somehow they had missed Gus, who was just another bobbing piece of flotsam without a light to mark him. At around midnight, Marty Myers, the highest-ranking of the survivors, ordered them to row on a course that would take them to within the patrolling area of land-based aircraft from Maine.

The throb in his shoulder had awakened him but, by that time, the boats were an hour to the west. He never knew if anyone had made off in lifeboats. From the information he could gather in his watery world, he could have been the only survivor.

However, just in case there was a rescue boat in the area, he switched on his small torch and began calling out. But after 15 minutes of this, his voice was ragged and he ceased it. At least it had taken his mind off his shoulder for a time.

As he glanced at the moon, Ginger's face and dancing body entered his mind and he suddenly wondered if anyone had given her the news yet. *Did they get my first message? Would they notice my missed transmission and send out a search party right away? Would Stokes come right out to the house and tell her or would he wait for a day or two to conduct a proper search?*

Breathing through another series of bad pulses in his shoulder, Gus glanced up at the stars and pulled himself around so he faced due west. Then he began swimming, slow, methodical strokes, favoring his left shoulder as much as he could manage.

As he swam, he thought of many things: Ginger's birthday, his crew, airplanes and sharks. The predatory fish were the last thing he needed to concentrate on right now but he could not shake the thought. This was, after all, the Gulf Stream and he had fished for tuna out in its warm waters enough times to know that where there was tuna, there were sharks. Suddenly, he felt naked and the trauma of his ordeal was translated into an overwhelming fear of being pulled down by something below.

*　*　*

"Why can't we submerge?" Fripp complained. "The enemy aircraft will be out soon."

Lothar dug his hands into the railing of the rubberized-steel platform as he scanned the star-studded horizon for signs of danger. There were four lookouts and the cross-like mast of the radar detector stood like a medieval talisman to ward off evil.

"Because we have another 60 kilometers to go and I want to make sure I get as much time on the surface before relying on the batteries. When we get close to base, there might be enemy activity and we might not get a chance to *schnorkel*.

"But you have nothing to fear, *Hauptmann*. Our new radar detector was developed to find the three-centimeter transmissions of the newer Allied ships and planes. If there is something in the area, we will know in plenty of time."

Fripp was still shaken up from his ordeal with the *Montauk*. Although he fared no better or worse than the rest of his guards and the young *Kriegsmarine*, his Prussian bearing would not allow him to think so. He was an officer, and an officer had to set an example.

He did, however, appreciate Lothar's concern for him after the attack even though he would dare not vocalize it. And he did have to admit that the commander was the perfect example of leadership during the battle and had saved their lives. This puzzled the SS man. To Fripp and his superiors, Lothar and his U-boat kind were rebels who did not symbolize the spirit of the Fatherland as set out in *Mein Kampf*.

Yet these U-boatmen threw themselves into battle against an enemy with far greater numbers and resources, in the fearless tradition of the Teutonic knights, a cornerstone of Prussian lore. *What then was this defective part of their character that they could not follow the principals of Adolf Hitler?*

"There's a small light to port, sir!" one of the lookouts cried. "It's too close to be a small ship."

"Slow to one-third!" Lothar commanded.

As the boat's speed diminished another man shouted, 'It's a man!"

"All stop!" Lothar cried, jumping down from the conning tower.

A surprised Fripp followed him. "Why are you stopping?"

"Didn't you hear?" Lothar replied, striding across the dark, rubbery surface of the deck. "There's a man in the water."

"But it's probably one of those aboard that enemy ship you sank," Fripp argued. "We can't —"

"We don't know that yet!" rebutted Lothar his eyes locked on the slowly bobbing light.

The sub slowed and passed within 20 feet of the man. "I'll get him!" cried one of the lookouts.

"Quickly!" barked Lothar, suddenly irritated at having his schedule altered.

The U-boatman dove into the warm water and swam to the light. When he reached it, he yelled, "I think he's dead!"

"Let's see who he is," Lothar responded, and the light began to move toward the ship. When they were at the gunnels, three more crewmen reached down to haul the body up. Lothar kneeled down and shone his own light in the man's face.

"You!" Lothar said in surprise when he saw Gus' face.

"Can't you see he's dead?" shouted Fripp, his face pulsing with anger. "Shove him overboard!"

Lothar said a silent prayer and set the body of his former enemy adrift. He thought of retrieving it again and shutting off the light, as a show of respect, but thought better of it and walked back to the conning tower. At least his body had a chance of being found.

"The patrols will be along soon," he sighed. Then into the intercom he said, "Prepare to dive and run off the *schnorkel*."

Fripp watched the diminishing glow of the small light for a few seconds and then turned to Lothar. "You knew this man?" he asked, his adolescent-sounding voice grating at Lothar's ears like the buzz of a horsefly.

"His ship was the one who damaged my first command," Lothar replied softly, glancing over his shoulder at the bobbing lamp on the ocean.

Fripp had read the reports and needed no further information.

CHAPTER SIXTEEN

Ashton Island

The potato harvest had gone well. With the trailer hooked behind the new tractor, Wyn was able to pitchfork the russets in one fluid motion. He then rooted around for orphans, sometimes having to pick them up by hand, before going on to the next plant. With the sun now dipping below the mainland he had completed almost an entire acre. Tomorrow, he would shake the tubers loose and toss the tops into the seaweed compost for next years' fertilizer.

Jesse had not meant to spy on him. She had merely gone over to Wyn's place to ask him over for dinner. Actually, it had been Wilbur's idea, and she offered several excuses why she should miss the meal. Unfortunately, like most children, she underestimated how well her father knew her and had stood in agony as he tossed away her excuses one by one.

There had been only one time in her life when Jesse felt the need to mistrust her father's judgment. That was six years ago when she was sent to her relative's home in Bedford to attend public school. For the first time in her life, she knew the feeling of betrayal and it had burned inside her for weeks afterward. Instead of a fond farewell for their 15-year-old daughter, Wilbur and Lottie had to hold back the tears when Jesse locked herself in her aunt's bathroom and refused to come out. In her eyes, the island was her own magical kingdom and her parents were ripping her away.

It was Christmas time before she would speak to them again when, upon reaching the island shore, a homesick and repentant daughter threw herself into her father's arms. Jesse never reacted that way again with her parents until this trip.

After her first long absence from Ashton, she began to realize that the world had many wonderful things to offer and that, as a maturing woman, she could live in the city and always have Ashton as her special vacation place. Her friends envied her for having Ashton, an island paradise that seemed to have so much more excitement and beauty than their own parents' summer cottages.

Unlike most of her classmates, Jesse did not want to get married right away, even to a son from a family of one of Halifax or Boston's leading families. She wanted to be a teacher and she was secure enough in her own mind not to be dissuaded by the fickleness going on around her. That self-assurance was not taught to her; it was absorbed, an osmosis that came as a result of growing up with parents who considered themselves a partnership of equals.

As Jesse watched Wyn start up the tractor and bring in the last load of potatoes, she reached for the letter in her jacket pocket. The message from Allan was expected, a correctly worded note, as only a lawyer could have penned. It explained the ramifications of their relationship, and that is was impossible for Jesse and him to continue to see each other if she was going to stay on at Ashton for the winter to help her father.

As if to diffuse the initial directness of the correspondence, he went on to say that he had been promoted to captain and was responsible for all the liturgical responsibilities for the regiment. In plain English, his contribution to the war effort entailed sifting through the regiments' official papers, picking out the ones that needed notarizing, and then affixing on them the seal of his father's law firm, Blakey, Corbett and Blakey. In other words, she thought sarcastically, Allan was too important to be wasted in combat.

In the letter, he had included a recent picture of himself, complete with his new rank. She stared at it, thinking that he did look handsome and somewhat dashing. The pencil-thin moustache was a new addition and gave him the air of an Errol Flynn. But Jesse could not find anything above his companionship that she would miss.

A feeling of sadness came over her as she placed the picture back into the envelope and crumpled it up. She took a deep breath and began walking down the hill. A minute later, she was at The Knob. In the last rays of the day, she saw the bronze, muscular form of Wyn seated on his tractor like some comic book hero on a strange beast. He was resting, sipping from a water jug at intervals as he surveyed the work left to do.

Looking at him from the back, his left arm looked normal, but when he shifted, she saw the stump that had once been his forearm and she felt a pang of remorse for him. She decided right then that, even if he had run in battle, the man had paid an awful price for it. Tears suddenly came to her eyes, ones that should have been shed over the loss of her boyfriend. However, instead of letting them flow, Jesse quickly dismissed the emotions and wiped her eyes, as she had done so many times in the recent days when her mother's memory came to mind.

Her father was a staunch supporter of Wyn's innocence. He believed none of the stories of his cowardice that he heard in Port Pleasant and curtly informed the concerned citizens to mind their own business.

Wilbur had been in three battles in the last year of the Great War and two nights ago, for the first time in her life, he spoke about them. He wanted to illustrate to her that things that happen in war can turn even the proudest and bravest individuals into clamoring, frightened animals. As he expected, she was shocked to hear of the deaths of his friends and others in the most horrible ways imaginable.

"Wyn told me about Dieppe," Wilbur had related toward the end of the conversation. "I made him tell me the truth about it because I felt, as his partner, he owed me his side, which ever way it went. Under those circumstances, he reluctantly obliged."

"How would you know if he were telling the truth?" she had replied.

"Because, after all these years a fellow gets the knack of sizing up another. You can tell by the way another man talks about war if he was actually there. Like all painful stories, this one came out in spurts and fits of anger, and a bit of crying."

"He cried?" she blurted, incredulously. She never thought he had an emotional bone in his body.

"Not the kind of crying that you nor anyone else who had never been in the same set of circumstances would imagine. More like an anguished sob here and there as certain things came out.

"You see, Jesse, memories of war aren't like thinking back on your aunt's summer picnics. They're flashes of faces, smoke, loud sounds and smells that come back to you. You try not to think about them or, when you do, your mind is geared to tellin' about the funny stuff — the guys with smelly feet or the ones that can't march straight.

"The rest, the awful things, are shut away where you can't get at them very easily. If, for some reason, you do want to let them out like I asked Wyn to do, then there's no way to adjust the flow like you would on a water pump.

"It's a perfect Pandora's Box. Things come out that you never remembered before. Things that you saw but your brain didn't register on at the time because they were so horrible. Things that you saw others do to each other that would make God almighty damn them to Hell for eternity. Things that you did to your fellow man that no amount of praying or giving to charities could be enough penance."

At that Wilbur had become silent, almost brooding. Then he got up from the table, his way of saying that the conversation was almost over, and added, "Wyn told me as much as his mind would let him, Jesse. But he didn't have to tell me no more. Because what he did say confirmed that I was a pretty good judge of horseflesh when he and I first met. And I also heard what he didn't say, which was just as important. So, Missy, Wyn ain't no coward. End of story."

She began walking toward the tractor, her feet feeling for the round stones as if she had never been down this part of The Knob before when, in years gone by, she could have flown down without disturbing a rock. Her mind was a mosaic of images and thoughts, like her mother's anaconda wallboard which was still plastered with photographs and small mementos: Wyn's intrusion on Ashton, her mother's death, Allan's letter, Jan Johansen's smile, her father's pain, and Wyn's confession.

Wyn reached over with his right hand to steady himself as he dismounted from the high tractor seat. As Jesse got closer, she saw a cluster of pinkish scars that seemed to spray from his left elbow. In an odd way, it looked like a tattoo of small rose petals.

Suddenly, as if an antenna on his back had warned him of an unseen presence, he turned around and confronted her. His boyish face was calm, almost inquisitive, and changed little as he recognized the identity of his visitor. As the last glint of sun bathed him in an orange hue, the sweat glistened on his chest and shoulders and his eyes sparkled like the rippling ocean beyond him.

"Miss Corkum," he announced, a slight smile on his face.

Jesse took a couple of seconds to compose herself. "Good evening, Mr. Parsons," she answered, her eyes trying to dodge his. They finally rested on his arms; how one was so huge and capped by a muscular shoulder and how the other, the one with the hand and lower forearm missing, was so much smaller.

"Can I do something for you?"

His question startled her out of her daydream. Taking a quick breath, she looked him square in the face. "Mr. Parsons, I was wondering if you would join us for dinner this evening?" Then she added. "There is some important business we have to discuss."

"Sounds serious," Wyn replied, noting the worry lines on her brow.

Jesse was surprised at her tone. She had not meant it to come out that way. It seemed that anything she said around Wyn was either being misconstrued or very blunt. With each millisecond that she thought of this, the more confused and angry she became.

"Well, it is!" she blurted, this time unabashedly, the thoughts of sympathy for the man waning with each second. "And if you weren't so damned irritating all the time maybe you'd be even likeable!" With that she turned and headed back up the slope, her feet knowing every rock.

This time Wyn followed her and caught up with her stride as they got to the top of the knoll. She saw him out of the corner of her eye but kept walking. He matched her step by step, the sea wind, absent from the hollow of The Knob, now bathing his body in a deliciously cool massage.

"So," he asked, still keeping up with swift steps, "can we stop before we hit the ocean? I mean, it might seem awful strange to you when I disappear below the waves while you keep on walking."

Suddenly, she halted and faced him, her fierce, brown eyes staring into his face. "There you go again!" she cried. "Every sentence you utter comes out an insult!"

Wyn's tanned face began to crinkle and his bright teeth showed through like the white beach rocks. Suddenly, he felt a chuckle rise within him, which, before he knew what was happening, built into a roar of laughter.

The feeling was so unexpected to Jesse that she just stared for a moment. Without knowing why, Wyn was totally immersed in a fit of mirth, the feeling of which he had not known for over two years. In fact, a thought went through his brain, a flash from April 1942, when his platoon had coerced Private Helmsley, an extremely handsome young man, to dress up as a woman. Using even more browbeating, they sneaked him into a British officers' canteen and watched through the window in uncontrollable laughter as waves of men made passes at him. This thought made him laugh even harder.

"You're mad," Jesse quipped, her forehead still wearing a frown. But her hand shot up to her face to stifle something that resembled a small titter.

"You're. . ." she tried, unsuccessfully. Then a wave of laughter overtook her.

* * *

"All right," Jesse said, her hand around the heavy mug of tea, "I agree that father needs a partner now ..." She stopped short of mentioning her mother's death. "I always knew he would get a permanent man, except that I thought it would have been later on, you know, long after I had married."

They had not gone back to the lighthouse for dinner, both feeling that they needed to settle their differences out of her father's earshot. She also had to show her father that she was making headway in her attempts to accept Wyn as part of Ashton. This was one of the terms of the bargain she had made with Wilbur in order to stay.

"And you were planning to ask the man you marry to come to Ashton to take up a new career as a lighthouse keeper?" Wyn asked.

He expected to be tongue-lashed for his unexpected intrusion into her story, but Jesse surprised him. Nodding sheepishly she said, "Now that I hear someone else say it, it does sound childish. I guess I was hoping Allan would . . . but that was stupid."

"Why, because he's a lawyer?"

"How did you know about him?" she snapped. Then, just as suddenly, she relaxed. "Of course, Father must have told you."

"Actually, it was your mother," he replied sipping more of his tea.

"My mother?" Jesse asked, her brows raised.

"She would have tea for me when I brought over the firewood, or lettuce from the fields, or mail," Wyn shrugged.

"You're full of surprises, aren't you?" Jesse chuckled, the feeling wearing off quickly. She was beginning to realize that his mannerisms were not meant to be rude, rather he was a brutally honest man unused to the platitudes in which she had grown accustomed to hearing around Allan's crowd. With most of Allan's friends in uniform now, it was hard for her to keep from chuckling aloud when they used borrowed phrases from British officers like: "How are you, old chap?" and "We'll kick the stuffing out of Jerry on this one, I'd say."

"Wyn, can I ask you a rather personal question?"

"Sure," he replied. "As long as it's not about why a single man, like me, has real toilet paper in his biffy."

"Really?" she laughed, imagining a scarce item like a toilet roll in a man's outhouse. "No Simpson's catalogue?"

"Nope. There's even a real toilet seat," he added proudly.

After that bout of laughter died down, she asked, "Would it be too forward to ask what rank you were overseas?" The question just came out, as easily as it did at one of Allan's friends' gatherings. *Everyone asked about rank, didn't they?*

"Not at all. I was a captain in the Hamilton Light Infantry," he answered nonchalantly, his angular face looking more mischievous without the added weight of their previous tension.

Jesse had known this from Allan's investigation but it did not seem to fit the man she saw across from her. "But —"

"Do I have a university degree?" he continued. "No."

He then took another sip of tea and, realizing that she was feeling awkward, said, "I was a sergeant when the battalion commander, Lieutenant Colonel Fairweather, pulled me out of the ranks for officer training. It seemed that, beginning in '40, a lot of experienced Canadian officers were being transferred to the British army on a program called CanLoan. Seems that the fellows running the war didn't think Canadians were going to be used for anything much except guarding the British shores so they wouldn't miss a few officers."

Wyn looked down at his mug and his voice cooled to the temperature of his remaining tea. "The Aussies and Kiwis were shipped over to fight in North Africa but, even though we saved their butts many a time in the Great War, the Brit commanders never thought we were good for anything except replacements. So, we just trained . . . and drank . . . and trained some more . . . and got into fights with the locals sometimes. That went on for three years. By the time June '42 came around, lo and behold, I was a captain."

Wyn looked up and the smile was back on his face, but his eyes were misty. Jesse wanted to reach out and touch him but thought better of it.

"Look," she said, "I know now that I've been wrong about a few things, and that I haven't really given you a chance. Father thinks you're the cat's whiskers so I have to believe that too."

For a moment she lost herself in his dark blue eyes, unsure about what was coming over her. She quickly put it aside and said, "So, why don't we agree to work together until Christmas time. After that, I'll be going back to teach on the mainland and father and I will have you trained on most of the lighthouse operations." Like a real estate agent confirming a deal she put her hand out.

Wyn reached across the table and took her small hand. It was a firm handshake and his fingers smarted. Seeing him wince, Jesse said, "I can work as hard as any man."

"Believe me," Wyn smiled, "I have no doubts at all."

*** * * ***

Gus had immediately recognized the voice of the man on the U-boat. When the large submarine had submerged in a rumbling torrent of frothy water a short distance away he had mixed feelings about whether his being left for dead was a good or bad circumstance. Because in the past 15 minutes the water temperature had dropped more than 10 degrees and for the first time he began to shiver. Still, he swam on; short strokes that were slow and sure, like those that a sloth might make if it were an aquatic animal.

For the first couple of hours, he busied himself with a search of the western horizon for any sign of the lifeboats. Every now and then he found some piece of floating wreckage but none large enough to allow buoyancy.

The coolness of the water had, at first, revived his sluggish brain, even causing him to look to the stars for salvation. To aid in his quest, he rolled over onto his back for a few minutes at a time. The Big Dipper was easy enough to find, as was its smaller brother whose tail was bejeweled with the North Star. He squinted to find the summer triangle of Arcturus, Antares and Vega, but then it occurred to him that they would have moved on by this time of night. Even his other favorite three-starred cluster, Vega, Altair and Deneb would not be visible at this late hour but he still searched. There was nothing else to do besides paddle.

One thing he did notice before too long was that his shoulder felt better. The swimming action must have reset the rotator cuff and the muscles tightened, which held it in place. As a result of the rifle accident, the bullet had blown away a small sector of the bony pocket, making dislocations easier when indulging in physical activity. His physical therapist had advised him to constantly work on the pectoral and deltoid muscles, the exercise helping it to stay in place during sports.

When the stars ceased to entertain him, Ginger entered his mind again. To keep his mind active, he acted out their first meeting; her fresh young face, the yellow chiffon dress, the smell of her perfume. He even smiled when the voice of someone at the dance class came to him. The remark had been, "Amazon," a reference to Ginger's height. The name of the man never came to mind, but he was glad that the guy had passed Ginger over for another dance instructor.

Gus never considered himself a Don Ameche-type and tended to shy away from asking women to dance. His true nature came alive in groups, whenever he and his friends joined a table of girls. Then he would let his humor win them over.

Ginger was a beauty and held all the men's attention until she got up and men saw how tall she stood. However, she had jokingly explained to Gus one night that if she could get them to the dance floor then she was in her element. On their first date, they were both more like dance instructor and pupil. A few dates later and he was on the road to becoming a competent dancer, and many of his friends were envious when they saw his new girlfriend.

From thoughts of her face, his mind drifted to the engineering blueprints of the Hamilton-class cutter that was to be his first offshore command. Everyday he would touch her keel and feel the rivets on her hull as metal fabricators shaped the tons of steel into a work of aesthetic beauty. In each area of the ship he saw the faces of the men who would make her into the proud fighting platform that she subsequently became. He saw the foam streaming down her bow and the green shards from the broken champagne bottle on her christening day: *Montauk*, she was called. It was as proud a day for him as the one when Ginger became his wife.

For very few wives, if any, would have let a man have another woman in his life the way Ginger let him indulge himself with the *Montauk*. She would listen to him for hours as he praised the virtues of the ship and her crew, even suffering through reams of engineering that meant nothing to her but, she knew, were important to Gus.

Dawn was fast approaching. Gus' mind puttered away on what he would do in the daytime. He was not hungry but water was a large concern as he would begin to get seriously dehydrated before too much longer.

Suddenly, his head struck something. When he rolled over he saw the coffin-like shape of a chest, and he recognized it as the box for stowing surplus life jackets and flak protectors on the deck of his ship. It was made of one-inch plywood, a container eight-by-four-by-four, and it towered above his prone form.

Gus reached up with his good arm and grabbed the lip. His other followed hesitantly, with the familiar grating feeling that accompanied the stretching of it. He then realized that he would have great difficulty getting over the lip with his Mae West, so he fumbled with the clips and spent the next few minutes getting out of it. Not entirely trusting the box he threw the life jacket inside before making another attempt to pull himself in.

With his flotation device gone, the wash of cold made him shiver again and it was all he could do to keep his hands steady. When he pulled on the lip, the box tipped a bit and made his job a little easier. Inside, he saw there were a few life jackets and, of all things, a grappling hook and rope. With his waist secure on the edge, he reached in and grabbed the metal hook, heaving it over the side in one throw. Then he inched himself into the box and rolled onto his back to keep his spine from hyper-extending.

Once completely inside, he found it dry except for the life preserver he had worn. With so many other ones around he jettisoned this one and began burrowing down until he was covered with the kapok jackets. Then he fell asleep to the rocking motion, his lips in thanks to God for giving him this box.

CHAPTER SEVENTEEN

August 23rd
2217 Atlantic Time

To Wyn, the evening was the best part of a late summer's day. The water was the warmest at this time of the year as evening winds blew from a southerly direction, enabling him to dress lightly when he went out in his kayak.

The large two-man canoe had been modified from a British Army collapsible he found washed up on Ashton last spring. It had a few tears in the rubberized canvas but seemed quite seaworthy. Wyn built a waterproof hatch up front and fortified the bottom for sliding against the sharp rocks of the islands and shoals in the area

While training for the Dieppe raid, he was put on an extensive course designed for cross channel commando raids on German gun emplacements and U-boat pens on the French coast. It was the brainchild of Combined Ops. One of the strategies was to load these collapsible kayaks on motor torpedo boats and then drop them off with their crews toward the French side of the English Channel.

Some forays were made to place mines on ships and were mildly successful, but his was one of many projects which were canceled and shelved. However, with the experience he gained, Wyn knew these small boats as well as he did his own rifle.

If someone, such as his now-deceased great uncle Jimmy, were to have asked him why he was going out tonight with the threat of post-hurricane storms brewing, Wyn would have had to answer that he had an inkling. On hearing that, Jimmy would have understood, as would many of the old-timers who worked the oceans for all their lives. Because, even with the new advances in meteorology, the fishermen on the South Shore still went by the tried and true ways that had seen them safely through many a bad storm. Each one of them stood by their hunches. That was the way it always was.

As he passed the shallows of the shoal his eyes moved toward Raddall Island. He had been listening to the radio reports from there on his short-wave. The Norwegians were still transmitting in code but Wyn was not interested in the content. He was listening because of this inkling. However, nothing seemed out of the ordinary. It was bunch of gibberish, just as it always had been — that is, unless you had the codebook.

He paddled past the northern tip of the island, the darkening skies and growing swells leaving no silhouette. The grip of his hand on the two-bladed paddle was dead center and his exaggerated strokes, needed to get the extra push on his left side, resembled the baton movements of a drum major. To prevent his hand from slipping when the handle got wet he had covered the oar with a piece of old inner tube.

It might have been the growing wind, or his imagination, but he swore he heard voices from the point of Raddall Island. He eased the kayak to the right and as the craft passed the long jutting finger of rocks and he saw a flash, a brief blink of yellow, like a quickly cupped match of someone trying to light a cigarette. Instantly, as he had been trained, he lay flat across the top of the kayak and let it drift.

* * *

"We're supposed to be speaking Norwegian!" scolded the largest of the SS guards.

"I can speak German quite well," chuckled the Norwegian, the man called Swensen. "Much better than your Norwegian, so why don't you take a break and relax?"

"Very well," replied the first, a husky sergeant named Nagel, who sounded as if he was in charge of the platoon. "But Deckler will have our balls if he finds out."

Another voice took up the cue. "Shit on him! What has he done for the Fatherland except make rockets? We sure could have used those rockets at Smolensk when the whole Russian front was collapsing. He just pisses around, wasting valuable time while Germany gets bombed to rubble."

"Shut up, Forst!" the first one replied in a loud whisper. "One more word and I'll have you reported!"

There was a short silence and then the Norwegian spoke. "Now, now, we're all in this together. When we light these things, America will sue for peace and we all can fight the Russians."

"What makes you such an expert, Swensen?" It was the second soldier.

"Oh, I'm definitely not." replied the Norwegian. "But I did my fair share of fighting, *Herr* Forst. Before you Germans landed in Oslo, we were working to discredit the bastard government that was in power and sow seeds of discontent. That was why you landed unopposed."

"Aren't you going to give credit to Göbbels and his Propaganda Ministry?" replied the senior soldier. "You're forgetting, I was one of the first to land in Norway. My grandmother lives there and told me that the newsreels of the bombing of Poland sickened the population."

"Was your grandmother a Norwegian?"

"No, she was Chinese." This brought ripple of laughter. "Of course. On my mother's side I'm Norwegian. That's why I was chosen for this mission."

"What does she think of you, Sergeant?" Forst asked.

There was another bout of silence. Then Nagel said, "I really love the old bear but she told me that Quisling and his bunch were a nest of traitors. I guess that includes you, Swensen."

"Nazism is not the same as Germanism," replied Swensen, ignoring the rebuke. "Nazism replaces the chaos caused by the corruption of ill-suited governments who rob our national purse and quibble about things such as whether or not to keep out foreign nationals. The Germans did not defeat Norway. We true Norwegians asked for help and *Herr* Hitler honored us by sending forces. Together we threw the British back into the sea at Narvik."

"So," Forst said, "how did it feel when Deckler had your fellow countrymen killed, ones with whom you ate, slept and played cards with for all those months?"

Swensen grabbed up a handful of rocks and threw them at the German's feet. "You should talk about such things!" he spat.

"We only kill enemies of the state."

"These men were enemies of *my* state, traitors aiding in fighting all of us!" Swensen's voice, although irritable, sounded confused and unconvincing. Then he added, "When we first rounded them up, Deckler didn't say anything about disposing of them. They were just to have been detained."

Nagel's voice came in after a brief lull. "I think we should be heading back now. Our patrol is almost over."

Without another word they all stood up, and Wyn saw their outlines for the first time. The swells were gaining in height and the dark water raised and lowered him like he was being passed from one gigantic hand to another.

"Hey?" asked Nagel. "What's that out in the water?"

Forst put his hand across his eyes, a useless gesture in the near dark. "It's probably just an old log."

* * *

Wyn pressed his face hard against the rubberized surface of the canvas kayak, so much so the vulcanized smell almost made him gag. He was sure that a shot would ring out next. Maybe he wouldn't hear the shot, just like at Dieppe. He never knew a 75mm shell had hit his landing craft until he woke up in a British hospital.

When it became clear that he had not been discovered, Wyn used his right hand to paddle the sea canoe away from the point and into ocean currents beyond the shoal. In five minutes he would drift far enough away that his silhouette would not be seen when he began using his paddle again.

* * *

Over the babbling of the incoming tide, as the rivulets ran over the rocks, Wyn could still hear the odd laugh from the retreating patrol. He paddled for a minute and then lay flat, his ears listening beyond the natural sounds for any hint that he might have been discovered: most urgently, the sound of a boat engine.

However, none came and, in time, he straightened up and positioned his kayak to round the point again. Going back would be easier because of the tide.

At first, he thought the floating object was a bait box that had swept overboard from a fishing boat during a storm. With a salvager's mind, he quickly appraised its value and whether or not it would be worth towing back. Wyn paddled over to it and pressed down on the lip to look inside. It was half full of life jackets. The stenciling on the side read: US Coast Guard.

Reaching into his forward compartment, he took the end of a rope and lashed it around the wooden handle on an end of the container, using a sheepshank to tie it down. Then he played out the rope so that there would be enough room to allow the stern of the kayak to avoid hitting the salvage en route.

The first few strokes with the paddle were the hardest. He dug the blades in, using his weight to get more torque. Then, just as a locomotive gets its train in motion, the box began to slide through the water, an un-streamlined bulk which bobbed back and forth making the kayak jerk and sometimes stop. More than once during the trip around the shallow shoals, Wyn wanted to cut it free.

Once he was around the point and heading for Ashton Island, the unwieldy barge settled into the current and moved effortlessly along side the kayak. Wyn put down his paddle and pulled the box closer so that he could maintain a modicum of control.

He kept a constant vigil, scanning Raddall Island for any signs that he may have been discovered. To his relief, he saw no lights and heard no boats from that direction.

Twenty minutes later, the keel of the kayak grounded on the sandy crescent and he hopped out and dragged the box onto the shore. As he drew his kayak up on land he thought he heard a noise from the box but dismissed it as someone dropping something on the docks at Port Pleasant, across the calm bay waters.

He positioned the kayak onto a wheeled buggy, which he had designed and built, and then he rolled it up the trail. Once at the top, 100 yards away, he veered left and there stood a low-slung shed, which fit the sea canoe and its dolly. A small door was shut behind and the water raft was now sheltered from all the elements. Then Wyn went home to fetch the tractor and wagon.

Since he had moved every rock on the trail, the tractor and the cart behind moved effortlessly down to the water's edge. He backed it up to the large box and pulled the tow rope around the front of the wagon. Here, a winch had been installed for loads just like this.

With each pull on the handle, a ratchet-type gear inched the box onto the trailer. In less than ten minutes, it had been loaded and Wyn started the tractor for the return trip.

The moon was high overhead now and The Knob was bathed in the silvery glow. When he turned off the engine he was greeted with the jabbering of annoyed black ducks, who were now flocking together to forage for the journey south. In less than a month, Wyn and Wilbur would be building blinds for the fall hunt. But for now, the waterfowl were welcome visitors waiting for their cousins from Labrador and points farther north.

Wyn backed the load into the shed beside his house, directly under the electric light. He fumbled with the switch and, feeling the click, turned around to face the barrel of a large pistol.

"Just stay right where you are," the man said, his voice like a nail scratching wood.

Wyn noticed that the intruder was a big man with a big face and a big gun — a Colt .45, American issue. He was standing up in the wagon and, when Wyn looked beyond the barrel, he saw the khaki uniform and four gold marks on his epaulettes. The man who was ready to kill him was an American naval captain.

After a tense few seconds, in which Wyn thought the American might pull the trigger, his captor finally asked, "Who are you and where the hell am I?" This was followed by a sigh and an off-handed comment. "That is, if you speak English."

"I do," relied Wyn, making no bodily move. Instead, he slowly turned his head around the pistol to get a better look at the man.

"You are on Ashton Island, off the coast of Nova Scotia," Wyn said matter-of-factly. "And I'm a Nova Scotian which, unless things have changed in the past week, makes you and me allies."

Gus stared at his hostage, looking Wyn's muscular body up and down. The missing lower limb registered with him and he slowly lowered his pistol. "I guess I have you to thank for pulling me out of the drink," Gus sighed.

"Actually, I was after salvage," Wyn admitted.

There was an awkward silence between the two men. Both were fatigued and were not embarrassed by their lack of friendly overtures so far. "Here," Wyn finally said, "take my hand."

With Wyn's help, Gus lowered himself to the ground and, for the first time in days, he managed a smile. "I'm Gus Lanton, captain, United States Coast Guard, formerly commander of the USCGS *Montauk*. We were torpedoed early last night about 50 miles off the coast. I must have caught a strong current to get me this far."

"I'm Wyn Parsons," Wyn said, shaking the man's hand. "I farm this patch of the island and help out at the lighthouse. Come on," he said, pointing toward the small house. "I've got some dry clothes. And I'll put some tea on."

"Just a gallon of water would do," sighed Gus.

CHAPTER EIGHTEEN

August 24th
1132 Atlantic Time

"We are two days behind schedule, *Kapitän*."

"That can't be helped. I cannot guarantee the integrity of the system unless my divers complete all the underwater tests."

Colonel Deckler slapped his gloves against his small hand. It sounded like a rifle shot in the small hut. Unlike the two SS guards, whose eyes twitched at the unexpected report, Lothar remained impassive.

"Delays," he sighed, the outburst having suddenly tempered. It was obvious to Lothar that it was more for the benefit of the guards as it was to display his displeasure. Being so far away from home had tempered his fanaticism. The absence of Nazi dogma was bringing out his real persona, which was that of a scientist. These small bursts of anger were meant for show, to remind everyone that the SS was still in charge, not the scientist, Müller, or the U-boat captain.

"You know, Stahl, with each new postponement, I can see Himmler putting another black X on my file."

He then chuckled, a low laugh without any mirth. "So even if the plan succeeds beyond our wildest hopes, I may still be liquidated because of the mere point that I delayed a few days."

The colonel sat down and stared down at a map of Nova Scotia. "Do you think they know we're here?" he asked, changing the subject.

"In my best estimation," replied Lothar, "no, I don't. We have been lucky, but we have also been diligent."

"True," Deckler continued thoughtfully, "but it's absolutely amazing to me that the Canadian authorities did not catch on to our ruse when we informed the Norwegian commander in Lunenburg that the departing crew had been invited to stay on at Port Pleasant as the guests of the town."

"Swensen handled that well," replied Lothar. "The commander in Lunenburg knows him as a compatriot and didn't suspect a thing. The crew is probably still having a good time there and putting it down to their own good fortune."

"Yes, well, if we don't get this project going in the next two days they will be missed," Deckler added, tapping out an American cigarette from its package and passing one to Lothar.

Deckler continued, lighting both his and Lothar's cigarettes. "Himmler is racing against time, and not just because the Allies and the Russians are advancing. Even though the nest of cowards, vipers and technocrats who planned the assassination of the Führer were successfully routed out, there are many others who, at this moment, are trying to seek a separate peace with the Americans and British to avoid falling into Russian hands. These military commanders and scientists may surrender *en masse,* taking away the negotiating tool that we have here. However, if we are successful, we can end the war on favorable terms and then all of us, the Americans, Germans, English and their Aryan allies, can join the fight to destroy Stalin's Slavic hordes."

Lothar was silent. The more Deckler spoke, the more his Nazi roots showed, effectively blotting out the image of the talented scientist that Lothar knew him to be.

"Come, show me how far they are now," he added, pointing down at the chart table. A blueprint was spread out over the chart and he had marked off certain points with red-tipped pins. The top of the sheet of paper read: *Sea Scorpion.*

Lothar studied the torpedo-shaped diagram and pointed to the bottom of it. "Two of my divers are now adjusting the ballast to compensate for the shifting currents. Too much weight, the pod might take in water from the top. Too little and it will wobble, throwing off the aim.

"The electric valves which control the flow of ballast water, in order to tip the pod upright, must be re-calibrated. The trip across the ocean might have jarred them. If the transference of water is too abrupt, the pod might flip upright too quickly and snap the guyline and electric cables."

"Noted," remarked Deckler. "When is the earliest that we can load the fuel?"

"Tomorrow night. Until then, the tide is gentle enough that we can anchor the pods to the ocean floor without a chance of throwing off the settings."

Deckler puffed on his Lucky Strike, his mind doing calisthenics. "Then we load the charges on Three and Four at tonight's land-based launch. Müller and my guards will handle that exercise so you need not be there. Just make sure Beust knows how to raise the pods to the surface so that they can be loaded."

There was a light pause while Lothar considered the plan. Then he asked, "What is wrong with the charges that were loaded in Kiel?"

"Stahl, that is none of your concern," Deckler snapped.

However, his mood quickly corrected itself and he added, with a smile, "I'm just joking. We are loading one of the pod rockets with messages from your old pal, Göbbels. Thousands of leaflets will fly down Wall Street spreading the bad news to New Yorkers that the city that they thought was so safe from the war is now a target, just like Berlin."

Lothar eyed him suspiciously. He wanted to ask another question but his instincts prevented him.

"That settles it," Deckler huffed. "And tonight, while the rockets are being loaded with their charges, Nagel's group will go on a scouting mission of their own to Ashton Island. They will cut the telephone transmission from the island and disable the radio. Then, they will go back tomorrow night and, at dawn when the light is extinguished, take care of the keeper and the others. By the time any one misses the light the next evening, we shall be 300 kilometers to the south. Nagel's men and the other *Kriegsmarine* will take the power boat out to sea and be picked up on schedule by *U-1409* to make their way back to Germany."

Lothar wracked his brain for an understanding of the situation. "Colonel, am I to understand that the lighthouse people are to be liquidated?"

"This is war, Stahl," he shrugged. "We have to take all the precautions we can."

"But they can't hurt us."

"That man with the one arm," Deckler said, puffing deeply on his cigarette. "He has been spotted nosing around the island in his paddle boat."

"Yes, I saw him yesterday afternoon. It's a kayak, an Eskimo boat. He goes out fishing in it and collects lobsters. He's never come close to the island, though."

"Would you like to bet the project on it, Stahl?" Deckler baited. "Is that what your *Onkle Karl* taught you?"

"No, of course not," Lothar replied, suddenly angry with Deckler for bringing in his uncle's name.

"Then, hadn't you better get your men ready to receive the two transports? Isn't that your assignment for this evening?"

* * *

"Swensen, I want you to accompany me over to the lighthouse," Lothar snapped.

The Norwegian balked for a few seconds, then asked. "Who ordered this?"

"Who do you think?" snapped Lothar, walking past him toward the leeward beach.

The two men walked past the steel pillars of the launch-towers, taking in the progress of Deckler's six-man rocket crew. The 30-foot rockets were like two giants at perpetual attention, their series of hoses and electric cabling forming a network of a man-made umbilical cord to the towers.

"Can you imagine it?" Swensen commented, his necked crane upward as he slowed to view the projectiles. "These things will go all the way to Boston, New York, Washington and Norfolk."

Lothar never answered him, preferring to exit the small clearing and get into the forest again. "Come Swensen, before it gets too dark."

When they were past the portal to the thick woods, Lothar suddenly stopped and spun around on the Norwegian. "Swensen," he said, calmly, but his face bathed with a look that frightened the Norwegian. "What happened to the weather station crew?"

"They are in Port Pleasant, as the guest of the mayor. Didn't Deckler tell —"

Lothar's action was swift. He drilled his fist into the man's soft belly, and Swensen doubled over with a sickening groan. Then he dropped to knees and threw up.

"No more!" he pleaded in a choking voice, fearing Lothar was going to strike again. After a minute he reached for a branch and pulled himself upright. He saw no change in Lothar's eyes.

"As you are aware, we arrived two days before you, while you were out settling the pods. Me, Deckler, three of the scientists and the SS guards. We had *Abwehr* information on the identity of the men and their commander in Lunenburg. When I approached the weather station, I told them I was on a ship from England where I served with a Free Norway patrol boat and our ship was docked in Shelburne. When the last man came back from his rounds I pulled my pistol and identified myself as an emissary of Quisling's government. Then Deckler's men came in and took them away for interrogation."

"Where?"

"To Deckler's hut. They were told to go in when their name was called and, when the interview was finished, leave with the guard by the back door to be tied and placed in the storehouse."

"What happened? Tell me!" Lothar glanced around him to make sure no one was lurking in the bushes.

"One by one, they were taken through the hut and led out the back door without being questioned. It was a ruse to keep them calm. Then Corporal Schmidt knifed each one as he came out. Then they were buried."

Lothar shook his head in disgust. "Your own countrymen, Swensen."

"It sickened me," he replied, his voice now a series of light sobs. "They may have been my political enemies, *Kapitän*, but I wouldn't have killed my own people. That Deckler, he's a —"

"Enough, Swensen," Lothar sighed, actually feeling sympathy for the man. In the time to come he might be faced with having to kill some of his own, only face-to-face. "Will you come help me warn the people at the lighthouse?"

"Warn them?" he asked nervously. "What if they escape? What about the rockets?"

"They will fly, Swensen," Lothar replied, a firm tone of certainty in his voice. "My aim is to get the islanders away from Deckler, just until we are safe and the rockets are fired."

The Norwegian nodded, his round, cherubic face brightening. "I will go with you then."

"We'll leave just after we unload the 'milk cows' around midnight. That is when I do my rounds in the boat, and they will never think about following me in the dark."

CHAPTER NINETEEN

August 24th
1146 Eastern Time
Radio Intercept Station
Office of Naval Intelligence (ONI)
Chatham, Cape Cod

"VALKYRIE x
SEA SCORPION/VICTORY
S PLUS 2 x"

"Well, this is the first ULTRA intercept that tells us the Krauts are up to something specific," remarked Vice Admiral Eugene Baker, tapping his Annapolis ring on the pewter ashtray. ONI chief-telegrapher, Ensign Robert Boggs, nodded in agreement, not willing even to twitch lest the admiral from Washington take it as a sign of disrespect. Officers from Washington went in and out of the wireless monitoring station, but never with as much brass on their epaulettes as this one, a big man who hailed directly from the White House Map Room.

"Mr. Boggs," he said, laying the sheet of paper on the desk. "Although you have informed me that I have all of what you know right here in this file, I want you to run over your procedure one more time for the benefit of my ailing memory."

Even though Baker was in his early 50s, Boggs doubted that there was anything wrong with the admiral's ability to ascertain and hold information. In naval talk, he was giving Boggs the chance to remember any bits of information — no matter how minute they were to him — and fit them into his statement.

"Well, sir," he started, pausing for a nervous cough and brushing aside his long brown hair. If he had known that any capital officers were scheduled to arrive at the somewhat casual station, he would have had it cut and worn a proper uniform. The shorts and T-shirt, as well as his smallish nose, made the 23-year-old telegrapher look like a teenager.

"I began hearing these particular transmissions at 2107 on August 10th. The signals were strong so, at first, I estimated them as S5, or originating from a very close location. But after rechecking, I found that the message was a copy of an earlier broadcast originating farther north. After going over several such transmissions, my colleagues and I came to the conclusion that the broadcasts were being picked up by a repeater station, somewhere in S5, and re-broadcast."

"That station being another sub that surfaces at a certain time, picks up the message and then relays it," remarked the admiral.

"Yes, sir," replied Boggs, his voice getting stronger as the interview continued. His nervous blinking of his eyes slowed, revealing the green irises.

"Go on, Mr. Boggs."

"Well, sir, we also concluded that the transmissions were being sent out on a diplomatic B-Bar signal, which told us that this U-boat was sending out diplomatic messages in a high-priority status."

"Yes, that is common practice. Keep going."

"The complete message was sent in three parts, each one lasting barely three minutes in length and separated by a few minutes. This one was the shortest and, as you can see, is just seconds.

"Then at 2131 hours, using standard procedure, we re-transmitted these messages to the US Naval Cryptographic Center in Washington. We received them back at 2243 hours with the request to verify the coding and destination address, which we did."

"Where was the destination address? The BdU in Bernau?"

"No sir, the codings weren't for Dönitz." After four years of tracking U-boats transmissions he was absolutely sure of this.

"Who then?"

"Uh, sir, I'm sure I'm not qualified to say —"

"I just made you qualified," Baker snapped. "Give it your best shot, son."

Boggs took a deep breath and said, "Heinrich Himmler."

"The fucking SS?" Baker blurted, his jowled face quivering for an instant.

Boggs never answered. He wished now that he had kept his speculation to himself. Life had been grand up here at Cape Cod. The operators and technicians were away from the mainstream bustle of a country at war and, in the summer, pretty girls numbered in the hundreds.

To Baker, a disgruntled capital officer who cringed when the names of Halsey, Spruance and MacArthur came up, Washington was too far away from a fleet command. While the others of his generation were mounting up naval victories in the South Pacific, his big sea war was over after US ships pounded northern France before, during, and for several days after the Normandy landings.

Even his fighting Dönitz and being part of beating the U-boats in the Battle of the Atlantic, as challenging a fight as any commander ever had, never captured the public interest as did Coral Sea or Midway. Now, except for a few pesky subs, the war was winding down quickly on the Atlantic Ocean.

Baker's mind tried to wrap itself around the larger picture. He had not reached this high plateau in the Navy for ignoring small details as mere coincidence. On August 15th, he had been briefed by COMINCH — the commander-in-chief — that the British Admiralty had been following the travels of a U-boat they had designated as "LT." The British reports claimed that it was heading toward the US side of the Atlantic and suspected it was on a special mission. As per its usual strategy, the sub was operating under radio silence. There was also a Ghost Track, another sonar reading that might, or might not, be another U-boat traveling in close proximity.

This coincided with a similar tracking by the US Navy of the movements of a U-boat designated by them as "RJ" or "Red Jig." The course was checked and "RJ" and "LT" — called Love Tare — were judged to be two boats on a parallel course. RJ was sunk by its trackers just east of the Grand Banks and turned out to be *U-1229*. This solved the Ghost Track.

Or did it? thought Baker. *U-1229* was a solid contact, not a smear on the screen. *How could a ghostly image suddenly become a sharp contact?* The *U-1229* proved to one of the new Type IXC/40 *Atlantikboot*, a formidable boat that in large numbers could begin the Battle of the Atlantic all over again. *Love Tare might have a partner.*

As Boggs stood waiting for his orders, Baker's mind reeled through reams of information. The longer Baker stewed the more nervous he became. Finally Baker said, "Thank you, Mr. Boggs."

The young ensign hesitated for a moment and then asked, sheepishly, "Sir, this may not be relevant to what I have already told you but a Coast Guard cutter was reported torpedoed two nights ago off Nova Scotia."

Baker stared at Boggs for three seconds and said, "Mr. Boggs, on my watch, everything is relevant."

After the ensign had left, Baker called the COMINCH.

As Boggs sat out on a sand dune and watched the choppy waters, he wracked his brain to come up with the significance of *Valkyrie, Sea Scorpion* and *Victory*.

The Great War was the first conflict where the chain of command was kept informed through the use of radio waves. As this type of communication was far from secure all parties began to use codes to ensure that their information was not being interpreted.

Before the Battle of the Atlantic got into full swing, the German crypto-analytic branch successfully penetrated the British and Allied Merchant Ship (BAMS) code, which wreaked devastating results on Allied shipping through the first years of the war. However, even though there was a significant amount of evidence to prove that the British codes had been compromised, they were not changed until June 1943 — after the Allies had broken the back of the U-boat fleet.

The Germans, on the other hand, began the war with a sophisticated code system using the Enigma machine, an electromechanical device much like a typewriter which was highly resistant to decoding. Before the war started, the Polish cracked the code and, when the eastern European country fell, transferred their information to the British.

At this time, Britain had their Government Code and Cipher School at Bletchley Park, a collection of professional intelligence people, chess champions and academics from all disciplines who became known as ULTRA. They began routinely cracking the Luftwaffe and Army codes but made no headway with the German Navy ciphers until the HMS *Bulldog* captured the *U-110* and, along with it, its code machine and relevant code books.

With each side reading each other's codes, the U-boat war became a game of one-upmanship until late 1942, when the Germans added a fourth rotor to their machine and the Allies became blind again. By April 1943, the Bletchley Park gang had solved the code which set up the biggest U-boat disaster of the war during the next month. However, even with devastating losses, Grand Admiral Dönitz refused to believe that the code had been compromised. The tables had been turned: the Allies finally realizing that their codes had been broken and the Germans believing theirs impregnable.

Boggs never knew this. However, he did know radio technology. And he knew that anyone clever enough to piggyback radio signals was an enemy who was not defeated by a long shot. And a personal emissary of that enemy was under the very patch of water that filled his vision.

CHAPTER TWENTY

August 24th
2134 Atlantic Time

Jesse stared across the table at Gus as if he were a ghost. The famished naval officer had just finished his third bowl of beef stew and was now sopping up the leftover gravy with a chunk of bread. Hunger knew no table etiquette.

"Wyn, we got to be sure about these men before we call the authorities," Wilbur said as he filled his pipe. "It wouldn't do no bit of good to have them arrested only to find out that it was really Norwegian you were hearing instead of German."

Wyn sat back in the chair and looked up at the ceiling for an instant. The small room was made smaller by the fact that, for the first time in ages, Wilbur had pulled down the blinds. He concentrated on the language spoken by the men for the third time. "Wilbur," he said, the front legs of the chair banging down as he leaned forward, "I'd stake my life on it."

Gus finally finished up and joined the conversation. "Mr. Corkum, even if what Wyn says turns out be a misconception, isn't it better to err on the side of caution?"

Jesse took a deep breath and slid into the conversation. "Jan Johansen is no Nazi. He's a Norwegian patriot. I think it's awful that you're all jumping to conclusions because of what Wyn thought he heard. He admits he doesn't understand German."

"*Much* German, Jesse," corrected Wyn. "I did study enough of it in commando training to learn common words and phrases."

"How about Norwegian?" she countered.

"Well, I'm not very well versed on that, Jesse," he admitted.

"Then how can you say it wasn't Norwegian?"

Wyn finally threw up his arms and said, "All I'm asking is to have them checked out. One phone call. Is that too much caution?"

"Miss Corkum," Gus added, "I came over here to report in, to let my people know I'm okay. I can place the call so that, if they are truly Norwegians, they'll think it was because of my suspicions."

"Well," Jesse shrugged, "I guess I wouldn't mind it done that way."

"That sounds fine by me," Wilbur said, reaching for the phone. He cranked the handle three times and then put it to his ear. Looking puzzled, he tried the procedure again. After a few more seconds, he said, "That's funny, the phone's dead."

Jesse took it from his hand and listened. Her expression told the rest that Wilbur's first words were true. "Maybe the underwater cable's damaged," she said, calmly.

"If that were so, Missy," Wilbur answered, "the electric lights would have gone out and I would have had to start the back-up generator by now. They're both run along the same line, you know."

Suddenly, everyone was quiet, their combined hearing power straining for outside sounds.

"Everyone stay here," Wyn cautioned as he stood up. "I'm going to take a look."

"I'll come with you," Gus piped.

"Fine," answered Wyn. "Wilbur, where's your duck gun?"

Wilbur left the room for a few seconds and then returned with the double barrel and a box of shells. Wyn shoved two of the paper cartridges in the breech and snapped it shut. Then, cradling the gun in the crook of his left arm, shoved a dozen more in his pockets.

"Aren't you being overly dramatic?" Jesse asked, as she watched Wyn gear up. Wyn just put his finger up to his lips and signaled her to stop talking.

Everyone was still, listening for the slightest creak. Finally, after three minutes of silence, Wyn whispered, "Jesse, you and Wilbur lock the doors. Don't let anyone in.

"Wilbur, do you have a Verey pistol in the storage room?"

"Yah, and lots of flares."

"Go get it and wait up on the upstairs landing. If you hear a shot, open the window and fire off all the flares you have in the direction of town."

"What if you don't come back?" he asked.

"Okay, if we're not back in 15 minutes, fire them off anyway."

Jesse tried to say something to Wyn before he grabbed the door handle but her mouth was suddenly dry with fear. Wilbur took her arm and led her to the room behind the kitchen.

Wyn lifted up the trap door to the root cellar. In the rocky ground, it was only five feet high at most. Wyn warned Gus to keep low. Gus took the flashlight from Wyn and began climbing down the steps. As Wyn stepped down he felt a hand on his left shoulder. A frightened Jesse looked down at him and said, "Please be careful." Wyn patted her hand and smiled and then lowered the trap door.

In the cellar, Wyn pointed the way to the outer door and they lifted up the crossbar. Then he turned off the light. Gus drew his pistol and nodded that he was ready.

Once outside, the lighthouse beam was like a giant sun. They scurried along the dark shadow of the house into the bushes to hide. After a few minutes of scanning the area, Gus picked out something beside the house. He pointed at the movement and Wyn sidled over to get a better look. Three figures were huddled under the front room window, the same spot from where Wyn and Gus had just exited. With each passing of the light they saw the intruders more clearly. They were wearing dark clothes and toques — and they had pistols.

"They don't look too friendly," Wyn whispered as he slipped back in beside the naval officer.

"What's your plan?" asked Gus, his voice like a low drone.

"Well, there seems to be only three of them," replied Wyn in a low voice. "I'll flank them to the right and post a challenge. If they don't drop their weapons, start pulling the trigger."

"Check," Gus replied. The warm meal had revived him, somewhat, but sleep was what he needed the most right now, not a fight.

Wyn slipped away and left the big man watching the silent figures. They were obviously waiting for a signal to go into the house. He got around behind them and crawled along a deer path to the edge of the clearing. The intruders were 30 feet past that point — no problem for a full choke 12 gauge with goose shot. He gently opened the breech to check his load and clicked it shut. Pulling back the hammers, he slowly stood up and waited for the light to pass.

"Hands up!" he yelled, causing the men to spin around quicker than he expected. A fusillade of shots rang out and bullets zipped by his head. The shotgun kicked twice into his right shoulder. Then all was quiet.

Wyn waited for the light to pass again and, when the beacon lit up the yard, he saw three lumps on the ground, none of them stirring. "Gus?" he called out in a loud whisper as he reloaded the shotgun.

"Check," was the reply and, in a few seconds, Gus was standing beside him. He thumbed the magazine release and cupped the clip in his palm, checking his remaining ammunition. Five bullets were gone, their reports lost in the loud shotgun blasts.

Gus snapped the magazine back in and they cautiously made their way over to the downed men, all the while searching the area for other intruders. Wyn turned one of them over and saw the man was one of the "Norwegians." He pulled at the neck of the man's bloody sweater and the steely markings of the SS came into view.

"Some Norwegians," Wyn breathed.

"I don't believe it," sighed Gus. "Hitler's boys, here?"

Both men heard the shuffling of rocks at the same time and hit the ground. A shot rang out and missed Gus by inches. Without another word, they scampered behind the house and another bullet hit the ground not far from Wyn's foot. Knowing full well they were being outflanked they raced for the woods again. A short time later they heard the report of a flare gun and saw the incandescent pink light.

Then there was another shot.

* * *

Jesse and Wilbur heard the fusillade of shots and scrambled upstairs with the flare gun. Shoving the window open, Wilbur pointed the Verey pistol over the tops of the trees and fired. The next thing he knew his chest was on fire and he fell back. Jesse prevented her father from hitting the floor but had no clue as to why he had suddenly slumped. Then, in the surrealistic glow of the pink flare she saw the dark stain on his chest.

"No, Daddy!" she cried, ripping open his shirt to reveal the dark arterial blood pouring out of a small hole in his sternum. She placed her hand on top of the source of the blood and tried to stem it by sticking her thumb in the hole. "No, you can't do this!"

Wilbur looked up, a puzzled look on his face. "You know it's funny, Missy," he said calmly. "Those bastards never got me in the last war so I guess this is my time."

"Don't say that!" Jesse bawled, "I can fix this . . . I can fix you!"

When she looked back into Wilbur's face, it was relaxed and his eyes were set, as if looking at a cloud well above her.

"No, no, no," she whimpered, wrapping her arms around him.

"Miss Corkum?" The voice was familiar.

She turned around to see Lothar walking toward her.

***

The flurry of shots surprised Lothar and Swensen as their boat slid against the beach. In the next instant, they were running toward the house with their pistols drawn. There, they saw Nagel and three guards stalking the light keeper's house.

More shots rang out and, suddenly, the area that used to be in the shadow of the lighthouse was lit up like daylight. As he rounded the house he saw a guard raise his pistol and fire.

"Stop!" he shouted, bringing his hand down hard on the man's arm. The pistol flew from the startled guard's hand and he grabbed the spot where he had been struck and began rubbing it. Another figure came out of the shadows and Lothar brought his gun up.

"What are you doing?" the man demanded. It was Sergeant Nagel. His clothes were dark and he wore a dark woolen cap on his head.

"Why are you shooting?" Lothar demanded. "These people have no guns!"

"No guns?" shouted Nagel. "Tell that to Forst, Schmidt and Lang. They're lying dead around the side of the house!"

Lothar ignored him for a moment and looked up at the window. There was no one there. In the next instant, he skipped up to the door of the house and, finding it locked, smashed the small pane of glass and opened the lock. He immediately dropped to his knees with his pistol ready to fire, but no one challenged him in the empty kitchen. Then he heard whimpering from upstairs. Climbing up carefully, he paused again to search for would-be assailants. There, on the landing, was Jesse holding her father's body.

"Miss Corkum?"

Jesse raised her eyes and regarded him for a moment. Then she returned her gaze to her dead father and began to cry hysterically.

***

"What did you think you were doing, Stahl?" barked Deckler, walking briskly up the path toward him. He had just inspected the bodies of his three men. Lothar never bothered to get up. He just sat on the step keeping an eye on Jesse. In her grief-stricken state, she had allowed Lothar to take his body downstairs.

"Nothing." he sighed, "Your men had already done it by the time I got here."

"Done what?" yelled Deckler. "Three of my men are blasted to shreds and you have nothing to say?"

Lothar stood up and faced Deckler, his eyes tired but still menacing. "I prevented your thugs from shooting a woman. So if that's what I did, then, that's what I did, Colonel Deckler!"

"I have told you many times, Stahl, you have no right interfering with SS business!"

"You mean murder," replied Lothar, watching Nagel's right hand, which rested on his black holster. "You murdered the Norwegians and you planned to murder these people. And I see you partially succeeded."

Deckler watched the areas which lit up when the light came around. "Any more interference from you, Stahl, and you will suffer the consequences!"

Suddenly, the rage in him increased and he threw his gloves to the ground. Pulling his Walther PPK, he pointed it at Lothar and said, "Your *Kriegsmarine* are on board the boat. What's to stop me from ending your meddling right now?"

Lothar seemed unperturbed by the pistol barrel. Even the maniacal look on the slender face of the officer did not make him flinch. "Colonel," he finally said, "do you know how a lighthouse works?"

"What do you mean?" Deckler snapped, holding the pistol steady. "Who cares about what that stupid thing does?"

"Oh, nothing," sighed Lothar, looking up at the turning lamp mechanism atop the tower. The mechanical noises became noticeable as they watched the revolving lens.

"It's just that in a half hour the gearing has to be rewound and the lamp oil checked. That's not too hard, but tomorrow night someone will have to light it up again and that takes a few skills. Skills, I might add, that the SS may, or may not, possess.

"And if that lamp doesn't light on schedule, people are going to start snooping around, people with airplanes and guns."

Deckler lowered his pistol. "I suppose you know how to operate this thing?"

"Why do you think I spent so much time over here?"

The next motion was so swift that no one expected it. Lothar grabbed the gun from Deckler's hand and then shoved it against the startled man's throat. With his other hand, he grabbed Deckler's head and wrenched it back. Nagel and the two other guards pulled their pistols and cocked them.

"Go ahead, sergeant," Lothar spoke through clenched teeth. "Shoot me, but I can still blow his head off!"

"Put your guns down!" pleaded Deckler. There was a reluctant pause and then three guns hit the ground.

"That's right, Deckler. You be a good Nazi and save your own hide, just like you bastards do in Germany while the Allies are bombing the hell out of our homes. If Hitler goes down, we all go down, is that what you think? Purify the master race by destroying our country?"

"What do you want?" asked Deckler, his voice strangled from the barrel in his throat.

Lothar began to laugh. "Want? Want?"

Then his voice became as cold as a tomb. "I want to do my job without you and Fripp, and the rest of your kind bothering me."

"Agreed," Deckler breathed, trying to swallow.

"I'm not finished yet," Lothar growled. He spun Deckler around and shoved the gun up under his nose. "When the rockets have been fired, I'm going to find you, wherever you are, and hang you up by your balls." Lothar let that thought sink in to Deckler's mind. Even in the cool breeze, the man was sweating profusely.

Lothar added, "Until then, here is what we are going to do. We are going to call a truce. I stay here and operate the lighthouse one more night. Beust will be waiting for my signal and then, just before dawn tomorrow, I will go out to his boat and continue the mission. Whatever you do with *your* rockets is up to you. Agreed?"

"Agreed!" breathed Deckler.

Lothar shoved him away as Deckler grabbed his smarting nose. He said and did nothing. With the U-boat skipper holding the gun he did not want to exacerbate the situation.

"Get out of here," Lothar spat. "I will send all communication through Beust. Until then, you and I need not talk. If you want to get word to me use the Aldis lamp or send Nagel here."

Lothar then regarded the sergeant and said, "You're not a bad sort, Nagel, if you took off that black uniform."

Without another word, he popped the clip from Deckler's gun and threw the Walther back to him. After he had holstered it, Deckler said, "You know that you are finished back in Germany?"

"We all are," remarked Lothar, unable to mask the sadness in his voice. "The only difference is, your kind doesn't know it yet."

CHAPTER TWENTY-ONE

August 25th
0829 Atlantic Time

Dawn came to Ashton Island in a shroud of gray as a fog bank moved into the South Shore. The intended tropical storm had swung northward and had missed Nova Scotia, pushing up a thick mass of mist and large waves.

It was also noisy. It seemed that a small herd of migrating harp seals had chosen the seaward side of the Knob to lie over from the storm. Their barking echoed off the lighthouse tower and outbuildings, and the din was a fitting soundtrack to bury a man whose whole life revolved around the ocean.

The lithe, muscular Swensen began digging the grave at first light, picking away at the large chunks of granite that were mixed in with the gravel. Wilbur's father had foreseen the need for burial space on the island and had made provisions for it by blasting out an area on the point just over the ridge from the Knob. He did not want to waste the precious dirt necessary to grow food so that the occupants of the island could have a final resting place.

Wilbur's grave was dug right beside the fresh one that held his wife, Lottie. Beside her were Wilbur's father, mother, and grandfather. Off to the side was a small one belonging to a pet dog, one which died when Jesse was nine. At the time, the interment in the family plot had lessened her grief.

Lothar had stayed with Jesse until she had fallen asleep. Then he had wrapped Wilbur's body in a sheet of canvas and, in good sailor's fashion, had sewn it up as he would for the body of a dead crewman. In his eyes, Wilbur Corkum, or any other man who dedicated his life to the preservation of others in peril on the sea, deserved a funeral befitting that of a naval officer.

"Should we go get his daughter?" asked Swensen, tossing the shovel up over the side of the grave.

"No, with the pills I gave her, she will sleep for a long time."

Lothar leaned over and grabbed the legs of the body and pushed them over to Swensen. The Norwegian slid the body into the grave and then pulled himself out.

The two of them stood over the shrouded figure and doffed their caps. Amid the quarreling of the seals they said silent prayers in their own languages, prayers that sailors in their respective countries had been saying over the graves of their own for centuries.

* * *

"Where do you think Parsons went?" Swensen asked, nervously looking over his shoulder. The seals had gone out to gorge themselves on mackerel and there was a ghostly silence to the place.

"He's on the island somewhere," replied Lothar. "His sea canoe is still in his shed and all the boats are accounted for. I doubt if he could swim far in that cold water with one hand."

"But where can he be? The *Kriegsmarine* have searched the whole island and there's no sign of him."

"He's a smart operator," Lothar said. "Wilbur told me that Parsons was a former commando who was wounded on a raid in France."

"So," sighed Swensen, "we are up against a bloody hero."

"That part is not necessarily true. It seems that the Canadian Army believes him a coward. Supposedly, he ran from battle and was thrown out of his unit after his arm healed."

"Do you believe that?"

"Eyes tell a lot about a man, Swensen," Lothar replied. "And if that is so, I think Parsons would have made a good U-boat commander."

Lothar kicked at a few tufts of grass, a sudden nervousness coming over him. "Did you see the bodies of Deckler's men?"

"They were blown apart by shotgun blasts."

"Yes, well I checked them over before we loaded them into the boat," Lothar continued. "Two appeared were killed by a shotgun. But one of those men, and the third, were hit with bullets from another source."

"So, you think Parsons was not alone?" Swensen replied, sharing Lothar's misgivings.

"You heard the shooting. It lasted barely two seconds. The man has only one arm. He couldn't have fired the shotgun and then drawn a pistol, ran, and fired five pistol shots from another direction, all in that amount of time."

Lothar put his hand in his jacket pocket and pulled out five brass shells. "I picked these up a good ten meters from where I found the shotgun shell casings. There's definitely a second man on the island and he could be an American."

"All that from some shells, *Kapitän*?"

Lothar held up one of the brass objects. "A .45 caliber shell. Pistol. United States officers' gun. The British and Canadians use Webleys. It's doubtful that Wilbur would have had one, nor Jesse. They're islanders. They have guns for birds and deer."

"But what would the Americans be doing here?"

"There's just the one, or we'd all be dead and Raddall would be crawling with Allied troops by now."

One of the *Kriegsmarine*, a bearded youngster, came up to Lothar and saluted. "*Kapitän*, we have searched the whole island and all of the buildings. There's no sign of the man. As you have requested, there are men watching all the trails and three more are guarding the man's house."

"Thank you, Karl," Lothar replied. "Tell them to keep sharp. The man we seek is extremely dangerous.

"Is the woman awake?" he asked.

"No sir, she's still fast asleep. The drugs you gave her were very strong."

* * *

Heinrich Müller was a small man who wore a lab coat and round spectacles. Seated in the small boat with two burly *Kriegsmarine* guards, he looked as if he were a child going out for a picnic on one of the other islands. At 37, he had never been out on the open ocean before and, while some of the others had been so terrified during the trip across the sea by U-boat and had to be sedated regularly, he sat calmly, keeping his mind busy with tasks, like going over propulsion tables for the project. Müller was one of Wernher von Braun's most capable assistants, a man whose whole life revolved around rockets.

If there was one thing that Müller knew during his long tenure at Pennemünde, it was that Deckler, although a competent researcher, was not to be trusted. He had witnessed the man's rages and his having ordered more than a few of the slave workers executed. Müller himself had also sat in jail waiting for the hangman's noose while von Braun's friends sought to free their associates. As he said to himself on more than one occasion, "When a man has resigned himself to die, a chemical change comes over his body. After that, he is forever calm. From then on he fears nothing."

So there was no anxiety in him when he asked Deckler if he could visit Lothar to finalize the fueling of the pods. The colonel, rather than eyeing him suspiciously, gave him permission and a time limit for the meeting. That was the extent of it. After all, Deckler remembered the frightened little man that he had arrested in Pennemünde with von Braun and the others.

Lothar sipped his tea as he watched the motor launch ride the large waves toward the rocks. He and Deckler had agreed that any contact with the island would be on the seaward side and out of sight of the mainland. This meant that his men had to receive a bow line from the rolling craft and haul it in over the slippery, seaweed-covered boulders. Then they had to secure it tightly lest the waves begin to ram it up against the rocks.

Müller shook off an offer of assistance from one of the sailors and stopped when his feet touched the largest of the boulders. He spoke briefly with one of the men and then headed up to the lightkeeper's house. After a polite knock, Müller walked in.

"Good morning, Heinrich," greeted Lothar. "I got your message."

"Good morning, Lothar," he replied, placing a briefcase on the kitchen table. His small head moved in rapid jerks like that of a sparrow as he inspected the room.

"Don't worry, Heinrich," Lothar chuckled, "Deckler does not have eyes or ears here."

Satisfied, the small man sat down on the chair and opened the briefcase. Leafing through a sheaf of papers he handed Lothar a document. "Look at this," he said, firmly.

Lothar read it through once, noting the dates and the official stamps of some officials he had never heard of before. After reviewing it again, he shrugged and looked up at Müller, whose bird-like face was set in a frown.

"Now, read the name at the very bottom of the page."

"Himmler?" asked Lothar. "So?"

"So, Lothar, this means that the contents of what I have in this briefcase have been approved at the highest levels."

Lothar shook his head slightly. He was a military man and did not like guessing games. This academic man, so skilled and learned in his field, was trying his patience with his condescending barbs.

"Look, Heinrich," he growled, "I have had a very bad couple of days and I haven't the time for this. Say what you came here to say."

The scientist nodded and retrieved another paper from the binder. "What I hold here pertains to the shipment we received from the submarine the other night."

"They were heavy boxes, that's for sure," Lothar interjected, now mildly interested.

"The heaviness was mostly due to the lead lining. It is used to protect the handlers from the effects of the cargo." Again Müller looked around the room anxiously.

"Lothar, have you ever heard of a special program we had up in Norway?"

"No."

"Well, before the war, a Danish scientist named Niels Bohr had set up a heavy water facility to produce an unstable compound to be used for the making of a highly destructive substance. When Germany took over the country, our scientists inherited the facility and began to produce the material for our own use.

"Unfortunately for them, Norwegian saboteurs destroyed the plant and all subsequent shipments. Their best estimates are that it will take Germany two years to get their program back on track."

"What has all this got to do with us?"

"The Japanese efforts have gone on unhindered and they are giving us some of their compound."

"Are you saying," asked Lothar, the exasperation evident in his voice, "that we are borrowing material from Japan to make this stuff?"

"Partly, Lothar," the nervous man replied. "One of the main concerns of this material is that it is highly poisonous. That is why it was packed in lead crates. If exposed to the air currents, it can infect a wide area in a matter of hours, causing sickness and death, depending how long one is exposed."

Lothar glanced at the window to Raddall Island and then back to the scientist.

"This is to be the payload for rockets, not explosives nor propaganda leaflets, right?"

"Yes Lothar," he sighed, looking like a tired Chihuahua.

Lothar stood up and sauntered into the small bedroom where Jesse was sleeping. He watched her for a few seconds as if trying to sort out his feelings for the Canadian girl, then he returned to the kitchen.

"Heinrich, why are you telling me this?"

The scientist looked down at his clenched hands as Lothar noticed the sweat on his forehead and bald pate. "Lothar, like von Braun and the rest of my colleagues, I am an engineer dedicated to the development of rocketry. When I first joined the group we were trying to make a rocket to reach the moon, not to bomb London. Now the fruits of our hard work are being used to kill people. None of us, not even you, a U-boat commander, are that callous.

"When this is all over, and it will be soon," he breathed, "I want to be a part of a new Germany dedicated to the peaceful exploration of the heavens. If we launch these vile weapons on the United States, Germany will be finished."

"Yes," agreed Lothar, "the Americans will double their bombing campaign and flatten every square inch of our country. Surrender will come at a high cost."

"It's much worse than that, Lothar," Müller said, his voice now trembling. "I know through my sources in Sweden that the Americans are very close to developing a bomb made of this material, one with the destructive capability to level an entire city."

The ring in Lothar's ring spun rapidly as he pondered the scientist's words. "Heinrich, this means if the rockets are allowed to fly …"

Müller stood up and dramatically grabbed Lothar's hand. The U-boat man had never seen him exhibit so much emotion before. "Berlin will disappear from the map of Europe. And their vengeance might not stop with one city."

CHAPTER TWENTY-TWO

August 25th
0921 Eastern Time
"ULTRA" Radio intercept,
Office of Naval Intelligence

Vice Admiral Eugene Baker read the transcript in private, having dismissed Ensign Boggs as soon as he had arrived with it. In this operation there was no chain of command. Boggs was the telegrapher and Baker was the ear of Franklin Roosevelt.

The communiqué was good, but only half good. *U-1229*, the *Atlantikboot* dubbed "RJ," had been successfully sunk by US Naval forces just east of the Grand Banks. The message stated:

> "TWO OFFICERS AND ONE PROPAGANDIST AMONG 41
> P/S FROM LOVE EASY x C.O. LOST x YOUR 1279 PARA
> 4 x LOVE TARE HEADING BAFFLING BUT BEST GUESS
> IS HE IS APPROACHING ST JOHNS AREA x"

Baker rapped his ring against the glass ashtray a few more times and then flipped the switch on the intercom. The smooth voice of Bing Crosby wafted through the tiny speaker. "Peg, could you send Ensign Boggs back in here?"

Boggs entered the room and saluted the admiral. The young ensign was wearing a neatly pressed khaki work uniform and tie, having shed the shorts and light denim shirt after his first meeting with Baker.

"This doesn't make the situation any better, Ensign," he growled, as if it were Boggs' fault that there were still two powerful subs heading toward American waters. "But you can bet Sixteen-Z will have a field day with this bunch when they bring them back home."

"Sixteen-Z, sir?"

Baker studied the young man for a few seconds and then said. "Look Mr. Boggs, you don't have clearance for this stuff, but since we're working together I'll authorize it here and now.

"Soon after their capture, all prisoners of war are interrogated, some more than others. ONI's Op Sixteen-Z deals with extracting information from them that we deem vital to national security. These U-boat sailors will go directly there. Unfortunately, time is not on our side and we might get a surprise from the Germans still out there before our guys get set up for interrogation."

Baker began tapping his ring again. "Now here's what's happening out there," he said — not to Boggs but to clarify his own memory. "Our boys are combing the area around Newfoundland. The Canadians have got every available aircraft flying, as do we, and we've also got the naval airship squadrons off Maine on full patrol.

"Mr. Boggs," he said, cracking his ring one last time on the ashtray, "there's got to be a reason, a few coincidences that might add up to a lead. So, I want you to go over all the intercepts again and see if a pattern formulates. That is, use your intuition, son, and see if we can't find those boats before Himmler gets a chance to unleash something ugly on us."

Then he slapped the intercom switch and the crooning of Crosby wafted through again. "Peg, get me Washington."

* * *

"Okay, Gus, it's time," said Wyn, shuffling into position. The dank basement smelled like moldy cement. In the blackness the illuminated radium face on his watch was like a large firebug. "Remember, if I don't come back before first light, you go to Plan B."

"Check." Gus replied. Suddenly, Wyn felt the butt of a pistol in his hand. "Take this."

"Thanks," Wyn replied, tucking it into his belt.

Gus struck the match and the small basement room became a bright yellow. Wyn reached up and carefully loosened one of the bricks on the top of the wall. When he nodded, Gus extinguished the flame and Wyn went to work extracting the stone block. A small scuffing noise signaled the block was free and Gus could reach up to help Wyn put it down. Then he repeated the process with the second one.

Wyn then felt for the shelf with his right foot and tested it again. When he knew it would hold him, he pushed down hard on his right leg and worked his torso through the small opening. Two minutes later, he was gone. Gus lifted the blocks back up and painstakingly put them back in their spot.

The narrow area that Wyn squeezed into was an old crawlspace built by the light keeper that was here before Wilbur's family came. The tunnel had been a trough to hold the footings of the first lighthouse, a wooden structure which contained the living quarters as well. Rather than tear the tunnel out, and not having the means to blast out a basement as the foundation for his new house, Wilbur's grandfather simply built the new structure on the old walls and extended it over the ground for 40 feet. That was why the house had such a small basement.

After the battle, Wyn had led Gus under the house and into the ditch. When the guards shone their lights underneath, it appeared as one dark, rocky area, with no sign of the long trench. Lothar had found the trap door and checked the cellar, but found nothing. Then, after all activity around the house died down, Wyn pulled the bricks out and led Gus into the basement. The opening had been made there for the dog to come in and out without it actually coming inside. Lottie never allowed animals in the house. And now that there was no dog, it was simply bricked up.

Getting to the kayak shed was not difficult. The guards were still nosing around, but not moving very quickly, seemingly tiring of the hunt when they surmised that the quarry was gone. Wyn quickly extracted the kayak buggy, thankful for having oiled the hinges on the shed and buggy wheels of the small, flat wagon. He gently took the canoe off the buggy and rolled it back in, shutting the door.

Then, he lifted the boat and moved a shoulder underneath, using his forearm stump to steady it. Pushing his large thighs to their maximum endurance he waddled down to the waters' edge under the shadows of the moon's glow.

* * *

It was almost 2200 hours when he crept into town. Alex Lloyd, the Mountie for the area, would be back in Shelburne by now. Wyn looked down the street and saw a light on in Sady's store. Trotting to the gate, he went around back and knocked lightly on the door.

A light came on and the door began to open. In his excitement, Wyn said "Sady, am I ever glad you're up. I've got to use your phone to —" He stopped in mid-sentence. For standing in front of him was Laura, in her nightdress.

"Wyn!" she cried, her eyes darting back into the house. "What are you doing here?"

"Where's Sady?" he breathed, his heart pounding rapidly.

"Didn't you know?" she asked, clutching her clothes tightly around herself. When she studied Wyn, she saw his clothes were dirty and torn. "We bought the store from Sady a month ago. She's gone to live with her sister in Shelburne."

"Who is it?" a man's voice demanded.

"Uh, just someone wantin' late groceries, 's'all." she replied nervously. "I'll handle it."

"Tell 'em to bugger off and come back at a decent hour," the man's voice replied.

"Sure!" she replied. Then to Wyn, she said, "you've got to go. If he finds you here, I don't know what'll happen."

Wyn regarded her face. It seemed older than the last time he saw her and her eyes were tired and wrinkled. His heart sagged for a moment, as he sought and then failed to find the soul of the feisty girl he used to chase in the park, the woman who, up to this very second, had been the one true love of his life.

"I'll go now," he mumbled. Without another word, Wyn turned around and began to walk into the darkness toward the gate.

Behind him he heard a commotion and a man's voice. "How many times have I told you not to go to the door after dark? Do want us to get robbed? Huh?" Then Wyn heard a loud smack and a whimper from Laura. But he kept on walking.

It was a few seconds later when he heard Barry Finer say, "Well, if you're not going to listen to me then you can listen to my cane again."

The sickening slap was followed by a louder whimper and plea. Turning around, Wyn saw the silhouette of Finer's cane going up and down among the moths and flying insects bobbing around the dim porch light. Laura was lying across the banister, trying to protect herself from the blows.

It took Wyn seconds to bound across the lawn and up the stairs. He caught the cane in mid-air with his good hand and, glancing down in the soft light, saw Laura's face and it sickened him. Laura's right eye was already swollen shut and a trickle of blood ran down her face.

Finer stared incredulously at Wyn, and then a sly grin came to his face. It was plumper than it had been a year ago and the smell of rum on his breath was overpowering. "Well, well, it's the gimp and he wants to play," he chuckled.

Wyn never replied. He simply ripped the cane out of Finer's hand and began whipping him with it. When a surprised Finer tried to recover, Wyn slid a leg behind him and shoved his large torso backward. The big man fell over the stair railing and onto the dirt path, a seven-foot drop, sounding as if a sack of potatoes had hit the ground.

As he tried to get up, Wyn was on top of him, pinning him down with his knees. He brought the cane around and caught Finer full in the throat. A moment later, Wyn dropped the cane and drove his fist into Finer's solar plexus. There was a gasp of air as Finer began having convulsions, making gurgling noises as he thrashed on the ground.

Suddenly, Wyn was aware of someone pounding on his back. It was Laura. "What are you doing to him, you animal?" she yelled.

Wyn spun around, grabbed one of her arms and said, "Laura, are you okay?"

Laura's swollen eyes appraised him as if he were a demon. There was no recognition in her mind of the boy who had been a constant companion for two years. Suddenly, her puffed eyelids widened and she broke free of him. Before he could calm her down, she ran into the dark street and cried, "Help us!"

People began running from their houses and Wyn could hear the slapping of feet on the boardwalk. "What are you doing, Parsons?" someone yelled out of the darkness, recognizing him under the porch light.

"I need to use a telephone, that's all," he pleaded, seeing Laura's crazed face under the street lamp. Bloodied and contorted in anger, he recognized the unmistakable sheen of hate in her eyes. Regaining her composure, she slowly walked over to her husband who was now still.

Then they heard Laura scream, a bloodcurdling yell that shocked him even more than her attitude. "Barry's dead! Wyn killed him!"

A stunned Wyn moved backward. Behind him, he felt people moving away in fear, people that he had known for years but, at this moment, never knew at all. And above all the clamoring were Laura's pitiful wails.

"I'm sorry about Barry," Wyn pleaded. "It was an accident. Someone call the Mounties. Tell them that there are Germans on the island. Get them to phone the navy or the air force."

Suddenly, Wyn felt a blow on his back and turned to see Bob Jarvis, his old baseball coach, preparing to swing a baseball bat again. "Yah, you see Germans all right," he shouted, threatening Wyn with the wooden bat. "All those ones you run from!"

"Please, Bob! It's true."

Jarvis yelled. "Let's get 'im!"

Wyn felt a rock hit his right shoulder, a glancing blow that stung. Another one just missed his head, and soon there was a volley of them. Fearing for his life, Wyn ran down the street and took refuge behind a tree.

"He's hiding behind that elm tree across the street!" the old coach yelled, moving in that direction. As the crowd approached him, Wyn stepped out with the .45 raised in his hand. They all stopped dead. "Cripes, he's got a gun!" Jarvis gasped.

"Yes, I do, Bob," Wyn replied, calmly raising the pistol. "And I'd shoot as soon as I'd look at you."

Wyn cocked the gun and the frightened crowd slowly backed away. "Now, go get the Mounties. Tell them I'll be waiting for them by the lighthouse! And they better bring lots of guns 'cause they'll never take me alive!"

With that the crowd noises stopped and they stared at him in horror. Wyn Parsons, once the golden boy of hockey and baseball in Port Pleasant was, in their eyes, a psychopathic killer.

CHAPTER TWENTY-THREE

August 25th
1722 Eastern Time
Radio Intercept Station
Office of Naval Intelligence

Vice Admiral Eugene Baker whistled *The Yellow Rose of Texas* for the third time as he waited for Ensign Boggs to arrive. Although slightly out of tune, there was a happy lilt to it and, during the last chorus, he swung it, putting in a jazz rhythm.

However, his jovial mood was a very recent occurrence. Until two hours ago, he had resigned himself to the fact that he would have to fly back to Washington and report that Love Tare would have to stay in a "Remains Open" state for the present. That was the designation that the British Admiralty had given the status of the rogue U-cruiser which meant, in layman's terms, that "We haven't a clue as to its whereabouts."

The searches had revealed nothing of Love Tare or the ghost image. And since President Roosevelt had an emotional attachment to northern Maine — because of the fact that his summer residence was at Campobello — the hunt for Love Tare was as important to the President as Patton's push through central France, and Baker knew this did not bode well for future fleet promotion.

However, Boggs changed all of that. He had sent him a note stating that, at 1600 hours, a Pan American Airlines clipper had sighted a submarine just south of Great Round Shoal Channel, seven miles east of Great Point, Nantucket. COMINCH had been notified next and two 83-foot Coast Cutters and two 110-foot sub-chasers were ordered to the area. In addition, a US Naval airship from ZP-11 Squadron out of South Weymouth was proceeding in that direction. The K-25, patrolling 60 miles to the northeast, was at the scene first and had surprised the U-boat on the surface.

Baker looked up when he heard the familiar knock on the door. "Come in Mr. Boggs," he said, his voice sounding lighter than it had been in days.

"Sir, here is the follow-up report on Love Tare."

Baker took the paper from Boggs hand and a wide grin lifted his jowls. "We got the sonofabitch, Bobby!" he bellowed, banging his ring against the ashtray. "Two down and one to go!"

"That is terrific, sir," grinned Boggs, glad to see this side of the bearish admiral. Re-reading the report, the young officer added, "There is no mention of a Yankee Search in this report, sir. Shall I send one now?"

Baker's smile receded and was slowly replaced by a more serious countenance. This mood of concentration lasted about 10 seconds before he stood up and walked around the desk. He put his beefy arm around the slender ensign in a fatherly fashion and led him to the window. As Boggs knew, the admiral exercised regularly and was in great shape for a man of his years. "You know, Ensign Boggs, after today I see a big promotion for you, one which will place you in some of the top spots in naval intelligence. A man of your fiber is what the Navy needs to help win the war for us in areas where we don't have such expertise. That is why, as of right now, I am promoting you to the rank of full lieutenant."

"Why thank you, sir," beamed Boggs, letting a grin turn up the corners of his mouth.

Baker patted him on the back and looked him square in the eyes. "You deserve it, son. Now get back to work. You'll be notified as to your new assignment."

Boggs' face dropped slightly. "New assignment, sir?"

"Oh, sure," replied Baker. "Promotions always come with new assignments."

"May I ask where, sir?"

"How about Hawaii?"

Bogg's eyes flipped wide open. "Thank you, sir!" he blurted, saluting the admiral.

"Don't mention it," replied a smiling Baker returning the salute. Then he added, "And Bobby?"

"Yes sir?"

"Let there be no more talk about searches, okay?"

* * *

Colonel Deckler woke up at 0613 on G-Day with his ego still smarting from his altercation with Lothar. As a result, he had a restless sleep and had arisen

13 minutes late. In response, he spent the last half hour snapping at any man who dared approach him.

In his mind this was going to be a glorious day for Germany. But, somehow, he felt a tug at his stomach, a foreboding that was uncommon to him. It was an ill omen, and he brooded for a few minutes before taking a quick breakfast of bratwurst and bread. He washed that down with hot tea, hoping to dispel the ache but it would not go away.

His thoughts went back to Heinrich Müller. For some reason, one which he could only put down to social stupidity, the diminutive scientist had ignored his morning rage and kept on working on his checks for the launches. This was most puzzling to him because, back in Pennemünde, Müller had always cowed to him.

After another cup of tea, Deckler went out into the launch area and studied the short engineer as he went over the details with the three technicians one more time. These young engineers were from the Elektromechanische Werke at Karlshagen, Pomerania, and were specialists in the field firing of rockets.

As would be the case with someone who had a great hand in developing the mission, the colonel knew the launch procedure so well he never needed a clipboard to check on figures. Only Müller and von Braun knew more than he about rockets.

The thought of Wernher von Braun caused him to swell with rage again. "Spoon-fed traitor," he spat as he went over to the launch station.

"Anything I should know about?" he queried. The three engineers saluted him in proper Nazi fashion but he ignored the gesture as he always had during the mission.

Müller regarded him with doe eyes and shook his head. "Everything is fine, colonel."

"Walk with me, Müller," he ordered, at which he began a slow pace toward the launch site. As Müller scurried to his side and joined his canter, Deckler asked, "What was in your message to Beust last night?"

"Routine," quipped the scientist casually.

"Except an extra word or two, I hear," Deckler baited.

The small scientist put his clipboard down and stared unflinchingly at Deckler. "If you mean the *Kapitän*'s greeting to his friend, that was a extra bit he wanted to put in."

"Why an extra bit?" Deckler asked, stopping and turning to face Müller. The rocket engineer was not intimidated.

"Because *you* found it necessary to isolate him from the submarine and he cannot signal it directly without breaking radio silence, which he would not do."

"What was the message, Müller?" he snapped, growing tired of the man. When they got back to Germany he would see that Müller was locked up with only his experiments to keep him company.

"Nothing of interest, just a U-boat greeting."

"U-boat greeting?"

"Yes," shrugged the smaller man. "It's a line from *The Kretschmer March,* a song written to honor Otto Kretschmer, one of Germany's greatest U-boat aces. There is a proud tradition in the *Unterseebootwaffe* that you may or may not understand. Many of them know any greeting may be their last, so they make it memorable. Any line from this song would be special to them, short and sweet."

Deckler just shrugged and observed the area. The guards had pulled down their tents and were now burying them in the dense underbrush. All surplus equipment was being crated for disposal in the ocean and extra boxes were ready for the launch instruments. As usual, the weather station was sending out its daily reams of information to Halifax, giving the Canadian authorities no inkling that Raddall was operating under any other circumstances. Tomorrow, however, there would be no report.

"Did the sound crews get the results they wanted?" It was question brought on by nervousness. He knew that the work had been completed within the week. After alerting the former Ashton lighthouse keeper that they were exploding a couple of mines, two explosions had been set off with the approximate decibels of a rocket launch and the results were good.

Swensen was in Port Pleasant to monitor the blasts. They sounded to him as dull thuds as the small forest on Ashton had absorbed most of the noise. These did not attract any attention except for a child who looked skyward.

Suddenly, Deckler wished he had a phonograph. He wanted to hear *Deutschland Über Alles* and some of the marches that thrilled him during the torchlight processions at Nuremberg and Berlin. To him, this was now Germany's finest hour. The greatest country in the world would strike back at its enemies in the traditions of the Teutonic sagas. *First New York, then Moscow and, finally, we will wipe London off the map and with it that fat pig Churchill!*

As Deckler daydreamed, he saw himself as a younger man, the one who walked into the Polytechnical Institute wearing his new, brown SA uniform and polished boots; who astounded his fellow students with his high praise of the new National Socialist Party and its amazing leader, Adolf Hitler.

He remembered his initiation into the SS, how the physical training had been foreign to him at first, and how cruel his instructors had been. But now, he revered their names. For they had brought him to this point in his life, one of dazzling glory. *The name Deckler will soar with those of Hitler, Himmler and Bismarck!*

"Colonel?"

Deckler looked down and saw the smallish face of Müller. "In nine minutes we can turn on the systems and proceed with the countdown."

"Uh, right," Deckler replied, the image fading. "Carry on."

CHAPTER TWENTY-FOUR

August 26th
0521 Atlantic Time

Lothar had allowed himself only four hours sleep but they were not restful. Nightmares plagued him, unnerving dreams of a city in which rotting skeletons lay everywhere. Some were in business suits or dresses, while many others were very small who clutched stuffed toys to their small bony breasts.

When at last he awoke, he took out his large valise and found a small pair of scissors. He carefully clipped his beard, especially the excess hair along his neckline.

He dressed in his tunic, complete with all his brass and gold decorations. Around his collar he gingerly tucked the medal ribbon of the Knights Cross with Oak Leaves and Swords, the revered enameled award resting just below his throat. As he inspected himself in the kitchen mirror, he then placed the white-crowned *Schirmmütze* of a U-boat skipper on his head.

"Well, Lothar," he spoke to himself, as his thin, furry face glared back at him. "What happens today will either lay the foundation for a new Germany or launch it into purgatory."

He then wheeled and walked back into the kitchen, taking a quick peek into Jesse's bedroom. To his surprise she was gone.

Before he could think of the places where she might have gone, one of the guards walked into the house and snapped a salute. "The woman is down at the shore, *Kapitän*. Should I detain her?"

"No, Paul," he replied, more of a sigh of relief. "Leave her be. There's nothing she can do to harm us. She's already been through enough."

"Then we are ready to go, sir."

"Excellent. Wind the counterweights for the lighthouse one last time and we'll leave this island for good."

The *Kriegsmarine* guard saluted again and jumped down the stairs. Lothar took one last look around at Lottie's kitchen, the bright yellow walls, the toll-painted edges and the porcelain tea figurines collected by two generations of lighthouse wives. Then he shut off the light and descended into the cool morning.

As he made his way down the cracked concrete walkway, he glanced up at the rotating beacon of the lighthouse and made a quick calculation on how long the lamp would stay lit. When he looked back down to the beach, he saw a dark figure standing on a bluff beside the path and knew it was Jesse. Instead of avoiding her, he walked right up to her side.

Jesse never looked at him, seemingly contented to stare at the velvet horizon. "You can be proud of yourself, Jan," Jesse said, her words a string of monotone phrasings. "Or whatever your real name is."

She was standing on one of the larger rocks on the promontory beside the lighthouse, a dark doom-like figure whose long poncho fluttered on the gentle sea breeze. Beyond her, the calm waves were a dark purplish color, like a field of moving stone.

She had awoken from the heavy sedation two hours before and had walked outside to stare at the ocean. There was no use in her trying to use the radio. The diode tubes had been removed the day that the telephone line had been cut. All the flares had been confiscated along with anything else she might have used to attract attention from the mainland. Her last hope had been to start a fire but when she went into the kitchen she saw a *Kriegsmarine* guard grinning at her.

"You sure had us all fooled," she continued. "Except Momma and Wyn. They both looked at you with a gypsy's eye. I might have listened to her, but I thought Wyn was just jealous."

"Lothar."

"What?" Jesse asked.

"Lothar," he replied. "My name is Lothar. Lothar Stahl. I am a captain in the German Navy, *U-Bootwaffe*."

In the leaden tones of the pre-dawn, Jesse's brown eyes were like dark pits which gave back a piteous stare devoid of any warmth or understanding. Light leaking from the huge beacon encased her in a bright cocoon for an instant and then whisked away. "Captain? U-boats?" she chuckled, a macabre lilt in her response. "I guess your type has to call themselves something that rings of respectability."

His eyes dropped for a few seconds and then popped back up in her direction. Her face reflected the purplish glow making it appear as cold as the dark waters.

"But Lothar," she went on, his name feeling funny on her tongue as she spoke it, "if you don't mind what a hostage thinks, I'd rather call you a murderous coward."

The two guards flinched at the slight. Chosen for their command of English as well as Norwegian, they felt embarrassed for their commander.

Lothar thumbed at his gold ring, making it spin around his finger. "If it means anything to you, Jesse," he finally replied, "I am truly sorry for the death of your father, and that others thought it was necessary to include your family in this mission. My men also feel bad for the incidents. We are sailors, not murderers."

"Well," Jesse spat, "the next time I visit my father's grave I'll mention that to him."

Lothar quickly checked his watch and glanced over to Raddall Island. There was so little time left to be with her, to comfort her. *If there were some way I could stay longer I might . . .*

"By the way," she added, the acid tone of her voice cutting through the loud lapping of the dawn waves. "You and your stooge made a nice job of the burial."

There was another anxious pause and then a voice caught Lothar's attention. He turned to see Swensen coming down the path. "Captain" he said in English. "Parsons must have escaped to the mainland. His canoe is gone."

"But if that was the case," Lothar replied, puzzled, "there should be patrols all around us. Surely, he must have alerted someone." Because of his concern for Jesse he was not as alarmed as he might have been.

He glanced back up at Jesse. Her eyes were becoming clearer in the dawn and revealing not hate but a deep sadness. He moved closer to her, feeling a pang in his chest. In a flash of hurt, he knew that his duty had once again precluded him of an opportunity for happiness. "The island is yours again, Jesse," he breathed, his voice barely audible over the lapping waters. "Goodbye and I wish you well."

There was a moment of indecision in Jesse's face. Then she replied, "Goodbye, Lothar." This time, oddly enough, her voice did not imply bitterness.

"Drop your weapons!" The command startled both of them as they turned to face the speaker. Lothar already had his Luger un-holstered and was slowly bringing it about.

"Don't make a move, Stahl, or you're a dead man." The voice was familiar to Lothar, but he could not put a face to it and it was too dark to identify him yet.

Two shots rang out and two sailors fell to the rocks, one writhing in pain. "I said drop the weapons or I'll shoot you all!"

The clacking sound of metal hitting stone echoed off the humming tower of the lighthouse as a sliver of light lit up the large figure of Gus Lanton. Lothar's eyes were like saucers when he saw Gus' big face.

"You were dead!" he moaned. "You were floating with —"

"No, I guess I wasn't," Gus replied. "I didn't want some Nazi sonofabitch finishing the job so I held my breath."

"Gus!" cried Jesse, rushing to his side. "You're okay!"

"Eric is dead and Paul is bleeding from his arm," Swensen reported, ignoring Jesse and Gus' big figure as he came closer.

Lothar stared at the body of his dead petty officer. Then to Gus he asked, "Can he put a tourniquet on Paul?" It was then that the light came around again and he found himself staring down the barrel of the Colt .45 he had identified correctly after last night's shooting.

"Sure," replied Gus. "I don't want him to bleed to death before he goes to jail." Then he added, "I know 1,000 of you would not be worth the lives of my crew, but I'm sure that what you can tell my superiors about those rockets might make my sailors rest easier."

"So, what now?" Lothar demanded.

"We sit and wait until the Canadians get here," Gus growled. Right then he would have liked to put a bullet in Lothar's kneecap.

Lothar stared at the serious face of the man who had bested him three years before. "We don't have time, captain," he announced, firmly. "We have to stop them now."

"Stop them? What do you mean by that?" Gus asked, suspiciously. "You seem to be forgetting which side of the swastika you're on."

"He means that the Germans mean to set off rockets on Raddall Island today, ones meant to travel to the United States," Jesse interrupted. "And they carry a poison far greater than anything the world has ever seen before. It's meant to kill the population of large cities."

Jesse turned and faced Lothar. "I was eavesdropping on your meeting with that little rocket guy."

"Oh my God!" Gus blurted, remembering bits of the conversation between Müller and Lothar as he huddled beneath the kitchen floor. From the few words of German he understood he was able to piece together the subject of rockets. But he had assumed they were referring to the V-1 attacks on London.

Turning back to Lothar, Gus cocked the gun and said, "You better start talking, Stahl."

"I'm afraid she is right, captain," Lothar replied. "I just found out last evening and I —"

"Quickly, from the beginning!" Gus snapped, waving the Colt. "Then, I'll decide what to do."

"Captain," Lothar said his eyes burning in exactly the same manner that Gus remembered on that night three years before, "there is no time for a long explanation. You have to trust me with an addendum to what Jesse said. And that is, this rocket, the one carrying the poison, is being targeted on New York."

"New York!" Gus cried, incredulously. "You have a rocket that will hit New York from here?"

"There are four. Two are to be launched from Raddall Island in one hour's time. The first is to hit downtown Boston. The second will detonate in New York City. Then, in two days' time, two more will be launched from special submerged pods. Number Three will be targeted for Norfolk navy yards and Number Four for Washington, D.C. All the rockets will carry the poisonous substance."

"Christ Almighty!" Gus gasped, his mind calculating the destruction. "Underwater rockets? What the hell're those carrying?"

"I would hazard to guess more of the poison," replied Lothar. "I can stop those later, if I'm allowed. But right now we have to get to Raddall."

Gus looked at the faces of Lothar and the stricken guard and said in a low drawl, "You people make me sick."

"Captain," Lothar replied, "whatever you think of me, or my country for that matter, is irrelevant now. We have to stop those rockets from being launched, for the sake of hundreds of thousands of your citizens who will surely die a horrible death."

Gus saw the lighthouse shake before the pain of the blow registered. Then his legs buckled and he sagged to his knees. He felt the gun being wrenched from his hands but was unable to put up a struggle.

CHAPTER TWENTY-FIVE

August 26th
Radio Intercept Station
Office of Naval Intelligence

"When was this sent out, Mr. Boggs?"

"1101 Atlantic Time. The local Royal Canadian Mounted Police sent the message to the Canadian navy base in Halifax, requesting assistance in apprehending a murderer who had fled to this Ashton Island."

Admiral Baker reviewed the communiqué again and looked up over his reading glasses at the earnest face of Robert Boggs. The young man was proudly sporting his new lieutenant bars.

"And tell me again why you think this is relevant?" Baker's voice was conciliatory, trying to convey to Boggs that his question was not meant to demean him. The young lieutenant had already shown "a talent for picking winning horses," as Baker had told his superior in Washington, and he did not want the man's magic touch to fade.

"Well, first, sir," Boggs replied, stopping to clear his throat, "this message comes from the S5 sector, the area where the ghost image was thought to have headed. To confirm this observation, I plotted a vector from the coordinates given by our forces and the British ULTRA Department. Also, I examined all Canadian radar reports, no matter how vague each contact was, and added them in. And what I found out was that, out of 28 contacts, 19 small hits were in this area."

"That's over 60 percent," replied Baker, seemingly unfazed. He took off his glasses and stood up, the breeze providing a cool relief to his sweaty underarms. "But you said small hits?"

"Correct," replied Boggs. "The Canadians passed them off as whales or schools of tuna, because the signatures were of that caliber. And rightly so. However, that Coast Guard cutter was sunk barely 50 miles east of these readings."

Baker studied the young man for a few moments and then said, "Call the Canadians. Ask them to put everything they got in that sector, and I mean everything that can fly or float!"

"Yes, sir," replied Boggs, snapping a salute. Just before he left, he turned and asked, "Excuse me sir, are we to designate this as a definite sighting?"

"Hell yes!" blurted the admiral. "In fact, call the search, NEEDLE. Because, if you're right on this, you just found our needle in a haystack."

* * *

The two *Kriegsmarine* guards at the house had died quickly. The first he knifed at the boathouse and the second he had hit with a heavy iron hook, bashing the unfortunate man's head to a bloody pulp with one powerful swing. As each man expired, Wyn felt a pain in his chest, an angry ache at the waste of human lives that this war had wrought.

The forest was black as he made his way from the Knob so the torch of the third guard bobbed down the path like an incandescent ball. Wyn hid behind a large bush and, as the man passed, stepped out and shoved the shotgun barrel into his face. The resulting action caused the man to drop the torch and hit his head on a tree.

The flashlight lay on the ground illuminating the attacker, a man who appeared to be in his mid-20s. It also lit up the shotgun and the two menacing barrels that pointed it at his eyes.

"Now, I know you understand English, so here's the deal. Your two friends are dead and you'll be shortly if you don't follow my instructions."

The frightened man, readjusted his boat-style *Schiffchen* and nodded slowly, the fear in eyes reminding Wyn of a deer in a car's headlights.

* * *

"Stahl, it will be a great pleasure to watch you hang when we get back to Germany."

In the murky dawn, the black SS outfit made *Hauptmann* Heinz Fripp appear as a miniature version of Deckler. However, although he always tried to make his voice sound lower, his size and the nasal tone of his words gave a comedic edge to his authority, a trait that Deckler would have never exhibited.

"Sergeant, see that this man is brought along as well," Fripp continued. "An American naval officer will make a fine prisoner."

Gus groaned as Nagel and a guard helped him to his feet. As big as he was, the blow to his head still affected his equilibrium, so he put up no resistance.

Fripp looked up at Jesse and gave her a half smile. "I apologize that we don't have room for another passenger," he said to her.

Lothar edged slowly over so he was between Jesse and the captain. Fripp just grinned. "Your heroics are commendable, Stahl, but we can't take any more chances. You wasted many opportunities for a clean approach to this mission so her life is on your conscience."

Seeing that Gus' hands were now tied, Fripp said, "Sergeant, take her into the lighthouse and dispose of her quietly."

Nagel hesitated for a moment. "But, *Herr Hauptmann,* she can't —"

"Do what I say!"

Jesse never moved as Nagel walked slowly toward her. She simply said, "I know what you are going to do and I'm not afraid."

The stocky Nagel stopped in his tracks and caught Lothar's eye. "Sergeant," Lothar said, "you once told me about Kursk, and how you fought hand-to-hand with Russian soldiers. You said that, instead of the inferior Slavs that needed to be exterminated — as your superiors had told you — they were men and boys who fought with the same tenacity as your *Waffen SS* regiment. They died without a whimper, but more took their place, succumbing to the same fate but never cowering, nor backing down."

"Nagel, get on with it," Fripp ordered.

"Nagel, they lied to you about the Russians," Lothar persisted, "and then squandered your elite regiments rather than listen to sound military reasoning and allow your commanders to withdraw to a more defensive position. So if they lied to you then, what makes you think that they are not lying about this mission?"

"Shut up, Stahl!" Fripp shouted, drawing his pistol and pointing it at Lothar's head.

"You are like us in the *U-Bootwaffe*, Nagel," he continued, ignoring Fripp's Luger. "You have always conducted yourself with honor. This man is a bureaucrat, a phony soldier."

Fripp cocked the pistol and jammed the barrel up against Lothar's forehead. "If you don't shut up, I will save you the trip back to Germany and kill you right here."

The SS officer suddenly felt his whole arm and the pistol go up in the air. He was surprised to see Nagel's rugged face a scant few inches away. Although not as tall as Gus, Nagel was broad-shouldered and very powerful. "He's right, Fripp," Nagel growled. "You have never faced battle and yet you can order us to kill women? You don't deserve to wear that uniform."

He expertly immobilized Fripp's hand and took the pistol from his lax grip. "When the colonel finds out," Fripp cried, his struggles brushed aside, "you will all be executed for this. Your families will be sent —"

Nagel threw a huge arm around Fripp's head and twisted. A sickening snap ended Fripp's sentence. Nagel then let the quivering body of the officer slide to the ground. "His kind are wonderfully brave when giving orders," Nagel shrugged, ignoring the man he had just killed.

Looking up to Lothar, the sergeant asked, "Well, *Kapitän*, so what do we do now?"

"We take the skiff to the island and stop the launch."

"And when do we rendezvous with the U-boat?" Nagel asked.

"I have already arranged that with Beust."

Lothar then kneeled down beside the stunned figure of Gus and untied him. "Captain, I'm going to leave you here with Jesse. I'm sure your authorities will arrive very soon."

Gus grabbed his arm. "You're really going to stop those rockets?" he uttered, his voice slurred and his head pounding with pain.

"Yes, I promise you, I will," Lothar replied. Then he added, "I don't know if it makes any difference to you or not, but I am very sorry for the loss of your ship and crew."

"Acoustic torpedoes?" Gus asked, flinching at the throbbing pain.

"I'm afraid so," Lothar replied. "But if they hadn't worked you would have killed us on your next run."

"We were that close?"

"Almost right on top of us."

Through blurred eyes, Gus stared at the bearded figure for a few seconds and finally said, "Godspeed." Then he passed out.

CHAPTER TWENTY-SIX

The Lighthouse

The sky was a gray mat when Wyn arrived at the lighthouse with his prisoner in tow. The beacon from the red and white tower still had enough intensity in the fast-approaching dawn to make the small wave tops sparkle gold. But there was no one around.

"Looks like your friends have deserted you," Wyn uttered, as the distraught German joined him in scouting the area. They walked down the path, having forgotten, at present, about their arrangement as captor and prisoner. When they got to the rocky shore they saw Fripp's body and a semi-conscious Gus.

"Jeeze Gus!" Wyn shouted, kneeling down beside him and examining his bandaged head. Out of the corner of his eye he saw the German back away and said, "Just stay where you are and you'll stay alive," he uttered "I'm pretty good with a pistol." The man froze.

"Where have you been?" Gus asked, his eyes trying to focus on Wyn.

"I bumped into an old girlfriend."

"That's great," Gus chuckled. "I'd hate to think you didn't have a good time while I was shooting it out with half the German army. I nailed two and one of Stahl's boys got the officer, there."

"Stahl?"

"Lothar Stahl, U-boat captain," Gus added. "Better known to you as Jan Johansen, the Norwegian officer."

"So that's his name," Wyn replied, shaking his head. "Where's Jesse?" he asked, suddenly looking around.

"She's up in the house hauling stuff together to build a bonfire."

Just then Wyn saw the flash of a fire through the window of the lightkeeper's house and his heart sagged. As the fire grew he saw the figure of Jesse standing outside, her body flickering with the light from the flames that were consuming her home.

"Here, keep the gun on him."

"Check," Gus replied, laying the pistol across his lap.

When Wyn got to the house he saw Jesse sink to her knees and spread out some framed pictures. "Jesse?"

She looked up from the mosaic of family photos and her eyes were brimming with tears. "I had to do it," she moaned. "There was no other way to warn anyone."

Wyn jumped to the shed and unrolled the firehose, letting it roll downhill until it was stretched out. Then he worked the valve on the hydrant and watched the hose expand like some giant worm. He raced the crawling bulge to the end and picked up the metallic end.

When he opened the nozzle, the brass fixture bucked in his hand and a long spray shot at the house nearly breaking the kitchen window. Then he put his shoulder to the fat hose and walked it into the kitchen of the house.

Fortunately, the fire was contained to a pile of rubbish and oily rags on the kitchen floor. As Wyn sprayed the bottom of this pile, smoke attacked his lungs and he had to pull back for a few seconds to get clean air.

It was then he felt someone pounding on his back and he saw the disheveled Jesse. "No, no!" she screamed. "They must see it. They must come out and stop them. They have to save the cities!"

The fire sputtered out and a thick cloudy of smoky water vapor poured form the kitchen. The floor was badly seared and the paint on the walls, cupboards and ceiling were blistered but everything else seemed fine, just in dire need of a cleaning.

"Why did you do it?" she cried as he shut off the nozzle.

Grabbing her in his arms he said, "They're already coming, Jesse." She collapsed in his arms and they stood there rocking for what seemed like a long time. When they finally moved apart, Wyn asked, "Where are the Germans now — on Raddall?"

Jesse nodded, her shock evident as she came to the realization that she had almost destroyed her family home.

"They left only 10 minutes ago." It was Gus.

"Fine. Gus you take the pistol. I've got this guy's machine gun —"

"I'm coming too," Jesse demanded.

Wyn looked over at the frightened German, whose eyes were now flitting back and forth between the two men. "Don't worry. We don't kill prisoners unless they act stupid. You can stay here because there's no other way off the island. But, when the angry mob from town comes out I'd suggest you hold your hands up high and surrender and not hide in the bushes. They'll have dogs and, if you do something stupid, they'll probably shoot first and then sort out the details."

The disoriented man just nodded.

"Good. Make yourself at home. There's tinned food in the cupboards."

CHAPTER TWENTY-SEVEN

Raddall Island

"Sir, there has not been a transmission from *U-1229* in over 37 hours."

Colonel Deckler looked past the dark trees and then back at the soldier clutching his headphones. In front of him was a radio transmitter/receiver perched in a suitcase-sized crate. "How is your equipment?" Deckler asked.

"It has been thoroughly tested three times over and there are no problems," the SS corporal answered. "We are picking up signals on many different wavebands, so our receiver is working up to standard."

"Then we go to the backup plan, as per our instructions. We forget the first boat and rendezvous with U-2900. Radio Beust and let him know of our change of plans." Deckler glanced down at the chronometer on his wrist. "Pick up will be at 0630."

Deckler turned to see a smallish man with a tanned complexion run into the weather hut. "Report?" he asked the soldier.

"The boat is loaded, colonel."

"Good. When the rockets are away, load the instrument consoles. Are the charges on the launchers set to go off five minutes after liftoff?"

"All confirmed, sir."

"Good. When they are destroyed, the Allies will never know what they were."

Deckler exited the rickety shack and shuffled across the flattened brown grass to where Müller was going over his calculations on a slide rule. The small scientist looked even smaller and less important in his U-boat coveralls. He never looked up but heard Deckler's footfalls. "Launch on schedule exactly for sunrise," he droned.

Deckler stopped and ran his eyes up the 35-foot monoliths, taking in the intricate web of cables and hoses that fed the launch engines. On his orders, red and black swastikas had been painted on each side of the four fins used by each to maintain stability. German engineering had brought these amazing creatures to life and he, Klaus Deckler, was going to shoot them out of the nest to wreak havoc on the enemies of his country.

"Heinrich," Deckler began slowly, a lump rising in his throat, "I just want you to know that your work has been exemplary and, well … what I mean to say is that I was perhaps too hasty in putting you up on charges back when …"

The silvery head of the diminutive scientist slowly tilted up from his clipboard and he looked Deckler dead in the eyes. "Colonel, everyone has to do something in this world," he said, his voice cold and lifeless. "For me it is rockets. For you, it is to make sure that people like me make them and fire them off for the purpose of killing people. Personally, I think your talent is wasted in that black uniform, but that is a discussion we will probably never have, isn't it?"

Deckler breathed deeply and said, "You always do it, don't you Müller?" he seethed. "Every time I try to be nice to you, you find some way to bite my hand."

"No, colonel, I do not," the small man replied calmly. "I am just being honest, and if that means offending you then you have my apologies for that. But it would go against all that I truly am to say what I don't mean, when I'm asked."

For Deckler, the gall of the man irritated him. "You are wrong, Müller, we *will* continue this discussion another time." Then he added, "For now, just launch the damn rockets."

"Beginning countdown at two minutes," the scientist said, as if the previous conversation had not taken place. He glanced over to the east, where a bright crescent was forming on the horizon.

* * *

Lothar, Nagel and Swensen stepped out of the boat with their guns drawn and ready. When they approached the first guard Nagel simply said, "Horst, lower you weapon." Though puzzled, the soldier complied.

"Now, I will give you a choice, but you have to be quick about it. Will you follow me or Deckler?"

The man grinned and clicked his boot heels together, "Why you, of course, sergeant."

"Good Horst, pick up your gun and come with us." The slightly built man, a veteran in his late 20s, nodded and fell into step.

Lothar leaned over to Nagel and whispered. "Are you sure we can trust him?"

"He was with me in Russia," the stocky Bavarian answered. "I would trust him with my life."

"Well, you're getting your chance right now," Lothar breathed. "Where are the others?"

"Waiting at the boat on the other side of the island," replied Horst. "When the rockets are fired they will go back to the area, remove the instruments and set charges to destroy the launchers."

The small group made their way into the clearing and there they saw the shadowy figures of Müller and Deckler. They were talking at first, and then Deckler walked away to inspect the rockets. Silently, Lothar's group crept in and came up noiselessly behind Deckler.

"It's over Deckler," Lothar said, grabbing the Colonel and spinning him around. But Deckler's expression was far from that of surprise, and Lothar suddenly felt a cold chill run down his back.

"I've been expecting you," Deckler grinned, a serpent's smile splitting his face. "Fripp was supposed to radio back the moment he arrested you. One of the guards heard the shots on the lighthouse island, and when we didn't hear from Fripp, I knew you had sprung a trap on him.

"Now, I've got a surprise for you and your band of traitors." In a move that completely took Lothar and the offers off guard, Deckler dove into some bushes. "Shoot them!" he bawled as he lay prone.

The rattle of pistol fire brought Lothar out of shock and he dropped for cover but was too late. A sharp pain shot up his back as he pitched over into a somersault and then lay still on the soft ground.

Deckler held up his hand for the shooting to stop and the cracking of pistol fire ended. There was not a sound from the bodies lying in heaps where they had once stood. The three shooters moved in and checked the bodies by kicking them. The soldier, Horst, moaned and another shot rang out, ending his life.

"Traitorous swine," Deckler barked. "Drag them to the boat and tie steel to their feet. We'll dump them overboard when we go out to the U-boat."

He looked over at the scientist and said, "Continue the countdown."

Müller just stood there, shaking, unable to move. "Müller," he said, drawing his own pistol, "I can do this without you, you know. It would just take more time."

"Yes, I know . . . Countdown continuing," Müller uttered.

CHAPTER TWENTY-EIGHT

Raddall Island

As Wyn and Gus leaned hard on the oars of the old lifeboat, Jesse kept the 9mm submachine gun pointed over the bow with the safety off. Water lapped against their feet from leaks in the old weatherworn craft and they were all glad that Raddall Island was not twice as far away lest the boat sink away from them.

His head still aching from the blow, Gus pulled on the old oar, catching splinters of bleached wood in his hands at first until the rubbing wore down the sharp burrs. Wyn worked the oar with his good right hand and the crook of his left elbow, his blade cutting as deep and as strong as the one Gus was using.

When they approached the boat landing, they suddenly got out of the shadow of the island and the sharp rays of the day's first sunlight hit them. But it was low tide and the floating dock was lying like a beached whale.

They spun the boat around and the keel of the lifeboat caught the rocks. Without a word, they all jumped out and waded to shore, their bodies crouched over to lessen themselves as a target. It was then that a terrific roar startled them and the ground began to shake.

"Get down quickly!" Jesse cried, her wet poncho bottom slapping the legs of her corduroys as she struggled up onto the rocks. The three boaters dove behind a large round rock just as smoke and vapor engulfed them. The ground began to shake with a heavy tremor and superheated air scorched their faces.

Wyn pushed Jesse's head farther into the rocky crevices and her nostrils balked at the odor of rotten seaweed. This was soon overpowered by the stench of burning wood.

Gus took a deep breath in the cool crevice and then popped his head up to glance over the rock. Through the lung-scorching air he saw that a large cloud had formed into a ball over the trees. Then a large cylindrical object pushed its way upward through the billowing mist with the golden sun of the morning glinting off its sharp tip. A sudden flash attacked his eyes and he slumped down in pain.

Wyn popped his head up and cupped his eyes. He sat in awe as the gigantic torpedo-shaped craft cleared the treetops and began climbing exponentially with each second. At the end of the vehicle, great swastika-embellished, red fins protruded cupping a brilliant yellowish-red flame, whose intense light was blinding.

Suddenly, the row of protective trees was bowled over from powerful detonation of the second rocket engine.

"Get down!" yelled Wyn, and they managed to squeeze in behind the rocks as the furnace-like blast passed overhead. A second set of vibrations rumbled the ground and the calm bay became a ripple of wavelets. Then the second rocket lifted off.

"Oh dear God!" Jesse uttered. "We're too late!"

All three shielded their eyes for a few moments and then craned their necks to see the rockets climbing skyward.

* * *

"*Wunderbar!*" Deckler cried from his perch, almost a half kilometer away, as the two vehicles lifted off and began their ascent. Watching with his special darkened spectacles, his heart was flushed with pride as tears came to his eyes. "We've done it, Heinrich!"

Müller was also watching the event, his goggled face giving him the persona of a cartoon character. Deckler wrapped an arm around the small man's shoulders and began to shake him ecstatically. Müller never moved. He just watched.

"All right, Heinrich," Deckler finally said, retracting his arm. "Get back to the console. Check that the gyro settings are still in place and then disconnect the unit so we can get it packed up. Beust will be surfacing in less than 10 minutes."

There was no word or movement from Müller. He just craned his neck farther backward to get a better look at the ascending rockets. A puzzled Deckler leaned over the console and glanced at the glowing cathode ray tube. After a few seconds of watching, he doffed his glasses and pushed the scientist away, caring to study the console himself.

As the reality registered in his brain, he looked over at the smaller man and then followed his line of sight skyward. The two airborne vehicles shone like golden needles as they climbed higher, their engine blasts appearing as sparkling balls, one below the other.

"This shows they still are heading straight up, Müller," he said calmly, not believing the instruments. "How can that be? They should be turning to the south by now."

Still Müller never spoke.

"Müller?" Deckler said, tapping him on the shoulder. "Look at this. They are not supposed to go this high!"

Klaus Deckler, correct in his uniform right down to the cap with the "death's head" emblem, threw his tinted glasses onto the ground and pulled the small scientist around to face him. "What is going on, Heinrich?" he asked.

Müller finally took a breath, almost coughing as tiny particles of residue from the scorched earth and trees tickled his lungs. "Colonel, our rockets are going into space."

"Space?" Deckler bellowed incredulously. "What do you mean? I set and sealed those gyroscopes myself. They were corrected for the coordinates of Boston and New York."

"I reset them," the scientist confessed.

"You what?"

"I reset them," he repeated, coolly.

"You sabotaged them?" spat Deckler, undoing his holster and pulling out his pistol in one moment. Then he shoved it into Müller's cheek.

"No," answered Müller, seemingly unfazed by the hostile action. "I found out about your payload and decided that poisoning Americans was not in the best interests of Germany."

Deckler stood frozen, his expression in total disbelief.

"And," Müller added defiantly, "I wished I had done that a few months ago when our A-2's were landing in London."

Deckler's pistol came down hard on the man's head. The scientist's goggles took the brunt of the blow but he lost his footing and fell on his back looking up at the maniacal countenance of the SS officer. Then he felt three bullets tear into his body, and it was suddenly hard to breathe. His vision, however, was clear, and the sight made him smile as the blood ran out of his wounds. His two birds were now heading into the stratosphere on their way to the heavens.

* * *

As Müller had calculated, the rocket engines burned out in 55 minutes. The rockets had reached a height of 100 miles into the atmosphere before they became two pieces of metal floating in the earth's orbit. Then, on May 8th, 1945, one day after the Allies accepted the surrender of the remaining German forces from Grand Admiral Dönitz, the rockets began to lose their orbit and enter the atmosphere, where they burned up in less than 10 seconds, their deadly payload incinerated and joining the tons of extraterrestrial dust that filtered down from the atmosphere on that day.

* * *

Lothar felt arms wrapping around him and his body being raised up. Just then his back began to burn like someone had stuck him with a branding iron. When he opened his eyes he saw himself moving over the rocks toward the motor launch. Then he was heaved over gunnels and landed on what he thought was a greasy pile of rags but in fact were the bodies of Sergeant Hans Nagel and Private Horst Shönig, the SS men who had turned against Deckler, and Swensen, the Quisling man.

As lay there he heard two loud explosions, which he recognized as the firing of rocket engines and a sudden sadness came over him. *It is all over*, he sighed.

He reached up with his right hand to check on his wound and was satisfied that the bullet had not gone through. Moving his back he cringed at the pain but found it was localized in the region of his right shoulder. He could move the arm but not far. It was his clavicle, he reasoned.

Next, he heard the stutter of a machine gun and a fusillade of pistol shots. Then he heard footfalls come his way. "Get moving!" It was Deckler's voice.

"But the *Kapitän*'s still alive," one of the SS guards remarked.

"Drag him out and shoot him again. Make it fast!"

* * *

The first bullet nicked the tree above his head. Wyn returned fire with the submachine gun. All around him were the blackened hulks of smoldering trees, too green to burst into flame but scorched enough so that the whole area looked like a forest fire had been through it. The burnt odor attacked his nostrils.

Five explosions in rapid succession made him dive for the cover of a rock as shrapnel whizzed overhead. When he dared to look up he saw a smoking tangle of steel that, he guessed, had been the launching towers. The fifth explosion had gutted the weather station, blowing its furniture and scientific equipment in a shredded mass out through the shattered window openings and causing the wooden shell to ignite.

Wyn fired at a fleeing figure and watched him pitch over. Then the Canadian was on his feet again. As he took the rapid steps, the sound of battle erupted in his ears, the screaming and yelling that had now become part of a nightly ritual in which he re-lived Dieppe in his sleep. Only it was happening to him now. His armpits became cold hollows and his scalp seemed to freeze. He shivered as if it were a January day.

He gave a quick look at the dead soldier. A full burst had caught him in the back and it appeared he had died instantly. This was another face that would greet him in his nightmares. Then he saw the wounded body of another man with goggles. Wyn thought him a child at first until he saw the thin moustache.

A commotion ahead distracted him and he looked up to see a boat loaded with three dark figures getting ready to leave. One of the soldiers was dragging out a body and he saw that the man he was carrying was the German who masqueraded as Johansen. The man cocked his pistol and pointed it at the prone body. As he did, Wyn brought the 9mm *Schmeisser* up..

* * *

Lothar found himself being dragged out of the boat and thrown against a rock on the shoreline. Looking up, he saw a Walther pistol being cocked. Behind it, he saw the face of Peter Zundel, an SS corporal, one of the original Pennemünde guards. "Sorry Stahl," he breathed, somewhat sympathetically.

Just then Zundel's body jerked and the gun flew from his hand in a spray of red. A bullet smacked against the bow of the skiff and several kicked up small geysers in the water.

"Get going!" Deckler shouted as the guard's body fell on the rocks. A private in the stern gunned the motor of the skiff and the craft groaned as a comber pushed it sideways against the rocks. A few seconds later the boat broke free of the restraining movement of the waves and began to gain momentum on the ocean.

CHAPTER TWENTY-NINE

Raddall Island

"You're hit," Gus said, lifting up Lothar's head.

"I'm fine," he replied, as Wyn fired off a long burst from the submachine gun. The bullets hit the water in a series of sprays well behind the speeding boat.

"It was worth a try," Wyn shrugged.

Jesse knelt down beside Lothar and pulled off his tunic. The back of his white shirt was greasy with blood. "It looks like it never penetrated the clavicle," she said, her emergency medical training popping into her head. Lothar ignored her. His eyes were on the horizon.

Gus lifted up the German Navy tunic, noticing for the first time the four solid rings on the sleeves and the medals. "Christ almighty," he breathed, "you're sure some sonofabitch with a submarine."

"Yes, well as one who has felt your depth charges," Lothar replied, flinching as Jesse cleaned his wound, "I would have to say the same thing about you with a ship."

Wyn was silent. He stared hard at the retreating boat and then quipped, "I would have to make a wild guess and say that a sub will pick them up."

"You are right," Lothar replied. "But what does it matter? The rockets were fired."

"Straight up to the stars," Gus offered, a grin widening to his face.

"What?" Lothar cried.

"One of the scientists, a little guy, told us they would disintegrate up in space."

Lothar smiled. "Müller, old friend, you did it!"

Jesse ripped the right sleeve off Lothar's shirt and rolled it into a bandage. Then she wound her scarf around his shoulder to hold it on the wound. "This should keep you from bleeding to death before they take you away," she said, her eyes set, as if in a challenge.

"Is Müller all right?" Lothar asked, craning his neck.

"I'm afraid he died," Gus shrugged. After a few seconds silence the thought passed and he said, "Now what can we do about the rest of the rockets?"

"Check those bodies," a heartened Lothar said, pointing to Swensen, Nagel and Horst as if they were sticks of wood. "See if any of them have a flashlight."

* * *

"Commander, there is a motor launch approaching."

Kapitänleutnant Sigmund Beust grabbed the periscope from his adjutant and scoped the western horizon. "Prepare to take her up," he said, beginning a wide pan to check for enemy planes.

"Take her up."

After a few seconds of a myriad of water sounds the watch officer announced, *"Turmluk ist frei, Boot ist raus!"*

"Very well, open the hatch."

* * *

"There!" Lothar shouted. "There's the U-boat!" The dark conning tower was nearly two miles away. "I have to get into the trees, so there is a dark background for the light."

Lothar began to get up and Jesse and Gus helped him the rest of the way. In his left hand he gripped the flashlight. Once situated, Lothar began clicking the light on-and-off in a series of Morse code flashes. It took two minutes before the signal was returned. Lothar cupped his eyes to ward off the glare of the rising sun and deciphered the coded message.

"Good, very good!" he beamed, suddenly heartened by the reply.

"What did he say?" Wyn asked.

"Kretschmer," replied Lothar, a subtle grin animating his face.

"Kretschmer?"

"It's a code that Beust and I worked out beforehand. It's named after *Kapitänleutnant* Otto Kretschmer, Germany's first U-boat ace and a good friend. He is a very modest man whom we called 'Otto the Silent.' He was so famous that a song was commissioned in his honor, one that the dockyard band used to play when our U-boats returned to base. He was captured and is now languishing in one of your prisons."

With that his eyes moved out across the sea to the small black object.

* * *

"There it is!" cried Deckler, pointing to the surfacing sub. The motor boat steered in beside the huge U-cruiser and the waiting hands of the crewman pulled the bobbing skiff in closer. Deckler's mouth hung open in amazement. The largest craft he had seen before was the Type IXC *Atlantikboot* on which he, Stahl, and the scientists had traveled across the ocean. With its two huge, armored turrets and eight heavy anti-aircraft guns, the U-cruiser looked more like a half-submerged destroyer than a submarine.

As Deckler was helped aboard, his eyes went skyward, to the twin vapor trials that went skyward. "What a waste," he breathed, as his feet touched down on the rubberized decking.

Beust was there to meet him. "Where's Stahl?" the big, furry U-boatman asked, his face like a quizzical animal.

"Dead," replied Deckler, shrugging. "He died bravely while holding off the Allies who stormed the island.

"You were lucky to escape, then?" Beust asked.

"Very lucky, now let's get moving," Deckler snapped, satisfied that his story was well told. "We have the next part of the mission to complete."

"*Jawohl*, Colonel Deckler." Beust then waved at two crewmen who, on a pre-arranged signal, jumped into the motor launch and started it.

"Where are they going?" Deckler asked, as the boat pulled away.

"Back to the island to retrieve Stahl's body," Beust shrugged.

"But I told you there are enemy —"

"True, but Stahl's ghost just signaled me and said that they are very friendly."

"What?" Deckler snapped.

Beust raised his hand again, and strong arms grabbed Deckler and his two remaining SS guards. The other SS soldiers and the technicians had come aboard on the previous launch and were quartered below. What Deckler did not know was that his men were locked in the forward cargo bay.

In the next instant, the colonel felt his legs being pressed together. He looked down to see the U-boat crewmen wrapping them with chains. "I'm an SS colonel! You can't place me in chains like this! When we get back to Germany, I'll —"

"You're not going back to Germany."

Deckler studied the man. His ape-like caricature, a look that Deckler had dismissed as being just short of dim-witted, transformed into one of fierceness. The Nazi scientist suddenly felt afraid.

"You would never turn me over to the enemy!" Deckler sniffed haughtily, glaring at the man in efforts to get him to back down.

"No, Deckler," Beust sighed. "They may be enemies of my country but I would not wish a man like you on them."

Deckler looked down and saw a U-boatman attaching a large grappling hook to the chain. He tried to comprehend the obvious but his logical mind would not accept it.

"Say hello to the lobsters for me, Deckler," Beust added, a lyrical overtone to his voice.

Deckler forced out an anguished cry and felt himself being thrown from the deck. The cold water hit him like a huge fist gripping his chest and suddenly his whole world was green. The heavy anchor and chains took him down slowly past the dark mass of the submarine and its twin propellers. Two other dark shapes were struggling close by him.

Then a motion picture of Deckler's life went through his mind: his exemplary marks in math and science in grade school; his Ph.D. from the University of Berlin; his meteoric rise in the rocket program, his marriage to Katrina.

However, for some reason that not even he could fathom, his promotions and commendations within the Nazi Party were absent. As hard as he tried to remember that part of his life, it would not show on his "screen."

Finally, his chest pounding, he let the reservoir of air burst from his mouth with one final scream.

* * *

A few seconds before the skiff pulled up to the rocks, one of the three *Kriegsmarine* raised his machine gun. Despite the fact that Lothar had assured him that the U-boat had been apprised of the situation, Wyn had his gun cocked and ready to fire, which made the German sailor nervous.

Lothar hobbled down to the craft with help from Gus and Jesse. The three Navy guards had never seen the enemy up close before and were reluctant to move from their position of superiority.

"Sie sind harmlos," Lothar chuckled and the men finally relaxed their weapons. But in reality, he was nervous. His sharp ears listened above the lapping of the waves for the drone of patrolling aircraft.

The U-boat man's light green eyes flashed in the sunlight when he turned back to face his new comrades. Jesse stood blank-faced, her hair laying on the breeze the same way Lothar had first seen it one month ago. Her eyes were misted but he knew it was because of the breeze in her face.

"Goodbye, Jesse," he said taking her hand for a few seconds and then letting it fall.

"Goodbye, Lothar." Tears came to Jesse's eyes. They were tears of sorrow: for her dead family, for the people killed, for the war and her lost life on Ashton Island. And for knowing that she'd never see this man again.

"Please stop them," she said, her voice choking, reaching for more to say but finding none.

Lothar just nodded. For to say any more now he would feel compelled to explain the meaning of the past few weeks: the mission, the rockets, his affections for her. There wasn't time.

When his eyes met those of Wyn, he asked, "You knew all along?"

"Let's say I suspected something."

"Was I that bad of an actor?" Lothar shrugged.

"I thought you were pretty good," Wyn replied. "But I think you should know that there is no *Jolly Witch* pub in Portsmouth."

Wyn lowered the *Schmeisser* and pulled the strap over his left arm. With his right he clutched the German's hand. "May we meet in better times," he said solemnly.

"I would like that," Lothar replied.

Gus was last. His mouth was dry and the words would not come out in the fashion he wanted. Lothar brought his left hand up and gripped the American's shoulder. "We are brothers, you and I," Lothar said, sternly, "men of the seas. I would be honored to serve with you on any ship. And when this war is finished we shall meet again."

Then, despite his pain, Lothar leapt into the craft and the motor groaned as it tried to propel the small boat forward. He never looked back.

* * *

The three weary figures watched as the conning tower of the distant submarine disappeared.

Wyn spoke first. "Lothar's going to dump them in the deep off the Continental Shelf." Then he asked, "but do you think this rocket scheme is over?"

"On this side of the Atlantic," Gus replied, turning around to look at the three bodies on the blood-splattered rocks who were now attracting the attention of some seagulls. "Britain, I hear, is taking quite a pounding."

Suddenly, the sound of an engine broke their weary spell and a motor boat carrying green figures came around the point. "Here's the cavalry," Gus said, relieved to see friendly uniforms. The boat pulled in close and one of them stood up and shouted something.

"What?" Wyn cried back. Then he saw the sten gun pointed at them and remembered the German machine pistol in his hand. He lowered the gun very slowly. The leader said, "Raise your hands and don't move."

Half of the soldiers who jumped ashore ran up to them with guns ready while three more scampered up the rocks to check the trees. They wore British-style pie-plate helmets with webbing and canvas putties over their ankles. The leader, a grim-faced youngster with an acne-scarred face, walked up to them cautiously. "I am Lieutenant Colin MacDonald. You are all prisoners of the Princess Louise Fusiliers."

"But Lieutenant," Jesse replied, pronouncing the rank "lef-tenant," just as he had said it, "I'm Jesse Corkum. My father runs, or ran, the Ashton Light, and these men are Wyn Parsons and Captain Lanton of the United States Navy."

"Coast Guard," Gus corrected her. *What the hell did it matter?* he thought.

"You Parsons?" the young officer asked, his brown eyes narrowing. Wyn nodded.

"Then you're the one we're after, then. The murderer."

"Murderer?" Jesse snapped, her temper rising. "This man is responsible for saving our lives and you call him a murderer?"

The young man shuffled uncomfortably. His training had never shown him how to deal with irate women and he glanced nervously between her and Wyn. "Ma'am, all I know is that I was ordered to bring this man in for the murder of a local citizen, Barry Finer."

"Finer?" Jesse snapped. "That vermin?"

"Well, Miss," the officer returned, "whatever he is to you, he's dead, and Parsons is wanted for his murder."

"As well," he added, "you will go with him as suspected accomplices. Once we're ashore, and back in Shelburne, we'll let my commander sort it out."

Jesse looked over at Wyn. "They want you for killing that drunk fisherman?"

"It's a long story," Wyn shrugged, as one of the soldiers knelt down and picked up the submachine gun.

"Holy smokes!" he cried. "This is a Jerry machine gun!"

Jesse ignored him. "Well, Wyn," she sighed, the rising sun attacking her tired eyes, "you can tell me all about it when I wake up in two or three days.

"Holy Jesus!" It was MacDonald. He was surveying the burnt area and the gutted weather station. "What went on here, another goddamn war?"

"In a matter of speaking," Gus grumbled.

CHAPTER THIRTY

The Atlantic Ocean

"Status, Beust?"

"Both pods have cleared the bottom and are at the right attitude," returned Beust.

"Very well. Maintain depth. Ahead two-thirds."

Lothar winced as the medic continued dressing his wound. The bullet, Jesse had told him, flattened against his clavicle and was easily removed. However, the bone was cracked and the muscle tissue around the area was severed. He would need to have it immobilized for a month to heal properly.

"Here is fresh shirt for you," Beust said as he kneeled down beside Lothar. A big grin split the black mass of facial hair. "I hear Argentina is wonderful this time of year."

"We sure as hell can't go home, can we?" Lothar chuckled. "I can just see Himmler waiting to greet us in Kiel."

"Kapitän," Beust continued, with a seriousness that dissolved the smile. "All of us in the crew know that Germany cannot win this war, and that we will be lucky if our country is not overrun by the Russians." Lothar went to say something but Beust raised his hand in a respectful manner.

"Please, hear me," he continued. "If your wish is to keep fighting, then there is not a man aboard — besides the SS goons we have locked up in the cargo bay — that will not go anywhere you want to take us, and fight anyone you decide we should fight."

"Thank you, I will keep that in mind. However, first we need to maintain this speed for 59 minutes before we hit the edge of the continental shelf. Then we dump the rockets in the deep water."

"So, surrender is not in your plans?" Beust continued.

"Maybe. I don't have a plan as of yet. As I said, my primary concern is to dump the pods. Because if we are captured with them, we could all be charged with war crimes, even if none of us knew that Deckler planned to use the radioactive material in the warheads. As the Americans say, 'possession is nine-tenths of the law.' We would be guilty by association."

"Propellers! Nineteen hundred meters!" It was the sound room. "There could be more than one set."

Lothar jumped up and winced as the pain stabbed through his shoulder. "Bearing?"

"Their course running is parallel to us," replied the sonar man as the short youngster pulled the plotter along the chart. "It doesn't appear as though they know where we are."

"Course change, eight degrees starboard, maintain speed."

The crew grabbed on to overhead pipes and bulkheads as the submarine made a quick turn.

"Are they turning, Heinz?" Lothar asked.

"We have two sets of signatures, now, *Kapitän*," replied the sonar man. "One is maintaining the previous heading and the other is breaking off to zero-five-one."

"They know where we are," sighed Lothar to Beust. "They're trying to flank us." He grabbed the intercom and yelled, "*Achtung!* Battle stations! That includes respirators."

Lothar grabbed hold of one of the funnels from the cluster on the bulkhead and yelled, "Open rear doors!" Then he grabbed the handles of the periscope and jammed his brow into the eyepiece. He picked out both attackers, two Canadian corvettes, the newer modified Flower-class attack boats that could easily outrun the U-cruiser with its trailing cargo. A flicker to the south caught his attention. It was the pterodactyl-like silhouette of a Consolidated PBY flying boat, as deadly a predator to U-boats as the prehistoric flying lizard was to its prey.

"Ahead full. We'll have to get as far as we can to the edge of the shelf and then fire the rockets."

"We are going to fire them?" asked an amazed Beust.

"We might be able to get them to the deep water that way. Besides, it might distract them enough for us to shed the pods and elude them," Lothar replied. "Check rocket firing systems."

Beust followed the cables from the firing box beside the periscope to the rubber fitting where it went into the pressure hull. Then he returned to the launch mechanism in the box and tested the complete circuit. "Circuits are working," Beust announced, thankful for his diligence at the rocketry school in Pomerania.

"All stop. Everyone silent." The twin Siemens-Schuckertwerke electric motors wound down like the decrescendo of muted sirens. Then the red emergency lighting came on.

"Initiate flooding sequence in pod ballast."

Beust threw two of the toggle switches up and watched two small meters above the firing box. The dials on the instruments moved upward. Beust toggled them down again when the pointers reached the thin, green crescent on the face. "Pods vertical."

"Adjust five degrees."

"Adjusting ballast controls for five degrees."

"Depth?"

"Depth is 20 meters," he replied, his eyes re-checking the face of the depth meter.

"Adjust to 15 meters."

Beust flipped another toggle switch and watched the meters just below the first ones. "Depth is now 15 meters."

"Initiate firing sequence … fuel on."

"Fuel is on."

"Range is now 1100 meters!"

"Oxygen on," said Lothar, ignoring him.

"Oxygen is on."

"Range is now 1,000 meters!"

"Prepare Tubes Five and Six."

Beust yelled the instructions into the funnel and went back to the firing box. Lothar peered over at him and saw the crude face of an ancient Teutonic warrior. "*Angreifen! Ran! Versenken!*" Beust shouted, and the U-boat reverberated with the cheers of the crew.

"Fire One!" Lothar commanded.

"Fire One!" was Beust's ecstatic reply as he threw the red switch. The U-cruiser began to rumble.

***

Corporal Jim MacKenzie, the second-engineer of PBY-5A Consolidated Canso A — a Canadian-built version of the amphibious American Catalina — spotted the periscope just before it was retracted by the U-boat crew. After relaying the information to the pilot, Squadron leader Allan Maitland replied, "Inform Y4 and the *Sackville* that we are now attacking."

Maitland pushed the nose downward and opened up the throttles. Although powered by two 14-cylinder, 1200 horsepower Pratt & Whitney R1830-82 engines, the flying boat was no speedster. Pilots often commented that the lumbering PBY "climbed at 90, cruised at 90, and glided at 90." It was an exaggeration because the aircraft regularly cruised at between 110 and 115 knots and could build up another 40 knots-per-hour in a dive. When Maitland checked the gauges the Canso was doing nearly 135.

However, if the U-boat had decided to stay on the surface and fight, then Maitland, as did all PBY pilots, had standing orders to back off and track the submarine. With the improved *flak* batteries aboard the newer boats, the Canso would be riddled with holes before being able to drop any of her four 250-pound depth charges.

* * *

Inside the first pod, the ethanol-oxygen mixture was ignited by an electric charge and the resulting blast of the rocket engine began melting the intricate wiring and tubing inside the cocoon. A millisecond later, the build-up of pressure nudged the projectile upward, its sharp nose tearing the rubber diaphragm at the top of the pod and propelling it out into the open sea.

Once free of its caged environment, the rocket surged upward through the water, its self-contained oxygen supply allowing the combustion to continue. Seconds later, it reached the surface, having traveled 44 feet in the process. The rocket then broke free of the ocean leaving a boiling wake in its path

* * *

"My God, what the hell's that?" Maitland yelled, wrenching on the controls so hard he almost flipped the top-heavy aircraft on its back. The Canso yawed and went sliding to starboard as Maitland caught the flash of a large star shooting past him, a mere 100 yards away. In the next instant, the turbulence from the rocket's vortexes lifted the starboard wing. Again, Maitland, his eyes spotting from the immense glare, recovered and had the aircraft flying level with 10 feet to spare over the dark ocean.

* * *

The cheering in the U-cruiser went on for about 10 seconds before Lothar shouted, "Fire Two!" Then, abruptly, it stopped, and everyone went back to their stations. Beust flipped the remaining switch and waited for the rumbling sound.

There was none. He calmly pulled it back and threw it once more, this time with more pressure. Nothing.

"Check the wiring!" Lothar ordered. Beust and two crewmen went back over the cluster of wires and, a minute later, he tried again. Nothing. There was an eerie silence where, a minute before, there had been exultation.

"There must be a malfunction in the pod. Does the ballast control work?"

Beust nodded. "Yes, the gauges show that the pumps are still active."

"Ballast to 50 percent."

"Ballast to 50 percent."

"Prepare to jettison Number One Pod."

Beust reiterated the command.

"Flank speed!"

The U-cruiser sprang to life and the electric motors tugged at the propeller shafts. In seconds the boat was moving through the water, dragging the remaining pod like a woman pulling a reluctant child down a street.

Beust checked the system again, but the result was the same. "Shall I jettison the remaining pod with the rocket, sir?"

"No, we're still on the shelf. We have to take it deeper."

* * *

"It's from the *Sackville*, sir," the second engineer informed Maitland. "Contact picked up again bearing two-two-seven. It is now proceeding to attack."

The HMCS *Sackville*, its depth charge crews at ready, raced to the location of the ASDIC readings and fired off its hedgehogs. Moments later the K-guns went off and then the stern charges rolled off the stern.

* * *

Two of the hedgehogs exploded right over the conning tower, surprising Lothar that the attack had come so fast. The sub shook and the lights flickered, but there was no damage. Then came the deadly sound of the ship's screws passing overhead with its deadly *swish, swish, swish* sound. While the others were frozen in tension, Lothar took out a stop watch from his jacket pocket.

"Dive!" Lothar yelled, clicking the start button on the watch.

The ballast tanks flooded and the planes tipped the bow of the *U-2900*, racing the barrels of death into the depths. One of the stern charges went past the submarine and, at 450 feet, the pistol drove the hydrostatic detonator into the primer core of the barrel-shaped bomb. Six hundred pounds of Torpex — half again as powerful as TNT — exploded, forming a huge bubble of super-compressed vapor which slammed against the pressure hull of the *U-2900*.

The tremendous blow threw everyone off his feet, the rattling of debris echoing down the hull long after the ear-splitting gong. Immediately water began spurting in from numerous breaches in the seams of the inner hull. The main lighting went off and it was replaced by an eerie blue glow.

Lothar's wounded shoulder sagged and he soon realized the blow had finished the job of breaking the clavicle. Pressing his teeth tightly together, he lurched over to the communications funnels. Cries for help intermingled with the sound of trickling water.

"All stop!" he bellowed, his voice wavering. Then two more depth charges shook the U-cruiser and the water began to run more freely. Lothar's ears were ringing. He knew by the severity of the detonation that, had this boat been an old Type VII, they would be going the bottom at this moment.

Beust was already up and checking the damages before the next two exploded. The aft torpedo compartment was a shambles with water pouring in through breach in the bulkhead. Two crewmen lay dead under two of the monstrous torpedoes. Beust allowed himself a brief thought about his two friends and then ran back to the control room.

"Sir, the aft torpedo room is flooding badly," he said, between breaths. "We'll be going down by the stern if we don't stop it."

Lothar stared at the bearded man, the tiny droplets of water matting the hair on his face. There had been another time when he had made this very decision and it had plagued him ever since. Now, and forever more, it was to be compounded with the one he had to make now. *Kretschmer and Prien, they had to make this choice; one lived and one died.*

He searched the faces of the scared, young men — some whose beards were so thin they could not have been more than 19 — and saw the future of Germany. They did not have to die. There was nothing more for which these brave youngsters should have to fight because it was not their war any more. The battle was not Germany against England, America and France. It was now good against evil — a quest to rid Germany and the world of Hitler, Himmler and his cronies. Maybe there would be a time in a new post-war Germany — however devastated it may be — where weak-minded men like Deckler or Fripp could never be molded into murderers.

"Blow the ballast," he sighed, as a rivulet of water trickled over his toes. "Take her up."

Beust looked into Lothar's green eyes for a second. There was no defeat in them, just a resolved fierceness. "Blow the ballast!" he bellowed."

Then he said, "Sir, are we to man the guns?"

"No," he said as the U-boat began to lurch and twist under the strain of distant depth charges.

Beust studied the tension on Lothar's face for an instant. Then he bellowed, "*Verdammte Scheiss!* Blow the ballast tanks!" His command echoed through the conn and a tremor ran through the U-cruiser as the pumps strained to push the water from the tanks.

"Get some large white sheets and get ready to wave them when the cargo hatch is opened."

"Yes sir, I —"

"And Beust, stand by to open the valves."

"Sir?"

"We're going to sink it here, with the pod," Lothar sighed, "Now prepare the men to abandon ship."

"*Alle Männer aus dem Boot!*" Beust cried.

* * *

"U-boat surfacing to the starboard side!" cried Corporal MacKenzie, the second engineer on the Canso.

"Attacking," returned Maitland, banking the aircraft.

When the black submarine broke the surface of the water, Maitland held the aircraft in a shallow turn and proceeded to circle it instead of dropping the depth charges. "For the love of Christ, Mac, do you see that big thing?"

"Roger!" replied the crewman, his voice wavering. "It looks like a bleeding battleship!"

Before Maitland could answer, the hatches on the deck of the great boat popped open. But instead of gun crews, the Canso crew saw white sheets.

"I don't believe it," sighed a relieved Maitland. The Canso skimmed over the heavily gunned U-cruiser, and every man on the aircraft leaned to starboard to see the leviathan.

"It's the *Sackville*, sir," Mackenzie finally said, breaking the spell brought on by the spectacle of the boat and the droning engines. "She wants to know why we are not attacking."

"Tell the *Sackville* that the U-boat is surrendering," Maitland grinned.

"Are we going home, now?" MacKenzie asked.

"No, Mac, let's hang around until our fuel gets low. We may never get a chance to see a monster like this again."

* * *

When the *Sackville* and *Regency* pulled up alongside of the rolling *U-2900*, the U-boat crew was already in their inflatable boats. Lothar was leaning against the railing of the *Wintergarten*, straining to hear the commander of the Canadian corvette as he spoke through a megaphone.

"My name is Lieutenant Alan Easton of the HMCS *Sackville*," the Canadian called. "You will evacuate your boat immediately and prepare to take on a boarding party."

Lothar nodded and waved at the man that he understood. Then he picked up the intercom mike and asked, "How's it going, Beust?"

"One last valve, sir."

The Canadian commander gave another warning and then two white-capped sailors pointed Lee-Enfield rifles at Lothar. He held up his hands but there was a grin on his face. A few seconds later, a whaler carrying a boarding party bumped into the rubbery side of the U-cruiser. His hands still up and his shoulder in great pain, Lothar went down to greet the sailors.

"Sir," he addressed the ensign leading the party in perfect English. "This vessel will sink in one minute and it will go down like a rock. So I suggest you not board."

The young Canadian officer looked back up at his commander. "They're scuttling it, sir."

From his perch on the corvette, the skipper could see the U-cruiser settling deeper in the water. He swore an oath and then waved at them to return.

"If you please, commander," the young officer asked. He was armed but his gun was holstered. Lothar noticed that there were no guns trained on him any more. It was an honorable gesture and he took it graciously. "Thank you," he said, and slipped down into the whaler.

A few seconds late Beust popped up out of the cargo bay so suddenly that an armed sailor from the corvette panicked and shot at the big, burly German who then toppled into the rippling ocean. Lothar immediately dove overboard and grabbed him, flipping him on his back to get his mouth free of the water. Hands reached down and pulled the big man and Lothar into the lifeboat.

Beust was coughing and his eyes were flitting around at the white-capped Canadian sailors. "Prop me up so I can see," he requested, his voice raspy. Ignoring his own blinding pain, Lothar tugged at his clothing to find the wound. The hole was in his chest and the blood was a pink froth. As it slid down his wet clothes it settled into a bright-red patch. Suddenly, bubbling noises from the U-cruiser caused everyone to look away from Beust.

The *U-2900* went down by her stern. Beust had blown the ballast of the remaining pod and it went down first — this time the child pulling at its mother to join it in the depths with its lethal cargo. When the waves were over the open cargo hold of the submarine, the conning tower disappeared quickly into a mass of bubbling water.

"Will you call my wife, *Kapitän*?" Beust asked, his voice a gurgling rasp. A large shadow ran over his face as the bow of the U-cruiser tipped up out of the water in one last gesture of defiance. Beust's eyes looked wild in the shade of the sinking boat.

"I will," Lothar replied, the noise of the air escaping through the submarine's hatches increasing into a long groan. He never tried to downplay the reality that Beust would die soon.

"Will you sing the song with me?" he asked, arterial blood now spraying over his beard with every cough.

Lothar hummed the melody of *The Kretschmer March* and Beust joined in. At the end of the first stanza, the big man's eyes rolled back and he stopped breathing.

The Canadian officer leaned over and said, "I'm sorry about your friend."

Lothar just nodded. The U-cruiser's bow disappeared in a loud waterfall sound and, when the bubbling died down to a steady gurgle, he began to hum the march to Beust again.

CHAPTER THIRTY-ONE

August 31, 1944
Shelburne, Nova Scotia

"**Barry Finer was as big an asshole** as I've ever come across, and I've seen hundreds of 'em come down the pike."

RCMP Sergeant Jim Everett tossed a sheaf of papers down in front of Wyn and then leaned back in his chair, stretching with both hands over his slender head. He wore a thin moustache which, topped off by a pair of liquid blue eyes, gave him an Errol Flynn look. "But you're a trained soldier in hand-to-hand combat —"

"One hand," Wyn corrected him, pointing to his stump.

Everett pushed forward and slammed his hands to the oak table. "Yes," he snapped, "and that's the only thing that's saving you from lounging in a Halifax jail right now."

His point made, the middle-aged Mountie relaxed a bit. He studied Wyn's face, his astute eyes resting on the pink, worm-like scar on his brow. "Wyn, I've known you a long time. Hell, I saw you pitch more times than I can think of right now. And I remember you scoring that double-overtime goal — the one that won the provincial championship — even better than I remember my own wedding day.

The big policeman sighed, waving his big hands around, "I was also there to clean up your house after your old man blew what little brains he had all over the ceiling."

The big cop got up from his desk and looked over at the constable, Alex Lloyd, standing guard. Like Everett, he was in his standard Mountie uniform with Sam Brown belt and a khaki tunic; the working version of the ceremonial red serge jackets of which the Mounties are so well known. His pistol was holstered and a lanyard from around his neck was attached to the butt of the gun. And on his head was the standard Mountie Stetson. "Get us some tea, will you, Alex?"

The Mountie hesitated for instant, whereupon Everett added, "He's not going anywhere with those leg irons." The constable nodded and left the room.

"All right, Wyn," he said sitting down on the desk, "let's get down to brass tacks." Seen close up, his blue eyes had a pale steeliness to them, matching the silvery hair and thin moustache. As he had witnessed a few times in his youth, Wyn again saw the formidable persona of the Canadian Mountie emerge from Jim Everett.

"I talked with Dave Saunders, the Crown Attorney in Liverpool. He agrees with me, and damn near everyone else around here, that Finer's death was no loss. The man was presently awaiting two court appearances for battery and two-thirds of the county was scared shitless of him. But he was shrewd. He'd never do anything that could tempt me to personally put a billy club to him. Cowards never do.

"So, off the record, if you want my opinion," he continued, "here's what you do." Everett leaned over so his voice was barely above a whisper. "Tell Saunders that you plead no contest and he will put in a recommendation to the judge that you serve one year for manslaughter."

"One year in prison?" Wyn sighed. After thinking about it for a few seconds, he asked, "Where?"

"Ashton Island."

"What?" Wyn's eyes opened so that huge white ovals appeared briefly.

"I spoke with Jesse Corkum and she says she needs a helper with the lighthouse," Everett went on. "As a government official, she asked if you could be released in her care to run the place, under the same type of plan they use with German prisoners for picking potatoes and such. Well, Saunders concurred. He will recommend to the judge that you spend your sentence running the lighthouse for her."

"Government official?" Wyn replied, a puzzled frown contorting his face. "She's a school teacher."

"Temporarily," Everett corrected him. "She'll finish off this school year at her position in Bridgewater while you serve out your sentence running the Ashton light. After that time, she'll take over the lighthouse duties and you can do what you like, because in the eyes of the law, you'll be a free man."

"She's going to quit teaching to do that?"

"Seems so," Everett replied. "Awful lonely job for a pretty girl like that, if you ask me."

Wyn looked at the hawk-faced man, one who had been a mentor to him in his younger years. "Yes, I guess it would be."

"So, are you going to take the deal?"

"And that's it? No jail time?"

"Put it this way," Everett said, leaning closer to him so as not be heard by anyone in the hallway. "A one-armed man kills a known bully in a fist fight. A man, by the way, who outweighs his crippled opponent by about 40 pounds. Do you think any lawyer of the Crown wants to take that to court to see if a jury rules in his favor?"

Wyn let the reality of his freedom settle in for a moment. Then he asked, "How's Laura doing?"

"Not good," sighed Everett. "The poor girl had been harassed by Finer for so long that she feels lost without him. It's like a dog whose owner beats him all his life and when the owner dies, the dog grieves because he knows nothing else. Laura's known nothing else for almost five years."

"I guess it would do no good for me to see her?" he asked, fishing for a reason.

"Legally, I'm afraid you can't," Everett sighed. "She's filed a court order against you. You are not to try to communicate with her, or her family, under the threat of prosecution. And on that one, I would have to concur."

He placed a hand on Wyn's shoulder. "This woman is not the Laura you used to know. Finer and her father beat that out of her. After you left for Hamilton to play hockey, that stupid asshole Johnson literally threw the two of them together."

"He never liked me, did he?"

"No, but Johnson liked money, and coerced Laura to marry Finer to increase the fishing production. With the war on, they sold every fish they could catch and made big bucks. Too bad Johnson died within the first year of a heart attack. That left Laura at the mercy of Finer, and you know she was never a strong woman."

"Yeah," replied Wyn, staring down at the shackles on his ankles, "none of us are that strong."

Everett took out a keychain and reached down to the metal on Wyn's legs. The steel ankle bracelets popped off and he slid them into the corner.

"Oh, I almost forgot," he added. "The Army wants to see you. It seems that they don't know what to do with you. Just when they have you pegged as a screw-up, a coward and a murderer, the American Navy phones up and says that they want to pin a medal on you for saving that Captain Lanton fellow."

"Gus got off okay?" Wyn asked, ignoring the part about the medal.

"Funny thing about that," Everett relied, scratching his salt-and-pepper hair. "An American officer and two big Marines landed in Yarmouth and they flew him out of town an hour later in *civilian clothes*. Not only that, the American authorities have asked the Canadian government not to publicize this little raid by the Germans. Seems it's been labeled Top Secret."

"But we all saw —"

"You may have," chuckled Everett, a sinister sneer washing over his face, "but if I was you, I would do as they ask and keep your tongue in your mouth. There's a lot of touchy people around RCMP headquarters in Halifax these days and a nosy person could get in a lot of trouble for mentioning it outside of this office."

"So what do they say happened?"

"Here's the official report," he said taking out his reading glasses. Lifting a sheet of paper off his desk he began to recite the words:

"On the morning of August 26, 1944, the Raddall Island weather station, manned by nine Norwegian nationals, was the site of two great explosions when fuel storage tanks were ignited by the careless shooting off of a flare. All nine, plus Wilbur Corkum, the lighthouse keeper on Ashton Island who was visiting Raddall Island, were killed in the blasts."

"That's it?" Wyn asked, incredulously.

"Yup," Everett shrugged. "It goes on to say that nine coffins were interred in Lunenburg cemetery. These contained the remains of nine men found buried where you said they would find them."

"What about —?"

"Wyn, that's all I know," Everett said curtly. "And you better forget all this stuff about Himmler and rockets and such. This shit does not exist, got it? That's the official line and, as a servant of the Crown, that's what I have to follow."

Wyn stood up slowly, his head in a fog. It felt good to have the leg irons off as he stretched his legs for the first time in four days.

Everett grabbed his round Stetson from the desk and pointed to the door. "Come on, Wyn, put it all behind you and take this opportunity. Let the ne'er-do-wells in Ottawa and Washington figure it out.

"Besides," he smiled, "there's someone waiting for you outside."

* * *

Jesse was wearing a light summer dress and her hair was pulled back into a ponytail. The hot sun of the last few days had darkened her face and arms to a rich mahogany color. She was not smiling but her eyes were bright and cheerful.

"Hi," he managed, swiping at the lock of reddish hair that the breeze had blown down over one eye.

"You look good," she said, instantly hating herself for a comment she deemed as insipid. "The food in there must agree with you."

"I always liked Shelburne," he replied. "So it stands to reason that their jail would be of the highest standard."

"So, I hear you are released to work on Ashton … at least while I'm still away teaching."

"After the papers get signed."

Jesse began to laugh, her curly hair shaking in convulsions. "This is awkward," she sighed. "It's hot, damn hot . . . so why don't we go over to the hotel and we'll have a beer to seal the deal?"

"Will they let you in?"

"Because I'm a woman?" she replied, haughtily. "They better. No hotel would dare refuse to give a bottle of beer to the new keeper of the Ashton Light."

"I guess not," Wyn replied, seeing that something was bothering her.

Jesse looked up into his face and said, " I want to say something before the alcohol clouds my thoughts."

She looked away and took a deep breath. The wind picked up her hair again and Wyn could see that she was fighting back tears. Finally she said, "Momma and Daddy were right about you," she said, her words interrupted by a sob. "I was so terribly bad to you and I want to ask you for your forgiveness." With that she turned away and wiped her eyes.

Wyn pondered her words for a few seconds and then answered, "No."

"What?" she asked after a short pause, not sure if she heard him correctly.

"I won't accept your apology," Wyn stated firmly, his eyes displaying no malice.

The words struck her like ice cubes. "Okay," she breathed, fighting to compose herself as she tried to decipher their meaning. "I'll be going then."

"What I meant to say," added Wyn, "was that it would be pretty lousy for us to start off our new relationship with an apology."

"Oh, I see," replied Jesse, a relieved smile coming over her face. She waved her hands in nervous gesture as it would to get more words out her mouth. "Uhm, then, you are going to take the Crown's offer?"

"I'd be a fool not to."

"Oh, right," she sighed. "I guess that does excuse you from jail time and all that."

"It also gives me time to get better acquainted with you on your visits to the island during your holidays," Wyn said, over the clanking bottles of a milk van as it passed them.

"Really?" she blurted. Then uttered, "I mean, yes, I guess it would."

Wyn touched her on the shoulder and she suddenly wrapped her arms around his neck. They held the embrace until they both needed to take deep breaths and they finally parted. "Does this mean you're going to like being my partner?"

"Uh-huh," she replied, adjusting her hair, and peering around to the passers-by by who had stopped to watch them.

"All right," Wyn went on. "Then can I ask you somethin' else?"

"Uh-huh," Jesse replied, not certain if it was the hot sun or the embrace that was beginning to make her dizzy.

"Who do I see to declare my intentions on courting a certain Jesse Corkum?" he asked, officiously.

Jesse's smile lit up her face. At first, she wanted to kiss him but seeing all the people around, she grabbed him by the arm and led him across the street toward the hotel tavern. "Just step into my office and we'll do some discussin'!" she piped. "You're buying the first round!"

THIRTY-TWO

Washington, D.C.
May 10, 1945

It seemed that every time Gus Lanton went to Washington he found the weather disagreeable. When he was there in winter, it was foggy and cold, and in the summer the humidity killed him. People had always told him that the spring and fall were beautiful but he never seemed to get invited at that time of year. Today was about as beautiful as any Gus could remember in any town he had ever visited and he hoped it was a good omen. Because this time he had come of his own volition.

The outer office of Vice Admiral Eugene Baker, Director of the Office of Naval Intelligence, was crowded with officers of all ranks, each waiting for their new assignments now that the war in Europe was over. Gus sat patiently in the waiting room reading the latest Mickey Spillane novel.

The conversations of the naval officers centered around their chances of getting ship commands in the Pacific, postings which would surely mean promotion and the opportunity to serve under some high profile commander such as "Bull" Halsey or Clifton Sprague. Two of those with battle experience talked of an opening in Admiral Nimitz's staff, an area of command that Gus new very well.

"The admiral will see you now," piped the young adjutant, snapping a salute as Gus stood. A second later, there was a prolonged shuffling as the 11 young men in the waiting room suddenly clamored to stand and offer the same gesture. Gus returned their salutes just as smartly.

Admiral Baker was deep in thought when Gus walked in, so much so that Gus thought he may be asleep. His jowls were much larger and his glasses seemed thicker than the last time they met, but three stars flashing on each shoulder and both collars of his shirt showed he had been very active.

When Gus reached the desk of the large office, Baker looked up and a big smile tightened the loose skin. "Christ in heaven, it's the hero of Surigao Strait in the flesh!" Baker stood and, ignoring Gus' salute, grabbed his hand as he brought it down, clasping it in a tight shake.

"Sit down Gus," he said, "and tell me how you got that Navy Cross."

"Well, sir, there's not much to tell," Gus shrugged. "It was dark. All I did was fire off a bunch of torpedoes and get my ship damaged in the process — by American shells."

"You always were a modest sonofabitch," chuckled Baker. "The way Oldendorf tells it, you took your destroyer against a line of capital ships twice. He credits your ship for blowing one Jap battleship in half and sinking two destroyers. That's a nice night's work!"

"Well, for starters," Gus explained with an embarrassed chuckle, "there were two other destroyers who went in with the *Jeb Stuart*, plus a pile of PT boats. Our torpedoes were just a few of dozens zipping through the water. Then Admiral Oldendorf's battlewagons and cruisers opened up."

Baker shook his head slowly, obviously in awe that one of his protégés took part in the most famous naval battle in American history. Gus Lanton, a man he had personally plucked from the Coast Guard not two months before the action, had been assigned a destroyer which became part of a giant US armada assembled to take back the Philippines from the Japanese. The attack was directed toward Leyte Gulf, a sea in the central Philippine archipelago, and began on October 20, 1944.

"Gus, you were in the right place in history. That goddamn Oldendorf catches Nishimura's battleships coming single file through the strait and crosses his T for him. Christ, that's what Nelson did to the French at Trafalgar and the British Navy did to Germany at Jutland in the Great War. It's a naval commander's dream come true. And you were there."

Since the very beginning of battles at sea using cannons, all admirals knew there was one position to always avoid: never let the enemy cross your "T." In theory, this phenomena usually happens in narrow areas, as in straits, where the line of ships cannot breakaway or move up beside one another to extract a greater firing power. This forms the stem of the "T." The attacking force then lines up at the mouth of the straight in single file — or in lines of two or three, if they have enough ships — and crosses the "T." All the guns on one side of each ship can be brought to bear on the lead enemy ship — which could be more than 20-to-1 in firepower — while he can only fire the front guns at one of his attackers. When the first ship is destroyed, the next one faces the same barrage.

"Three different radar men show that your ship was in the right position to nail the *Yamashiro* when she turned to avoid Oldendorf's ships. No one was near that lone destroyer you nailed, or the one you chased until it ran aground. I'd say you earned your pay."

But Gus never thought so. The *Jeb Stuart* was hit three times by Japanese fire. Then the ship was crippled when targeted by confused gunners on American ships before Oldendorf gave the order to cease fire. Twenty-seven of his men died on those blood-spattered decks that night.

"So, how was Hawaii?" Baker asked, abruptly changing the subject.

"Wonderful," Gus replied, with a smile. "My leg mended well and they did some more surgery on my shoulder. It got roughed up some."

"Well," Baker chuckled, "the Germans couldn't kill you and you dared the Japanese to, and they missed. Now you got your first star and a great big bauble, who else you gonna take on?"

Gus never spoke at first, his basset eyes resting in a forlorn gaze. Then he said, "Admiral, I need a favor."

"Name it," Baker replied, leaning back into his chair, the brass stars on his khaki shirt twinkling in the sunlight.

"I want to visit a German POW named Captain Lothar Stahl."

"Stahl?" he replied, a puzzled look coming over him.

"Yes, sir," Gus continued. "If you remember, he was the commander of that submarine that went down off Nova Scotia last August, when I was stranded there."

"Gus," he growled, "that stuff was sealed tighter than a nun's pah-toot, and it will be long after you and I are gone from this earth. 'Nough said."

Baker's stare never wavered. It was evident Baker had drawn a line in the sand and no officer with any sense would have ever desired to go near it, let alone cross it.

"I know that, sir," Gus replied, unfazed by the changing tone of Baker's voice. "Look, admiral, I don't wish to stir up anything that will cause you or the Navy any problems. I just want to see him for 10 minutes."

His posture unwavering, Baker breathed deeply, his large torso raising like an inflating tire. He then held his breath for a few seconds before he blew it out through his mouth, his lips fluttering as if he was imitating a horse for a child's amusement.

"Damn you, Gus," he said, in a softer tone than Gus had expected, "you got the world by the ass right now. A guy with your experience and shithouse luck couldn't do anything less than retire with two stars — even if you sat on your ass for the rest of the war. So, why the hell do you want to screw it up now?"

"I owe it to him," Gus replied. "*We* all owe it to him to see that he's all right."

"Wait a minute, Lanton!" Baker exploded. "Don't you go sayin' that me, nor any other American, owes some swastika-wavin' sonofabitch a goddamn thing! You reading me, sailor?"

"He could have launched those rockets on us," Gus persisted. "Instead, he scuttled them, saving tens of thousands of lives — maybe even much more than that."

"Get this straight!" Baker bellowed, his heavy ring smacking the oak desk with a crack like lightening. *"There were no rockets.* Understand? This Stahl character put ashore a raiding party which wiped out a Norwegian weather station, resulting in loss of life. The Canucks knocked out the sub and the crew was captured. Then they cleaned up area with foot soldiers. End of story."

Gus nodded thoughtfully. Baker was just repeating the official explanation from the previous fall. "I understand completely, admiral," he nodded amiably. "And I will concur with the explanation given. That being said, then there should be no problem if I visit this *German raider*, should there?"

"You're pushing this, Lanton," Baker replied, his face as solid as stone. "You're pushing for a lowly captain's position in the Aleutians. And you can live like a fucking Eskimo for the rest of your life."

"Fine, if that's what it takes," Gus said calmly.

Baker threw up his arms in frustration. "You're a real pain in the ass, you know that, Lanton?" he added, shaking his head. "You mean you'd risk your rank, your whole career, to see a fucking Kraut?"

Gus never answered. His heavy brow and unwavering eyes, like brown pearls, communicated his thoughts.

"Well, Jesus Christ almighty, I must have been pretty dense to have grabbed you out of the Coast Guard when there were others who could have done just as well."

Gus knew that he was moved from the Coast Guard both as a reward for his actions and to get him away from the area until the White House could come up with an official line for the German action off the coast of Nova Scotia. He also knew that the incident would have to be kept from the public for a while, but he never thought the people would be hidden away.

"Ten minutes, sir," Gus pestered. "Then I'll never mention this again."

Baker subconsciously slid his ring off and began tapping it on the half-full ashtray, which made a *clank* sound each time it connected with the tray. Then, many seconds later, he brought it up and slammed it down like he was judge hammering with a gavel. The dark, thick glass cracked at the onslaught and the dish-like tray split into two pieces. Ignoring the damage, Baker picked up his pen and thumbed the nib. It stay poised over the paper for a moment, while the admiral reached over with his other hand and picked up his glasses. Sliding on his spectacles he began to write.

After two minutes of writing, he looked up and slid the paper at Gus. "He's in Boston at the Charles Street Jail," he grunted. "This will get you in to see him."

Gus picked up the document, briefly examined it, and then looked up at the frowning, bulldog face of Baker. "Thank you, sir."

Baker ignored his gratitude.

Gus got up and saluted. But Baker continued to glare at him.

* * *

The trip had been a long one in the Navy PBY. The pilot had chosen to take the lumbering aircraft around a massive storm front and land in New York, before going on to Boston the next day.

The old stone building, known locally as the Hub, was a time-worn, three-story brick building that fronted on Charles Street across from the Charles River. When he approached the guard station, he found a mildly hospitable welcome. The two burly Marines saluted correctly, but stood in his way until he showed them his credentials. They seemed even bigger in their in white helmets, Sam Browns and spats. Billy clubs and pistols were their only sidearms, but the guards inside the shacks brandished Thompson submachine guns. Upon seeing his documents, they let Gus pass without another word or smile. Rank had no meaning here, except the rank of their superior officer.

What Gus had found out from Canadian authorities was that the *U-2900* survivors had been transferred from Shelburne to Halifax where they were mustered and screened for interrogation. Those deemed not to have significant information were transferred to the prisoner of war facility on Citadel Hill while Stahl and seven specialists were flown to Boston. That was where Canadian control ended.

Gus climbed the stairs and found himself in a three-tiered prison, much like those he had seen in the movies. The interior walls were made of cinder blocks with solid concrete separating the cells. The place smelled of moldy concrete and small whiffs of urine. Another guard was in the middle of the first block, and he perused Gus' papers.

The officer, a thin lieutenant in khaki uniform, stood up and saluted as he approached. "Good evening sir," he said, reading the papers Gus handed to him. "Floor two, sir. They're all kept up there. But your man isn't here right now."

"He isn't?" Gus asked. "Where is he then?"

"In the hospital, across the street." Gus looked out the window and saw the large complex.

"What happened?" he asked, turning back to the young man.

"I guess he got sick, sir," the man replied, with a sly grin.

Gus shot a glance at his assistant, a petty officer, and then turning back to the officer he asked, "What's your name?"

"Lieutenant Harvey Adams, sir," he replied, with the cocky grin still stuck to his face.

"Well, Lieutenant, where's your commanding officer?"

"Commander Jenkins? Upstairs, sir, with the other Kraut prisoners."

"I see," Gus grinned back. "They're making them feel at home then?"

"Nah, all that stuff is pretty well finished. A couple of Sixteen-Z guys used to be here doing the interrogations but only one guy comes around now."

"I see," Gus replied. "Thank you, lieutenant." He then committed the man's name to memory. This was one man he wanted to see transferred to the South Pacific for duty in some job suited to his talent: something like grave registration or supervising the mess on an oiler or some other transport vessel.

Two officers were speaking to one another when they saw Gus' stars and snapped to attention. "Admiral?" the one with commander's stripes asked incredulously.

"Rear Admiral Lanton," Gus replied, handing him the papers.

"I'm Commander Jim Jenkins," he replied perusing the documents. Then he said, "Oh, Stahl, he's across the street. Tried to commit suicide with a sharp stick to the throat. Lieutenant Ferguson got to him in time."

Ferguson looked around nervously and then saluted again. "Nice to meet you sir. If you would excuse me, sir, I have my rounds."

When he had gone, Gus looked past Jenkins and into the guard shack. "Mind if I go in?" he asked.

"Not at all, sir," he replied, nervously, following Gus in.

It took Gus only four seconds to guess what went on in this room. On the table was a set of brass knuckles and on the wall were strung a series of crude electric wires. The place smelled foul, the faint odor of urine, feces and vomit still lingering.

Backing out, he stared at the commander. "Jenkins, where is the rest of the crew?"

"In the next block. They like the view."

His small chuckle was met by an approving nod from Gus.

"Well," Gus said, taking a deep breath of the dank air, "I guess I should be going," he said, smiling. "When is your shift over?"

"Oh, not until 0830. I have some papers to clear up."

"Great," beamed Gus. "I'll be back."

Then he added, "So, Stahl's in the hospital across the way?"

"Boston City. You can't miss it, sir."

* * *

"This is quite unexpected, sir," the officer remarked. He was an older man, a career Marine officer with a row of medal ribbons on his shirt. Again, rank would not bowl anyone over if the papers were not correct. Colonel Forbes rubbed his salt-and-pepper brushcut, perusing the first document as if it held some long-lost secret to finding a pirate's treasure.

"This seems in order, sir," the colonel finally said, his gravelly voice reverberating down the corridor of the hospital ward. "But the situation has changed since he went in here."

"How so?" Gus asked, trying to hide his irritation. He had kept his basset face looking chipper for so long the muscles in his cheeks were tiring.

"Well, since his suicide attempt, OPNAV has set the security level higher," the man shrugged.

Gus studied the man for a moment and then asked, "Colonel, where did you serve?"

"Guadalcanal, Tarawa Atoll," he shrugged. "Got hit in the hip, so they ruled me unfit for combat."

"Tough fights," replied Gus sympathetically.

"Yeah," he replied, "but if the truth be known, Admiral, I'd rather be back there. All this know-how on fightin' Japs is going to waste."

"How bad were you hit?"

Forbes stood up and walked in a circle, a noticeable limp interrupted his stride.

Gus studied the man for a moment and said, "What if I told you I might know someone who could get you back to the Pacific?"

Forbes eyes lit up when he heard the words. "I'd say you must be a magician, sir."

Gus wrote down a name and phone number down on a piece of paper and then his own name. "Give me two days and then call this man. He's back in Washington now and carries a big stick in the Marines."

Forbes eyes widened when he saw the name. "You know McNulty?"

"'Dick-Eyes' McNulty and I spent Christmas in a hospital ward at Pearl."

Forbes belly laughed at the name. "Not too many people outside the Marines would know the Colonel by that name."

"So," Gus prodded, "can I get a few minutes with the guy inside?"

Forbes took another look around and then nodded. "Sure," he smiled.

* * *

Gus saw the intravenous bottles first and then his eyes dropped to the sleeping figure in the bed. His head was bandaged over one eye and there was a cast on his left arm. At most, he weighed in at barely a hundred pounds.

As Gus got closer, he saw the urine bottle and catheter and the heart monitor. Lothar's face below the head bandage lacked the familiar beard. It was round and purple, and his mouth line was crooked. His breathing was more of a rattling sound than the even hiss of a sleeping person.

Gus slid a chair over and sat close to him. He reached over for Lothar's free hand and saw a disfigured claw. After hesitating for a moment, he gently picked up it and held it in his own palm. His eyes began to mist.

"Good Christ, Lothar," he breathed, "what have they done to you?"

Lothar's swollen right eye opened to a narrow slit of brown and the recognition was instantaneous. "Gus," he said in a raspy voice. "You look good for an old sailor."

"I wish I could say the same for you," Gus replied, rubbing the man's hand gently. Two of Lothar's knuckles were lower than normal and his pinky flopped as if there were no bones in it at all.

"So, you are an Admiral now?" Lothar went on. "I'm glad your navy recognizes a good man with a depth charge."

"I'm getting you out of here," Gus blurted, barely able to contain his disgust.

Lothar squeezed Gus' hand as best he could and pulled his frail body off the pillow. "No, Gus, you must leave it alone. You must not ruin your career over matters which do not concern you."

"Concern me?" he asked, incredulously. "You saved our lives and —"

"What they are doing is correct," Lothar went on, his voice coming and going in intensity. "I led a group meant to sabotage your war effort and was captured. They have every right to try and get me to speak about the mission and its objectives but have I told them nothing and will continue to tell them nothing. That, my friend, is war." Then his head plopped back onto the pillow.

Gus shook his head in amazement. "But —"

"How is your wife?" Lothar asked, the corners of his mouth turning up in a smile.

"She is fine. She's home in Bar Harbor, waiting for our child."

"Really?" Lothar's eyes sparkled for the first time.

"Yes. We're adopting a boy," holding back a flood of tears.

"Congratulations!" Lothar chuckled. "This makes me very happy."

Then he raised himself up again and brought his right arm around. In it was a gold ring. "This is the ring that my uncle gave me after the raid on Scapa Flow. Gunther Prien and whole crew of *U-47* were given them. Except for the Nazi symbol, it is an honorable medal. I want you to have it."

Gus took the ring and examined the intricate pattern, a U-boat with *47* on the conning tower, running over a British flag. "This is a wonderful gift, Lothar," he breathed, "but I feel it should go to your family."

"They were all killed early last year in an air raid. There's just Uncle Karl's family now and, with two dead sons, they will have had enough of the war by now without another bauble to remind them of it."

"It's over, you know," Gus said.

"I know," Lothar tried to grin. "I was given special treatment in honor of that occasion."

"Bastards," Gus uttered, holding the ring in his palm as if it were a delicate piece of crystal. "I can get you out and back home, you know," he said, more to raise Lothar's spirits.

"And the US Navy will be deprived of a great commander," Lothar replied. "Go and be a good father and a good leader. That will make me the happiest."

"What of your crew?"

"The interrogators realized right away that none of the crew knew anything more than their little part of the mission. After a few weeks they were shipped away to a camp. Eight more are still upstairs but they are the remaining SS that Beust had already arrested. They did not know very much about the operation either but, being SS, the Americans are holding them until more information is gathered from German files."

"Who interrogated you?" Gus asked.

Lothar shook his head. "As I told you, Gus. This does not concern you."

A shudder went through his frail body and he gripped Gus' hand tighter until it passed. "Goodbye, my friend," Lothar sighed, obviously weakened by the pain.

With that he fell back on the pillow and his breathing became erratic. Gus ran out to the nurses' station to get help.

* * *

It took Commander Marty Myers two days to get to Boston by car. He met Gus at the Biltmore Hotel, and then both men spent the first day getting caught up on where their career paths had taken them since the *Montauk* went down.

While Gus had been idling in the cellar of Wilbur Corkum's house on Ashton Island, Myers and his string of lifeboats had been picked up forty miles off the coast of Maine by the USCGS *Cowslip*, a 180-foot Cactus-Class lighthouse tender. After a month's furlough, he was promoted to lieutenant commander and given command of the USCGS *Mayflower*, a new cruising cutter, which was presently in at Portland for sonar refit.

This was good news for Gus, because Marty was the first man he called out of a list of 10. Marty had since been given his third full stripe and the lieutenant had been dropped from his rank. He was now a full commander.

After a fine halibut dinner in the hotel restaurant, where they got caught up on old times, the two comrades went upstairs and changed into civilian clothes. Later, when the two officers went out the back entrance and into the alley, they looked like two dockworkers going home after putting in some overtime in at the yard.

* * *

O'Reilley's was a thriving watering hole on Charles Street. The Irish-style pub was a rectangular box squeezed between Maggie's Rooming House and O'Toole's Bakery, with a long bar down one side and two rooms at the end: a bathroom and the office, which served as a gambling room.

It was usually crowded from shortly after the five o'clock whistle at the dockyard to nine, when even the hardiest of customers went home. On Monday at 10, just an hour before closing, there were the die-hard clients, a dozen men who were either single or who never felt the need to go home to their families.

John Kerrigan was one of the latter. Despite the fact that he had a wife and three school-aged children at home, he preferred his crowd to his family. The big man always stood at the same place at the bar and woe betides anyone who dare take his place. His face was handsome, with just a couple of scars above his eyebrows and a slightly crooked nose to show he had once been a boxing champion in the US Navy.

McParton was also husky although two inches shorter than the six-foot-two Kerrigan. He always wore a black tie on his white shirt and metal armbands to hold up his sleeves and show off his powerful forearms. The rest of the bunch were and odd mix of customers from the neighborhood.

When the two dockworkers walked into the near-empty bar, all nine heads turned and 18 eyes glared. One of the strangers was as big as Kerrigan and the other a normally built, six-foot man. The place smelled of stale beer and cigar smoke.

McParton personally welcomed new customers with a smile and a handshake, but not at this time of night. This was the sacred hour with the boys.

"Sorry, the bar's closed," he announced, his face a stone mask. The combined glare of the rest of the patrons seconded the proclamation.

"Oh, that's okay," said the tall one. "We didn't come here to drink. We came here to see a man named Kerrigan, John Kerrigan."

Kerrigan instantly straightened up and shoved his glass of Jameson aside. "Who wants him?"

"Oh, just a couple of nobodies who want to say hello," the taller man went on. "Would you be him?"

"And what if I was?" challenged Kerrigan, puffing up his shoulders. His dark blue eyes narrowed, focusing like a gunsight on the intruder. The big stranger had bushy eyebrows and a sad-looking face, and Kerrigan had already decided that this was the man's night to get it re-arranged.

"Oh, well, if you were him, then I'd have to tell you that you are a filthy coward who beats up on defenseless prisoners," the man shrugged. "Then I would have to add that you need a good shot of your own medicine. But that's only if you are him."

McParton saw the crazed look in Kerrigan's eyes and reached over and touched his shoulder. "Now, now, Johnny, calm down. If the man's lookin' to get beat up, let him go somewhere else. I'll handle this."

As McParton lifted up the end section of the bar and walked through, the rest of the bunch stood up in a threatening motion. "I want you to leave, now!" McParton said. "Otherwise, we'll throw you out."

"Hey, no problem." returned the bigger visitor. "I'll just wait outside for Kerrigan. I'm sure a man such as he would not want people to go around saying that he is coward, now would he?" With that, the man wheeled and left, his friend watching over his shoulder to make sure that they would not be rushed.

Outside on the side street, the two men prepared themselves for the suspected onslaught by taking off anything that could be grabbed in a fight. Then they waited. The night was misty and fresh after a sudden shower and the pavement had a black sheen. The lights of Boston formed a bright shroud overhead and the bustle of machinery supplied an eerie drone.

Just then the door burst open and John Kerrigan leapt down the stairs with the other eight patrons and McParton in tow.

"Well, sir," Marty Myers, said very lowly in his southern drawl, "I think you got his attention."

As the big man burst forward, Gus said, "So, you're the famous Johnny Kerrigan?" Gus stood with his arms straight down at his side, his jacket cuffs resting on his palms.

"And what if I am?" Kerrigan announced stopping 10 feet away from him. He was as tall as Gus and about the same build. The others spread out around him in a line, their fists clenched.

"Then you and I have a score to settle."

"We do, do we?" Kerrigan grinned. "What about?" His hands slipped into his pocket and came out slowly.

"Knuckle dusters," whispered Myers, and Gus nodded.

"About how you beat up men who can't defend themselves."

"And how would you know about that?" Kerrigan returned, his grin still broad.

"A little birdie told me."

Kerrigan stepped forward and said, "Well, maybe this little birdie's friend needs plucking."

"Pluck away," challenged Gus.

Without taking his eyes off Gus, Kerrigan cocked his head to his friends and said, "This should take about 10 seconds." A hearty laugh followed his announcement.

Kerrigan raised his hands in a classic boxer's pose and walked slowly toward Gus, a small glint on his right fist confirming what Myers had suspected. Gus stepped back slowly, his eyes on his attacker, ignoring the bar patrons who were slowly moving out on the flanks. In a minute, he and Myers would be surrounded.

Gus let him get within five feet before letting the baton drop from his sleeve. And before Kerrigan saw the billy club, Gus whipped it through the air right across Kerrigan's face. The sudden slap was accompanied by a sickening crunch. As Kerrigan cried out in pain, the club came back and caught him on the right temple.

The man bawled and his legs buckled. But instead of falling, he steeled himself to it, and then charged. Gus was expecting this and moved aside with the agility of a bullfighter, bringing the round, black stick down hard on the man's head. Kerrigan's feet lost their traction and he dove to the pavement, scraping his chin to the bone.

It was at that moment that McParton rushed in with the others but Myers was waiting. The familiar clicking of a gun stopped them and they looked to see a Colt .45 in his hand. "One more step, gentlemen," he said, "and I start aiming for kneecaps."

"But he's —"

"He's getting a wake-up call," Myers answered, his gun readied in both hands. "Now, everyone, get on the ground and spread your arms out!" The eight men knelt down on the wet pavement and gingerly laid flat.

"I'll kill you!" Kerrigan threatened, raising up on his knees. Gus answered by punching him hard on the back of the neck. The wounded man's face slammed against the pavement, breaking his nose.

When he rolled over, Kerrigan's face was streaming blood. His jaw was broken and a low pitiful moan rose from him. "What do you want?" he groaned, trying to think of a way to recover and come at Gus.

Gus knew what he was up to. "If you twitch, I'll smack you again."

"No, no," pleaded Kerrigan, his voice having a nasal tone as blood ran out his nose and mouth. "I won't move. Just don't hit me."

"All right," Gus said, agreeably. "Let's talk."

Kerrigan nodded, his hand supporting his injured neck. "Sure."

"Good, but you just stay where you are and I won't have to hit you again."

Kerrigan nodded, and two large globs of blood dropped from his nose onto the slick, black pavement.

"Now, here's what I want you to do," Gus said, low enough so only Kerrigan could hear. "First, you will go to the hospital and get yourself checked out. Even *I* don't want you dead.

"Next, tomorrow morning, you phone into work and say that you fell down a flight of stairs and the doctor will confirm that you are too banged up to work." Kerrigan agreed.

"Then, after you get out of the hospital, you will request a transfer from OPNAV."

"What?" Kerrigan blurted, wrenching his head up, his cry causing the others to look up from the ground. "

"Faces down, assholes!" sneered Myers, the gun still at ready.

"I said, you will resign from OPNAV," Gus repeated.

"But, I've got —"

"You'll have nothing if you don't do what I say, Kerrigan," Gus warned him. "I know everything about you, and I know your commanders in OPNAV."

"That's top secret!" Kerrigan said. "I don't discuss that with my family or these guys. I've got clearance to —"

"Not anymore," Gus continued. "You're gone from that hole."

"What do you mean, gone?"

"Just what I said. I got friends upstairs, so if you try to pull a fast one, I'll know. And instead of shuttling toilet paper in the South Pacific, where I hope you end up, I'll make sure you're a lowly lieutenant wiping the ass of some SNAFU-riddled captain in the Aleutians." Gus liked Baker's threat and it felt good passing it on. "You got me, sailor?"

"You're not a fucking dock —"

"I am the man who will make your life miserable if you don't take my advice," Gus threatened. "So, what'll it be?"

Kerrigan's head was a mass of blood now, his eyes like two white grapes peering through the sticky mess. "I will," he sighed.

"Good," Gus replied in a good-natured voice. "Now my partner and I will be on our way."

Kerrigan sat up and saw Myers' pistol. Just from the way he held the gun, the battered man knew Gus' friend had military training. "Hey," he said, his voice breathy, "You have to tell me."

"What?" asked Gus, shoving the billy club under his jacket.

"Was all this all over that fucking Kraut, Stahl?"

Gus suddenly leaned over until he was inches from the bleeding man's face. Myers tensed as if he expected his friend to hit the man again. Instead, Gus handed him a clean handkerchief.

"What goes on in that jail is a disgrace to the United States Navy," Gus breathed, menacingly, "and I know a dozen guys who would risk their rings to sail a destroyer up the Charles River and blow it off the face of the earth."

Kerrigan felt another tinge of fear as he considered his assailant's face. During his many years of brawling and boxing fights, he had seldom witnessed such a mixture of strength and menace in another man. What he failed to recognize was another, more compelling trait in Gus: compassion. However, people who never possessed the quality, rarely saw it in another person.

"You see, Kerrigan, believe or not, we're supposed to be the good guys," Gus continued. "The reason we're fighting this goddamn war is to defeat countries which think it's their God-given right to take over another one by force, and then imprison their people and use torture on prisoners-of-war. But sonofabitches like you and your kind at that jail leave a smell on the achievements made by our forces and the Allies – a goddamn stink."

Kerrigan wiped his nose again stuck the handkerchief over his cut eyebrow. "I don't know what your beef is mister," he groaned. His face was now swollen round and his eyes were slits in puffy, dark balls that used to be his eyelids.

"We're just doin' what our superiors want – to get information," he said, accusingly, "and you beatin' the shit outta me ain't gonna change nothin'."

Gus never said anything in response. He was contemplating the damage he had inflicted on the man, and he almost felt sorry felt sorry for him. But knew better than to let his guard down. To relax his menacing posture would be construed as weakness and his point would be lost on the man.

So what yah gonna, do, beat the shit outta everybody?" Kerrigan pouted.

"You just do what I say, Kerrigan," Gus replied as if not hearing his question. "Or the next time I won't be so pleasant."

When Gus finally straightened up, a diligent Myers holstered his pistol. "Nice meetin' y'all," he drawled with a wave to the men lying on the wet pavement. "Now y'all have a nice evenin', you hear?" There was a slight smile on his face, as if he were parting with friends.

As he and Gus slipped into the shadows they heard Kerrigan's strained voice. "You can't beat up everyone, you know!"

When they were out of earshot, Myers suddenly asked, "Was it on account of those freighters in '41?"

"What?" asked Gus, his mind still on Kerrigan.

"You know, when Stahl was huntin' those freighters. Is that when you began takin' up causes?"

Myers knew he was pushing the point but the evening had brought out many questions about his old commander that he never had the chance - or the guts - to ask. This was one of them.

"No, Marty," Gus returned in a surprisingly congenial tone. "It all began a long time ago, with some elk high up in the Rockies."

Myers stopped and cocked his head as if the words would filter into his brain with some sort of meaning. Then he shrugged and began walking again.

A half minute later he finally said, "I kinda figured it'd be somethin' that needed a few bourbons to explain."

*　*　*

The reality hit Gus as soon as he saw Forbes' face. The big marine officer was standing in the lobby with his cap down at his side, his face set in a frown. Understanding the seriousness of Gus' wordless look, Myers stopped and let his friend proceed.

"When did it happen?" Gus asked, not bothering to offer a greeting.

"This afternoon," sighed Forbes. "OPNAV took his body out and loaded it on a truck. That's all I can tell you."

Gus looked down at his shoes for a few moments, a great sadness weighting on him. Forbes' face turned to one of sympathy.

"Admiral," Forbes added, "I found this in his hand when the nurse called me in. He produced a gold, circular pin with a miniature submarine lain across it. "What is it?"

"It's a German Submarine War Badge." Gus breathed, taking the bauble. "You get it after your second patrol."

"I thought it was something important like that," Forbes sighed, rubbing a hand over his brush-like head, "so I snagged it for you."

"It's important to me," Gus returned, fingering the medal.

Sadly, he looked up at the old Marine's chiseled face and added, "And I won't forget this."

EPILOGUE

Raddall Island Bird Sanctuary
August 25, 2000

The mackerel were running close into the point, drawing in a pod of Minke whales who churned up the water with their strong tails before turning and gorging themselves on the stunned fish. Closer to shore, harp seals picked up on the fish that the small whales chased into shore. Crying seagulls, hovering patiently overhead to grab a half-eaten morsel, added to the racket of the barking seals.

"Wow! Look at the whales!" cried nine year-old Jenna Lanton, jumping up and down as each Minke flipped and splashed in the rippling blue waters.

"Yeah, holy mackerel!" laughed her twin sister, Clara. The two girls, dressed in designer sweat suits clambered over the rocks to get a better look.

"Don't get too close to the seals," warned their mother, Sally Lanton, a former farm girl from Iowa. Her blonde hair was in French braids and resisted the heavy afternoon gusts. "And mind the signs that say where the birds are nesting. Don't bother them." The girls just nodded and went on their way.

"This is really beautiful, Gramps," Gary Lanton announced as he surveyed the point. He was a sandy-haired 33-year-old computer consultant who lived in Dallas. Many people said he was a spittin' image of his dad, Richie Lanton.

Beyond the point was the long, low-slung silhouette of Ashton Island with its familiar white lighthouse with the red and white checked top.

"Sure is," smiled Gus, taking a deep breath. At 87, he was still a tall man and his hair was as thick as the day Ginger married him, but now white as mountain snow. His worried look, so prevalent in his younger days, had transformed into a clown-like grin, the big ears rounding off the comedic touch. But his chestnut eyes were still sharp and, after last spring's laser surgery, his sight was that of a man half his age.

Ginger Lanton had aged gracefully. She kept her hair long and dyed silver, which seemed to keep her looking like a woman in her 60s. She and Gus still danced on a regular basis, which accounted for their high level of fitness. They were grandparents to two children, although only Gary and his family could get the time off to come. Marty was in China on assignment with the State Department.

Gus peered around the island and noticed how different it looked. The trees had been cropped back to provide the luxurious grass for the piping plovers to nest. Except for the large rocks on the point, this could have been one of many islands he had seen in his long lifetime.

Gus had done well by the US Navy. When the Japanese surrendered on September 2, 1945, he was on the deck of the USS *Missouri* in Tokyo Bay, not 40 feet from General Douglas MacArthur. He had stayed on in the service after the war and survived the downsizing of the American fleet. He received a second star in 1950, when war broke out in Korea, and retired as a full admiral in 1955 to spend more time with his 11-year-old son.

From the early 50s to the mid-70s, he owned a fishing boat, using his son, Richie, as his mate until the boy went off to college. Richie graduated in engineering from M.I.T. in 1964 and married his Bar Harbor sweetheart. They had two children: Gary and Marty.

During his studies, young Richie had enrolled in the naval reserves and was chosen for pilot training. Tragedy struck in late 1969 when Richie's A-6 Intruder was shot down over North Vietnam. He and his navigator bailed out and were held in a prison camp. Unfortunately, Richie's injuries were too severe for the hospital to handle and he died Christmas Day. He was 24 years old.

Richie's sons brought Gus and Ginger out of their despair. Even though his wife, Sandra, remarried, she was as much a daughter to them as she had been before, and Gary and Marty spent much of their time over at their grandparents' home.

"I think that's them now," Ginger remarked, cupping her eyes to ward off the sun.

"Late as usual," quipped Gus, his penchant for punctuality not having tempered over the years.

The Canadian Coast Guard helicopter, fire engine red in color with a diagonal white stripe, hovered above the pre-designated landing area on the opposite side of the small island and then set down. A sport utility vehicle picked up the passengers and drove them the half mile to the point where Gus and his family were waiting.

Wyn and Jesse Parsons had also aged gracefully. At 80 and 79, respectively, they had married in 1946, after a two-year partnership on Ashton Island that had many of the local mainlanders shocked. Wyn and Jesse eloped and settled down on Ashton to raise a family of four, all of whom went on to have families of their own. Now, Wyn and Jesse had three great-grandchildren.

In 1953, they moved to the mainland, passing the light off to the Department of Transport, and bought a farm outside Shelburne. Jesse went back to teaching, retiring in 1981 at age 60.

One of the biggest moments in Wyn's life was in 1972. As a veteran of Dieppe, he was invited to a reunion in England where Lord Louis Mountbatten was the host. When the ceremonies were over, Wyn was invited in for a private audience with Mountbatten. After 30 years, some sealed German documents pertaining to the raid had been opened revealing that a platoon of men had "come in under a hail of our gunfire and had snatched away wounded soldiers from the seawall."

The German commander who witnessed the platoon's charge went on to say, "It was the bravest action I have ever witnessed." In light of this new information, Mountbatten used his influence to have Wyn exonerated for his previous conviction and Queen Elizabeth pinned the Military Cross on him later in that same year. When he left Buckingham Palace, Wyn sat down on the sidewalk and burst into tears.

Then he and Jesse got on an airplane and flew back to Canada, just in time to catch one of the charters going over to Moscow for the second leg of the 1972 Canada-Soviet Summit Series hockey championship. Jesse had never seen him so happy.

"About time you lazy Bluenosers got here!" Gus bellowed, as the truck stopped in front of them. "And watch out you don't step on the damn birds!" he added sourly. "You know what big feet you Canucks have."

Wyn just ignored him and leaned over to kiss Ginger. "If it wasn't for Viagra, he'd be pretty useless, wouldn't he?"

"And then some," grinned Ginger, wiping a tear from her eye. "It's good to see you two again."

"Always great to see a beautiful woman ... even if she is married to a grumpy old man," Wyn chuckled.

"Sorry we're late," Jesse said. "We stopped off at Ashton to see Mom and Dad's graves." Jesse Parsons was a graceful senior with a face barely touched by wrinkles. Her hair was short, which made her look years younger. "Gus, Ginger, it's been too long!" she squealed hugging Ginger.

Taking the cue, Gus threw open his arms. "Oh, there's a pretty girl," he said, pushing Wyn aside and hugging Jesse. Turning to Wyn, he said, "Kiddin' aside, Wyn, I always loved your mug." Then the two men embraced.

"Where's your family?" asked Jesse, wiping her eyes.

"Over watching the whales," Gus answered. "Them and the seals are putting on quite a show."

"How're yours?" asked Ginger.

"All out west," Wyn shrugged. "What can you do? That's where the money is."

Wyn had shrunk a bit, and his face was as rugged as Gus', who was eight years his senior. The sea air and the farming life added heavy crevasses to his skin. But his eyes were still a dazzling blue and the mop of white hair hanging rakishly across his eyes gave him the look of eternal youth.

The four of them stood together a long moment and then it was Gus who finally said. "Let's go over and see him."

* * *

It had been nearly a year since a joint venture by Trident Research & Recovery of Framington, Massachusetts, and Sub Sea Recovery of Portland, Maine, located the wreck of the *U-2900*. In doing so, their submersibles had filmed some odd-shaped "half-submarines" on the bottom trailing behind the silt-covered German U-boat. They had followed leads from de-classified documents which helped them discover a Type XI-B U-cruiser off the coast of Cape Cod, Massachusetts. This proved once and for all that this type of submarine, previously dismissed as not having been in operation, had, in fact, patrolled off the east coast of America.

The area around the *U-2900* was extensively photographed and tested for radiation. The pod showed signs of radioactive material. Gus became aware of this information through an acquaintance at Trident Research and immediately went about to set the record straight about Lothar Stahl and the crew of *U-2900*.

* * *

They stood as timeless sentinels, four old people on a day blessed with the sun and a warm prevailing wind. The identically adorned headstones of nine Norwegian sailors stood in perfect symmetry on the promontory overlooking the point, their country's flag engraved and painted on each one. Just beyond that was a new gravesite, one with a shiny headstone that read:

Lothar Karl Stahl
U-2900
April 16, 1911 - May 15, 1945
Knight Cross with Oak Leaves, Swords and Diamonds - Germany
Cross of Valour - Canada
Presidential Medal of Freedom - United States

* * *

It was Wyn who finally broke the silence. "That must have taken some doing to get him here."

"Oh, I found out where they put him back in '45," Gus shrugged. "Potter's Field. I marked the spot and then looked in on it from time to time. Then, after the documents were declassified, it was a cinch. I spoke with the State Department and the German ambassador, and they had a pow-wow with a U-boat survivors organization, and all of them concurred that it would be a fitting monument."

"Sorry we couldn't have been here when he was laid to rest."

"Well, except for some of the U-boat men who came, it was a media circus," Gus spat. "All they did was scare the damn birds half to death."

He stared into space. "Nah, it's better this way," he went on, "with just four of us. Your government was great to close off the island to let just us and the kids on today. Hell, this has become a shrine for German tourists so we'd had no peace out here today."

Jesse knelt down and rubbed the stenciled indentations of his name. "I remember his eyes and the way he spoke," she said softly. "He was a gentle spirit with a warrior's heart."

"That's beautiful," Ginger offered, dabbing her eyes. "I never met him, but I lived with him most of my life, through Gus."

Gus wiped his eyes as well. "Well," he said, abruptly, "let's put this thing in and go have us that lobster and corn boil you promised."

Gus checked the small tin box before closing it. Inside its velvet confines were Lothar's gold *U-47* ring, his Submarine War Badge, Wyn's Military Cross and Gus' Navy Cross. "Do you think he's got enough friggin' medals now?" Gus laughed, snapping the lid shut.

"Gus!" squealed Ginger. "Don't profane this place."

Gus ignored her and knelt down on the concrete surface. A small rectangular hole had been left in the granite stone. He placed the tin box inside the opening and then reached over and picked up another small block of granite.

It fit tightly into the hole and was machined so perfectly that the smooth surface of the block matched the headstone. Only someone who knew that there had been a cut in the stone would have noticed it.

"Look at that!" Gus beamed. "Damn, Wyn, your fellow sure cut that nicely."

With Wyn and Ginger's help, Gus rose to his feet. Then he stood at attention and saluted. Wyn joined him.

As they slowly made there way back to the jeep where the Lanton family waited, Gus stopped suddenly and said, "That a new arm, Wyn?"

Wyn twisted the life-like artificial left hand around to show him. "Yup. Got it last month. See? The fingers move and everything."

"Boy, that's clever," Gus nodded, walking in a fast hobble again.

A few seconds later, he said, "Say, did I tell you about my new shoulder? It's plastic. I can lift . . ."

THE END

AUTHOR'S NOTE

Although this book is a work of fiction, it is to some degree based on events that either happened as stated or ones in which the technology was available to carry out the operation. For one, the success of the V-series rockets on London in 1944-45 gave the Nazis the idea of taking this terror campaign to the east coast of the United States. There are many references to support this contention.

Next, the interrogations of U-boat prisoners by a sector of OPNAV (US Naval Headquarters Command) — called Op.16-Z — at the Charles Street Jail in Boston did happen. One such interrogator, Jack H. Alberti, a former concert pianist, was especially ruthless and one of the characters in this book depicts Albert's sadistic talent of extracting information from U-boat crews.